THE THESPIAN SPY

SEDUCTIVE SPIES
BOOK ONE

CHERI CHAMPAGNE

Jacket design and illustrations by Deana Holmes

Editing by Zara Kramer, Rachel Schoenbauer, and Heather Stewart: Pandamoon Publishing

ISBN: 978-1-7777443-0-4

 Formatted with Vellum

For everyone with a wild imagination and an adventurous heart.

PROLOGUE

ary Wright took a deep, calming breath as she paused at the top of the spiralling stone staircase. The dungeon of the castle ruins was still and cold, and the eerie calm sent a chill of apprehension down her back. She knew he was here. Gabriel was here, and he was hurting.

On silent feet, she tread slowly down the narrow stairs. She trailed her fingertips over the rough, damp stone wall at her side, guiding her way around the curve of the perilous steps. She blinked, attempting to acclimate her eyes to the darkness as it slowly engulfed her.

She adjusted the sheer cloth of the harem costume draping from her arms so the delicate material would not tear on the ragged rock face.

A loud, familiar clap of skin against skin echoed through the passage below, harshly breaking the silence. Her stomach clenched as a cry of pain and a choked groan swiftly followed. She must think of a plan to free him. But what? This costume hardly afforded many secret compartments for concealed weapons, as scant as it was.

Her costume...

Why of course! A slow smile stole over her lips. Her *costume*! When short on weaponry, one must know how to use all at their disposal. Mary would rescue Gabriel and save their mission with just her knowledge and her ridiculous costume.

She hastily removed two pins from her loosely fashioned chignon, allowing her curling auburn locks to fall over her shoulders and to her waist. She surreptitiously slid the two slender pieces of metal beneath the cuff at her wrist.

Pulling the elaborately beaded and embroidered vest from her shoulders, Mary slipped it down her arms and dropped it regretfully to the stone steps, discarding one of the only modest elements from her costume and leaving her bosom all but entirely nude beneath the fine lace of her bodice.

She pasted an insipid smile on her lips and forced her eyes to dull into witlessness before trundling noisily down the remainder of the stairs.

Torches lit the landing where one guardsman stood beside the large oak door leading to the dungeon. The large man was all too easily distracted by the dusky points of her nipples stretching the sheer material over her bosom. He stared openly at her, eyes glazed over and mouth agape. Predictable man. Mary winked seductively at him as she lifted the large piece of wood barring the door and pulled, stepping back to allow the door to scrape open on creaky hinges.

Striding sensually over the threshold, her heart nearly stopped at the sight before her. Gabe sat, shirtless and bloody, on a hard, wooden chair. His wrists were pulled behind his back and imprisoned by manacles, his shoulders bulged with strain, his body was shiny with perspiration, and his face...*oh, his face*. Swollen. Puffy and splattered with his own blood, the poor man.

Mary forced her heart to beat normally and willed her mind and body to follow direction and stay in character. The guard outside closed the door behind her with a decidedly ominous *thunk*.

She drooped her eyelids and curled her lips back in an aroused grin as she placed her hands on her waist, deliberately displaying her flagrantly-exposed figure. Cocking one hip, she allowed her belt of shining coins and bells to jingle.

"Oh yes," she lowered her voice to a husky thrum. "Please tell me I can join in this erotic game."

CHAPTER 1

Cumberland, England, July 1795—twenty-years ago

THE SWEETLY WARM wind blew through young Mary Wright's deep auburn locks as she ran hell-bent through the fields of bluebells. Her lungs laboured to drag in each gasping breath, her heart thundering mercilessly in her chest. With each leaping step, her dirt-stained skirts wrapped more tightly around her knees and calves, but she hardly took notice. She was being chased! Being pursued by...by...a dreadful pirate!

Mary released a shouted laugh of glee at her own genius and forced her legs faster.

Yes, the fearsome pirate White Beard. No. Not frightening enough. *Murderous Jack*! Yes, definitely the name of a dreaded pirate. He and his men knew that she, and only she, held the secret to the fair maiden's magic and the counter-spell that would unlock the horrible curse that had been placed on said pirate. But Mary would never tell. Even were she to be captured and held prisoner on Murderous Jack's ship, the...

the...Squalling Angel, *yes*, and tortured daily, she would never tell.

She frantically glanced over her shoulder. The pirate captain and his band of thirty men...no...*seventy* men rose over the crest of the hill behind her.

There was no chance of escape.

She drew in a deep breath and let out a lilting scream, but a fresh gust of wind carried it away just as quickly as it was expelled. But screaming was of little use. No one would come to save her. The wicked serpent witch, Alexandra, had imprisoned her love, the devilishly handsome Prince Sebastian.

Mary sent another glance over her shoulder. A lock of hair caught at the dampness on her forehead, briefly obscuring her vision. *My downfall at the hands of my own hair!*

With her vision compromised, she failed to spot the rock imbedded in the ground before her. The large toe on her right foot connected painfully with the small, jagged stone, the material of her slippers scarcely providing any protection. The incident propelled Mary forward into the waist-high bluebells, her cry of shock and agony rolling over the hills around her.

GABRIEL ASHLEY finally managed to escape his governess' notice. She was advanced in age and rather fond of drink, so all that was required was patience, and he was able to slip away once she fell into a liquor-induced sleep.

He tossed his favourite conch shell up in the air and caught it in one hand with a grin. Father had brought it for him the last time he'd returned home. It wasn't a tin soldier, but it was from father, so it was special.

Gabe strode past the estate gardens and began to wander through the tall grass, before he cringed at the throb of pain from the sore bruise on his rear. His older cousin, Fredrick, the nasty blighter, had delivered a punishing kick to Gabe's bottom while calling him *mixed blood* with a nasty sneer. Gabe frowned. Everyone treated him poorly because he was half Scottish. His aunt and uncle jeered at him and called him "half-feral," and he'd overheard his uncle's acquaintances call him a "thing" while grimacing in disgust. Gabe could hardly change his blood, *blast it*.

He took a bite of the biscuit he had palmed from the kitchens before leaving his uncle's estate, savouring the fluffy, buttery taste. He took solace in the familiar flavour. Mama made the best biscuits in the whole of the world.

Gabe kicked a tuft of long grass as he strode up a small hill. The sun shone gaily from its happy perch in the sky, the heat from it a comforting change from the coldness at home.

Swallowing another mouthful of biscuit, Gabe put his lips to the tip of his conch shell and blew, and a faint *honk* mixed with his sputtered breath came from the wide opening on its side. Father said that when his lungs were stronger, he would be able to make a louder noise.

A light gust of warm wind blew, further mussing his mass of curling brown hair. He had wandered far from the estate, but had not yet reached his favourite, secret spot. He marched over the hills and through the reaching bluebells which nearly topped his thighs. His secret forest lay just over the crest of the last hill.

A muddy white spot in motion on the next hill caught Gabe's attention. He squinted against the brightness of the sun. A girl...a *waif* of a girl, surely no more than four years of age, running headlong through the tall blue flowers. Her red-tinted brown hair glowed like fire in the sunlight. Gabe's chest tightened at the fear on her features.

Gabe's eyes darted over the vacant hills. The little waif appeared to be running from something or some*one*, but there was nothing in sight.

She swung her head around to glance over her shoulder. Her high-pitched scream carried to him on the wind and his heart dipped in his chest. Gabe's feet began to move of their own volition in the direction of the running child. She seemed to push herself ever faster as she cut a hasty path through the fragrant flowers.

She darted her head around again, then made a misstep. *No.* Another scream split the air, the shrill sound piercing his ears, before she fell, disappearing into the bluebells.

Without conscious thought, Gabe broke into a run. The warm wind blew his blue coat open to flap behind him and ruffled the curling mop of brown hair atop his head. The song of the birds flying overhead, the rustle of leaves from the nearby trees, and the *whoosh* of wind past his person all faded from his consciousness as he ran toward the fallen girl.

He skidded to a stop as he saw the small thing lying flat on her back among the flowers. She gazed back up at him with wide, tear-filled, steel grey eyes. His heart gave another odd bump. She blinked those startling eyes, fresh tears skidding over her temples and into the hair above her impish ears.

Gabe tore his gaze from the small girl to glance around them, searching for whatever had frightened her and feeling an odd surge of protectiveness welling within him. Whoever had frightened her would have to face *him* if they wanted to get anywhere near his waif.

He returned his gaze to her mud streaked and tearful form among the beautiful flowers. "Are ye well?" he asked in his faint Scottish brogue.

She pulled her lower lip between her teeth, more tears welling in her eyes as she valiantly nodded. Brave gel.

"Where are ye hurt?"

Lifting up on her elbows, the waif rose to a sitting position and wrapped her hands around her foot. Tears spilled over her eyelids, and she sniffled.

"May I have a look?" He raised his eyebrows in question.

She hesitated but nodded again. Lowering himself to his knees beside her, he put his conch aside and took her small foot in his hands. He slid her mud-caked slipper off and looked at her foot. Gabe hadn't the faintest idea what to look for, or why he had offered in the first place, but something about his faerie waif compelled him to offer his help.

Her big toe had become red and swollen. "It looks painful," he said, as though it would somehow help. "I cannae tell if it's broken or nae. If ye want, ye can come with me back to my uncle's estate and we can summon the physician."

She hastily shook her head, looking fearful once more. A brief, puzzled frown marred his forehead before he forcibly cleared it.

"What is yer name?" he asked.

"I'm Mary." Her small voice barely reached his ears.

He smiled. "Hello, Mary. My name is Gabriel Ashley."

"No," she said, a little louder, a slow smile curving her lips.

Gabe frowned into her grey eyes. "I beg yer pardon?"

"You are Prince Sebastian, escaped from the clutches of the evil serpent witch, Alexandra, just to save me. And I am charmed."

Gabe wrinkled his nose. Was the girl daft? "Prince... *What*?"

Her smile finally grew to split across her pale, freckle-specked face.

"Prince Sebastian," she repeated as though he was hard of hearing. She shifted into a seated position beside him as she pulled her foot out of his grasp. She replaced her muddy stocking and slipper back over her pale skin, grimacing at the pain the simple movement caused. "Prince Sebastian is my one true love and he has now saved me from the dreaded pirate, Murderous Jack!" She flung her hand high in the air as though holding a sword aloft and gazed into the glinting sunlight. "He drew his sword and slashed the pirate through the heart," she stabbed her fictitious sword through the air, "his blood spurting over the ground and a sickening gurgle in the cad's scurrilous throat!"

Gabe winced. Bloodthirsty lass. "How old are ye?" he asked.

She lowered her arm and looked at him with innocent eyes. "Six. But when I marry Prince Sebastian I shall be three and twenty because I would prefer to spend my youth at balls dancing with all the gentlemen instead of wasting those years bearing children."

"Verra decided fer so young a girl." Gabe felt the dampness of the ground seep through the knees of his breeches, but determinedly ignored it...despite how cross it would make his uncle.

"Decided, indeed," she agreed with a quick nod. "How old are you, then?"

"Eleven. Nearly twelve."

"You talk funny," she noted. Her head was tilted at an angle of curiosity, making Gabe believe she had not meant to insult him.

"Me mum is Scottish. Me—*my*—da is an English naval captain."

"But if you live with English people, doesn't your accent go away?" A gust of wind blew around them, picking up several locks of Mary's loose auburn hair and flicking them around her small oval face.

"I ken how te speak without my accent, but I choose not te."

She lowered her chin to rest it upon her raised knees. "It seems to me that you prefer to speak with your accent. If you wanted to speak like an Englishman, you would not struggle so, switching between the two."

He frowned, not particularly liking this conversation.

"What of *your* speech?" he asked, "Why do you speak so well but are out of doors without a nanny or governess, and are covered in dirt?"

"Why, 'tis simple, of course!" She smiled over the tops of her knees. "My Papa is a crofter on Baron Winning's land and Mama is learned and wishes for me to make an ad—" Her nose wrinkled as she struggled to find the correct word. "Advent... advantat...advant*ageous* marriage one day—"

"To a prince, of course," Gabe interrupted.

"Yes, to a prince. So, Mama bought books with Papa's earnings and makes me read and do my maths." She grimaced in distaste. "I despise math." Her face brightened. "Shakespeare, however, is very pleasing. Indeed, I could read his plays all day."

Gabe's eyebrows rose. "Ye are verra young to enjoy such advanced reading."

Mary tipped her head sideways and gave a shrug. "Well, Mama helps me read," she amended. "But I do so enjoy it."

"A lover of theatre, are ye?"

"Yes!" She bounced awkwardly on her bottom. "Mama says I'm a thes...thesepi...thisp..." She huffed an exasperated breath.

"A thespian?" he asked.

She pointed at him. "That's it! A *thespian*," she mimicked his accent with a grin.

"My uncle is Baron Winning," he said to the theatrical young waif.

"Oh!" Her lips formed a small *O*. "We are neighbours, then! Would you like to play with me?"

Gabriel gazed at Mary, warmth at her open and immediate friendship spreading through his chest. Who was this young girl to so willingly accept him despite his half-Scottish blood, to smile so freely and guilelessly at him without rancour? The other children of the nearby village sneered at him or spoke about him behind their hands when he passed, but this little girl, so warm, so inviting, not only accepted him, but seemed to like him.

"I would," he replied. "But what about your toe?"

Without thinking, he poked at the injured appendage, and the waif yelped in pain.

"Ach! I'm sorry, Mary. I didn't mean te—"

"I'm well enough," she said, her voice wavering.

Thick tears formed in her eyes and streamed silently down her cheeks. Gabe's stomach knotted. He felt awful for having caused her more pain.

He wanted to help, but didn't know what to do, then an idea occurred to him. Picking up his conch shell, he held it out to her.

"Here," he offered. "Have this."

"Thank you!" Mary wiped at her tears with the back of her wrist. "What is it?"

"It's a conch shell. My father gave it to me, but he's given me other things, too. This one can be yours."

He turned the pink shell over in his hands, and the waif's eyes widened as she saw its opalescent interior.

"It's beautiful," she breathed. "It's treasure!"

Gabe laughed. "See, here?" He pointed at the tip. "You can blow in it, and it will make a loud noise."

The lass pressed her mouth to the hole and blew. A weak, awkward *honk* came out the other end, and Mary laughed delightedly.

Gabe's chest warmed at the sound and he easily returned her smile. "Would you like to see my secret spot?"

Her smile turned uncertain and the realization of what he had said made him laugh. His head fell back and loud peals of laughter erupted from deep within his narrow chest.

"I'm...sorry..." he said between chuckled gasps, "that is not...what...I meant."

Another sweet smile broke over her lips. "You are very handsome when you laugh. I think I love you."

Gabe's stomach buzzed like a swarm of flying ants at her words, but he didn't know why. He took the feeling to be something good, so he kept his smile. "Thank you. But what I meant to say was that I have a secret spot that I go to in the forest. It's very pretty and I thought you would like to see it."

"Yes!"

"But first, we should get you back home and call a doctor for your toe."

CHAPTER 2

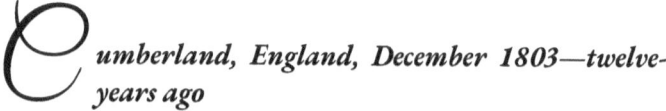

umberland, England, December 1803—twelve-years ago

BRACING herself against the frigid winter air, Mary sorrowfully strode down the snow-covered cobblestone street in the town of Carlisle.

Pulling her cape closer together to ward off the cold and adjusting the heavy basket on her arm, Mary huffed a sad, misty breath, the air curling and evaporating before her eyes. She strode through town, the morning sun hiding behind grey clouds, as she purchased items that her father had put on his list. She had already paid a visit to the local produce vendor, and she was on her way to buy meat and milk, when a sight halted her in her tracks.

Her pulse sped as she watched Gabe from across the snow-dusted street. He was with his mother outside the confectionary speaking to Mrs. Smithe and her three daughters.

Mary had not spoken to Gabriel since his father's funeral, though even that had been brief, as his uncle, Lord Winning, deemed it below his nephew to associate with a poor crofter's daughter.

Captain Ashley had been laid to rest in the family's cemetery a sennight ago, having passed away while at sea. Poor Gabriel had not seen his father for several months before the Captain had died.

In the eight years that Mary had known Gabriel, she had only met the Captain once, but he seemed an affable sort of man, certainly one who loved his wife and son very much. And for that, Mary had adored him.

But while the Captain's passing was indeed sad, it was not what affected Mary's mood so drastically. It was Gabe. She was unsure what had caused it—perhaps it was his time spent at school or his changing maturity—but whatever the cause, he had become distant with her. No longer did she spend hours in the kitchens of his uncle's estate watching Gabe cook, and gone were the days engaged in playful banter, cloud-watching, alfresco luncheons, and rousing tricks on unsuspecting neighbours.

It hurt a great deal more than she could ever have imagined. She very much feared that she was losing her best friend, the boy with whom she'd shared her first—and only—kiss, and the boy that held her heart.

Mary had tried to retain Gabe's interest, but while he had behaved normally with her, she had gotten the distinct impression that he was bored with her company.

Her eyes sharpened on Gabe as he stood in close conversation with the two handsome young women.

The Misses Smithe were closer in age to Gabriel than Mary was; he at nineteen and they at eighteen, seventeen, and fifteen. Not only were they more mature and distinguished than Mary, but they were a great deal prettier, as well.

Mary was only fourteen, and with her auburn hair, freckled cheeks, and still-childish figure, she worried that other girls would garner Gabe's attention before she could repair their friendship.

Gabriel laughed at something one of the girls said and Mary frowned, jealousy burning hotly in her gut. The need to know what they were saying warred with prudence in her heart.

He laughed again.

Damn prudence, anyway.

Making her way stealthily across the cobblestoned street, she carefully avoiding a carriage that rattled by. She hid herself between two buildings, keeping herself deep in the shadows.

Their voices carried to her from their position in front of the confectionary a few paces away.

The Misses Smithe were not only beautiful, but they were handsomely attired as well. All had pale blue walking dresses that poked out beneath navy cloaks over sturdy boots. Their blonde ringlets framed their rosy-cheeked faces and were topped with wide-rimmed periwinkle bonnets that brought out the colour of their eyes. One might think they were triplets if they did not know them.

Mary looked down at her own attire and felt another surge of envy. She wore her mother's old brown day dress and black cloak, hemmed to fit Mary's height, and her bonnet was simple straw, personally embellished with sprigs of holly.

"So, it is true, then?" The eldest Smithe daughter was saying. "You are moving to Scotland to be with Mrs. Ashley's family?"

A hoarse shout caught in Mary's throat, unable to be released. *No!*

"I am afraid it is," he replied, his voice low and rumbling and entirely devoid of his Scottish accent.

Tears welled in Mary's eyes. Gabe was leaving? It couldn't be! It just couldn't! Why had he not told her? Mary bit her lips together to keep a soul-deep sob from escaping. What was she going to do without Gabe?

"We have spent the past fortnight preparing for our departure," he was saying.

Mary's heart thudded sickeningly in her chest, her stomach knotting uncomfortably. *He knew*? Gabe had known for a fortnight that he was leaving and yet he hadn't told her?

"Do tell us, Mr. Ashley, who will you miss the most?" The middle Miss Smithe batted her long blonde eyelashes over her crystal blue eyes.

Mary hated her immediately.

She hated Gabe's overconfident, proud smile even more. "I cannot claim to miss one of you fine ladies more than the other; you will all be dearly missed in my heart." He placed one of his broad, gloved hands over his chest. "I do not know how I shall go on without you."

Mary forced herself to roll her eyes with a nonchalance that she most certainly did not feel. *Oh please*. What drivel! *Hurtful* drivel.

The Misses Smithe tittered behind their hands, the youngest sporting a pretty blush. Mary never looked pretty when she blushed; she just turned blotchy.

"What of that skinny, freckled, ginger crofter's daughter you always seem to hang around with? Will you miss us more than *her*?" The oldest Miss Smithe said, her reddened nose wrinkling.

Mary closed her eyes at the insult. She was not a *ginger*. Her hair was more brown than red, for pity's sake! And certainly not orange. And as Papa said, there wouldn't be anything wrong with it if it *were* red.

She waited expectantly for Gabe's response. He would leap to her defence, she was certain. They had been best friends for eight years, after all.

"Most assuredly, Miss Smithe," he said.

Mary's mouth dropped open, her breath fogging the air in front of her, then dissipating, just like her hope. He could not have said what she just thought she heard.

"Miss Wright was pleasing enough to run about a meadow with when I was a young lad, but she is not at all refined like you fine ladies; far too interested in the theatre," he said with a modicum of distaste. "Alas, she is still but a child in leading strings with a head full of fancies."

He could not mean it! She peeked her head around the corner of the building to assure herself of his jest...but one look at his face and she knew he was in earnest. Foolish hope.

One trembling, gloved hand rose to cover Mary's chest, just above the heart that now lay shrivelled beneath. He had slain her. Broken her heart just as easily as performing his morning ablutions. As though it were just another part of a rather ordinary day.

Mary pressed her back against the cold brick of the confectionary building, one arm still hooked through the basket of food for her papa. How could Gabriel say such an awful thing? Did he truly believe what he said about her? Oh lord! Did he always talk about her thusly when she was not around to defend herself?

Embarrassment mingled with the pain in her chest. Did everyone believe her to be a lost puppy following the older fellow around?

Suddenly the ache in her chest was too much. Turning on her heel, she hurried through the narrow alley and out onto the next street. The moment she was free of the confining alley, she picked up her skirts with her free hand and ran, ignoring the biting cold air that rushed painfully into her lungs and the heavy weight of her basket on one arm.

What did she need with Gabriel Ashley, anyway? His uncle, his school, and the pressure of society were all telling him that he was too far above her station to give any further notice to her. He would grow to be a gentleman, and she would always be the daughter of a poor crofter on his uncle's land.

"Bah!" she shouted, her voice carrying on the icy wind behind her.

A sob escaped her as she ran, and fresh tears wavered before her eyes. Damn Gabriel Ashley! He was moving to Scotland and she would never see him again, so what did it matter what he thought?

But it does matter!

She loved him, and he had broken her heart! The scoundrel! The cad! The rogue! He had not even told her that he was going to move away! *Damn Gabriel Ashley! Damn him, damn him, damn him!*

CHAPTER 3

*E*dinburgh, Scotland, September 1807—eight-*years ago*

THE PAPER CRINKLED in the twenty-three-year-old Gabriel's hand as he reread the article in the English newssheet.

...MISS MARY WRIGHT'S performance of Ophelia in the small country theatrical was unparalleled to that of even the brightest actresses of London. A true thespian. Mark my words, ladies and gentlemen; this young woman will soon grace the stage of the Theatre Royal, Drury Lane, and will outshine all before her...

GABE SET the paper aside and took a swig of his ale. The hard, wooden chair on which he sat creaked as he shifted his position, though the sound was overpowered by the boisterous, drunken laughter of the other men in the dirty pub. Gabe was journeying back to his mother's clan, though what tied him to those people anymore, he couldn't say. His mother had died of fever two years past, along with his mother's sister and elderly great aunt.

He'd felt compelled to return to Lord Winning's—now his cousin Fredrick's—estate in Cumberland, but his reception had been ill, indeed. The arrogant man of five and thirty was just as he remembered him to be. Frederick had lifted his lofty nose in the air and superciliously declared Gabe unworthy of setting foot in his presence.

Being kicked out of his cousin's country seat with threats never to return did not surprise him. It was what he had done after he had been kicked out on his arse that had surprised him, even days later. He had gone to the Wright crofter's cottage.

It had not changed in the four years since he had left England, though it had decidedly fewer occupants. Mary's mother had died from the same fever that had claimed Gabe's mother, Mr. Wright was out working the land, and Mary was nowhere to be found. He'd remained for a short while, as he'd wished to see Mary, but after two hours of awkwardly hovering outside the cottage, he'd had a change of heart.

He did not know precisely how or why it had happened, but somehow, he had lost her friendship. He'd sent her the odd letter over the past years, but either she had not received them, or she had deliberately not responded. Gabe suspected the latter.

He glanced down at the paper currently resting on the table next to his hand. He had known of Mary's ambition to become an actress, but he had hoped it was a passing fancy. His hand fisted on the table, his knuckles whitening. He knew she would be a wonderful actress, but *by God*, those women were treated as tarts at best. It sickened him to think of Mary being pursued by young fools just looking to lift a girl's skirts. Mary did not deserve such treatment.

A churning heat began to fester in his gut. The feeling smacked of jealousy, but he assured himself it wasn't so. It had been so long since he had seen Mary—

"Oi!" His thoughts were cut off by a deep grunt at his elbow.

Gabe turned his head to look right up into the glittering eyes of a furious giant.

"Ye fook me wife?" the giant growled, the low timbre of his slurred voice vibrating through his chest.

Gabe took one last gulp of the sour brew in his mug and gently returned it to the coarse surface of the table. "Can't say as I 'ave."

Their voices had garnered the attention of the other patrons, each curious face aimed in their direction, clearly eager to witness a good brawl.

"I ken ye 'ave!" The large man poked Gabe on his shoulder.

"Ye're wrong, big man." Gabe rose from his seat to stand nose to chest with the giant. "I donnae wish te fight ye."

The giant's lip curled back, revealing blackened teeth and foul breath. Then, without further preamble, the man's large fist swung at his jaw.

Gabe ducked swiftly out of the way, his opponent's fist swinging uselessly over his head. With deceptive speed, Gabe jabbed his opponent under his ribs with extended fingers, then punched the man's face with a well-placed fist. The great giant fell chest-down and winded to the repulsive wood-planked floor of the pub. Without giving the man an opportunity to rise, Gabe pressed one knee between the man's shoulder blades and pulled his arms backward. The beast roared.

Gabe brought his head closer to the man's ears, but far enough away to not contract the lice the man likely had.

"When a man says 'e doesnae wish te fight ye...donnae fight 'im." He pushed his knee deeper between the man's shoulders, eliciting a grunt from between his bared teeth. "And I didnae tup yer wife."

With an extra jab of his knee, Gabe rose. At least forty pairs of eyes stared back at him, and not all of them were benign. He quickly drew some coins out of his coat pocket and placed them on the table. He snatched up his paper—and inside it, the article written about Mary—nodded to the gaping men and hastily made his retreat. Best to make himself scarce before someone else decided to challenge him.

Gabe passed through the neighbouring innyard and into the stables. The fresh scent of hay and manure filled his senses as he strode calmly toward his mount Hunter's stall. Gabe pulled the door open and entered, patting Hunter's neck, before turning to the wall, and reaching for where his saddle was hanging.

"You have fine form," a male voice rumbled behind him.

"*A Thiarna Dia!*" Gabe called to the deity in Gaelic as he swung around in surprise, fists at the ready.

The tall, lean man no older than Gabe himself rested one shoulder against the door of Hunter's stall, a confident grin on his lips. He wore all black, nearly blending into the shadows, his suit of clothes of the highest quality. *A toff,* Gabe sneered the word in his mind.

"Goddamnit, man! Donnae surprise a soul like tha', ye ken?" He lowered his fists, but remained alert. The man's easy manner told Gabe that he wouldn't attack, but he would be prepared nonetheless. "Who are ye?"

The man in black pushed away from the stall door and sauntered another two steps toward Gabe and his mount, Hunter shifting nervously at the stranger's advance.

"Noted," the grinning man drawled. "My name is Richards and I have a proposition for you."

Gabe shook his head. "I've nae interest in any schemes."

"This is no scheme. I was recruited by the King himself."

Gabe raised an eyebrow. "Recruited?"

"Yes. And if you are amenable, I have a modest training program at my estate in..."

Gabe sliced his hand through the air, cutting Mr. Richards off. "Nae. Whate'r it is ye're tryin' te fool me on, I'm nae interested."

A piece of paper appeared in Gabe's hand.

Gabe raised an eyebrow. Mr. Richards was deceptively silent in his movements and on his feet. What sort of man was he?

"My documentation, sir." The man had the audacity to wink.

Gabriel looked at the fine parchment lying in his palm and turned it over. The royal signet had been pressed into the wax seal. He arched an eyebrow at the smiling Mr. Richards before he ripped open the seal with his index finger and opened the missive.

This document does hereby royally certify that Colonel Kieran Richards... His eyes scanned the parchment, and his doubts swiftly fled.

"Ye're a *spy*?" He lifted his incredulous gaze toward the mysterious, smirking Colonel Richards.

"Don't bandy that about, wot?"

"If ye're a..." he slid his gaze quickly around the stables, then focused on the spy in black in front of him. "Then wha' do ye want with me? I'm nobody."

"You are not nobody, Mr. Ashley. You are a man of good breeding with knowledge, capability, and are able to take down a veritable giant with just your hands." His eyes glittered. "You are honest, you have learned how to control your accent—or at least affect an English one—when you feel like it, and you are not a stranger to hard work. The Secret Service is very interested in you."

Gabe was nonplussed; his eyebrows rose nigh to his hairline. "Ye know me?"

The horse in the next stall shuffled his hooves against the straw-covered ground, kicking up the fresh scent of manure and hay.

Colonel Richards casually shrugged one shoulder. "I cannot very well recruit men that I do not know."

Gabe took a moment to wrap his thoughts around the fact that this man had obviously been having Gabe followed and had likely questioned his family. It was invasive. It was prying. It was...rather flattering.

Despite the impetuousness of this potential decision, Gabe was intrigued. "Ye deem me worthy, then, aye?"

Richards' grin grew into a full smile. "I do, Mr. Ashley. Training is intensive and rather time consuming, but you would learn how to easily traverse this world; how to blend in with the highest of society or the lowest, depending on where you are needed." He raised one gloved hand and patted Hunter's neck.

Gabriel did not know what to think of this man. The documentation was indisputable; the man was a spy for the crown, and for some unknown reason he wished to recruit Gabe.

Oddly enough, Gabe was intrigued by the notion. After his fisticuffs with the giant in the pub, he'd intended to mount Hunter and ride away...but he had nowhere to go, no one to seek refuge with.

Richards hadn't mentioned it, but Gabe suspected that there was one aspect of Gabe's life that was likely a very appealing aspect of his potential recruitment: few attachments.

Both of Gabriel's parents had gone to meet the good Lord,

and no one else particularly cared whether he lived or died. He had no siblings to speak of—only a few odd members from his mother's clan that lamented his half English blood—and his disreputable cousin who likewise hated his half-Scottish blood. He was alone.

A vision of Mary Wright flashed through his mind's eye, but he quickly brushed it away. She might have cared about him at one point in their lives, but that time had long since passed.

Accepting this man's offer for recruitment would change his life, would give him a new purpose.

"I'll do it," he said.

CHAPTER 4

arlisle, England, March 1808—seven-years ago

"WILL THAT BE ALL, THEN, GUS?" Mary wiped the damp rag over one of the pub's roughened tabletops, then brushed a strand of hair away from her cheek with the back of her wrist.

"Aye. Ye can go on home noo, Mary." Augustus, the Hog and Toad's heavily-set owner waved her off, his Scottish burr thick and rumbling.

Mary eagerly hurried behind the counter at the far end of the large, open pub and removed her work-worn apron. It must have been at least half of four in the morning, for all the pub's patrons had already ventured drunkenly home and Mary's eyes felt like someone had thrown sand beneath their lids. She placed the damp rag and her apron over an old wooden stool, eager to depart her place of work and return home to Papa.

That evening's performances had gone as well as could be expected for her modest pub plays. She smiled to herself. Just over a year ago, someone had come into the pub and watched her perform. He had been so impressed with her that he had invited her to join his cast in Shakespeare's *Othello*. Since then, she had worked both at the pub and in the local theatre. Combined, she worked all the days of the week, sometimes in both places in one day. It was trying, but she was rather proud of herself. The pub was by no means a pleasing position, but it paid well enough to help support Papa and to save a few meagre coins.

One day she would have saved enough coin to travel to London to become a *true* actress.

"Yer earnings," Gus grunted as he neared her.

Mary accepted the precious coins and quickly placed them in the pocket of her threadbare cotton dress.

"Thank you. Good night, Gus." She pulled her out-of-style pelisse off the peg beside the rear door and slipped her arms into the sleeves.

"G'night, Mary." He lifted one thick, callused hand to tug on his forelock.

She turned to smile over her shoulder at the large man as she looped the buttons through their awaiting holes. She pulled her black mantle off the next peg and put it on as well, the dark material covering her to the very tips of her half boots. The mantle disguised her well enough in the darkness of night, though Mary rarely saw a soul on the streets of Carlisle so late—or early—to warrant any amount of concern on her part.

With one last wave, Mary lifted the hood to cover her dark auburn hair and opened the door into the night. She pulled her mantle closer together at her throat as the cold wind threatened to seep within. She had forgotten her gloves that morning, but it hardly mattered. Her hands were so badly callused from her work, no glove could protect them from chapping in the cold air of winter.

She hurried herself along the cobblestoned street, her soft footfalls echoing off the short, narrow buildings around her. It had been two days since the last rain, but the dampness still hung in the air, giving the night an eerie, light fog that seemed to hang about the ground around her ankles. The chill raked its cold fingers up her calves and down into her half boots, making her long for the hot coals in her father's modest fireplace.

The moon hung lazily in the sky, casting its milky-silver glow over the land. While the sight was beautiful, it had become commonplace for her. What she truly longed for were the beautiful sights of London.

She knew what actresses faced in London, how they endured lurid advances and were treated as whores or taken as mistresses. Mary believed herself of a strong constitution, however, and could withstand such advances. Being an actress might have its challenges in London, but not only would it provide a living for her and enable her to live life in the company of others, it would also allow her to fulfil her life's passion of performing.

Perhaps one day she would marry and have children, but she was as likely to be a man's kept mistress as a smithy's or a cobbler's wife. Such was a fine enough life for her.

"Ooooh," a breathy exclamation came from somewhere behind her.

Mary swung around to see three silhouettes stumbling out of the innyard and her heart skittered in her chest. They were men that Gus had forcibly removed from the pub earlier in the night, as they'd begun to verbally abuse the other patrons.

She quickly turned around and increased her pace. Mary had had experience dealing with drunken men and inappropriate advances, but such had always been in the public eye and with fewer men to defend herself against. She had no desire to fight these men off on her own, so she sped along the cobblestones.

"Look-ey wha' we got here, gennelmen," one of the men slurred.

Mary turned to look over her shoulder as one man slipped on the damp cobblestones and fell to his knees on the hard ground of the thoroughfare. The other two men brayed with laughter at their fallen comrade, and Mary quickly turned and continued.

At the curve in the road was a tall stone archway that led to the long, narrow path to the fields of Lord Winning's estate. The walls of the walkway were nearly shoulder-height, and opened up into the night's sky, and at the end of the path was an iron gate. Such a narrow route could increase her peril, but it was the only way home without turning back and walking toward the intoxicated toffs.

The men's laughter swiftly died. In the silence, she could hear their footfalls coming up behind her, the fallen man evidently once more on his unsteady feet.

"It'sss the *wench* f—from the pub." The voice was much closer now.

Mary had always disliked her role as the pirate wench in her pub performances, but Gus was adamant that she continue in that role once per week, as it brought in customers. Mary was now more certain than ever that it attracted the *wrong* sort of customers.

"Wha' should we do with 'er? Eh?" one of the other men said.

"I think weee should t—tup 'er, wot, wot?"

A shiver went up Mary's spine. She closed her eyes and sent up a prayer that the "manoeuvres" that her father had taught her once she had begun work at the pub actually worked to fend off these drunken louts.

"Hey, preddy wench, stop a minute!" The voice was yet closer, almost upon her heels.

Mary sped her pace.

"Hay! We wanna t—talk to you!"

She had finally reached the narrow, stone arched passageway that led out of town when a heavy hand clamped down on her shoulder. Mary swung around, leading heavily with her knee. It knocked him squarely in the cods and he fell to the ground with a groan.

"Oi!" one of his friends shouted.

Then she was surrounded. She had the urge to look about frantically for someone to save her, but she firmly tamped the impulse down. No one would save her. The street was vacant and even if it wasn't, the likelihood of someone coming to the rescue of a pub "wench" and amateur actress were slim if not non-existent. No. She must save herself.

"Come, come, whore, you know you wanna lift your skirts for us fine blokes," a man behind her said, a waft of his whisky-soaked breath reaching her nose.

"Yesssh," the other sneered, "we'll even pay ye for it."

The injured man still writhed on the ground, his hands clutched at his man bits.

"Let us sthee your purdy face..."

Suddenly her hood was removed from her head in a *whoosh*, her wild hair loosening haphazardly. The man behind her tugged harder and her mantle fell entirely from her shoulders, leaving a wash of frigid air to steal over her body.

"Cor!" one of the men exclaimed. "I get 'er first."

Moving on instinct, Mary spun on her heel and ran.

Then, they were on her.

Heavy breathing came from behind her as one arm snaked around her waist. The man pulled, forcing her back against his chest. Mary struggled even as his other arm came to join the first, his grip tightening. Her elbows connected with his ribs and her fists pounded at his forearms to no avail. The black-guard grunted as she made impact, but he held fast.

The other two men rounded in front of her, reaching for her skirts, the injured man evidently recovered. She kicked her legs, trying to connect with anything sensitive.

The tip of her half boot hit one man's shin. "Damn it!" he roared.

Desperate, Mary flung her head backwards, directly into her captors' nose.

Several muffled curses rent the air as he released her to cover his injury.

She staggered away, then picked up her skirts and ran. She sprinted as fast as she could through the narrow pathway that led to Lord Winning's estate, her breaths coming in panicked pants. The passage was too long. Too far. She couldn't gain enough of a head start from these attackers.

Disembodied huffs of breath followed closely behind her as she ran. Her pulse raced almost painfully in her chest, her throat and lungs felt seared with cold as she laboured for each gulp of air. It ached. It burned. But she pushed herself on.

The gate to Lord Winning's fields was just up ahead. If she could but reach it...

A hand clutched her elbow and wrenched her arm backward, sending screaming pain up into her shoulder, and forcing her into an abrupt stop. She swung around, prepared to deliver another knee to this man's parts, but he anticipated her movement and blocked her with his own knee.

Mary scoured her mind for the other manoeuvres she had learned for defending herself, and in a last-minute effort, Mary stiffly extended her fingers and jabbed them just below the juncture point of one ruffian's ribs. That earned her a brief respite as he wheezed for breath, but one of his hateful companions quickly took his place.

His large hand gripped her jaw, his fingers digging deeply

into her skin, pinching her cheeks together and forcing her lips to purse.

His blood-soaked lips curved back to reveal startlingly white teeth. "*You*," he said, his voice dripping with malice and his breath reeking of drink and the metallic zing of blood. "You will suffer for this."

The next moments were a blur of agony. She kicked and fought as much as she could, taking solace in the evil villains' grunts of pain as her fists and heels connected with their soft flesh.

The sound of quick footfalls registered in the back of her mind, but her thoughts were focused solely on her own defence.

A swift movement caught her eye as one of the men drew a fist back to deliver another blow to her face. Mary grimaced and squeezed her eyes tightly shut, preparing for another blazing burst of fire to radiate through her head.

"Release her," a cultured voice brimming with controlled rage said from somewhere beyond her assailants.

In that instant, Mary's bravery fled. Even though her arms were suddenly free, Mary didn't move. She clapped her hands over her ears and kept her eyes squeezed shut, flinching as warm liquid splattered her. The sounds of muffled shouts, thuds, cracks, and all manner of other nause-ating noises could still be heard through the barrier of her hands.

Then it was silent. The only sound she could hear was the beating of her thudding heart and her panicked breathing echoing in her ears.

Something lightly touched her shoulder and she shrieked, cowering where she knelt. Then there was nothing, once more. No touch, no noise, just calm. And patience. Whatever manner of person it was that had interrupted what could very possibly have ended with not only the loss of her virtue, but very likely her demise, one could at least credit them with patience.

With a deep breath to fortify her courage, Mary cracked open one eye.

"Do not be alarmed. I will not harm you," the cultured voice said softly from the shadows. *Or is he the shadow?*

She opened her other eye and gazed into the darkness. The assailants were gone; vanished as though into thin air. The only evidence that there had been anyone there were the splatters of blood over the walls, ground, and on her person.

She licked her swollen lips and whispered, "Wh—where are they?"

"I took care of them. You do not need to fear them any longer."

Mary nodded, but Lord knows she hadn't the faintest idea where he would have deposited the three drunken, malicious devils.

"Thank you," she said.

A hand shot out of the darkness and she flinched. Then she realized that he meant to help her to her feet and she blushed. "I'm sorry." Her voice wavered.

"There is no need to apologize to me. You have just been through an ordeal and have every reason to not trust me. I am a stranger in the dark."

Mary jutted her chin in defiance at her own fear and accepted his hand, allowing him to assist her to her feet. She felt oddly unsteady, but the man shrouded in darkness remained silent and patient as she gripped his arm to right herself.

"Your cloak, I believe." He extended his free hand, and hanging from his two outstretched fingers was her mantle. "I am afraid that it may be torn beyond repair, however."

Indeed, her mantle appeared to have been rent nearly in half; it must have been rather more threadbare than she had thought. After what had just transpired, however, the loss of her mantle was hardly of any significance. "I thank you again, sir." She draped the ruined material over the wall of the passage. Perhaps she would bring it home and use it as washrags.

"My name is Richards, Miss."

"Pleased... Well," she amended, "under the circumstances, pleased to meet you, Mr. Richards. I am Mary Wright."

The milky moonlight shone over the man's dark hair and shadowed features. She could easily be frightened by his imposing presence, but something about him compelled her to feel safe. Part of it, she was certain, was due to the fact that he had just rescued her from a terrible fate.

He affected a bow, quick and rigid.

"You defended yourself most admirably, Miss Wright. You displayed knowledge, skill, bravery, and the willingness to defend yourself. This may sound inopportune and perhaps inappropriate, but I have a proposition for you."

Disappointment crashed over her, but she could not muster the strength to be outraged—or flattered. She felt rather disheartened that the man had only saved her out of a desire to bed her himself. Despite how kind Mr. Richards appeared to be, however, she had no interest in becoming a man's mistress at present.

"While I appreciate your offer, Mr. Richards—"

"I would like to teach you."

Mr. Richards' words overlapped hers and she was not certain that she had heard him correctly. "I beg your pardon?"

"I manage a small...education program at my estate in Brampton. I have several students under my tutelage there, where I teach them skills for defending themselves, language, history, accents..." His teeth shone silver in the moonlight as he grinned. "Reconnaissance, sleuthing, interrogation, espionage, infiltration, and the handling, loading, and use of all manner of weaponry."

Mary's eyes grew wide, and her disappointment fled. *He's bamming me. Surely he's bamming me.*

But what if he wasn't? What if he *was* a...a *spy* who taught spies? Or, even worse, what if he was a spy for the *other* side? She could not abide inadvertently joining the fight *for* England's enemies.

A folded piece of parchment appeared before her eyes. "My documentation," he said. "Though I do not know how well you can read it in this light."

Even if the sun was shining brightly in the sky, Mary was not certain that she could read it anyway, her eyes being as tired as they were. She rubbed her index finger over the wax seal, feeling the design in the indentation. The royal crest, unmistakably.

Anticipation bubbled through her midriff at the thought of learning the skills to defend her country, to defend herself. But what of her plans for the future? What of her hope of becoming an actress?

She hugged her arms across her stomach in an attempt to ward off the frigid air, the parchment crinkling in her hand.

"I thank you, Mr. Richards, but as much as I would like to—"

"I apologize for interrupting, Miss Wright, but there is something I should like to add before you make your decision."

She nodded, waiting for him to continue.

"There is one additional advantage to becoming a crown spy. Once your training is complete, you may take on any position in London, be it as a governess, maid...or actress. Whatever you decide, we will ensure that it comes to fruition."

Mary stood frozen. Her dreams could be realized, as simple as that? With one stipulation; that she become a spy.

Could she do it? Could she become a spy for England? She hugged her arms closer around her middle, the cold and humidity of the night seeping easily through her pelisse and dress, soaking deep into her skin. She was chilled, weary, aching, and injured; she wished for nothing more than a bracing wash with a rag, a cup of watered-down tea, and her lumpy but warm bed.

But...what if she could have *more*? What if she could be further educated and acquire a position as an actress in London? She could provide for Papa as he aged, realize her dreams, *and* live comfortably.

There was no question.

"I would be pleased to accept," she heard herself say, the puff of her breath against the cool air turning to a wispy cloud of fog before her eyes.

Another grin from Mr. Richards veritably shone in the darkness. "I am pleased to hear it."

THE FOLLOWING HOUR WAS A WHIRLWIND. Mr. Richards escorted Mary home, ensuring that she understood the importance of her silent tongue. She wished that she could tell Papa the whole of the tale, but as Mr. Richards so aptly pointed out, any connection that an enemy may make to loved ones could end poorly, indeed.

They reached her and Papa's modest crofter's cottage where she slipped inside to pack her meagre belongings; two dresses, one set of underthings, a pair of half boots, and the beautiful conch shell that had been gifted to her by Gabriel.

She reached between her mattress and the hard-packed earthen floor and retrieved a small pouch of coins. Where she was going, she did not require her savings. This evening's earnings, where it currently rested in her pocket, ought to suffice for funds. She then strode toward the worn tabletop near the kitchen to one side of the cottage, and placed the pouch atop it, the coins inside clinking. She retrieved a treasured sheet of vellum and penned a note informing Papa that she was to journey to London for a wonderful opportunity and would write and visit soon. She then placed the note beside the pouch and returned outside to Mr. Richards.

It was significantly brighter than an hour before, the moon slowly fading with the lightening of the sky. The air still held a strong chill and Mary shivered, lamenting the loss of her mantle.

Mr. Richards' gaze flicked down to her attire, then back to her face.

Mary looked down at herself for the first time since her incident with the three men and she could not help the gasp that escaped. Her pelisse and bodice were torn enough to expose the tops of her breasts and a great amount of blood splattered her front, from exposed bosom to the tips of her half boots.

"Oh dear," she said. "I fear this is far beyond repair."

He cleared his throat. "We have a modiste and tailor in residence at my estate—Grimsbury Manor. I will have Mrs. McPhee attempt to fix your dress if you like, or she could be commissioned to fashion you an entirely new wardrobe. The choice, of course, is yours."

Mary looked up at him, amazed. What an ingenious notion. She was, however, short on coin.

She gently shook her aching head. "I fear that my dress will have to go. I have two more in my bag, however; they will have to do until I can earn more coin."

His grin returned. "I failed to mention, Miss Wright, that our modiste will not work for *your* coin. I employ her just as I do the cook. You may request of her any number of gowns and she shall make them." His gaze turned meaningful. "If you are to become an actress, you will require a vastly different style of dress. But you shall learn all of that in your lessons."

Mary nodded, a delighted smile on her lips.

"Are you ready?" Mr. Richards asked.

Mary looked at him. In the dim light of early dawn, she saw how very handsome the man was. He was tall, lean, and had dark waving hair and a grin that surely broke hearts wherever it was brandished. *Her* heart, however, was unmoved. She supposed that was for the best.

"I am ready."

CHAPTER 5

*B*rampton, England—three-hours later

MARY JOLTED AWAKE WITH A GASP. She blinked the blur of sleep away from her eyes, forcing herself to focus on where she was. A carriage. She looked across the well-appointed equipage and saw the ever-grinning Mr. Richards on the opposite velvet-covered squabs.

It all came flooding back. Her work at the pub, walking through the darkened streets of Carlisle, the three men, what they nearly succeeded in doing to her... She shivered. Then she recalled Mr. Richards' rescue and subsequent offer. *Goodness.* Was she mad to be leaving her home to journey with this strange man? She had only known him for mere minutes before she agreed to get in a carriage and travel alone with him, evidently without a care for propriety.

Her gaze slid over his guileless features. He was absurdly handsome, but it was not his attractiveness that compelled her to trust him. It was some other mysterious quality that she could not quite put a name to. Even so, she was most assuredly mad for agreeing to this scheme.

"You awoke just in time, Miss Wright," he said, his eyes glittering with...mirth?

Mary turned to gaze out the window and her jaw dropped briefly before she could catch it. Mr. Richards' estate, she presumed. The sun shone over the white marble façade, lending it an ethereal glow. It was four—no, *five*—stories tall and had marble columns on either side of the massive oak front doors.

"Grimsbury Manor is grand, is it not?"

"I should say so," she whispered, never taking her gaze from the largest home she had ever seen.

"It was passed down to me by my grandfather several years ago. I'd never had the pleasure of seeing it while he was alive, but I know that he would not wish for it to sit unused. Alas, I turned it into a school...of sorts."

The footmen leapt down from the back of the carriage, rocking the equipage with the shift in weight. One opened the door and lowered the step while the other pulled her sack of belongings down from the back. A waft of cool air entered the carriage, bringing with it the crisp scent of an imminent snowfall.

Mr. Richards exited first, then held his hand out to help her down.

"So solicitous." She grinned, and immediately regretted the action, for it pulled at her split lip. Cringing, she touched the tips of her fingers to the cut.

Compassion lit his eyes. "We have a live-in physician. I will have him examine your wounds."

Mary gazed at him in awe and deep appreciation. This man had *truly* thought of everything when he'd created this school for spies. "I thank you, that would be very much appreciated."

He nodded. "Shall we?"

With a sweeping gesture of his arm, Mr. Richards allowed her to pass.

The gravel of his front drive crunched beneath her half boots as she approached her future. The door swept open several long moments before she reached the top step of the grand marble stairs. A man in an official-looking butler's uniform stood stoically just inside the door, while three footmen with powdered white wigs stood in waiting, presumably to take her pelisse or jump to do their master's bidding.

She stepped across the threshold and stopped to stare in wonder. The foyer was swathed in white and gilt, the marble floor reflected the light through the windows and the candles in the high chandelier. The ceiling stood two stories above her head; it was domed and ornately painted with cherubs and clouds, all surrounded with gilt leafing. Her breath was nigh stolen from her very lungs.

A sudden *boom* shook the ground beneath her feet and rattled the chandelier above her head, the dangling glass bulbs tinkling lightly. The explosion caused her to jump and, to her embarrassment, squeak. She spun around toward the still-open door. "What in heaven's—"

"Target practice, Miss Wright," Mr. Richards said, a half-smile playing on his lips. "There are targets set up for any number of weapons practice. As you can hear, there is a class in session."

He winked at her and she was struck again at just how handsome the man was. He certainly had a devilishly charming air about him. And goodness, but he couldn't be much older than Mary herself.

"Isaac," Mr. Richards said to a waiting footman, "see that Miss Wright's belongings are brought to the Red Room." He turned to her, his grin still in place and his hands linked behind his back. Clearly a man at his ease. "Our bedchambers are decorated in an array of colours, and yours is the only one swathed in red. Also, our students double as members of staff; mostly maids and footmen, unless they have a particular skill that they wish to expand upon.

"I would take you on a tour of the classrooms, but I suspect that you would prefer to see the doctor and perhaps have a nap."

She touched the tip of her fingers to her swollen cheek. It had only been four hours since she had been so brutally handled and the mention of a nap nearly sent her into a swoon. "That would be lovely, thank you."

He inclined his head. "Of course. We will tour tomorrow. I will have Stevens here show you the way." He motioned to another of the footmen nearby with only the slightest raising of his dark eyebrow. Amazing how some men could command with just one look. "Summon the physician, if you will," he added.

Voices came from down the hallway, but the others ignored them. Mary was curious, despite herself. What other manner of men and women had begun training to become spies? Were they all commoners? Gentry?

"Welcome, Miss. I am Bramwell Stevens," the charmingly handsome footman with beguiling golden eyes said. "Your room is this way."

He turned to leave, but was stopped by her softly inhaled exclamation.

From the doorway to her right came three young men, all dressed finely in dark coats and trousers. But it was the man on the left of the three that made her heart stop within her chest and her stomach flip over and over in a tumbling roll. Lord, but the years had treated him well, indeed. Much to her consternation.

43

"Ah," Mr. Richards said unceremoniously, evidently unaware of the emotional turmoil churning within Mary. "Here are some of our students now."

The men looked up, then bowed appropriately to their superior.

"Hugh Haddington, Colin Greene, and Gabriel Ashley, this is Miss Mary Wright. She will be joining our fascinating school. Miss Wright, Mr. Haddington, Colin Greene, and Mr. Ashley have been with us for just over six months."

Mary saw the precise moment that Gabe recognized her. His arched brown eyebrows reached to his hairline, his eyes wide as saucers, and his mouth opened in a silent *O*. It had been years since she had seen him, and despite her self-assertions that he no longer held any control over her, she felt a significant amount of hurt, anger, and she was ashamed to say, embarrassment, just at the sight of him. He had broken her heart as a young girl and clearly her heart had not yet recovered.

"Charmed, Miss Wright," Mr. Haddington bowed politely, an openly pleasant expression on his fine, pale features.

Mary could not help but give him a small smile in return, her lips pulling and splitting unpleasantly.

Mr. Greene grinned at her, his dark eyes dancing as he bowed. "A pleasure, I'm sure."

She curtseyed to both of the men. "Likewise, I'm sure, Mr. Haddington, Mr. Greene."

"What in the *bloody hell* is *she* doing here?" Gabe finally burst out, his fiercely scowling face a mottled red. His Scottish accent seemed to have apparently faded entirely over the past years.

Anger took the foreground in Mary's emotions. How dare he imply that she hadn't the right to be there?

"It is a pleasure to see you as well, Mr. Ashley," she said, her voice brittle with sarcasm. "I am sure that Mr. Richards has a reason for recruiting me, just as he had a reason for recruiting *you*."

Gabriel ignored her to gaze accusingly at Mr. Richards. "You brought *her* here?"

The others around them watched, enthralled, as Mary stepped forward, determined to have Gabriel speak directly to her. "Yes, he brought *me* here."

Still refusing to look at her, Gabe's frown deepened. "Into *this* life, you would bring her? What could she possibly have that is of interest to you?"

Mary's gasp echoed through the grand foyer. Hurt lanced through her heart once more.

This time Mr. Richards responded. "Not that it is your place to decide who is recruited and who is not, Mr. Ashley, but Miss Wright is not only an accomplished actress and well-versed, contributing member to society, but just hours ago she defended herself most admirably against the onslaught of three impudent ruffians. Her bravery, knowledge, and skill are to be commended, particularly for someone without the proper training. As you know, I do extensive research on my recruits. And I do *not* make mistakes."

Gabe's eyes had widened further—if that were possible— as he turned his gaze to lie fully upon her. "*Good God*! What happened?"

Gabriel's gaze travelled over her torn and blood-soaked dress and pelisse, his face wreathed with horror. Mr. Haddington and Mr. Greene, however, gazed at her with growing admiration glittering in their eyes.

Mary felt only hurt, anger, and exhaustion. She had slept but a mere three hours on the carriage ride here and nothing before that.

"My pardon, Mr. Stevens," Mary said, her spine stiffening, "but I should like to see my room now."

The young footman appeared beside her. "Of course, Miss Wright. Do follow me."

With her head held high, Mary straightened her skirts and followed Mr. Stevens up the grand, curving marble staircase. Damn Gabriel Ashley anyway.

CHAPTER 6

ondon, England, mid May 1815—the present

GABRIEL ASHLEY GRIMACED as he pulled his loose-fitting white muslin shirt over his head. His ribs continued to pain him something fierce. It had only been a sennight since the Bonaparte-supporting turncoat attacked him in the Mason family's house in town and left him in a cellar to rot. Hydra had been perpetrating a plot to lure out traitors among Hydra's men by using his sister by marriage as bait. Lord knew that had been a mistake. Lane Mason, the Earl of Devon, his staff, and family save for one sister, had withdrawn to a safe house while their home was filled with Secret Service spies.

Gabe had been working as the cook during the scheme and had been jumped from behind while preparing tea. The stitched gash from his right ear lobe along his jaw line to his chin still stood out in stark relief from the drawn pallor of his skin. But it was not his jaw, head, or his ribs that caused the majority of his aches. No, indeed. That honour went entirely to Miss Mary Wright.

He cursed to himself as he tucked the tails of his shirt into his trousers then slipped his brown waistcoat on and began to fasten the buttons. Ever since the attack on his person, Mary had visited him daily, her face wreathed in concern and her charms all but bursting the seams of her maid's uniform.

He *really* needed to get out of town. This was Mary, for God's sake, a friend—*if* one could even consider their association a friendship—and nothing more. He had made the foolish decision many years ago to leave his childhood fancies behind, Miss Mary Wright included. He had thought himself far above the patrons of Carlisle.

Soon after he had left Cumberland, however, Gabe had deeply regretted his decision. Mary's friendship had been dearer to him than he had realized, but by then it had been too late. He had already lost her.

Then confounded Richards had brought her to the school to become a spy. Damn the man, he knew how Gabe felt about her; Gabe had talked about her on the journey all the way from Scotland. The man had *known* what Mary had meant to him when he had recruited her and yet he'd done it anyway, the cur. Gabe didn't want her there. She didn't belong in this kind of life; she was so much better than any of them. She was better off without him, without spy work... Damn it, she was better off without *him* in her life. She should be living peacefully in some cottage somewhere, safe with a husband and a passel of children. Instead, she spent her days doing dangerous sneak-work, her afternoons and evenings working in the theatre in front of hundreds of salivating men, and her nights doing Lord knew what with her next mark. It made him ill. And, confound it, it made him angry.

He met his own blue gaze in the mirror in the corner of his temporary guest bedchamber and ran a hand over his haphazardly curling brown hair. If he stayed in town, Mary's attentions would surely kill him. Another curse escaped him.

"If your injuries continue to pain you, Gabe, you are more than welcome to stay on," a voice intoned from the open doorway.

Gabe turned to see his superior, Sir Charles Bradley—or as they called him, Hydra—leaning against the doorframe.

"Ta. I thank ye verra much, sir," Gabe said, allowing his natural accent out and pulling on his mud-coloured woollen coat. "But I am well, I assure ye." Or as well as he was going to be under the circumstances.

"Even though Lord Devon, the rest of my family, and household servants are returned to town, there are those of my men that are staying on, if only until they receive another assignment. And of course, there are the other injured men who all have rooms here, or at the other town house. So believe me when I say, Gabe, that you may stay if you wish, whether in the kitchens with cook or as a guest in recovery. This house might be full, but I rather enjoy a busy home. You are more than welcome to remain."

Gabe nodded in acknowledgement and appreciation. "My thanks again, Hydra. But by my troth I am well. The others are far more injured than I; Barrows still has yet te awaken."

They stood in silence for a moment, each pondering their own worry for the other fallen. During the scheme, several of Gabe's fellow agents—and Gabe himself—had their identities compromised...and then the attacks had begun. Young Harris, a new recruit just out of intelligence training, had been shot in the shoulder on his first assignment. Greene had been stabbed in the back, and Barrows suffered with a severe head injury.

Gratefully, the French spies responsible had been dealt with appropriately and would no longer be a threat to the other Crown spies or Hydra and his new family.

Hydra's blond eyebrows furrowed. "Yes, well..." he cleared

his throat. "If you are well enough, preparation for a new assignment in Eastbourne begins tomorrow. If you decline I have another man in mind."

The hum of anticipation buzzed through Gabe's veins. He needed to get out of town, to get into something sneaky and dirty, to get into the thick of enemy territory and take them out from within. And...to get away from Mary. Damn but she distracted him something fierce.

"Aye, I am well enough te take on an assignment."

Hydra jerked his shaggy blond head in a single nod. "Very good, then. It's a partnered assignment and the briefing is tomorrow at dawn."

Gabe's lips curved upward in a grin. "I will see ye then, sir."

"Oh, and Gabe?"

"Aye?"

"You had better practice your English accent. You are going to need it." Then he was gone, the small guest bedchamber in the Devon town house empty once more.

A log popped in the fireplace behind him and Gabe turned to smile at his reflection in the tall mirror, the act pulling painfully at the stiches along his jaw. But he paid it no mind. He was going on another assignment. An *infiltration* assignment if Hydra's warning to practice his accent was any indication. Damn, but he hadn't done infiltration in some time. He couldn't deny that he was excited.

He'd become used to speaking with an English accent while he was in school, and he often used it during assignments. It had gotten to the point where his habitual accent was a mixture of Scottish and English, though when emotions were involved, he switched fully to Scottish.

"Ve*ry*," he practiced to his reflection as he tugged the final knot in his starched white cravat. "Did*n't*. Y*ou*."

"I haven't heard your English accent in some time."

Gabe's heart slammed in his chest at the cultured female voice behind him. He swung around.

"Damnit, Mary, donnae sneak up on me like tha'!"

Her soft lips turned downward in a pretty frown. "Oh pooh. And you were doing so well."

Gabe suppressed the swell of pride that her words provoked.

"Wha' are ye doing here, Mary?"

The joyous glint to her steel grey eyes fled and Gabe felt as though he'd lost something precious.

"I came to see how you fared, but I can see you are well." She affected a shallow curtsey. "Pardon me for intruding, sir. Good day."

She turned to leave but something made him stop her. "Mary, wait," he called.

She froze in the doorway then turned to face him, an expectant expression on her lovely features.

Gabe let his gaze travel down her attire. She was dressed as a maid as she so often was when she was here. The drab black and white frock should dull anyone's ardour, but with her dark auburn hair veritably shining beneath her mobcap and her voluptuous charms straining against the material across her chest, any man would want her. And, damn it, so did he.

His covetousness warred with prudence within him and he ran his hand agitatedly through his already dishevelled hair.

Mary's eyebrows rose expectantly. "You really must spit it out, Gabriel, my rehearsals begin in three quarters of an hour."

Anger immediately burned in his gut as her words shook him out of his reverie. "Mary, ye shouldnae continue at the theatre."

A delicate frown creased her brow. "I do not wish to have this argument with you again, Gabe. You know how I feel about being an actress."

"Aye, I ken ye are a *thespian*," he sneered the word, feeling like a petulant child, "but te let—nae, *encourage*—men te ogle ye then te use yer wiles..." That familiar, hated fury gnawed at him again... It was like a festering wound that wouldn't damn well heal.

MARY WRIGHT BALLED her hands into fists as she stared down the man that had once been a dear childhood friend... whom she had thought she would be with forever.

Curse her romantic heart anyway. The man had crushed it long ago and best she remember that.

"It isnae right," he said.

Mary knew what he thought. He believed the same thing that everyone else believed. She was an actress, after all, and most actresses were considered as good as high-priced whores by London society. Of course, she used that to her advantage in her own way, but while she may not be as pure as the driven snow, she was most assuredly a maiden. Not that Gabe would believe her if she said as much.

Instead, she made the same argument she had made countless times. "It is not as bad as you believe. I love being an actress and I love being a spy. In addition to that, it is the perfect identity for a woman in the Secret Service; men will tell me anything I wish, as they believe me too dimwitted to understand its significance."

"Ye may believe what ye say, Mary, but yer treated as a common doxy."

Hurt laced through her. "Yes, of course you would belittle my position in such a manner. Because I could not possibly be capable of separating my spy life from my true self, yes? Of *course* not," her voice veritably dripped with sarcasm, "I will just lift my skirts for any man that walks through my door, like a harlot. Think you I do not understand the difference between the acquisition of intelligence and becoming a man's lover?"

His eyes widened slightly in alarm. "Nae, I didnae mean—"

"You have said quite enough, Gabriel. At least I now know what you truly think of me." With a stubborn ache in her chest, Mary spun on her heel and hurried from the room and down the hall to the hidden servant's passageway.

Curse Gabriel Ashley anyway.

Mary forced her legs faster down the passage. Would that she could return to her modest apartments and sleep the day away. But no, she must be professional. She would put aside thoughts of her aching heart and would do as she was taught.

Tonight was the last performance of *Lover's Vows*—written by the talented Mrs. Elizabeth Inchbald—at the Theatre Royal. She would conclude her role with one last assignment—as long as Hydra had a mark for her.

Gabe thought that she used sex to glean information from her marks, but while she did use her sensuality, she by no means had intercourse. After the incident with the men in Carlisle, Mary had become hesitant and nervous around men, which put a damper on her lessons. As a means to harness her newfound fear of men, Mary wished to use their own barbaric nature against them.

Per her request, Kieran Richards—or as the spies in the Secret Service fondly called him, Hermes—had introduced her to a very unique instructor. Mary now knew how to bring men fulfilment with the sway of her hips or the tip of her finger.

Her newfound knowledge did not entirely remove her fear and trepidation, but it certainly gave her the confidence to face men and know that she could use her body and mind to control any circumstance that she might find herself in.

She made her way down the narrow servant's stairwell and

through the winding passage until she reached the stone façade of the back side of a fireplace. She lifted her hand and thudded her fist three times on the warm stone, then waited. She could hear the soft footfalls on the other side of the thick stone before a responding thump. Mary quickly rapped twice, paused, then rapped thrice more in their practiced routine.

A gust of air blew at the tendrils of hair sticking out from beneath her mobcap as the stone fireplace swung out like a door on hinges.

"Mary!" Hydra stepped aside to allow her to pass him into his study. "You know you may come in through my front door."

"That may have been the case when it was just spies in residence, sir, but with your wife's family and their servants returned, I believe it would be prudent of me to observe the traditional roles of a downstairs maid."

He nodded. "Quite right, Mary. Quite right. And your prudence is appreciated." He closed the hidden passageway with a quiet *whoosh* then returned to stand before his leather chair behind a great oak desk. "As a matter of fact, I am glad you came. I have a small matter to discuss with you."

He gestured to the chair across from him and Mary gratefully took a seat before he took his own. She had anticipated that he would wish to speak with her for, beginning tomorrow, her cover position as an actress would be put on hiatus. And as the war with Bonaparte was still very much active, the need for her sort of intelligence was imperative.

Mary's gaze travelled over the furnishings while she waited for Hydra to speak. His study was rather ordinary; bookshelves with books lined two of the four walls, dark wooden panels covered the others. A tantalus with glinting glass bottles of liquor stood in one corner, and a settee and two armchairs rested before the fireplace. Small trinkets and vases ornamented the two small round side tables and the fireplace mantle, and a large painting of men on the hunt, proudly mounted on their horses while hounds bound before them, hung on the wall behind the grand desk. The two tall windows on either side of the painting allowed the sun to brighten the darkly appointed room, lending it warmth.

The room smelled of leather book bindings and sandalwood soap.

"I have an opportunity for you to take on a new role," Hydra's deep voice shook her from her observations. "There have been reports from some of our men of suspected traitorous activity among our past marks. I must confess, after first learning of this, I was hesitant to send any men out to investigate, particularly after the leak of information, and subsequent attacks."

"But the parties responsible were—"

"I know, Mary." Hydra raked his fingers through his hair. "They were all dealt with, and our identities protected. It was merely a residual fear, I assure you. Our duties must now return to normal, and that means new assignments.

"There will be a briefing for you tomorrow at first light."

A new role. Could this be for a position as actress, or would she get to practice her infiltration? She very much wished to know. But regardless of the position, Mary was anxious for something to do.

"I will be there, thank you," she said. "As you must know, tonight is the last performance of *Lovers' Vows* before rehearsals for my next role in *The Devil to Pay*." She clasped her hands together in her lap. As many times as she had asked this question, she always felt a mite uncomfortable at its significance. "Is there a mark you wish me to seek out this evening?"

He cleared his throat. "As a matter of fact, yes. I have it under good authority that the Earl of Reddington will be attending tonight's performance..."

"Consider it done, sir." She moved to rise, but Hydra stopped her.

"One more thing, Mary."

She looked at him expectantly.

"This task is unique, yet crucial to your next assignment."

Mary nodded, intrigued.

"You are to obtain an invitation to a house party that your mark is attending at Kerr House in a fortnight. I hate to ask it of you, Mary, but you *must* acquire that invitation, whatever it takes."

She'd never had to exert much effort in obtaining information from men, but garnering an invitation posed a challenge that she was eager to conquer.

"I will do all that I can, sir," Mary said.

"I have every confidence that you will. Though as this assignment is time sensitive, I will require the result before the morrow." He raised a hand in a placating gesture. "Rest assured, you needn't make the short journey to me; I will come to you. Our signal will remain the same."

Mary nodded, another lock of her auburn hair falling from beneath her mobcap. "Very good. I shall expect you."

CHAPTER 7

*T*he brilliant light of candles shone all around her, lighting the stage and the hundreds of faces that watched, enraptured by the performance. The occasional cough or clearing throat were the only sounds but for the act. The theatre was filled with the merging of scents, from melting tallow to freshly-sprayed perfume. Mary loved it.

But right now, Mary was not Mary and her fellow thespian, Mr. Murray, was not Mr. Murray. Enacting Act two, Scene two of Mrs. Inchbald's *Lovers' Vows*, she was Miss Amelia Wildenhaim and he was her very dear Papa, the Baron, with whom she currently spoke about matrimony. She was in love with Mr. Anhalt and engaged to Count Cassel.

"You put me out of patience," the Baron said. *"Hear, Amelia! To see you happy is my wish. But matrimony, without concord, is like a duetto badly performed; for that reason, nature, the great composer of all harmony, has ordained, that, when bodies are allied, hearts should be in perfect union."*

In that moment, Mary did something she had never before done. She dropped character. She said her lines, naturally, but she was certain that it sounded dull to the audience, as her thoughts were elsewhere. On Gabriel.

How could he be so cruel? She was not a lightskirt—not that he would know, she supposed. He had never witnessed her acquiring intelligence from a mark; he did not know that her cover did not involve taking a different man into her bed each night.

She determinately suppressed a scowl. And what if she *did* take lovers to her bed? Men did it with startling—and abhorrent—regularity. Why should she not enjoy the delights that were reportedly found in the marriage bed?

Focus, Mary, she told herself. *This is the last performance. Focus.*

Still in a daze, she completed the scene, each line going quicker than the last. Before long, the third act had begun. She was not in the first scene, but she stood to the side and observed. In the next moment, the curtain dropped, and she went on stage, ready to play her part.

The first few lines were easy enough. Her *love*, Mr. Anhalt, was a splendid actor.

"*A very proper subject from the man who has taught me love, and I accept the proposal,*" she said.

"*Again, you misconceive and confound me,*" Mr. Anhalt said.

She replied in a carrying voice, "*Ay, I see how it is—you have no inclination to experience with me "the good part of matrimony:" I am not the female with whom you would like to go "hand in hand up hills, and through labyrinths"—with whom you would like to "root up thorns; and with whom you would delight to plant lilies and roses." No, you had rather call out, "Oh liberty, dear liberty."*"

"*Why do you force from me, what it is villainous to own?*" He stepped forward and earnestly gripped her shoulders. "*I *love you more than life—oh Amelia!*" Mary did not hear the remainder of his lines, for she was lost in thought once more.

Curse Gabriel Ashley for that. What she would not have given, at one time, to hear Gabe say such a thing to her. Love... What a simple yet unattainable thing.

She must banish Gabe from her thoughts. She was a thespian...and she was a spy. She pushed her shoulders back and notched her chin higher.

I am Miss Amelia Wildenhaim, she told herself. *I love Mr. Anhalt...*

THE DIN WAS nigh deafening in the back rooms of the Theatre Royal in Covent Garden, but Mary did not pay the crowd of actors, actresses, and their many admirers any mind. She had eyes for only one man.

She spotted him immediately across the crush and started toward him. She wove between the many bodies, the cloying scent of perfume and warm perspiration assaulting her senses. The chandeliers hung high above, lending a cheerful glow to those below.

Her mark turned his back to her as he whispered something into Mary's fellow actress, Kitty's, ear. The girl giggled, a pretty blush on her pale cheeks.

Mary's lips curved upward in a self-assured smile as she reached his shoulder. She hastily adjusted the gauzy shawl about her elbows and gave an extra tug to the bodice of her already daring evening gown. She had the frock specially made to entice; she wore no petticoat, so the fine green striped silk of her skirts perfectly accentuated the outline of her body beneath.

It was entirely wicked.

With deliberate sensuality, Mary trailed her first finger from her mark's wrist to his shoulder. This had the desired effect of taking his attention away from Kitty.

"Why, Lord Reddington," Mary purred, "you do look fine this evening."

His lascivious green gaze turned to encompass her and his smile broadened. "I must return the compliment, Miss..."

"White," she gave him her stage pseudonym.

"Miss White. My, what a charming name." Turning his back on Kitty, he faced Mary fully.

She bit back a laugh at Kitty's pout. The young actress was better off without this man in her life anyway.

Mary ran her fingers over his narrow shoulders and down his chest, earning a shudder from her mark. She grinned openly at him. He appeared to be nearly thirty years of age and was rather startlingly handsome. He had wavy blond hair, emerald-green eyes, a strong jaw, patrician nose, and a wicked smile. He also smelled of liquor and was—if her previous experience was any indication—obviously easily seduced. This was going to be quicker than she had thought.

Deliberate coyness and artificial naiveté were stratagems that Mary often employed, but she knew from the moment she had set eyes on Lord Reddington that such tactics would not win her the desired reaction. Idiocy, yes. Wanton abandon, naturally. Blatant sexuality...absolutely.

She winked at him, her smile seductive as she leaned her breasts against his arm and stretched up to press her lips to his ear. "Come to my dressing room," she crooned provocatively, "and you will experience something beyond your wildest imagination."

Mary pulled away from him the moment she felt his breath quicken, and with one last heavy-lidded glance, she spun about to make her way back through the crowd, exaggerating the sway of her hips. She knew he would follow. No man of his ilk could deny his curiosity when a woman made such a bold statement.

Winding her way through the side and back corridors, she passed the scene painting and storage rooms, the Royal Saloon, and several other dressing rooms before she reached her own. The room was of generous size and stringently tidy. A chaise and a French privacy screen concealed two corners of the room, and the third was filled with her wardrobe, dressing table, and looking glass. The walls were a pale pink, though devoid of any art. The light in her dressing room was deliberately dim, with only one sconce and a candelabra lighting the space.

Mary moved to stand near the chaise and turned in time to see Lord Reddington hurry into the room after her.

"Do close the door, Lord Reddington. I trust you would not wish us to be observed by every passer-by."

His breath came rapidly as he closed the door.

"Have a seat, won't you?" She indicated the chaise.

"I believe I was promised an unforgettable experience."

Insolent pup. "And indeed, you shall receive one. *Sit*."

He did as she demanded and draped himself casually on the lush red velvet cushions.

Cocking her hip to the side, she slowly pulled her thin shawl from her elbows, and ran the fine material through her hands before stopping to grip each end in a tight fist. She approached him slowly, swaying her hips with each step, and leaned deeply over him, bringing her breasts alluringly close to his face. It was only as she drew away that he realized that she had tied his wrists together with her shawl.

"What—?" His jaw dropped open on the word as she put her hands to her front-opening bodice and began to pull the ribbons loose. "*Ooooh*..."

Dipping one knee, she flicked the opposite hip upward, then did the same on the other side. *Dip, flick, dip, flick.*

She began a rhythm with her hips as she pulled her gown away to reveal the sheer material of her chemisette. It did little to cover her as it hugged her curves like a second skin, but that was the object. Beneath the chemisette were two strips of material, one covering her breasts and the other wrapped around her hips and bottom, completely covering her *feminine* area.

The seduction had the desired effect. Her quarry was enraptured by her movements, utterly captivated by the swivel of her hips. And the evidence of his interest strained the falls of his trousers.

Excellent. This is going to be easy.

She stepped out of the gown that had pooled at her feet, and she brushed it aside with her slipper-clad toes.

"Where," he gritted out, "where did you learn to do that?"

"This?" She flicked her hip.

Ever so slowly, she ran the backs of her fingers over her hips, trailing them lightly over her waist, up the sides of her breasts, neck, and further, until her wrists touched high above her head.

Lord Reddington licked his already glistening lips and nodded jerkily.

She saw no harm in telling him—at least *part* of the truth. "As a young girl, I came across an actress from a foreign land. She taught me all there is to know about this style of dance. She had been part of a harem for many years."

"H—harem?"

She winked saucily at him. "Yes."

Then she began to dance.

GABE BROUGHT the mug of ale to his lips and took a long swill before plunking it back down, the contents splashing over the rim and onto the polished tabletop. He sat in a private dining room of Brooks' Gentleman's Club; it was a favourite meeting place for Gabe and his select few friends, as it afforded them privacy and anonymity when they used their aliases.

The dining room was of diminutive size, with just one round table that sat four and a sidebar with liquor and assorted cured meats and cheeses. Gabe was certain that if he stood in the centre of the room and stretched his arms out from his sides, he could touch each wall with his fingertips. It was, in essence, a cupboard. But it served their purpose and the keeper of the establishment ensured that this room was always available for Gabe and his friends' use. The walls and ceiling were covered in dark wood and were lit by candles on the sidebar and table.

Gabe took another gulp of the bitter ale. He would much rather it be a scotch, and he would much rather drown his sorrows in an entire bottle, but he had to report to Hydra at dawn and did not wish to be ill from drink.

Bloody hell.

Only one woman had ever shaken him in such a way and Gabe suspected that only one woman ever would. Mary. The chit never listened to him. If only he could make her see that she was wasting her life away with sneak-work...

"Something is weighing in your thoughts, my friend. Feel at your ease to unburden yourself to me."

Gabe lifted a sardonic eyebrow to his long-time friend, Colin Greene, and took another gulp of ale.

"You are welcome to believe me insincere," his friend continued, "but I assure you I am in earnest. We have been friends—the best of friends—for many years, and I—"

"Ye sound like a wee lassie, speaking of feelings so," Gabe

grumbled, interrupting. He knew he was being an arse, but he didn't care.

Colin took a quaff of his brandy and grinned. "That may be so, old chum, but speaking of feelings never fails to win favours from the fairer sex." He winked at Gabe over the rim of his snifter.

Gabriel shook his head. His friend was nothing if not popular with women. "Quite right." Gabe's lips curved upward in a tight grin. "You and Hugh were always very popular with women."

The light in Colin's dark eyes dimmed slightly at the reminder of their missing friend.

Gabe, Colin, and Hugh Haddington had been the best of friends since they began their spy education at approximately the same time.

"Have you heard any news from Hydra?" Colin asked.

Gabe shook his head. "I've expressed my concerns to Hydra on countless occasions since the night of Hugh's disappearance. I had even volunteered to be a member of his search team, but Hydra insisted that I remain at my post."

As much as he adored his position in his life as a spy, Gabe would surrender everything just to find Hugh alive and well again. Gabe certainly hoped that the men sent searching for him would find him soon.

"To Hugh," Colin muttered, tipping his snifter.

Gabe nodded. He hoped that Hugh had found himself a woman and eloped, rather than what Gabe suspected after the attacks on their fellow men.

He lifted his gaze to observe his friend across the table. Colin was dark where Hugh was light: his hair, eyes, and humour.

Much like Gabe, Colin was recovering from a recent attack. Gabe was uncertain of the details but knew that Colin had taken a dagger wound to his back on his last assignment.

As distressing as his life in the Secret Service, tonight Gabe's thoughts were on a different troubling subject. Tonight his thoughts were on—

"Miss Mary Wright," Colin blurted.

Gabe's gaze shot to his friend. "Pardon?"

Colin shook his head. "You have not heard a word that I've said, have you?" He thumped his snifter a little too hard on the tabletop and frowned at Gabe. "You might have success-fully—albeit briefly—distracted me, but I will not be pushed aside. I gave you the opportunity to speak freely, but you did not take that chance. Now I have to be blunt with you, to the devil with the consequences."

Gabe didn't know what to make of his friend's abrupt displeasure, but as he was stunned into silence, he waited for Colin to continue.

"It has been *seven years*, man! Yes, she is in a demanding field of work, and *yes*, she likely beds a different man every night, but what right have you to dictate what she does with her assignments—or with her body for that matter? She chose to accept Hermes' offer of a certain education; she was not forced into it against her will." Colin's frown deepened. "If you had wanted to save her from this life—from *herself,* or so you say—then you should have taken her to bed and taken her to wife years ago and been done with this entire mess. But you didn't, because you're a coward."

"Oi!" Gabe bristled.

"*No.*" Colin pointed a finger at him. "I'm not finished with you yet and it's about time that you listened to the advice that I've been giving you. You have been miserable since she walked through the doors of the Brampton Estate and I'm tired of looking at your dour expressions. I would say this is from only my perspective, but everyone who knows you sees it as I do. You have two choices," he marked them off on his fingers. "One, you forget about Miss Mary Wright; tup a whore, bed some married or widowed chits, join an orgy, I don't care. But do whatever it takes, bed as many women as you can to rid her from your thoughts..."

"And choice number two?"

"Take Mary for your own." Colin tossed the last finger of his brandy down his throat with a slight grimace, and then rose. "Until you make a decision, do me a favour and don't seek me out."

With that, Colin straightened his coat and disappeared through the dining room door. Had he just lost a friend? Gabe allowed that quick shot of pain to briefly hit his heart. Colin would come back.

Take Mary for your own. Gabe ran Colin's words through his mind as he was left alone in the small room. But as alluring as the idea was, Gabe knew that he could not be with Mary. He had ended the friendship that they'd shared many years ago and there was no chance of rekindling it now. Most particularly after the way he'd treated her over the past years. He was beastly, he would admit, but damn it, she would not listen to reason!

He shook his head. Bedding Mary—even if she would accept him—wouldn't solve anything. He was not consumed with thinking of her because of any desire for her, but for a concern for her safety. Colin did not know of what he spoke. What Gabe needed to do was to find a way to convince her that being a spy was too dangerous.

There had been moments in the past years that he'd thought that perhaps he and Mary could share a professional working relationship and he could accept her presence in the Secret Service, but something always happened to change his mind. Too damned often, men were hurt, killed, or abducted. Hell, Gabe had nearly died on his last mission, Greene had been stabbed in the back, and Hugh was bloody well missing entirely! No. It was far too dangerous for Mary to live this life.

66

He would think of a way. This evening was the last performance of *Lovers' Vows*, so he knew that Mary would not have an assignment for some time. During her hiatus, Gabe would go to the country on his own assignment, taking a much-needed break from being around her. By the time he returned, he would have had the time to think of a way to convince her.

Yes. A solid plan, indeed.

CHAPTER 8

"*Good God*! Miss White, you *must* become my mistress." Lord Reddington rose from his seat on the chaise, his wrists still tied and the damp spot on the falls of his trousers evidence that her plan had worked.

Mary was rather surprised at how quickly her *task* had been completed. Ordinarily it took men at least a half of an hour to be fulfilled without a single touch, but Lord Reddington had found completion within ten minutes.

She smiled at him, her eyes crinkling in the corners. "I am mistress to no one."

"Then you must say yes. Be my mistress."

She had been propositioned by many men and her answer with Lord Reddington would be the same as the others. Mary shook her head. "I will not become a mistress. I prefer the freedom to choose."

"Then I shall come again tomorrow. And the day after..."

Curses. The man was determined. Though...that might work to her advantage.

Mary slipped her chemisette over her mostly nude form and sidled up close to him. "La, what a persistent man. You may come back, Lord Reddington," she said in a throaty whisper, "but my answer will remain the same." As she pulled away, she slid her scarf from around his wrists and draped it over the decorative mirror of her dressing table.

She heard him stand behind her before she felt his body press against her back, his arms curving around her middle to pull her tightly against his front.

"Please, dearling, call me James. I long to hear my name on your lips." He spun her in his arms, turning her so he could see her face as she spoke.

The corner of her mouth curved up. "James," she whispered.

"Mmmm," he hummed, squeezing her tighter against him. "Louder."

She reached around her back to clasp one of his hands in hers, forcing him to loosen his grip. Bringing it slowly upward, she used his hand to caress her hip, her waist, and then between their bodies to graze her chest, finally reaching her deliberately chosen final destination. She lightly grazed his fingertips over her pouted lips, then she pulled his forefinger into her mouth and bit the tip. "James."

A grunt of satisfaction escaped him as he pulled her to him once more. He wedged his face in the soft area between her neck and shoulder and inhaled deeply. "A good friend of mine is hosting a house party in a fortnight." His voice was muffled against her skin. "Tell me you will accompany me."

She placed her most charming smile on her lips. "*That*, my lord, I will most certainly do." She lifted an eyebrow as she placed her hands on his shoulders. "*However*, I will not go as your mistress and I insist that we arrive separately."

"Come now, love, you don't know what you're missing." His liquor-scented breath wafted over her and she suppressed a grimace. Ever since her horrifying experience all those years ago, she had a vehement distaste for all spirits, particularly those riding upon the breath of a man.

Mary raised an eyebrow once more and began to pull away from him.

He tightened his hold. "I concede!" he said almost desperately. "I concede, minx."

She dazzled him with a bright smile. "I would be delighted to attend. Thank you."

Suddenly, the door swung open and a man tumbled in, falling to the floor. Startled, they both jumped. Lord Reddington released her, causing Mary to stumble backward.

"I say!" Lord Reddington exclaimed, red faced.

The man staggered awkwardly to his feet, the stench of brandy seeping from his clothing and filling the air around him.

"I say, get out, sir! This room is taken!" Lord Reddington removed the hat still resting on his head and placed it discretely over his pelvic region as he stepped away from Mary.

The intoxicated man looked around, bleary eyed, at his surroundings. His bright clothing was rumpled, but of fine quality, his black hair was wavy and haphazardly styled atop his head, and he sported the dark outline of several days' growth of beard.

Mary stepped toward the confused man with a mind to help, but Lord Reddington placed a hand on her arm to hold her back.

"Did you hear what I said, sir?" Lord Reddington's voice darkened.

The man turned bloodshot blue eyes in their direction, his gaze sweeping them both from head to toe. A slow grin spread across his lips. "Oooh...I geddit." He brought a hand up to touch the tip of his index finger to his nose, but missed and poked himself in the eye. "Bl—bloody hell!" He blinked rapidly, losing his balance and knocking into the stool in front of her dressing table. "Shhhh!"

He righted himself again, though still unsteady. "Having a liddle fun, eh?" He winked both eyes, his grin growing to show perfectly white teeth. "I don' wanna interrupt!" He wiggled his fingers suggestively and suddenly Mary felt the urge to smile.

The intoxicated man turned to leave but tripped over his own foot and fell face down onto the floor.

Lord Reddington cursed soundly and stepped forward, clearly at the end of his patience.

"No," Mary stopped him. "Leave him. I know how to deal with drunken men. I can summon some of the stagehands to assist with removing him."

His lordship looked from Mary to the man lying unconscious on the floor, clearly wishing to take his leave, but reluctant to appear uncaring. "It would be unseemly for me to leave you alone here with him."

"Oh, la!" She smiled broadly at him. "I assure you, Lord Reddington, I am fully capable of handling myself with this man. The moment you take your leave, I shall summon a stagehand."

Mary felt the urge to laugh at the look of relief that crossed his features. Evidently expending any effort not involved in a seduction was unworthy of his time. His indolence in this instance was rather to her advantage.

"If you are certain," he said.

She smiled at him. "I am certain."

"Very well. I shall send 'round a messenger with the details of the house party."

Mary ran her hand down his arm to gently squeeze his lace-clad wrist. "I wait with bated breath, my lord."

With one last glare at the slumbering, inebriated man and his hat still placed strategically over the falls of his trousers,

Lord Reddington made a hasty departure. Mary waited until she heard his footfalls fade far down the corridor before she closed and locked her dressing room door.

Turning, she placed her hands on her hips. "Must you have arrived so early, Hydra? I despise having to make excuses."

A low rumble emanated from the heap upon the floor before the grinning and decidedly sober Sir Charles Bradley rose to his feet to face her, his gaze carefully focused on her face. Hydra had seen her thusly on several occasions during assignments and he always had the graciousness to not draw attention to her scanty attire.

"It says little for the man that I anticipated an early evening for you, Mary."

Poorly hiding her grin, Mary clucked her tongue at him as she strode to the privacy screen to retrieve her dressing robe. "That is ungenerous of you, Hydra."

He laughed. "Indeed, it is." His laughter died as he quickly sobered. "Despite the soft side that he may show potential lovers, Mary, the man is a villain."

She emerged from behind the screen with her robe in place and the rope firmly tied. "I believe you. I always do."

He nodded, his arms crossing over his chest. "I gather you have garnered an invitation to the house party?"

"I did." She sat on the stool before her dressing table, then opened a container of rose scented cream and dipped her finger in. "Is that what my next assignment will be?" She turned to face him as she rubbed the cream over her hands and forearms. "You mentioned a 'new role' this morning."

"Yes. We will discuss the particulars at first light."

Mary wondered briefly at his evasiveness but pushed the thoughts from her head. Hydra was her superior. He had a reason for every assignment he sent her on and she trusted him implicitly.

She nodded. "Very well."

"I would discuss it with you now, but I expect you desire sleep."

"I do," she conceded. If tomorrow was the beginning of preparations for a new assignment, she most certainly required sleep.

"I brought my carriage," he said. "I would be pleased to drive you home."

A genuine smile split her lips. "Worried over me, Hydra?"

"As a matter of fact, yes. Far too many of our men have gone missing or have turned up injured or dead of late. As well as I know you can handle yourself with some men, Mary...I daren't contemplate it if you were to come upon the *wrong* sort of man, particularly in great numbers."

Mary's smile faded. *He truly is worried for my safety*, she realized. "I would be grateful for your escort; however, I must begin packing my belongings."

Hydra shrugged one shoulder. "I would be pleased to loan you my carriage and two footmen to assist you in packing after our meeting on the morrow so that you might retire earlier tonight."

"I would not wish to impose..."

"It is no imposition at all, I assure you." He grinned. "Besides which, Bridget would have my hide if I allowed you to do so on your own."

He smiled to himself at the mention of his new, very pregnant wife, and Mary could not help the small burst of envy that sprang through her. Would that she could have a man who adored her as much as Hydra adored his wife.

"Thank you, Hydra."

Mary pulled a gown and underthings from her wardrobe, then disappeared behind the privacy screen.

Foregoing the use of stays or a corset, Mary put a simple gown of brown over her shift and petticoats. It was not a gown one would see among the gentry, to be sure, but it was one of her favourites. It reminded her of chocolate.

Mary grinned as she fastened her stockings to her garters.

She slid her feet into her slippers and pulled her pelisse over her dress before emerging from behind the screen. Hydra straightened from his relaxed position by the door as Mary retrieved her matching brown bonnet.

"Will you not do your hair?"

Mary could not help but tease him. "Is it really that dreadful?"

She laughed outright at the look of alarm on his features. "Be at ease, Hydra, I plan to wear a bonnet." She knotted her hair at the base of her neck and placed the bonnet atop her head, tying the ribbons beneath her chin.

Hydra held an arm out to her and she accepted, allowing him to lead her through the corridor and out the rear entrance, where they found his carriage waiting.

The cool May night air held a refreshing crispness, devoid of fog. The moon shone gaily in the sky, high above them, the stars demanding acknowledgement with each twinkle. Such was an amazing—and rare—sight in the heart of London, for the evenings were often filled with the dark haze of coal smoke.

They entered the well-sprung equipage, and Mary took the rear-facing seat while Hydra lounged comfortably across from her. The ride was silent yet contented, each lost in their own thoughts.

Outside, carriage wheels clattered over cobblestones and coachmen called warnings to one another. The streets were dense with traffic, the equipages en-route to return their passengers home from balls, soirees, and the theatre. It made Mary grateful that her apartments were an easy distance to the Theatre Royal on Drury Lane.

An image of Gabriel's scowling face at her choice of location raced to the foreground of her mind and she frowned in return. He had never been approving of her choices. Shame on her for allowing his admonitions to affect her so. And, dash it, shame on her for allowing him to monopolize her thoughts.

She had embarrassed herself in the theatre this evening. While the audience might not have noticed her drop of character, Mary certainly had.

The carriage rolled to a halt before her modest apartments, the springs bouncing as the footman descended from his rear perch before the door swung open, bringing with it a gust of cool night air. The footman lowered the steps and Mary gratefully accepted the young man's hand as she exited.

She turned to gaze into the dark carriage, where she could see her superior's outline against the window. "I am much obliged, sir. Good night."

He nodded. "Until tomorrow, Mary."

"Oh, and Hydra?" She paused. "You make an excellent inebriate." She closed the door with his laughter ringing in her ears.

CHAPTER 9

The sky was brightening with hues of mauve and magenta as Gabe rapped on the side door to an old pub in Cheapside, the sound echoing through the narrow alley in which he stood. A rat skittered back to its home in a small pile of rubble not ten feet from him and Gabe's lips curled back in distaste.

An answering knock thudded thrice against the thick wooden door, recalling Gabe's attention. He rapped twice more and the door swung open.

"Hydra," he said, affecting a shallow bow to his superior.

"You are just in time, Gabriel. We've only just arrived ourselves."

Gabe had been partnered for assignments before, often for espionage, sabotage, or reconnaissance work. He wondered what Hydra had in store for him today.

He winced at the painful pull at his ribs as the two of them walked down the narrow hallway. The air in the hall was close and stuffy with the scent of smoke, which seeped through the walls from the front rooms.

They reached the closed door at its end and he could hear the high notes of feminine voices. Gabe's curiosity piqued.

"Enter, if you will," Hydra said from behind him.

Gabe pressed the latch and pushed, a plethora of floral scents assailing his senses in one gust. The room was bright, and Gabe blinked, allowing his eyes to adjust to the sudden light.

What he saw then stopped his heart.

"*Wha' the devil?*"

At his exclamation, Mary spun about, her half-clad form in high relief against the tight fabric of her shift and bosom-lifting corset, and another woman for whom Gabe hardly spared a moment's thought, dropped a measure of fabric. Gabe turned to gaze accusingly at Hydra, but the man had already entered the room to approach Mary.

"Close your gaping mouth, Gabe, and make a choice," Hydra glanced at his pocket watch before replacing it in its home in his waistcoat. "Come in and learn the details of the assignment or leave the position to the next available agent."

Gabe clenched his jaw, his heart beating thunderously in his aching chest. *Mary. Half nude. Oh Lord...*

"Shouldnae Miss Wright put on some clothes before we begin? She is nae decent!"

For the first time since he entered, Mary spoke, "I am hardly indecent; I am not nude for pity's sake. Mrs. McPhee was brought down from Brampton to measure me for my costumes and I didn't wish to delay her. Surely this is nothing you haven't seen before, Gabe." He frowned, and Mary rolled her eyes heavenward. "Very well, if it offends your *delicate sensibilities*, I will put on a robe." She turned to Mrs. McPhee. "My apologies, madam, but this must be suspended until our meeting concludes."

The older woman nodded and quietly left the room as Mary slid her arms through the sleeves of a thin cerulean blue dressing robe. She tied the sash in a knot about her waist and sat in the rough, threadbare armchair before the fire, an invisible cloud of rose-scented air rising with the motion.

Gabe tamped down on his inappropriately—yet justifiably —lustful reaction to her scantily clad form as he sat in the highboy across from Mary. He watched her from the corner of his eye. She appeared so out of place in this tattered environment; the once-jade velvet window dressings now torn and coloured a nondescript brown from years of coal and cigar smoke. The other fabrics about the room had met the same fate, the green and blue brocade rug worn through from years of being trodden on, the chaise and chairs, formerly adorned with thick fabric, were now nearly worn through; everything was bedraggled and smelled its age. Though at the moment, their smell was overpowered by Mrs. McPhee's saccharine perfume and Mary's alluring rose scent.

And there Mary sat, at her ease, in a robe and very little else. She belonged in a room of overstuffed silken cushions, surrounded by fragrant flowers and trays of fruits...which he would feed to her one by one before they shared the lavishly ornamented bed...

Damn, there his lust went again. He *must* stop thinking of Mary on such terms. Or better still, he should take himself as far away from her as possible.

"As you both might have surmised by now, this is an infiltration assignment." Hydra said, pulling Gabe from his thoughts. At some point in his musings, Hydra had settled himself on the chaise between Gabe and Mary, facing the fire.

An ill feeling began to fester in the pit of Gabe's stomach. He knew from the nature of an infiltration assignment that he was to play a role, but now that he knew of Mary's involvement, Gabe felt dread begin to seep into his bones.

A file of paper appeared at his elbow. "Your character profiles and the dossier for our suspected targets." Hydra nodded at Mary. "Mary has already gained entrée into the house party, and though she was not invited to bring a guest, Gabe, you will attend with her, should you choose to accept."

"A house party," Gabe mused. If Mary had garnered an invitation during one of her *evening assignments*, that did not bode well. "Might this be the sort of house party in which—"

"In which your sensibilities will be put on high alert," Mary cut across him, her gaze challenging.

Gabe's gut clenched. *Surely not*.

Hydra nodded. "This is delicate and highly dangerous. You must remain in character at *all* times."

Character? Oh God, no... Gabe flipped open his file, his heart freezing at what he saw on the first page. "My *mistress!*" he burst out. "*Wha' the devil do ye mean by this, Hydra?*"

"I beg your pardon!" Mary said, a tantalizing frown on her deceptively angelic heart-shaped face.

Hydra's blue eyes darkened, his voice lowering to an ominous level. "You speak out of turn, Gabriel."

Gabe stood, tossing the dossiers on the chair behind him before turning to pace the tattered rug. He took a deep breath and winced, the floral scent suddenly overwhelming.

Mary's cover was abhorrent enough without adding *mistress* to her list of sins. She did not belong in the world of spies. She did not belong in other men's beds. That thought arrested him, but he quickly dismissed it. Mary belonged married to an ordinary man, and that man was most certainly *not* Gabe.

This assignment was all wrong and Mary's role in it was...

Gabe drew himself up. "My apologies, sir." Gabe affected a shallow bow.

Biting the inside of his cheek, Gabe tried to keep in what else he wished to say, but one glance at Mary's downcast expression made him ever angrier. "Mary cannae do it! Put another female agent in her place if ye will, but nae Mary."

"*I* am the one who procured the invitation," Mary's quiet voice sliced through him with each syllable. "It would hardly be acceptable for another woman to go in my place."

"Very well, then," Hydra rose to remove the dossiers from the highboy Gabe had vacated, then tapped them against his opposite hand. "I had a mind to give the assignment to Greene from the first, but something compelled me to offer it to you. I can see now that I was wrong." He turned to Mary. "Are you amenable to completing this assignment with Colin?"

Mary nodded, pride stiffening her posture. "I am prepared to complete the assignment with any man of your choosing for my partner, sir."

Gabe's heart pounded harder, the beats thundering portentously in his ears. *No!* This was not how this was supposed to happen! Mary was not to go on this assignment at *all*, but with Colin *sodding* Greene? What if their faux relationship of man and mistress turned into something *more* while they shared a bedchamber? *God!*

An odd, panicked fluttering began in his stomach, the likes of which he had never felt before. He didn't think he could even put a name to the horrid, foreign feeling. He could not let Colin take the assignment. Not his oldest friend and his best friend together. Alone. Sharing the same bedchamber...

A throat clearing drew him from his distressing musings. "You are dismissed, Gabe. I shall contact you when I have an alternate assignment," Hydra said.

"Nae! I cannae allow Colin te replace me. *I* will go on the assignment with Mary."

Mary's stomach continued to churn as she watched the exchange between Hydra and Gabriel. How could he be so unfeeling? He implied, not just within her hearing but very obviously in front of her, that she was unfit and not skilled enough to carry out this assignment. *Insulting* did not begin to describe how his words had affected her. Painful and hurtful were both good words, as well.

She was just as experienced in the field as he; her knowledge and skill might differ from his, but she was certainly as capable.

"You just refused the assignment, Gabe. I do not respond well to minds being changed on a whim," Hydra rumbled.

"This is nae a whim, I assure ye, sir. I was just trying te look out fer Mary's best interest."

"*Best interest*?" Mary burst out, standing, her dressing robe swishing as she did. "I daresay you would rather work with Eliza, Amelia, or one of the other women, but I assure you I am fully capable of doing what is necessary to complete this assignment successfully. I—"

"Aye, I believe tha'," Gabe snarled.

Mary reared back as if struck. *Goodness*, it even felt as though she had, but not on her cheek, no. This blow was arrowed directly at her heart. "You believe me a *whore*?"

"*Enough*!" Hydra roared as Gabe flinched, though Mary did not know if it was from her words or Hydra's harsh voice.

"Gabriel, you overstep," Hydra's voice lowered. "Mary is the lifeblood of this assignment and is fully capable of carrying it out with or without you by her side."

"I would prefer without," Mary interjected, garnering the attention of both men. "Clearly Gabriel does not believe I am capable of being a part of this assignment, and I would not wish my partner to have so little faith in me. I will, however, gladly go with Colin."

Gabe scowled at her. "I think nae." He turned his gaze on Hydra, "My apologies, sir, fer my impertinence. It was wrong of me. I intend te make right my mistake by completing the assignment with Mary. I promise te nae allow my personal feelings or opinions to jeopardize the attaining of our goal."

Mary waited for him to apologize to her, but when it was not forthcoming she felt another stab of hurt.

Hydra nodded. "Very well."

"Just a moment!" Mary exclaimed. "You cannot honestly consider sending him with me after what he has said."

Hydra made an odd placating gesture. "He *is* an excellent candidate for the position, *and* he has been on this sort of assignment before. Colin specializes in sabotage; he does not have the same experience." Hydra turned his attention to Gabe. "Are you certain you will be able to fulfill your duties? You do not believe your injuries will impede you?"

"Certainly nae, sir," Gabe bowed his head. "They pain me only slightly; I will return to normal before the date of the house party."

The expression on Gabe's face told Mary differently. Evidently, he was willing to push past his pain in order to take this assignment. He likely only wished to keep her away from "sin" and save his pride. She shook her head. How demeaning that he should believe that he would act as her governess.

Mary straightened her shoulders. If Hydra deemed it necessary for Gabe to accompany her on this assignment, then she would prove to Gabe that she did *not* require his protection and that she *was* as capable an agent for the Crown as he.

"Very well," she said, her eyes shooting daggers at Gabriel and determination stiffening her spine.

Hydra clapped his hands together with one loud *crack*, seemingly at his ease with her displeasure. "Brilliant. Shall we begin?"

With the dossiers still in Mary's hand, she resumed her seat, adjusting her dressing robe over her knees. She watched as Gabe accepted his own set of dossiers from Hydra and both men sat.

"Let us start from the beginning." Hydra leaned forward, his elbows resting on his knees and his hands joined between them. "Recently, some rather important intelligence documents have been purloined from our operatives, several of whom protected the documents with their lives."

Mary looked through her own paperwork as Hydra spoke.

"The documents contain code keys," he continued, "battle maps, and war strategies. We know *why* and *when* they were taken, but we do not yet know who took them, where they have hidden them, or to whom they will pass the information along. There are three suspects attending the house party at Kerr House. Viscount Kerr," he listed them off on his fingers, "the Earl of Reddington, and the Marquess of Hale. I have Stevens already stationed as a footman in Hale's household, but keep an eye on Hale as well, if you will." He frowned. "Though I suppose I should call him *Sir* Stevens as he's been knighted, but for our purposes, he's still simply Stevens."

Thoughts and plans began to turn themselves over in Mary's mind. She had already begun a rapport with Reddington. It would, therefore, be simple enough to extract information from him. It would require more work, however, to glean information from the others, as she would need to gain their trust...or at the very least remove herself as a potential threat in their mind.

"Mary, you will keep your stage pseudonym of Miss Mary White. Gabriel, you will attend as Mr. Anthony Spencer, English wastrel, rogue, inveterate gambler, and youngest son of Sir Peter Spencer. Mary is your mistress. You will use any and every opportunity to search safe boxes for hidden documents, glean any information you can from servants or the attendees themselves, and uncover any additional supporters or cohorts of Bonaparte."

"Aye," Gabe grunted.

Mary nodded. "Of course, sir."

"Mrs. McPhee is creating costumes for Mary to wear and will do tailoring for Gabe's wardrobe. When she re-enters, have her measure you both. I have already given her direction on what the costumes shall be." He clapped his hands on his knees. "Any other information is available to you in your dossiers. Do you have any questions?"

"No, sir," they said in unison.

Mary slid a sideways glance toward Gabe. The man made her furious, but she could not help admiring him. He was everything practical; not a stitch of lace on his cuff, his brown, curling hair cut appropriately short. And his clothes... My, but his clothes fit him like a second skin, fitted perfectly to his broad shoulders, narrow waist, and, she was ashamed to have noticed, his perfectly sculpted bottom. All over, he was trim yet muscular.

She had seen plenty of men beneath their clothes, but she would wager that none of them compared to him.

Stop it, you ninny! She shook herself. How could she think such indecent thoughts about a man as hard-hearted as he? Why, only minutes ago he insulted her terribly. Indeed, she should hate him. She *did* hate him.

Her spine stiffened, along with her resolve. By the end of the house party, Gabe would be forced to recognize his folly and apologize for his continuous discourtesy toward her. Mary was going to take charge of this assignment and show Gabe how capable she truly was.

CHAPTER 10

*N*early a fortnight later, Mary's back rubbed against the squabs as the carriage jolted around a corner. The rumble of carriage wheels and the thunder of the horses' hooves was muffled by the dirt road on which they rode. They were only minutes outside of London with their long ten-hour journey still ahead of them. The sun had not yet risen, but the sky was alight with early morning colour...or rather, *most* of the sky. Bright pinks, purples, and reds shone through the window on one side of the carriage, while the other held the portentous gloom of an oncoming rain.

Gabe had wanted to take the journey in two legs, five hours per day with one restful night in between. If one could call a night spent next to Gabriel restful. It would have required a night's stay at a roadside inn and Mary couldn't abide it. Upon arrival at the house party, she would be required to act as his mistress—in the public eye *only*—thus their sharing a bedchamber. On the journey, however, it was not strictly necessary, and rather an unnerving prospect for Mary.

All night. Alone. With Gabe...in a bedchamber. Mary had

thought that she was prepared for the intimacies required of her but behaving in such a way with *Gabe* felt distinctly... *Goodness*, she didn't know how it made her feel. Uneasy? *No.* Nervous? *No.* Anxious? *Not exactly.* Eager? She didn't think so.

Well, whatever the name of the emotion roiling within her, it boded ill for their assignment unless she could harness it in her grasp, could take control of her tumultuous emotions and not allow them to dictate her actions.

Her chest pressed against her tight corset as she inhaled the combined scent of her rose cream and Gabe's aroma of fresh soap and crushed cloves filling her lungs.

This assignment was very important to King and Country, not to mention the lives of the many men in the war. Mary could not let them down.

The past fortnight had been filled with costume fittings for her and fittings and language practice for Gabriel. Mary let her gaze slide upwards toward the man himself as the carriage rounded a gentle turn. He was attired exactly as his position required of him: finely tailored blue superfine tailcoat that matched the startling blue of his eyes, dove grey waistcoat and breeches that seemed to make his hair appear darker, crisp white starched cravat and shirt, lace cuffs, and high-topped hessians polished to a shine. His curling brown hair was tousled *just so*. He was Mr. Anthony Spencer, youngest son of Sir Peter Spencer, ne'er-do-well, gambler, and man foolhardy enough to attend a house party without invitation on the arm of an actress.

But he was still Gabe to her—the handsome, bewitching, heartbreaking scoundrel Gabriel Ashley.

Tightening her cloak further against the early morning chill in the coach, Mary slid to one side of her seat and turned her gaze out the window. It was much safer than staring at her fellow passenger. Indeed, but for the sky, the passing rolling hills, trees, and shrubbery, there was not much to see but for her own reflection in the glass.

She pressed closer to blow her breath against the glass and wrote her name in the condensation.

Then, of course, her mind wandered. And where else would it wander to—again—but the man seated across from her? Curse him for dominating her thoughts. But no matter how much she cursed him, there he was.

She closed her eyes and briefly allowed herself to remember. The warm summers in his secret spot in the forest, having alfresco luncheons out among the flowery blooms, chasing each other over the meadow, cooling their feet in the lake bordering his uncle's estate. It had been heaven being friends with him as children. She had loved him since the first day they had met, and even for a short time after he left.

His abandonment had been truly heartbreaking. She had built their future up in her mind for so long that suddenly learning that he did not return her feelings had crushed her more than she cared to remember. She might despise him now, but as much as she hated to own to it, somewhere deep inside her was that young girl with hope in her heart.

Her eyes snapped open to see her own reflection gazing back at her in the window. She would not allow herself to dig that deeply into her core. She was liable to not like what she found there.

She had hoped sometime after her recruitment in intelligence training that she and Gabriel could become friends once more. But those hopes were dashed anew with every unkind word he uttered to her.

The equipage slowed to take another turn, and her shoulder pressed into the side of the carriage before it righted itself and picked up speed once more.

Mary covered a yawn with the back of her hand, her eyes

watering in exhaustion. She had not slept well last night but for thoughts of Gabriel...

Gabe had believed that she did not belong in the school from the first. He was adamant that she was not capable of completing assignments as the other spies, and he certainly had never said anything positive about her position as an actress. It hurt that he did not believe in her.

Her lower lip trembled embarrassingly and she tried to hide it by turning her face further into the window. She hoped that Gabe hadn't noticed, but then, what should it matter? He had no interest in what she thought or what she felt. It was times such as these that she wished she visited her father more often. He always knew the right thing to say to brighten her downtrodden moods.

A small smile replaced her dour expression. She knew what Papa would say if he could hear her morose thoughts... *Come on now, Mary, my pigeon. Lift up that chin and face your troubles head-on. Troubles are afraid of bravery. Be brave and you will conquer all.*

Her chin turned up a notch. She'd agreed to this mission, and she would prove to Gabriel that she was just as capable as the other female operatives.

GABE WATCHED DISCRETELY from across the carriage as an array of emotions played across Mary's face. He felt a little part of him break inside when he saw her chin tremble, but only moments later it was replaced with a small grin.

Then his heart stopped entirely, for he had the sudden, intense urge to kiss the smile from her lips. *What would her lips taste like?* He wondered. He burned to find out.

But once he did solve the mystery of what taste her lips held, he knew he could not stop there. He would want to taste her neck, to trail his lips downward and over her collarbone. He'd kiss the valley between her breasts, trail his tongue over the sensitive tips of her nipples, then move downward into... *no*. He shook his head in an attempt to knock that thought out.

Gabe brought one ankle up to rest upon his opposite knee, deliberately covering the ill-timed bulge in his breeches. The carriage interior still remained dim, but Gabe could not take the risk that Mary would see, for then she would know the direction of his debauched thoughts.

What was the matter with him? There was the fact that he had not been with a woman in nearly a month; perhaps that was his problem. He sighed. He would not get the opportunity for the next fortnight, either, for he was supposed to have a mistress in Mary and he was on a mission to root out French spies and recover some very important documents. He most certainly was not going to fraternize with the enemy.

His hooded gaze flicked over Mary once more. Her cloak covered her gown, but Gabe knew what was beneath. Their costume maker had spent days creating their wardrobes. Ordinarily Gabe wore clothes befitting a gentleman farmer: nothing foppish, no lace, and muted colours. Mary typically wore modest dresses of faded colour over well-worn half boots, her costumes as an actress aside.

Today, however, they were in character. Gabe was an English dandy and Mary was...well, she was...*indecent*. The red gown beneath her cloak only brightened the colour of her hair and the low décolletage all but revealed the tops of her areolas.

The optimistic appendage in his breeches leapt. Damn, but he should have taken himself away from her. *Far* away. He was some kind of fool for allowing this farce to continue from the first. He should have stood by his assertions and refused to allow Mary to attend.

Another thought that had been plaguing him for the past

fortnight reared its ugly head once more. Mary had seemed *zealous* in her desire to take on the assignment with Colin over him. Could it be that she wished to partner with Colin with the hope to begin an affair in *truth* with the man?

The thought made him ill. Mary as Colin's mistress? A shiver travelled down his spine and a pit settled heavily in his gut. Gabe knew enough of Colin's prowess with women to know that it was entirely possible that Mary had taken it into her head to be infatuated with the man. But Gabe didn't like it.

A shudder wracked Mary's body and Gabe turned his attention to her once more. Her eyes had slipped closed but her body still trembled. Was she cold? Had she fallen asleep?

"Mary?"

She shivered again but there was no response. He sat up to remove his coat before leaning forward and draping it over her, tucking it under her chin. He resumed his seat and closed his own eyes. It was to be a long journey and he would prefer to be in unconscious oblivion and rise at least somewhat rested than sit here lusting after a woman that he could—should— never have in his bed.

THE BONAPARTE SPY sat in the leather wingback chair behind the large mahogany desk, looking through corre- spondence.

"Other guests have arrived, wot?" his man asked in an irri- tatingly cheerful manner.

"It would appear so," the spy said. "Mr. Jenkins has the maids and footmen bringing luggage up to the rooms as we speak. There are several more to come. As a matter of fact, I am looking through their correspondence at this very moment." The crinkle of parchment echoed through the quiet study as the spy opened a new missive. "The actress, Miss White, is to arrive before supper, but... What is this?"

"Eh wot?" The man withdrew an elaborate, gold inlaid snuffbox from his inner breast pocket, and flipped it open.

"The actress is bringing her protector, it seems. A Mr. Spencer. Do you know him?"

"Can't say as I do." He dipped his overlong little finger nail into the white powder and brought it to his nose.

"Hmm. Better tell the others to keep an eye on him."

"Very good, very good." The man sniffed and snorted before scratching at his bulbous nose. "But, uh, do you think it was wise to invite so many of us here? Seems suspect, eh wot?"

The Bonaparte spy laughed cruelly. "No, idiot. A house party is not suspect, it is expected. If I arranged the meeting at a pub or club, *that* would be suspect. A house party is the perfect façade. The meeting will go on as scheduled."

"Very good, very good."

CHAPTER 11

The first thing Mary became aware of was warmth. She kept her eyes closed and enjoyed the comfort of the carriage's gentle rocking and the calming warmth that engulfed her. She listened to the muffled *clip clop* of the horses' hooves and the wheels rolling over dirt and gravel, the *pitter-patter* of rain atop the carriage's roof, the gentle snore of the— *just a moment—snore?*

Mary's eyes snapped open. A frown crossed her brow as she attempted to assess the situation with her mind still in a sleepy fog. She looked at the empty seat across from her and her frown deepened. *Is that my seat?*

Another snore came from above her head and Mary started. *Who—* Before she could finish the thought, she tipped her head upward to see Gabriel, eyes closed and mouth agape. Further awareness crept up her spine as she realized that Gabe's arms were wrapped tightly around her. *Oh goodness!*

Before allowing herself to think on just how contented she had felt, she gently pried his arms from around her and very nearly leapt to the opposite seat. It had been many years since she had felt a blush rise to her cheeks, but she was most certainly familiar with the sensation. She had crept onto his seat—onto his *lap*—while she was sleeping, for pity's sake! And he in his shirtsleeves, of all things.

When had that happened? She glanced around the carriage and saw his rumpled coat in a heap upon the floor.

"That won't do," she mumbled.

As silently as she could, Mary bent to retrieve the rumpled coat, shook it out, then leaned to drape it across Gabe's chest.

Just as she stretched her arms out, the carriage hit a rut, jolting her forward and onto Gabe's chest.

"What?" Gabe sputtered, his arms rising in defence.

"Shh—shh," Mary soothed. "I'm sorry to wake you." The blush already staining her cheeks flamed brighter as she pulled away to resume her seat. She adjusted her skirts then folded her hands primly on her lap.

Gabe brushed off the awkward moment by putting on his coat and placing his tall hat on his head. He pulled out his pocket watch and examined the timepiece.

"How long has it been since we last changed horses?" he asked, his English accent impeccable.

"I don't know. I only just woke, myself." Mary raised a hand to pat at her falling coiffure. She must look affright.

It was customary for females to wear bonnets whenever they were out of doors, but Mary often eschewed that particular practice. It had been said by many that it was the red in her auburn hair that fuelled the fiery, defiant nature in her. Mary was not so certain. But as she was wont to refuse to wear a bonnet, so was her pseudonym, Miss Mary White. It was daring, bold, improper, and yes, defiant.

"Do not bother to fix your hair," Gabe interrupted her thoughts.

"Whyever not?"

He scratched a finger over the still-fresh scar along his jaw as he glanced out the window. "I believe we are nearing Kerr

House. It works well with our characters that you appear dishevelled. The other guests will assume that I had my way with you on the journey."

The moment the words had left his mouth, he appeared to regret them. The air in the carriage became thick, forcing Mary to simply nod her agreement and gaze out the window to the sleeting rain. More than once, Gabe shifted his position in his seat.

How were they to complete this assignment if they were not comfortable behaving as man and mistress? Mary was an accomplished actress—if she said so herself—but even moments ago she could not stop the blush that rose to her cheeks at having nestled closely to Gabe so innocently in her sleep. Something must be done. They were nearing Kerr House and had very little time left to discuss it.

She licked at her dry lips and sat straighter in her seat. "This will not do."

His dark brows met above his crystalline blue eyes. "What will not do?"

"The discord between us. It is palpable!" He appeared stunned for a moment, and she continued. "Do not look so surprised, Gabriel, I know that you do not like me, and believe me incapable of doing my duty to the Crown—about which," she pointed a finger at him, "I mean to disprove you. But if we are to even come *near* to being successful in this scheme, we must be believable as man and mistress." She raised her hand to stop him from interrupting. "You must become accustomed to being in close quarters with me, touching me...even kissing me. For pity's sake, you've had mistresses, I'm certain, you know what outward appearances would be expected of us at such an event."

Gabe appeared positively ill.

"Lord, you're very nearly green, Gabe, are you feeling well?" He gave her a jerky nod and she continued. "Very well.

But you understand my meaning, yes? We must push past our hard feelings and act as though we are very thoroughly absorbed in each other."

The carriage rolled onto the gravelled drive to the estate and Mary hurriedly finished what she wished to say. "You shall call me Mary, darling, dearling, sweetheart, or some other pet name, and I shall call you 'Tony' or a pet name of my choosing. Though now that I think on it, is there a name you would wish me to call you?"

GABE GAZED at Mary in a state of disbelief and partial arousal.

She thought he did not like her? That he believed her unfit to be a spy? She had it wrong. All wrong. It was because he *did* like her that he thought she should not be a spy...and perhaps that was also the reason that he wished to be away from her. Not for *lack* of esteem, but for *too much* of it.

And what of her feelings for *him*? She mentioned pushing past *their* hard feelings...

"Sorry, darling." Her eyes sharpened. "We have quite run out of time."

Without further warning, Mary was across the carriage. She lifted her skirts, straddled his lap, and pulled open the ties of her cloak to reveal her daringly cut red gown.

Arousal. Swift and hot, and undeniably thrilling. Sensations jolted through him as he stared, wide-eyed at the upper swells of Mary's breasts. With a grunt of frustration, Mary grabbed his hands and placed one on her left breast and the other at the back of her neck. Gabe's breath caught in his throat as Mary arched her back and closed her eyes in apparent bliss. *Oh Lord*.

He inhaled deeply of her rose scent, the flower coiling in

him and catching somewhere near his heart. He could feel the heat of her through his gloves and their layers of clothing. She was hot. And damn it, so was he.

The door swung open, bringing in a waft of fresh, damp spring air, and Gabe's arousal fled instantly. This little show was not inspired by a sudden attack of want for him, then. How oddly disappointing.

"Beg pardon, sir," the red-faced footman said, averting his eyes. "Should I close the door again?"

Gabe pasted a cock-sure smile on his lips and patted Mary's bottom. "Not at all, lad. Off you go, sweetheart, it would appear we've arrived."

Mary bit her lip seductively as she dismounted and Gabe's heart skipped a beat. This might very well be more difficult than he had ever imagined.

Gabe sat back as Mary accepted the footman's hand and descended the steps, while another held out an umbrella to protect her from the rain. He waited a moment more before following her out.

As he exited, Gabe looked dispassionately at the grandeur of Kerr House. Mr. Anthony Spencer would not be awed by the red brick façade, grand columns surrounding the portico, myriad glowing windows, countless puffing chimneystacks, and expansive surrounding gardens that, even in the dense sheet of rain, was marvellous to behold. No, indeed.

"La, what a grand home!" Mary exclaimed, grinning up at the front entrance.

Gabe gripped her hand from beneath her gaping cloak and wrapped it around his elbow, the footmen flanking them with cover as they strode up the wide staircase. One side of the double-wide front doors opened to allow them entrance. Several footmen in bright, canary yellow livery stood to the right of the door and another man of advanced years in orange livery detailed in yellow—one could only assume he was the butler—stood to the left.

The scent of melted beeswax and vinegar cleaning solution hit him like a slap to the face upon entry.

The man in orange bowed. "Welcome sir, madam. Mr. Spencer and Miss White, I presume?" His voice echoed in the grand space.

"Quite so, quite so," Gabe said as he took in the ostentatious foyer.

White marble and gold flake abounded in the two-story entry. A double winding staircase encircled the far end of the room, leading to the second story landing.

The man held out his hands and Gabe and Mary automatically began handing him their outer wear: Gabe's hat and gloves and Mary's gloves and cloak.

"My name is Mr. Jenkins," the man said, "I am his lordship and her ladyship's butler. Do follow me, if you will, and I will lead you to your room."

With jovial smiles, Mary and Gabe followed the aging butler up one side of the marble staircase to the second floor. While Mary was fully established in her role, Gabe's thoughts were consumed with what had just occurred in the carriage. And he was mightily displeased.

He followed numbly as his thoughts pestered him. Did she behave in such a manner with all the men she came across at the theatre? She was certainly practiced in the art of seduction and the ways of enticing a man, which would lead him to believe that yes, indeed, she had used such wiles with other men. Gabriel was just one of many.

A thunderous frown crossed his features before he could conceal it. Gabe was grateful that no one had witnessed it. But damn it, Mary's position as an actress and spy rankled.

"Here we are, the puce room. One of our finest." The

butler swept one arm into the doorway, allowing Mary and Gabe to enter first.

The guest bedchamber was indeed puce. *Exceedingly* puce. The wall coverings, window dressings, bedclothes, carpet, even the furniture's upholstery were the same dark shade. Without the light coming through the open window and the bright firelight, the room would be black as night with the gloomy trappings and dark wood furniture absorbing any possible natural light the room would hold.

"*La*, what a beautiful colour!" Mary breathed, running a fingertip over the puce velvet bed curtains.

Hardly, Gabe thought. It was a hideous reddish-brown. He did not know very much French, but he knew that "puce" came from the Latin word "*pulicem*," meaning "flea-colour."

Two footmen entered with their trunks and placed them on the floor at the foot of the bed.

"I am afraid that the lady's maids are all occupied at the moment with the other ladies just arrived and preparing for supper."

Mary waved a hand through the air. "Oh, that is quite all right. I am rather used to dressing myself."

With a nod, the butler continued. "The washbasin and a fresh pitcher of water are on the washstand under that window there," the butler pointed to the far wall, then nodded toward the privacy screen in the closest right corner of the room, just before the bed. "That screen conceals the privy and other necessary instruments for your ablutions. The wardrobe is through those doors," he pointed to the far-right corner of the room, where a set of doors stood closed.

"Thank you, sir," Gabe said. "I believe we are able to find the rest on our own."

"Very good, sir. Of course. If you have need of anything, please let one of the footmen or maids know, or you are welcome to speak to me or Mrs. Jenkins, my ladywife and housekeeper to Lord and Lady Kerr."

"You are too kind sir," Mary said sweetly.

The butler nodded. "Dinner will be served in just under two hours, Sir, Miss." With an eye-crinkling smile the man left, closing the door behind him.

The latch clicked, echoing through the room.

"What a sweet man." Mary veritably floated to her trunk and flipped it open.

"Indeed." Gabe finally allowed himself the frown that had been begging for release. He strode purposefully for the decorative puce washbasin and splashed some water from the pitcher inside. The fire in the hearth filled the room with warmth, its light flickering over the chaise and armchairs that sat closest to the fireplace.

"And how nice that he works in the same household as his wife. That is rather rare, you know."

Gabe removed his cravat and pulled open his collar. "How happy for him," he grunted.

Mary whirled on him, all fiery displeasure. Gabe fought a groan as he glanced at her reflection in the mirror. He quickly bent, putting his face toward the water.

"What is it that displeases you so, *darling*, the kindly elderly man and his wife's contentment in life, or the *calamitous* happenstance of your being here with me?"

Gabe picked up a towel and dabbed at the droplets on his freshly washed face and neck. He could not very well answer her question without sinking deeper into whatever hot water she had placed him in.

Then her words came back to him... *I know that you do not like me... You must become accustomed to being in close quarters with me, touching me...even kissing me. For pity's sake, you've had mistresses, I'm certain, you know what outward appearances would be expected of us at such an event.*

No, Gabe had never had a mistress. Lovers, of course, but never a mistress. Too messy, too needy, and a damn sight too expensive for what one gained in return. He had never been particularly fond of the idea of someone sponging off of him for sex, money, and jewels. It smacked of desperation. He had also never been desirous to put anyone in a position of danger, which, as a spy for the Crown, he would inevitably do. But he did know what would be expected of him on this assignment, for appearances sake. So as much as he would like to disabuse Mary's belief that he did not like her, now was decidedly *not* the time

She was correct, however, that they should continue this assignment not only as amicable partners, but with a common understanding of what was expected of them.

He turned, strode back to stand before her, clasping her hands in his. He determinately ignored the jolt of awareness traveling up his arms and the goose flesh that followed in its wake. "My apologies, Mary. My behaviour has been unpardonable."

Shock lined her features as she gazed at him in silence.

He chose his words carefully, for one never knew when one would be overheard. "This journey did not begin as well as it should have, but I am very pleased to be here with you, sweetheart."

Awareness dawned and Mary's surprise turned to understanding. She notched her chin higher and cut him a withering glance. "I should hope so, Tony."

He bent to kiss the back of her hands. "Come, darling, we must prepare for supper. Let us unpack."

CHAPTER 12

*M*ary slipped the corset over her chemise and held it with one hand against her chest. She did not wish to have to request help from Gabe, but without a lady's maid available, she had no choice.

In all the years that she had been an actress and a spy, never once had she had a man perform such a personal service. Most of her own gowns were front lacing and as she often went without a corset or stays, she rarely required help to dress. At the theatre, if a costume required such under garments or if a gown buttoned in the back, she had another of the actresses aid her. But not a man. *Never* a man.

She stepped out from behind the puce privacy screen, catching Gabe's attention with the movement.

"May I have help with my laces?" she asked.

He stood in stony silence, his jaw set.

"Please?" she added.

With a curt nod he rose from his position on the chaise and strode toward her. She quickly gave him her back. After a brief pause, she felt the tugging of her corset laces as he efficiently tightened them.

His fingers brushed at her back ever so slightly, but the shock of it was thrilling. Heat radiated off his body and his breath teased the hair of her half-fallen chignon. Mary closed her eyes, briefly allowing the sensation to flow through her.

She had used intimacies and desire to glean the information she required from men aiding Napoleon, but never had she felt the same passions in return. Always, she had been able to separate her own feelings from her actions with each mark. Being as busy as she was with both her position as an actress and as a spy, she had never been courted by a man, never been a man's mistress...had never been kissed by a man that was not a mark, but for Gabriel's kiss when she was the tender age of ten and on-stage kisses with fellow actors. Each moment she had spent with a man had been in service to Crown and country.

Why did this feel so different? Why was each innocuous touch so intoxicating?

Mary was very aware of Gabe's deep breathing behind her, each exhalation seemingly closer than the last and each bringing with it the scent of crushed cloves and the gentle tickle of the springy, curly hair at her neck.

Mary gasped at the sudden thundering of her blood.

Gabe's hands faltered, then hesitated. "Are you well?" he asked, his tone deep and flat.

Mary cleared her throat, reigning in her composure. "Yes, of course. That last one was a bit tight, that is all. It is well now."

Gabe grunted, but did not answer. It was just as well, for she did not wish to explain further. She did not even know if she *could* explain the sudden maelstrom of...desire—*surely not!*—that she had just felt. But what else could account for the sudden dampness in her palms, the fluttering of her heart, or the warmth growing in her middle?

A frown creased her brow. It simply was not possible. She

might miss Gabe's friendship and continue to be hurt by his curt comments, but she did not—*could* not—desire him on an intimate level. It must merely be her underlying awareness that she was playing his mistress. Indeed, that must be it. It was her character, that was all.

With one last tug, Gabe stepped back, a waft of cool air rushing in to take his place. "Done. Now, if that will be all..."

Mary spun to catch him as he stepped away. "Wait!"

He turned to face her, his expression closed and distant, his blue eyes as hard as ice.

She flicked her tongue out to wet her suddenly dry lips and his gaze dropped to follow the motion, his jaw tightening. A nervous flutter pushed its way into Mary's stomach. She hardly knew what to do; was he so dissatisfied with her, then?

"My gown buttons in the back." She cleared her throat. "Could you...would you mind buttoning me up?"

His displeasure was evident in every taut muscle of his body, but he nodded nonetheless.

As quickly as she could without ruining her dress, Mary stepped into the coquelicot gown. It was the same colour as her travelling frock, but Mrs. McPhee had said it was an attractive shade against her skin and it brought out the red in her hair. Mary was pleased to have brought them with her for the house party.

After drawing her short cap sleeves up her arms and letting the skirts fall attractively over her hips and legs, Mary put her back to Gabe once more. This time his movements were brisk, each button put through its hole with expert swiftness. Mary hated to think how many times he had performed such a task for a woman. Why it bothered her, she did not know. Gabe was entitled to bed whomever he chose; it was not for her to feel any amount of... *No.* She would not even put a word to the feeling, for she knew it was not true.

As the last of her buttons were done up, Gabe swept his

hands dispassionately down her sides, straightening the gown for her in what Mary knew he assumed was a helpful gesture. But what it did was send a wave of faintness through her. She bit the inside of her cheek and closed her eyes to quell the dizziness. Gabe, apparently sensing her distress, gripped her waist tighter.

"Whoa, Mary. Are you well?"

Mary forced herself to step out of his reach and turned to face him with a saucy grin.

"Of course," she said lightly. "It has simply been too long since my last meal. I am well."

He eyed her warily but seemed to accept her excuse. Mary swept past him with a rushed "thank you" and sat at the dressing table across the room to fix her hair.

She breathed a sigh of relief when Gabe resumed his seat on the chaise. Her stomach was abuzz with nerves, but she gritted her teeth and forced herself to change the direction of her thoughts.

Although she had years of practice of doing her own hair, and was rather quick at creating ravishing curls, her hair was stubborn. However speedy her ability to put it up, it just as easily came down. It frequently fell out of her chignons, but as her pseudonym, Mary White, she needn't be concerned, for at this particular house party, all manner of wickedness, impropriety, and debauchery was not only accepted, but encouraged.

Her stomach fluttered once more, and she pushed past it, working her fingers through her hair, until it was done. In mere minutes, she had a smart, attractive twist to her hair with curls draping downward like a weeping willow. She placed several pearl-tipped hairpins throughout her hair then twisted her head to view the effect. It was well, indeed.

Distraction was just the thing. This was a different sort of role, that was all. Mary was nervous about the job. She merely needed to focus on the familiarity of her performance, mentally separate herself from the fact that she was working intimately with a man that clearly despised her, and complete the mission.

She opened her rose scented cream and swiped at the bottom of the container, not willing to allow any of what remained to go to waste, no matter how much she looked forward to opening the new scent she had just recently purchased. She rubbed the cream into her hands, dabbing some on her neck.

With a grin on her lips, she reached into her green velvet box and pulled out a string of pearls from among her other jewellery and placed them about her collar, followed by a matching bracelet. She raised her gaze to look once more at her reflection in the looking glass, but her breath caught on a gasp.

There was Gabe gazing back at her reflection, stark hunger in his gleaming eyes. Mary's heart flipped over then began to beat a staccato rhythm against her ribs. Her breath came fast, her chest rising and falling with each ragged gasp. She could feel her breasts swell with want in some sort of anticipatory instinct, while her *mons* flooded with welling desire.

Then, with a blink, the expression was gone. Just as quickly as it had appeared, it disappeared, replaced by genial contentment.

His mask was firmly in place, but Mary could not forget that expression. Indeed, the look of raw want on his features was etched in her memory. But what should she make of it?

Her own desire began to recede, and she willed her heart to return to its normal rhythm.

"Shall we?" He held out his arm.

Mary forced a smile and took in his attire. He was dressed appropriately for dinner in a black coat and trousers, starched white shirt with lace cuffs and collar, and green striped waistcoat with an emerald cravat pin winking jauntily at the base of his neck.

Mary swallowed past the sudden lump in her throat—what of that? "I should love to, darling."

It took them several minutes, and the help of a footman, to find the parlour where all of the guests had gathered to wait for supper.

They spotted the butler just outside the door, awaiting the guests so as to announce them as they entered.

"Ah, Mr. Spencer and Miss White, how very good that you have found your way here." The butler smiled. "I trust your room is to your liking?"

"It is very well, indeed," Gabe said, inclining his head in appreciation.

The old man's wrinkles deepened with his smile. "I shall announce you."

WHAT A SUPREMELY ODD BUTLER, Gabe thought. Very unlike any other he had seen in the house of a Lord of the realm.

Mr. Jenkins swung open the door to the parlour and announced in a carrying voice, "Mr. Anthony Spencer and Miss Mary White." He quickly retreated from the room, allowing Mary and Gabe to pass...into the den of wolves.

As they entered the room, each pair of male eyes was riveted on Mary. Not that Gabe could blame them; she was stunningly beautiful in her dinner gown. Gabe, himself, had to rein in his inappropriate lust at the sight of her. But the fact that Mary's beauty was obvious did not make Gabe feel any better about other men eying her with lust.

The room only held nine people, but it felt like so much more. Two men remained seated at their entrance, both hindered by the large-breasted women on their laps. The remaining two men stood, along with three women. Of the two women standing, the buxom brunette was very obviously a female of ill repute, while the other looked to be a woman of good standing. And the third...

The tall, black haired woman glided toward them with a predatory smile on her lips. "Welcome to my home," her voice flowed over them like silk. "I am Evelyn Black, the Viscountess Kerr."

Gabe affected a deep bow as Mary curtseyed beside him. "Very pleased to make your acquaintance, my lady," they said in unison.

She nodded serenely in return. "Likewise, I'm sure." Turning, she gestured toward one of the men with a woman on his lap. "Allow me to introduce my husband, Lord Kerr."

The man in question bounced the blonde tart who laughed merrily and gripped him tighter.

The Viscountess laughed at her husband's infidelity as though he were a mischievous young lad. "As you can see, we are all very *open* here."

Evidently, Gabe thought. But then, he had expected such displays at this particular house party. Which was just one more reason that he was thankful that *he* was the one to accompany Mary, and not Colin. It was also another reason why he should have taken himself far, *far* away from Mary. She was too tempting by half.

Lady Kerr winked. "We hope you are able to keep up with us." Before giving them a chance to respond to that lewd innuendo, she continued, "The other man with his mistress on his lap, and the ever-present Scotch in his hand, is Lord Pondridge." The man paid them no mind as he kissed a path up his mistress' neck. "This fine gentleman is Mr. Cecil Piper."

The man with nondescript brown hair and dark eyes bowed. "Pleased to make your acquaintance, eh wot?"

"And the last gentleman in the room," Lady Kerr continued after their bow and curtsey, "is someone I believe you are already very *familiar* with, Miss White..."

An absurdly handsome man approached from across the room, a charming smile on his lips. He had desirable blond hair and deceptively laughing green eyes. Gabe hated him on sight.

He hated him more as the cad gripped Mary's hand in his. But instead of kissing the backs of her fingers, the man had the audacity to lean in to kiss her cheek...and linger there far longer than strictly necessary, even for such an intimate gesture.

"Lord Reddington," Mary breathed. "I am so pleased to see you again."

"Oh, my darling, Mary, do call me James. You know how I love to hear my name on your talented tongue."

Mary's lips curled in an infuriating smile. Gabe's gut churned.

"James," she purred.

The man's eyes rolled backward briefly, and Gabe could swear that red began to spot his vision.

"I am *so* pleased that you accepted my invitation." Reddington looked pointedly at Gabe. "I see you've brought a friend."

"Oh yes!" Mary jumped as though she had forgotten he was there. Damn her. "This is my *very* good friend Mr. Anthony Spencer. Tony, this is Lord Reddington."

The man frowned, but mirrored Gabe's bow. "*Very* good friend, is he?"

Mary had the grace to appear shamefaced. "Yes."

Reddington placed a hand dramatically over his heart and staggered as though struck.

"You wound me, Mary!" His behaviour was playful, but

Gabe saw the steel in his eyes. The man gripped Mary's hand tighter. "I thought you would be 'no man's mistress.'"

Mary nodded apologetically. "It seems that I was persuaded."

Reddington tugged her closer to him. "Perhaps you could be swayed in your choice of protector?"

That was it. Gabe had seen enough. He stepped forward and slid one arm around Mary's shoulders, pulling her into his body. "She has protection enough at the moment, your lord-ship, but she thanks you for your kind offer."

Frosty green eyes glinted at him from between sandy blond eyelashes.

"Dinner is served," Mr. Jenkins intoned from the doorway.

Just in time. Gabe had been tempted to pound the fellow's face and spirit Mary far away. But that would be counter-productive to their purpose.

Focus, Gabe. We are here to uncover a French spy and recover stolen documents.

The eleven of them paired off by rank. With the customary male to female pairs—with one odd woman out—the low-ranking females outnumbered the ranking males.

Lord and Lady Kerr led the group to the dining room. Much to Gabe's chagrin, Lord Reddington paired with Mary, while Gabe was saddled with a Mrs. McArthur, Reddington's mistress.

The dining room was just as ostentatiously appointed as the other rooms he'd seen in the home. Two chandeliers hung high above them and bright sconces lined the gilt and green velvet covered walls. The couples took their seats at the table, which glittered with silverware and sparkling flutes of champagne.

Gabe sat between Mrs. McArthur and their hostess, with

Lady Kerr on his right. Mary sat directly across from him between Reddington and the hawk-like Lord Pondridge.

A hidden rear door to the dining room burst open, five footmen entering in a row, each holding two dishes. They positioned themselves each between two guests, then, in unison, placed the dish in front of the diners.

Gabe looked down at his dish. It was a bowl of what Gabe assumed was intended to be brown onion soup. But what sat before him was murky broth with floating bits of onion, coated in a thick layer of an abnormal oily substance.

Good God. Even *he* could create a better soup than this. Of course, he'd learned to cook from his mother at a young age, and held a great fondness for it, but he was by no means a famed cook.

The soft clinking of spoons against bowls and muttering voices filled the expansive dining room as Gabe dipped his spoon reluctantly into his "soup" and took his first taste.

The liquid sloshed nauseatingly on his tongue. Though his taste buds—and sense of self-preservation—rebelled, he forced himself to swallow. Indeed, it was far worse than he'd first assumed.

Gabe's gaze flicked upward to see how Mary was enjoying the first course and his stomach roiled threateningly. Mary sat happily in intimate conversation with Lord Reddington, their heads close together, thick as thieves, each ignoring their revolting onion oil water.

Reddington's gaze slipped downward to Mary's plunging décolletage before he whispered something in her ear. Gabe fought the thunderous scowl that threatened.

Lady Kerr leaned toward him and Gabe reluctantly pried his gaze from Mary's distressing circumstance to turn his attention to the lady at his side. "Do tell me, Mr. Spencer, how you convinced Miss White to become your mistress; I was under the impression that she would not take on a protector."

Gabe gave her a toothy, cocksure smile, still seething over Mary's apparent admirer. "The same way I have gotten all of my mistresses into my bed, my lady." He winked at her. "Considerable skill."

"Mmm." Her voice had a throaty resonance. "My lover has yet to arrive to this little house party... Perhaps you should pay a visit to my bedchamber so you can show me just how *considerable* your skill is." She ran a finger around the rim of his shirt collar, scraping the underside of his jaw with her nail.

Gabe hid a grimace at the sharp pain.

Blazes. She could very well have drawn blood.

Swallowing down his revulsion, Gabe forced his smile to grow and his eyes to warm.

He opened his mouth to inform her that he would consider her offer—though Lord knew he would never sleep with a woman not only so high above his station but one so overpoweringly irritating—but his reply was cut off by deep, boisterous laughter. Through the main dining room doors came five late-arrivals.

The scraping of chairs echoed through the room as the diners rose to greet the guests.

The first man to enter was a nearly forty, portly, well-dressed fellow, likely of the peerage. He entered with a petite, young, red haired woman who was very clearly his mistress, for she hung adoringly on his arm. Behind them was another man, though this one was vastly different from the first, where the former was tall and round, this man was short and slender. Gabe gazed at him with a critical eye. He was likely not a peer but dressed far above his station. He, very like Gabe's disguise, was dandified in his attire. He must have a wealth of funds, as he entered with a woman on *each* arm. Both were buxom blondes and both tittered unattractively as Gabe bowed over their hands.

Lady Kerr moved to stand beside Gabe, "Mr. Spencer, this is Lord Sheffield and his very good friend, Lady Kellings."

Gabe bowed to the rotund Lord Sheffield. "A pleasure to make your acquaintance, my lord, my lady." Gabe bent over Lady Kellings' hand, but before he could pull away, she extended her slender fingers to rub them across his lips.

Taken aback by such a brazen gesture, Gabe missed the name of the blonde mistresses of the second gentleman. He sketched a brief bow, nonetheless. He did not fail to catch the name of the gentleman, however.

"A pleasure to make your acquaintance, Mr. Jackson," Gabe bowed to the short, slender man with orange hair.

Gabe then watched as the group was introduced to Mary. She was perfect, her character completely in place. Of course, she lived her actress persona more often than Gabe cared to contemplate.

Her lips curved seductively upward at something Lord Sheffield mumbled quietly to her and Gabe clenched his jaw. It was time to uncover the traitors here and take Mary away from this place entirely.

CHAPTER 13

*M*ary took another bite of the nearly inedible jugged hare that sat mostly uneaten on her plate. The others around the table seemed not to notice the ghastly fare, but Mary certainly did. Goodness, even the stews that her mother used to make with little to no food and scarcely any broth were more appetizing than the slop currently sitting on her plate.

A heated waft of breath brushed her cheek and Mary suppressed a shiver of disgust.

"You look ravishing in red, dearest," Reddington whispered against her ear. "I scarcely recall if I have said as much already this evening, but I confess your beauty quite addles my senses."

He had been bothering her throughout the entire meal, but Mary accepted it as her due. She must encourage the men enough to discover their hidden truths, after all. She was here on an assignment and she would succeed. No matter what.

Mary put her fork down and turned to smile up at Lord Reddington with a demure tilt to her brows.

"Why, James, you flatter me."

He pressed a hand to his chest. "Upon my life, I do not."

A group of footmen entered and removed the diners' plates, while a second group entered to put another odious course in its place. It seemed to be an attempt at partridge fricassee, but Mary was not certain.

She hastily took a sip of the deep red wine in her glass and replaced it on the table. For a moment she watched in a daze as the candlelight played on the swirling liquid.

"My lovely Mary," Reddington's lips touched her ear, "tell me you feel it, too...this *heat*."

Alarm shot through Mary's stomach, but she carefully hid it. Hydra had said that this man was not respectable and likely had ill intentions, and she was inclined to believe him. The nightmare of her experience as a youth flashed through her mind... *You will suffer for this...*

As the memory of that night assailed her, she did as she always did and used her fear to fuel her determination.

A sense of peace stole over her as she considered her plans. Reddington wished to have her as his mistress, as much was evident. She could never give herself to Reddington—not willingly anyway; she morally refused to give her body to a traitor of the crown. Mary would rather give herself to a man she loved...whenever and whomever that would be. She was, however, more than willing to use any *other* means necessary to garner the required information. Perhaps she could tease it out of him.

She turned to Reddington with a sultry tilt to her lips, her eyes filled with desire. Then a voice cut through her awareness.

"Mr. Spencer," Mr. Piper called from down the table, a piece of partridge balled to one side of his open mouth, "why is it that I have never heard of you before now? Seems a trifle odd, eh wot?"

Mary looked at Gabe, who was unfazed by the inquiry. He returned her gaze with a coldness to his eyes that she had never seen on him before. The sight sent a shiver of unease down her spine. His frigid expression swiftly changed to one of self-assured complacency as he turned his head to look down the table.

"Yes," Lord Kerr put in, his expression stony and his gaze suspicious, "do enlighten us on your mysterious past, Mr. Spencer."

Gabe's lips cracked a slow smile. "I wouldn't say it's mysterious," he began. "I spent thirteen years travelling with my uncle in the Americas."

"Mmm," Mrs. McArthur hummed. "Adventurous, indeed."

Lord Sheffield swallowed his bite of partridge, then asked, "What made you decide to leave from the first? Did you not enjoy life in England?"

Gabe's smile turned sly, and his eyes crinkled in the corners. "There was an inn near my familial home that employed a *very* lovely barmaid..."

A few of the men around the table began exchanging grins and knowing glances.

"Needless to say, a few months after reaching my eighteenth year, my father felt it was necessary to ship me off."

"So now you are returned," Lord Kerr said before sipping at his coffee. He swallowed. "What brought you home after thirteen years?"

"My uncle left this earth to meet the good Lord, and I made the decision to return. Father was not happy to accept his ne'er-do-well son back into his home, so I took residence here in London. Alas, I met Mary a sennight ago and was enchanted."

"Aye, Mary does enchant," Reddington put in. "We must convince her to put on a performance while she is here."

A chorus of encouragement from the men filled the room and Mary feigned modesty. She had anticipated the request and had Mrs. McPhee create two new costumes for just such an occasion. He was playing perfectly into her plan.

With a shy nod, Mary affected acquiescence. "If you wish it, then I shall."

"Huzzah!" Reddington exclaimed.

Mary caught Gabe's cold gaze from across the table and another shiver ran down her spine. She fought down her own frown as she turned back to her meal. A pox on Gabe and his ever-present disapproval.

"What happened to your face, Spencer?" Mrs. McArthur said from beside him. She ran her index finger along the line of the red scar on the side of his face, her eyelids heavy. "It looks frightfully dashing."

"That story is not so amusing, I'm afraid. I stumbled through my previous mistress' home one evening after a night of revelry and found myself in the kitchens with hunger gnawing at me. A dashed stool came from nowhere and I fell, slicing myself on the way to the floor."

"I love the Americas," Lord Sheffield said, either oblivious to the change of subject or ignoring it. "I've been there several times myself; I never could get enough of their women." He wiggled his eyebrows suggestively, earning a laugh from some of the other guests. "In fact, there was this one woman—"

Mary missed the remainder of his lewd anecdote as dessert appeared before her. Immediately her mouth began to salivate. *This* must be why Lord and Lady Kerr kept their cook in their employ. The smell alone was enough to make Mary swoon.

Practically famished from a lack of eating the dinner's courses, she dipped her spoon in the exquisite lemon cream and brought it to her mouth. *Oh heavens!* The explosion of lemon zest, the citrus zing, and the sweetness of the cream combined to make the most sinfully delicious dessert she had ever tasted.

Reddington's lips brushed the underside of her ear as he

breathed, "Keep making sounds like that and I will have to tup you right here...in front of everyone."

Mary's eyes snapped open—when had she closed them?—and realized that every man seated at the table had his gaze on her. She must have made a noise, but she was not certain what that noise was. Clearly it had been loud enough to gain the attention of the table.

Mortification would have swamped her had their shock-lined expressions not enhanced her purpose. Lowering her gaze to her bowl, Mary determinately ignored them and returned to her delectable dessert.

Slowly, the others resumed their private conversations and bawdy joke telling.

"Mary, say you will come to me tonight." Reddington's scotch-scented breath wafted around her.

The man's whispering in her ear had become vexing, indeed. She put a placating smile on her face as she turned to him. "I do not believe that Tony would take kindly to my abandoning him in a strange home."

Reddington inclined his head toward Gabe's seat across from them. "I do not think it would be such a hardship. It seems as though your *Tony* is occupied."

Mary's gaze swung toward Gabe and her stomach plummeted. He was indeed *occupied*. Lady Kerr leaned so far over him that she may well be on his lap. The woman ran her fingers repeatedly up and down his chest and over his smoothly shaven jaw, whispering in—nay, *biting*—his ear. He laughed charmingly at something she said, and Mary's stomach knotted. *Goodness*, could she be jealous? Of another woman with *Gabriel*?

Oh dear. She must rein in her emotions immediately. Jealousy had no place in the heart of a spy, and she certainly could not afford to make any mistakes. For all she knew they were surrounded by the enemy. Any leak in her façade, any misstep, could put their lives in jeopardy. Whatever her apparent soul-deep feelings toward Gabe, she must let them go. He'd crushed her heart years ago, surely she could stomach seeing him with another woman—*any* woman. Indeed. She should hate him, not be harbouring amorous feelings for him.

Curse it. She was a spy. And she had work to do.

GABE TOOK a deep swill of his wine and wished it were something stronger. Lady Kerr and Mrs. McArthur would not leave him be, and he had work to accomplish. Lady Kerr was all but on his lap and her offers for sex were becoming anything but subtle. Mrs. McArthur, however, had placed her hand on his thigh sometime during the course of the hideously unpalatable jugged hare and had not removed it since. In fact, she seemed to be sliding it ever so slightly upward with each passing minute.

He *must* focus on the mission at hand... If only these curst women would desist their pawing and petting and let him concentrate on discovering who had stolen the documents.

The suspected traitors that Hydra had named were, firstly, the Marquess of Hale, though he had yet to arrive and Sir Stevens was reportedly already watching him for suspicious behaviour. Secondly, the Viscount Kerr—

Gabe turned his gaze to the head of the table, two seats to his left. The Viscount appeared at his ease, resting against the back of his chair, a glass of wine in one relaxed hand and a spoon in the other. He exuded confidence and held himself in the manner of a man entirely assured of himself and his position. Gabe believed Hydra justified in his suspicions of Kerr. The man had to be hiding something.

The third suspect listed was the Earl of Reddington.

His gaze flicked toward the blasted Earl and again he felt a jolt of displeasure through his gut. The man was a scoundrel and a rogue and Gabe wished Mary would keep well enough away from him.

Lady Kerr said something provocative in his ear and Gabe gave a responding noncommittal grunt.

Mary tittered at something *the cad* whispered in her ear and Gabe frowned. Lord knew what despicable acts she had had to perform for the man in order to receive an invitation to this sennight of sin.

"Goodness," Lady Kerr murmured in his ear, "what a severe look upon your handsome face." She leaned in closer. "Forget about the actress, darling, and leave her to James. My lover would not mind sharing me..."

Gabe did not hear the rest of the lady's sentence, as Reddington sidled closer to Mary, raising his arm to drape it over the back of her chair. He cupped the back of her head, mussing her striking auburn hair, then pressed his lips to her neck in a series of small kisses.

Gabe saw red. Anger, swift and blistering, sizzled its way through him, forcing him to his feet, his chair scraping against the wooden floor and gaining him the attention of the other guests.

Thinking quickly, Gabe pasted a genial smile on his lips and clapped his hands together jovially. "I believe I would enjoy a glass of port and a good cigar."

"Here, here!" Mr. Jackson waved a bejewelled hand toward the dining room door. "Send the ladies off to the parlour or somesuch and leave us to our port, cigars, and manly conversation."

"So we can talk about how good the ladies are between the bedclothes," Lord Pondridge flapped his hand drunkenly, his blinks slow and heavy. Gabe supposed he could be trying to wink suggestively, but he was not certain.

Lady Kerr rose, forcing the men and the remaining ladies

to their feet. "Come, ladies, let us adjourn to the drawing room and leave the men to their manly business." She turned, leading the ladies from the room, but looked over her shoulder at them just before her exit. "Say only kind things about us will you gentlemen? We women have excellent hearing and are unforgiving upon receiving scrutiny."

With one last wink from Lady Kerr, the women were gone, Mary with them. Gabe was grateful to see them go. Not only was it a relief from Lady Kerr and Mrs. McArthur, but also from the startling torture of seeing Mary flaunt her charms and flirt with dangerous men.

Gabe resumed his seat as a footman placed several boxes of cigars and a flagon of port upon the table.

"Fine ladies, eh wot?" Mr. Piper brought his snifter of port to his lips and took a drink.

The viscount bit the end of his cigar, spitting the tip on the floor beside his chair. "Fine, indeed." He reclined in his seat, his shrewd gaze encompassing every man at the table.

Gabe poured himself a dram of port and lit his own cigar. He had never been one to drink to excess or enjoy filling his lungs with smoke, but for the purposes of his character, he knew he must.

"Are yourshs twinths, Jack...son," Lord Pondridge inquired, his words slurred and his eyes half-lidded, "or just shishers?"

Mr. Jackson's self-satisfied smile grew at the inquiry about his mistresses. "Twins, as a matter of fact. Found them at Lady Haversham's."

"Is that across the road from Madame Bordeau's?" Lord Sheffield asked, his chins wagging.

Gabe was familiar with both houses of ill repute. They were known for their excellent drink and their clean women. Gabe had frequented them with Colin and Hugh on countless occasions, though seldom partook in the female company within. There was just something not quite...*right* in his mind about paying for a woman's attention; it smacked of desperation, and Gabe preferred to know that the lady is actually interested in *him* and not his money.

Mr. Jackson inclined his head. "Indeed, it is. Has the best women."

"I much prefer actresses and opera singers, myself," the Viscount Kerr drawled. "The thrill of the chase."

"And they're less costly, eh wot?" Mr. Piper grinned.

"And skilled," Reddington threw his head back. "Good God, you lot haven't the faintest idea what that woman is capable of."

Gabe wrestled with his mounting rage, fighting to keep his expression one of calm and neutral confidence.

"I'll wager Spencer does," Lord Sheffield wheezed, wiggling his thick eyebrows suggestively.

"You lucky sod," Reddington grumbled. "You must share her."

Gabe's jaw clenched involuntarily. "*Must* I?"

"I understand your reluctance," the devil incarnate said. "If I had access to that woman's charms—and remarkable abilities—on a nightly—nay, daily—basis, I guarantee that we would not leave the bedchamber for months. She is unique, to be sure.

"But indeed, we all share here," he continued. "You're welcome to have a go at my mistress in exchange for a night with Mary." Reddington took a drag of his cigar and blew the smoke upward. "Mrs. McArthur does some amusing things with her titties."

Gabe choked down a draught of his port in an attempt to swallow past the tightness in his throat, and the fury scorching him. What was happening to him? Why did he feel such intense...*feelings* when it came to the thought of Mary with other men? The answer hung just out of reach.

Gabe already knew that Mary was unique, but not in the way this cad implied. Mary was a free spirit, a talented actress, and a loving, caring, and extraordinary woman with a wealth of heart and knowledge. She was so far beyond the reach of all the men in this room. Hell, all the men in London. She did not deserve to have these witless, self-admiring, traitorous scoundrels salivating over her.

But that was not what his character would do. If they were discovered, their lives would be in great peril. He must *be* Anthony Spencer, despite how it galled him to do so.

"I suppose that decision would be up to the lady in question," Gabe drawled. "I can hardly arrange a rendezvous on her behalf."

A slow, predatory smile grew on Reddington's lips and Gabe immediately regretted his answer. He should not encourage the villain to pursue Mary...nor should Mary urge him on with her feminine wiles.

He took another gulp of his port and a deep draw on his cigar. What had happened to his plan to convince Mary to end her spy life? Had he not vowed to make her see the error of this life she led?

He shook his head. He knew what happened. This damned assignment. He had a feeling that something like this would occur; Mary would be objectified and hunted by the predators of the house party.

They should never have come.

CHAPTER 14

ary nearly choked on her own saliva as she fought to contain the shock of these women. She liked to think of herself as a relatively open individual, but these women were discussing things that were...well, vulgar. She knew for certain that no woman in polite society discussed such things, but aside from being shocked at their bold crudeness, Mary found the conversation almost amusing. Particularly due to their setting.

The group of nine ladies sat in a semi-circle facing a low-burning fireplace in an all pink, all floral drawing room. The walls were papered in the same floral print as the cushions and carpet. It was a highly feminine and overwhelmingly delicate setting for such a lewd discussion. And how odd that they would gather here; Mary thought that drawing rooms were reserved for greeting callers.

"I have never allowed a man to do *that*," a buxom brunette, whose name Mary had missed, said.

"Whyever not?" a thickset, handsome blonde woman asked, shock lining her features. "It is highly pleasurable."

"But your *tits*?" The brunette appeared unconvinced.

"Come now," the Viscountess Kerr put in, "be adventurous! It is ever so enjoyable and it gives you a great *view*."

Lady Kellings pouted. "I think Lord Sheffield would kill me if we tried it."

Mary tittered along with the other women. Mary despised tittering, but her grin was natural and wide.

Lady Kellings sat forward. "I am serious!"

The women laughed harder, Mary's laugh becoming genuine.

"Not only is my bosom too small for his cock to fit in between, but the weight of his body would surely crush the life out of me."

Roars of laughter echoed off the walls of the drawing room. Mary wiped a tear that had gathered at the corner of her eye, the awkward image the woman's words provoked causing her to laugh harder, despite the crude nature of it.

As the laughter died down, Lady Marpol, Lord Kerr's mistress, turned to the Viscountess Kerr. "Speaking of men's *sizes*, your husband is rather small."

Lady Kerr grunted, "I know. I'm surprised you put up with him at all."

Lady Marpol shrugged. "I do not mind so much, but sometimes I wish I could find another, *larger...*"

"Oh yes, I know. My lover is larger—though not by much —but he has yet to arrive and I am in dire need of entertainment. Which brings me to the question I have been positively *bursting* to ask all evening..." She turned to Mary with a look of unnatural earnestness. "What is it *precisely* that enamoured Mr. Spencer to you?"

Something about Lady Kerr's intensity struck Mary ill. As much as she wished to call Lady Kerr a traitor and have her taken into custody by the crown simply for her attraction to Gabe, she knew she couldn't. But instinctively, Mary knew this was a baited question and much hung in the balance of her answer. Which brought her to another dilemma. Would the ladies see through her falsehood if she answered as her true self? Or would they believe the lie as truth?

"His prowess? His charm? His handsome appearance?" Lady Kerr continued.

Mary thought quickly. The answer was simple. She was not Mary Wright, spy. She was Miss Mary White, actress extraordinaire and great seducer of men, legendary for her ability to bring a man to fulfillment without a single touch, and mistress to Mr. Anthony Spencer, gambler and Lothario.

She must also be careful of how she presented herself among these women. They may be open to any manner of debauchery and often silly, but that did not mean that they were not capable of treason. Particularly Lady Kerr. If Mary wished to avoid suspicion herself, she must exude not only the erotically sophisticated actress, but a dimwitted one, as well.

So, the issue remained; what would Mary White say?

She thought quickly, the patter of rain upon the room's windows the only sound breaking the fraction of a second of silence.

"La, what a question! Have you seen the man?" Mary winked. "Tony not only has the body of a Greek god, but," she closed her eyes in apparent rapture, her face tilted up to the ceiling, "knowledge of a woman's body, and stamina that is unrivalled by any other of my lovers. Superior in every sense." She waived a hand through the air. "That, and straight, white teeth. I cannot abide a man with dirty, uneven teeth."

The ladies tittered, but Mary noted the shrewd sharpness in Lady Kerr's coldly laughing eyes. Mary's suspicion heightened. Something was definitely not right about Lady Kerr.

"Oh, Lord, neither can I!" Mrs. McArthur exclaimed, a cringe on her lips

"I once had this lover that knew..."

Mary listened with half an ear as one of Mr. Jackson's

blonde mistresses began an open discussion about past lovers. Mary added in her own answers on occasion, and laughed and smiled where appropriate, but her thoughts were elsewhere.

She must find an opportunity to speak with Gabe about her suspicions of Lady Kerr. Now that she thought on it, she should also speak with him about the dark looks he had been giving her over supper. He needed to learn to control his facial expressions, if not his temper.

"The evening may now begin!"

Mary caught herself from jumping at the booming voice from the doorway. She turned to see a grinning Lord Reddington strutting into the room, his arms akimbo. The other men swiftly followed.

Oh dear. Gabriel's expression was thunderous.

Mary leapt to her feet and hurried over to him. His expression did not alter as she pressed her hands to his chest and raised her lips to his ear. "Be careful of your expressions, *Tony*. You give too much of yourself away."

Thank goodness he listened, for his expression turned to one of congenial contentment.

"What say we play a game of whist?" Lord Sheffield wheezed, his nose whistling as he breathed.

Lord Kerr sat at the round table in the far-left corner of the room with a deck of cards already in his hands.

"Play," Mary whispered to Gabe.

With one last enigmatic glance at Mary, Gabe sat between Sheffield and Lord Kerr as Mr. Piper sat across from him. Mary was at a loss as to what to do until Lady Kellings lowered herself to Lord Sheffield's lap. *Of course*.

With an ease belying the sudden fluttering in her stomach, Mary moved to stand between Gabe's legs and then sat upon his right thigh, her left arm draped lazily across his shoulders.

There was no denying the sudden heat she felt. Gabe was hot all over through his clothes, and his warmth sent shivers of tempting delight through her. *Dash it all!* Mary did not wish to feel such tinglings and melting dampness in private places when it came to Gabriel. He was not fond of her and she was certainly angry with him. Indeed. *Very* cross.

Oh pooh. Who was she trying to fool? Sitting on Gabe's lap was very nearly a dream come true. She only *wished* it wasn't, for she knew that along this path lay another broken heart. It had already happened once with Gabriel, it was inevitable that he would break her heart again if she gave him the chance.

For now, however, she was Tony Spencer's mistress in tandem with her job as a spy. Perhaps—perhaps she could use this card game to her advantage as a way to lure the other men into confiding in her. Yes, what an excellent plan!

GABE CLENCHED his jaw and played his two of hearts. *Was it a two? Or was it an eight?* Blast. He didn't know. He was far too distracted by Mary's tongue in his ear.

Good God!

Her fingers played with his cravat pin before she trailed them down the front of his waistcoat and down to his—

His eyes rolled briefly backward before he choked on his own saliva.

Mr. Piper laughed openly at him, "She's too much for you, wot? Quite the tigress from what I hear."

Gabe fought a scowl as he continued to cough. Mary's "legendary" prowess with men was not something that Gabe wished to discuss. Nor listen to. Ever.

Having concluded his fit of coughing, Gabe gripped Mary's wrist, removing her hand from its precarious place on his upper thigh and returned it to her own lap.

Her lips brushed his ear and his cock leapt in response.

Damn the woman but she was addling his brain something fierce.

"It is your turn," she whispered. Bloody hell, he could smell the lemon cream on her breath, which only fuelled his ill-timed lust.

Ye cannae have Mary, he told himself. *Mary is nae fer ye.*

He played his ace of spades, but damn if he knew what card was played last or what was trump.

Mr. Piper groaned. Gabe supposed it was a bad card to play, then, if his partner was disappointed.

"That was the last rubber," Lord Sheffield said around his cigar. "Kerr and I win!" He panted happily as he bounced Lady Kellings on his lap. The poor woman's teeth rattled with the movement.

"I think I'll drown my sorrows in my latest mistress, wot?" Mr. Piper rose from his seat.

"What *is* her name, anyway?" Lord Kerr drawled.

Mr. Piper raised an eyebrow. "She has large breasts. Does her name matter?"

Gabe forced himself to laugh jovially along with the other three men while he was privately disgusted with the man's comment. Gabe felt sorry for any woman ill-fated enough to become his mistress.

"Is there room for me to play?" Lady Kerr appeared beside them, her hand on the back of Mr. Piper's chair.

"Indeed," Lord Sheffield grinned wolfishly, the crease in his chins deepening. "Have a seat, if you will, my lady."

Lady Kerr sat across from Gabe as his partner while Lord Kerr shuffled and dealt the cards. Gabe tried with all his might to concentrate on the game and the other players. He should be watching for anything suspicious or malevolent in their behaviour, not lusting after his faux mistress. Mary knew the high stakes of this assignment, so why was she doing every-thing in her power to distract him from their purpose?

"It is your bet, Mr. Spencer." Lord Kerr tapped the surface of the table agitatedly with the tip of his index finger.

"Pay attention to the game," Mary whispered against his neck, as her lips kissed a trail down from his jaw to his shirt collar then up again.

Gabe clenched his jaw against the tempest of desire washing its way through him in gale after gale, and placed his bet of five pounds onto the table. They were playing a steep game, but Gabe was not concerned about funds, he was concerned about crucial documents being put into Napoleon Bonaparte's hands.

If only he could concentrate.

"Play your four of diamonds," Mary whispered against his earlobe as she dug her fingernails into the back of his skull.

How the devil could she pay attention to his game and he could not? She wasn't even looking at the table! *Ah, yes.* Of course. She did such things on a nightly basis, while he had been celibate for these long weeks. Arousing men was an ordinary practice for the ever-talented Mary.

The resentment that suddenly shook him to his core dampened his desire enough for him to play the game. For a moment.

The tip of her tongue traced the edge of his ear, sending gooseflesh over his skin.

That was it. He'd had enough.

He placed his cards face-down on the table, then gripped Mary's head in both of his hands as gently as he could. He pressed his own lips to her ear and breathed, "You are distracting me from my purpose. Now be a good girl and discreetly question the others." He pressed a quick kiss to her cheek, then pushed her off his lap with a swat to the bottom. "Off you go, sweetling. Let me play some cards."

With a pretty pout, Mary left the card table to join the others who lounged in the seating area. Lord Pondridge had fallen asleep on the chaise and was now snoring loudly with his disappointed mistress on his lap. Lord Jackson sat with one mistress on each thigh while he alternately kissed each of their necks. Mr. Piper had pulled out his elaborate, gold snuffbox and was sniffing the white powder from his little finger's long nail, while his mistress looked on. And Reddington... He had been lounging with his own mistress, Mrs. McArthur, but now turned his attention toward Mary.

Damn. Gabe had not considered that this might happen. But he ought to have. Perhaps it was a curse that he happened to be facing the seating area and not sitting with his back to it.

Mary walked past the settee on her way to an armchair when Reddington set aside Mrs. McArthur and pulled Mary onto his lap. Mary squealed and Gabe clenched his jaw tighter, the ache nigh unbearable.

"Come, love, and give me some of that attention that was wasted on Spencer," Reddington smoothed the backs of his fingers over the underside of her jaw.

Focus on your mission, Gabe. Do not let Mary and that villain distract you.

He looked at the table and tried to make sense of the cards placed there. As his turn came around, Gabe placed his knave of clubs down and hoped it was the right one.

His gaze flicked back up toward Mary to see her hands running over Reddington's chest.

Those hands should be on my *chest*, he told himself. *They* had *been, don't ye remember, ye fool? Ye kicked her off yer lap...*

Aye, he remembered. He remembered her kissing a path up and down his neck and along his jaw, whispering game advice or warnings in the same ear that she had licked and nipped. He remembered her hands travelling over his body, heightening an altogether unnerving awareness to his senses.

That same awareness began to sizzle its way over his skin.

He was too hot. Pulling at his collar, Gabe cursed the quick frown that troubled his brow.

He had to focus, blast it!

He played a two of...damn, he didn't know. Was it even a two?

Mary's peal of delighted laughter echoed through the room as Reddington pressed his mouth to her neck. Gabe's gut flipped over.

How was he to get any investigating done while Mary behaved like a common trollop?

As luck would have it, just that moment the rubber ended, and Gabe rose, not caring that he had lost dreadfully. "I am out."

With purposeful strides he moved to stand before Mary and Reddington, his hand extended and a forced lustful tilt to his lips. "I feel the need to retire, love."

Several of the men chuckled or hooted while the women exchanged knowing glances.

The vile Reddington tightened his grip on Mary's waist, jealousy written plainly on his features. "Why not let Mary remain down here for a little while longer, Spencer?"

The anger burning within him threatened to spill over. Gabe had to concentrate to keep his English accent as he spoke. "Because she is *my* mistress and I require her *now.*"

Someone whistled long and high behind him, but Gabe ignored it.

Obviously sensing his agitation, Mary pried Reddington's hands from her person and accepted Gabe's hand.

He frowned at the tingling sensation caused by her grip. Something must be wrong with him. Perhaps he *should* see a doctor. This was not normal.

Gabe helped Mary to rise, then with a showy flourish, lifted her into his arms, disregarding the twinge in his still-healing shoulder.

More hoots and whistles echoed behind them as he swept Mary from the room. He did not bother putting her on the floor when they reached the hall but kept her in his arms and hurried through the corridors until they arrived at their shared bedchamber.

He did not allow himself to stop to dwell on the warmth and the comforting weight of her in his arms, either. No, indeed.

CHAPTER 15

*M*ary felt the wash of cold air envelop her as Gabe set her angrily to the ground. He quickly closed their bedchamber door behind them then turned to face her, a dark scowl marring his handsome features.

"What the *bloody hell* was *that* about?" he hissed.

Mary frowned in return, hurt by his anger. "I'm afraid I do not know what you mean."

He gestured wildly toward the door and whispered heatedly, "*Tha*! Yer behaving like a whore ready te lift her skirts fer any man te offer!" His accent slipped through his practiced veneer.

Pain sliced through her chest, sending ripples down to her fingertips. "There you are, calling me a whore again," she whispered back. "Somehow you seem to have mistaken me for a *lady*. I am not highborn; I am a *spy*, Gabriel, and an *actress*. It is my job to behave in such a way."

"Aye! Tha' is precisely my argument." He pointed at her. "Ye should no' be put in this position from the first, Mary, it isnae right."

No matter how many times she had heard him say so, it

133

still hurt to know that he did not believe her capable of being a spy. "I have just as much of a right to be here as you do, Gabe," she said, her voice growing in strength as she warmed to her topic. "I was offered this life and I accepted wholeheartedly. This is *mine*, whether you approve of it or not. It is decidedly *not* your choice what I do with my life and my body.

"Why is it," she continued, incensed, "that it is acceptable for a man to have lovers and mistresses, and it is okay for *those* women to tup as many men as they please, but it is not acceptable for me?"

Gabe flinched at her coarse language, but she continued anyway. "What is it, exactly, that has you so upset? Do you believe I will fall in love with one of them? Do you believe me capable of switching my alliance to join a traitor?"

"Nae," Gabe grumbled, appearing discomfited.

"Then what is the issue, pray?"

Gabe stood mutely, his mouth a thin line and his eyes devoid of emotion. "Reddington is very likely a traitor, and fer all we ken, a man capable of unknown evils. And he wants ye." He stood straighter, as though he believed he found the winning argument. "He even suggested tha' I share ye with him. He said tha' everyone 'shared' here."

Mary could almost laugh. "I am aware of Reddington's wish to bed me; what do you suppose he was whispering in my ear all through supper?"

Gabe's jaw clenched. "And ye encouraged him."

How could she make Gabe understand? "I was trained for this, Gabriel," she continued in hushed tones. "I went to school just as you did. I learned how to defend myself and how to use this very sort of undesirable situation to my advantage. Which is precisely what I aim to do. If I can bring these men to not only desire me, but to believe me flighty and unintelligent, then they will confess any number of sins in a belief that gloating will gain them my favours. And, should that fail to work, at the very least I am able to distract them while you search for the documents."

Gabriel's disposition was positively thunderous as he scowled at her from under his dark eyebrows. "I do no' like it. I do no' think ye should—"

Mary shook her head, cutting off his argument, both hurt and tired of the entire issue. "You gave up any claim to give me advice when you abandoned our friendship, Gabriel."

If he clenched his jaw any tighter, Mary was certain he would chip a tooth.

He turned away with a mumbled "verra well" and pulled his coat from his shoulders.

Mary turned to do the same, removing her slippers and stockings then pulling her night rail out of the small wardrobe that they shared. "By the way," she glanced over her shoulder at him, "you may wish to focus on your accent. You seem to have forgotten it."

That statement earned her a grumble as he draped his waistcoat over a chair and began to unknot his cravat.

"Would you please unfasten me?" Mary gave him her back.

There was silence for a moment, and Mary began to wonder if Gabe would ignore her request and she would be forced to sleep in her gown and corset, but then she heard the shifting of fabric behind her.

The moment his hands touched the buttons at her back, Mary was swamped with need. She was brought back to those moments she spent on his lap and a furor of nervous fluttering erupted in her stomach. She must admit, at least to herself, that all of the teasing done to him had not *all* been for the sake of their cover identities. She could easily have simply sat atop his knee and whispered a few words in his ear. Instead, she had allowed herself those moments to satisfy her curiosity. She had never before felt such emotions while teasing a man, let alone ones so very *strong*. She wanted to explore...to taste...to nip...to take as much out of the experience as she could possibly manage.

Mary bit the inside of her cheek to keep from sighing.

Her buttons undone, Mary held her gown to her chest as Gabe set to work on the ties of her corset.

She took that moment to correct her wayward thoughts.

Gabe did not even like her, let alone harbour intimate feelings—or even warm feelings—for her. In fact, Mary was quite certain that he thought rather poorly of her, if his constant comments about her being a *whore* were any indication.

Mary cleared her throat of the sudden lump that had lodged itself there and changed the topic.

"I believe that we may have reason to include Lady Kerr in our list of suspects," she whispered.

Gabe's hands paused briefly before he let out a hoarse laugh and finished with her corset.

"What is so amusing?" She turned to face him as she removed the loosened articles and hung them over the same chair he had used.

"What in God's name," he said, correcting his accent, "makes you think that Lady Kerr is a potential suspect?" He was not smiling, but she could hear the barely suppressed mirth in his voice and saw the slight crinkle beside his eyes.

Mary listed the reasons off on her fingers. "She gives me long, calculating stares, she has an excellent bluffing expression as noted by her gameplay, she asked what *precisely* it was that enamoured me to you, the shrewdness behind her gaze, and..." she crossed her arms defensively as he cocked an eyebrow at her, "I have a feeling about it. Instinctually."

He shook his head, laughing. "Have you any notion of how mad you sound?" He lowered his voice, "Lady Kerr is *not* a spy."

Incensed, Mary stepped toward him, her hands on her hips. "You only believe her incapable of treachery because you cannot give credence to her flirting with you only to gain something."

"*You* only believe her capable of treachery because you cannot give credence to her flirting with me *at all*."

Mary grit her teeth at the ring of truth to his words and shook her head. "This is not merely a matter of feminine competition or jealousy, I assure you. I have no desire to be intimate with you *or* to renew our friendship," she lied. "Ours is purely a business association and nothing more. So you may trust that when I say I suspect Lady Kerr of wrongdoing, my opinion is unclouded by emotion."

GABE GAZED AT MARY, his stomach knotted so painfully he was certain he would be sick. This entire discussion had bound him in an emotional coil, wound so tightly he did not know which sensation to trust.

A *business association*, indeed. Whatever Mary thought, Gabe knew that those youthful years of friendship were more than mere childhood reveries. He just didn't know what they *did* mean. Or how he should behave towards the woman that continued to muddle his thoughts.

He clenched and released his jaw before he shook his head. "You are wrong, Mary."

His gaze bored into hers as his mind worked, his throat tightening. Something was there, but the answers were just out of reach. He didn't yet know what he wanted out of his *association* with Mary, but it wasn't a damned business transaction.

With one last searing glance, Mary turned her back on him and went about her nightly ablutions. Gabe watched her as she moved, both gracefully and almost...mournfully. The shadows cast by the flickering fireplace dancing along her spine like a wicked marionette. Gabe was suddenly very aware that she was mostly nude, her only article of clothing the thin chemise that clung to her every curve.

Cursing himself for even looking, Gabe removed the remainder of his outer clothing and draped them over the nearby armchair. With agitated movements, he snatched a pillow from atop the turned-down bed and tossed it atop the rug before the hearth. He lowered himself to the floor wearing just his smallclothes and curled his knees up to lie on his side, keeping his back to—and his eyes away from—Mary.

"Would you like a blanket?" Mary said from behind him.

"No," he grunted. "The fire will keep me warm."

"As you wish, then."

His gut still in turmoil, Gabe forced his eyes to close against the brightness of the flickering fire.

CHAPTER 16

The sound of sloshing water brought Gabe slowly awake. He blinked the sleep from his eyes, his gaze slowly focusing on the banked fire in the hearth. The anger and hurt that he'd felt last evening came rushing back

Blast.

He rose slowly and stiffly, then stretched. His position on the puce rug last night had not been as comfortable as he had initially believed it to be. It had been, however, necessary.

His spine *cracked* and *popped* as he bent over to retrieve his pillow, the sound gaining Mary's attention.

"Oh!" She smiled at him as she turned from the wash-stand. "Good morning!"

Damn her and her cheery disposition. "Good morning," he grumbled, keeping his eyes averted from her mostly nude and freshly washed form.

He tossed the pillow beside hers and lowered himself to the bed after it, pulling the counterpane over his lower half. As much as he hated to feel the warmth on the bedclothes left by Mary's body, he knew that they must keep up appearances, for Mary was a martinet for appearances. She'd reminded him of his slipping façade several times already during this assignment. And she was right. He ought to be more careful. A man and his mistress would not sleep separately.

Glancing toward the opened window, Gabe noted the early hour. The sun was low on the horizon, its bright, cheerful rays mocking his dour mood. Gabe defiantly closed his eyes.

Mary cleared her throat. "I am pleased that you are awake. I must dress and I require the help of a maid."

His eyes snapped open, but before Gabe could ponder the sudden tingling sensation racing up and down his chest and Mary's oddly formal choice of words, she walked toward the bedchamber door and tugged on the thick, corded rope hanging there.

"I thought there weren't any maids available." Gabe raised his arms to rest beneath his head, propping himself up so as to better see Mary while they spoke.

"Not yesterday, no, but I should think that there would not be many other guests awake at this hour."

"Why are you awake so early?" Gabe asked.

Mary moved to the chest of drawers and withdrew a pair of stockings from the top drawer. "I thought to break my fast —if it has been prepared—and then venture out of doors for a bit of fresh air."

"You're going to interrogate the gardener, aren't you?"

Mary raised a cautionary brow at Gabe as she bent to slip on her stocking. "Whether I am or am not going to speak to the gardener is..."

Gabe did not hear the remainder of her sentence, as all thought—and blood—rushed away from his head. The angle of Mary's low-cut chemise as she bent gave him a full view of her bouncing beauties...those swaying, rounded, orbs of milky pleasure. Gabe knew instinctively that they would look exactly like that as she rode him. They would hang just above his face and he would lift up to suck one into his mouth. He would bite and lick, and she would moan and sigh. *Bloody hell*. He would—

"Have you heard a word that I've said?"

Gabe blinked, his fantasy dissipating like smoke before his eyes. Pray God she didn't notice his cockstand beneath the thick counterpane. He lifted one knee for the sake of his modesty...and his pride.

"Beg pardon," he said, his voice thick. "I must have missed that last bit."

Mary placed her hands on her hips, the movement only accentuating her slender waist and—God help him—her stirringly wide hips and generously rounded bosom.

"I have been detailing my plan to discretely speak with the servants then search the house, while you have done nothing but gaze at me with a vacant expression."

"My apologies, Mary. Though..." Gabe thought of the men on the evening previous, wolfishly sniffing after Mary's skirts. "I do not believe you should search the house alone."

She huffed an exasperated breath and bent to put on her other stocking. "I hardly require a governess to follow me about."

Gabe forced himself to focus on the conversation rather than be distracted by her luscious breasts and his eagerly aggressive arousal.

He must convince her that whoever the spies might be within this house, none were to be trifled with. "If you are caught, Mary, you must have a means of escape. If we are together, a plausible reason for being in an odd part of the house would be easier to concoct. If you are discovered venturing off alone, you will become suspect immediately."

She rose, her bottom lip pulled between her teeth as she gently chewed on the soft flesh. "You make a fair argument."

Gabe's gaze lowered to her newly swollen and glistening bottom lip as she spoke.

My God, wha' is wrong with me? Mary is nae fer ye, lad, Gabe told himself. *Yer supposed te be convincing Mary tha' spying is too dangerous, nae lusting after her like a randy lad with his first promise of soft female flesh.*

A light knock sounded at the door, disrupting his inner rebuke.

"Come," Mary called.

The door opened to reveal a timid, softly rounded maid of medium height and dull auburn hair hidden beneath a mobcap. She quietly shuffled in, curtsied, and held her hands nervously in front of her abdomen.

Mary, obviously sensing the maid's distress beckoned the girl to her. "Thank you for coming..."

"Eleanor Mable, Miss. You can call me Eleanor." The maid curtsied, sending a shy sideways glance toward Gabe, then quickly averting her gaze.

"Eleanor. Thank you." Mary motioned toward the wardrobe. "Would you be so kind as to help me into the tyrian purple morning gown?"

With another uneasy glance at Gabe, the maid did as she was bid and turned to look in the wardrobe.

Gabe wished he could put the girl at ease and let her know that unlike the other male guests at the house party, he had no interest in taking advantage of the female staff. Poor gel likely got harassed more often than not in her position. She was a handsome female with an attractive face and shy, if not fearful disposition. Just the sort to attract the wrong sort of man.

But Gabe was in character. He was Anthony Spencer; a carefree rake who did not spare a second thought for *the help* or their thoughts, needs, or feelings. They were there only to serve.

So, Gabe settled in, propped his back with the bed's

pillows and watched as his mistress and the lady's maid covered up Mary's sinfully alluring curves, all the while trying to rein in the inconvenient lust that rode him nigh to the brink of madness.

GABRIEL WAS *VERY* adept at playing his role of lover for the sake of public opinion. He sat, unmoving and fairly brimming with arousing predatory covetousness, as he brooded from the bed.

Mary wished she knew what he was thinking. Probably lamenting ever having agreed to this scheme and wondering how quickly he could extricate himself from her presence.

The thought made her frown at her reflection in the mirror.

"Is it not to your liking, miss?" the sweetly dispositioned maid asked, a troubled expression marring her handsome features.

Mary forced a smile. "Oh no, dear, I was simply lost in thought. My hair is perfectly suitable."

"I could try somethin' different. Maybe looped braids?"

"I am very happy with the way you are doing it." Mary's smile deepened. "I am partial to curls."

Eleanor's face brightened as she turned back to her work.

As though by habit, her gaze slid sideways—to nothing. She blinked and returned her attention to the mirror. She'd never even noticed the habitual motion before, but now that she didn't have her conch shell to look at—which sat on her chest of drawers at home—the habit was rather more apparent. Odd as it was, the shell brought her comfort and a sense of calm; it reminded her of a time when she was truly happy with Gabriel.

The devil himself shifted in her bed, and Mary willed her

gaze to remain on her own reflection, as Eleanor's hands worked magic with her untamed hair. And decidedly off of Gabe's muscled chest. *Lord what a chest*. How was it even possible for a man to have a chest such as his? How did a man's body even get so...so...*powerful*? She had seen many a man's nude body in her position, but never had she seen a man with as many muscled hills and dips as Gabe possessed. He had not an ounce of fat or droopy skin anywhere on his person, she was certain.

One—obviously depraved—part of her wanted nothing more than to run her hands, lips, and tongue over every muscled mound of his torso until every square inch had been explored and tasted. While the other—clearly more sensible—part of her told her wicked half to *shut it*, forget about Gabriel and his stunningly, arousingly beautiful body, and turn her attention back to her assignment, because she knew that there was absolutely no chance that Gabe would return any sort of positive sentiment, let alone wish to bed her.

The moment that thought entered her mind, she regretted it.

Bedding Gabriel.

If the feelings he brought out in her were any indication, it would indeed be pleasurable. She was attracted to the blasted man, but if she possessed any amount of good sense, she should flee from him as fast as she could go. Their assignment notwithstanding, something compelled Mary to torture herself by staying close to him.

Focus, Mary. Spies abound.

She turned her open, trusting gaze up to Eleanor as the maid put the finishing touches on her chignon. "How did you come to be a lady's maid, Eleanor?"

"Oh, I'm not, miss. I'm a downstairs maid, but since there's so many ladies needin' their hair done and gowns mended, I was sent up to 'elp."

Mary nodded in understanding. "I've toyed with the idea of giving up the theatre and becoming a maid," she lied. "How do you find the work?"

Eleanor's fingers froze as her gaze turned down and a telling blush stained her cheeks. Poor girl.

"You do not have to fear being honest with me, dear," Mary soothed.

With an oddly wiggled shake to her head, Eleanor continued working with Mary's hair. "The work is not hard if'n you 'ave good shoes and a sturdy back, miss. It's the—" her gaze flicked upward toward Gabe's reflection in the mirror as he sat relaxed in the bed. The maid's lips pressed tightly together before her tongue darted out nervously to wet them. "The work is right fine, miss."

Mary would have questioned her further, but her behaviour toward Gabe spoke volumes where her words did not. Eleanor was afraid of men...for reasons Mary suspected were deleterious to the maid's self-worth, emotional stability, and disposition.

Mary suddenly very much wished to eviscerate Lord Kerr for allowing such despicable behaviour to take place in his home and for not taking better care of his staff.

"There you are, miss." Eleanor stepped back to admire her work. "Pretty as a paintin'."

Mary smiled at the maid's flattery. "Thank you, Eleanor. It takes magic fingers to tame my hair."

"It were nothin', miss. Will that be all?"

Mary had scared her off with her questions, then. Her smile slipped, but she put it firmly back in place. "Yes, thank you. You may go about your duties, Eleanor."

The maid curtsied and hurried past the bed and out of the room, closing the door quietly behind her.

The moment the latch clicked, Gabe leapt from the bed,

his bare feet hitting the floor silently as he dashed across the room to the wardrobe.

Mary swivelled in her seat at her dressing table to look at him. "Good heavens, you're in a hurry."

"It takes you women so damned long to get yourselves put together," Gabe grumbled.

"I beg your pardon, but you were fully able to get yourself dressed *while* Eleanor was helping me."

He rejected her comment with a quick jerk of his head. "Would ruin the illusion and break me from character."

Mary chewed her bottom lip. "I see your point."

Gabe stepped into his fine dove grey breeches, leaving the falls open while he pulled a shirt over his head and tucked them into the top of his breeches.

"What about a valet?" Mary asked.

Gabe paused while buttoning his falls. "Now I see *your* point." A heartbeat passed before he shrugged one shoulder and retrieved a cream coloured waistcoat from the wardrobe. "It is quicker when I dress myself. Besides, I cannot abide by someone fussing over every detail of my wardrobe."

Mary nodded as Gabe began buttoning his waistcoat over what Mary now knew to be a remarkably beautiful chest.

"Why are you in such a hurry?" She ignored the nagging jealousy at the back of her mind at the thought that he might be going to see Lady Kerr.

You should not *be jealous. Ninny.*

He gave her an odd frown that was lined with an emotion that Mary could not quite interpret. "*You* are dressed. We must break our fast, then begin the search for those documents."

"Ah," Mary brightened. "I had thought about that as I lay abed last night, and I thought that an excellent place to start might be the guests' bedchambers."

Gabe froze in the act of pulling on his coat, a fearsome

frown marring his features and turning his blue eyes as cold as ice. "I think not."

"Whyever not?" Mary asked in disbelief. "Surely you see the cleverness of the thought. Any man with sense would hide those documents somewhere close to them, and where is more personal than a man's bedchamber?"

If it were at all possible, his scowl darkened even more. He pointed a finger at her. "I will not have you sneaking into men's bedchambers, do you hear me?"

"But it is—"

"I said *no*. It is too dangerous for a woman to do such a thing. If anyone is to search the men's bedchambers, it will be me."

"But what excuse will you have for being there? If I were to search, then at least I have the option to flirt my way out of any suspicion they may harbour for me. *You* will...what? Use brute force?"

His jaw clenched. "I will think of something." He pulled a cravat from the chest of drawers and slid it under his shirt collar. "First we will search the study."

Mary scoffed. "That is far too obvious."

Gabe clucked his tongue then whispered, "You are not thinking like a spy, Mary." He finished tying his simple cravat knot then turned to sit on the edge of the bed where he had placed his hessians. "Have you considered that there might be hidden drawers? Secret compartments? A strong box?"

Mary twisted her lips in thought. "But would not a cautious spy already be aware of the opposition's knowledge of such hiding spaces and therefore take precautions to protect their secrets?"

Gabe stepped into his shining black hessians, then stomped his foot to the bottom of the boot. "We will search anyway, if not to rule it out," he grunted.

Mary stood, her tyrian purple morning gown settling

around her. It was not a colour that she had ever worn before, but the modiste had certainly chosen a colour that made her grey eyes sparkle. Mary supposed that had been the objective.

Gabe spared her not a glance as he stood to run his hands through his curling brown hair. Would that she could do her hair so easily and have it look as fine.

"We will do our searching together."

Mary tilted her head to observe him better. "If that is your desire, then so be it."

His hands stilled then dropped to his sides as he turned to stare at her. Barely banked fire burned behind his eyes. She wished she could hear his thoughts.

He abruptly stuck his elbow out to her. "Shall we go down to break our fast?"

CHAPTER 17

*G*abe felt himself tense as they neared the morning room. The sound of uninhibited laughter and answering titters echoed through the hall. It would seem that they were not the first guests to awaken.

Pasting a self-assured smile on his lips, he affected a jackanapes swagger and pushed open the door to the breakfast room. A nauseating waft of the presumably inedible fare curled up to his senses and he hid a cringe.

Without breaking stride, he led Mary into the grand, lavishly appointed morning room. This one was more absurd than the others they had seen of yet. The walls were draped in gilt wall hangings, the white floors were polished to such a high shine that they reflected everything in the room as though it were a mirror, and small cupids holding fruit smiled down on them from the painted ceiling.

Egad.

They greeted the others in the room but halted when a new man rose from his seat at the table.

"Mary!" The man boomed as he spread his arms wide and strode toward them.

Mary smiled in return and accepted his buss to her cheek. Gabe clenched his jaw to keep from loudly protesting and sweeping Mary from the room.

"Won't you introduce me to your friend?" the cad with auburn hair and striking green eyes asked.

Mary's grin widened at the curst man. "Of course! Tony, this is Mr. Anthony Spencer."

Gabe's confident expression slipped as he was momentarily nonplused.

"Tony, this is Anthony Walstone, Viscount Boxton."

"Two *Tony*s, eh wot?" Mr. Piper laughed from his seat at the long table.

Gabe affected the appropriate bow and said the customary things, all the while he was seething at the knowledge that this man and Mary already knew each other. The question was, *how* did they know each other? Did they have an *association* such as the one Mary had with Lord Reddington?

Perish the thought.

Gabe had heard of Boxton through his dealings—or *incidents*—with Hydra's family. Hydra's sister, Miss Annabel Bradley—now Lady Devon—had been courted by the man over the past season. From what Gabe had gleaned, Boxton was a right bastard and ended up forced into a loveless marriage after being caught doing unspeakable acts to his loathsome future wife.

"Tell me, how do you know each other?" Gabe cursed his quick tongue the moment the words escaped his mouth. He did not want to know the answer to that question.

A slow, predatory grin grew on the man's lips and Gabe felt his pulse begin to hammer in his temples.

"Oh, we go *way* back, don't we, love?" He winked at Mary, and Gabe had to resist the urge to punch the man in the nose. "But I thought you would not take on a protector, Mary." He turned to Gabe with a jaundiced eye.

Mary gazed at Gabe with adoration, her hand running up and down his coat sleeve. "Tony knew precisely what to say and what to *do* to alter my opinion on that score."

"Do stop," Lord Reddington grumbled around a mouth full of food from his seat at the table. "You'll make us all jealous."

"Yes, come in and eat," Lady Kerr intoned from her seat beside her husband at the head of the table. "I saved a seat for you, Mr. Spencer."

Lord Boxton raised a critical eyebrow at Gabe. "It seems that my lover has taken a liking to you..." his gaze flicked to Mary and back, "*and* the woman whose favours I, and dozens more, have very nearly begged for. You must be something special, indeed."

Damn. He had not meant to attract so much attention. That would not be conducive to their anonymity once this assignment concluded.

He shrugged a shoulder and affected a confidence he didn't feel. "What can I say? I learned some very *interesting* things while living abroad."

"Will you lot quit your blathering and sit your arses down to eat?" Lord Sheffield wheezed, his extra chin jiggling as he spoke. "The food is getting cold and your chatter is setting me off my feed."

"And that's damned difficult to do!" Mr. Piper laughed.

Gabe silently gripped Mary's elbow and led her to the sideboard where they both filled their plates. Nothing appeared or smelled appetizing in the least, but he swallowed past his repugnance and selected the lesser of the evils: nearly spoiled fruit and a slice of toast.

He sat next to Lady Kerr as she had requested, and Mary sat between the scurrilous devils, Reddington and Boxton. She smiled and flirted as she ate, laughed or turned her warm grey eyes on them when they whispered something in her ear, and batted her lashes at what Gabe could only assume were appropriate times. Damn them. Damn them all.

Why did it bother him so? Could it truly just be that he did not wish for Mary to be hurt? He was not certain that he wished to learn the answer to that question. He had best not dwell on it.

"We have ruins on the grounds of Kerr house, Mr. Spencer." Lady Kerr leaned in close to him.

Gabe forced himself to swallow down the dry toast. "Do you, indeed?"

She nodded, her black hair remaining perfectly in place with every movement. "We do," she purred. "You must come for a private tour."

"*I* should like a private tour, my lady," Lord Pondridge said, a Machiavellian gleam to his eye, while pouring a dram of brandy into his goblet.

"Drinking at *this* hour, Pondridge?" Mr. Jackson raised a perfectly manicured brow across the table at the hawk-like Lord.

Pondridge waved a fork at the man and his twin mistresses, one on each knee. "*Whoring* at this hour, Jackson?"

With a wink and a wicked grin, the slender, red haired dandy laughed. "Touché."

"Speaking of which," Reddington put in, "you said you might perform for us, but what must we do to convince you to perform for us *tonight*, Mary?"

"Yes, Miss White," Mr. Piper spoke before she could respond. "We have heard so much about your fascinating skills, it would be a shame not to honour us with a sample."

Boxton's eyebrows rose nigh to his hairline. "*Perform*?"

Mary's smile was a bewildering combination of demureness and seductiveness. Bloody perfect. "If you wish it, then I shall dance tonight."

"Dance, is it?" Lord Kerr sipped at the steaming coffee in his cup.

"Oh!" Boxton turned to gaze at his lordship, his green eyes wide and almost frightfully zealous. "You would not believe what Mary is capable of, Kerr. She does things that are simply...indescribable! The movement of her hips—"

"Don't give away the enjoyment of it with your ham-fisted descriptions, Boxton," Reddington cut in. "Let it be a surprise."

"Yes. Yes, of course. But I'll wager you have never seen the like."

"I'll take that wager," Lord Kerr said.

Gabe wanted to slap the cocksure smile off of Boxton's face.

"One hundred quid."

Kerr raised an eyebrow. "Are you certain you can afford to lose such a sum?"

Boxton laughed loudly, his voice echoing off the walls of the large room. "I can afford to *win* such a sum, I assure you."

Lord Kerr turned to look at Mary. "What say you, Miss White? Should I take the wager?"

Mary winked at him. "That, my lord, is for you to decide."

He pursed his lips for a moment then nodded at Boxton. "You have yourself a wager. One hundred pounds that this young actress cannot do anything that I have not yet seen."

Boxton clapped his hands in premature victory.

It took all of Gabe's will not to howl his fury to the room. Each word these idiots spoke brought his anger higher. Hell, Gabe could not recall a time when he felt as angry as he has in the past four and twenty hours.

He must be ill. Perhaps he had the ague; he certainly felt warm. *But no*. The ague would not make one angry. Mayhap he was going mad. Madness was not found in his family, but he supposed it must begin with someone.

One of Jackson's mistresses giggled as he kissed his way up her neck, cutting the sudden silence and breaking into Gabe's maudlin thoughts.

"Who is game for a hunt this morning? The weather is fine if not a bit damp from yesterday's rain, eh wot?" Mr. Piper leaned back in his chair and pulled out his snuffbox.

Lord Pondridge tapped his lap and his mistress rose from her seat beside him to straddle his thighs. "I do not ride...a *horse*." He winked and his mistress tittered.

Gabe suspected that Pondridge didn't ride because he was always too drunk to stay atop his mount.

"I love a good hunt." The Viscountess Kerr dabbed daintily at the corners of her lips then placed her napkin beside her plate.

"Capital!" Mr. Piper clapped his hands in one loud *crack*.

Lord Kerr swallowed a mouthful of coffee. "Once we've concluded the morning meal, everyone that wishes to ride ought to don the proper attire. It would seem that a hunt is on."

AN HOUR after the morning meal, Mary pulled Gabe's earlobe into her mouth, scraping the little nub against her teeth as her tongue lapped simultaneously. She behaved as the other mistresses did, casually draping over her lover's lap, toying with his lapel, hair, and teasing him with lips and tongue. She attempted, with all her might, to act as though Gabriel were just another "mark" and allow her body to move without her emotions being entangled. But as much as Mary tried, she could not be detached from what her body was doing with Gabe.

He was warm and hard, and he smelled of clean skin and the arousing gentle scent of soap and cloves. Touching him and smelling him did something to her senses that compelled her to not only continue, but to do *more*. Much, much more.

Gabe's voice rumbled as he spoke, the vibrations tickling her lips as she kissed the underside of his unshaven jaw.

Good heavens!

Male laughter cut through her shameful musings and she turned to see young Eleanor standing in the middle of the parlour, evidently having brought in a refill of the men's refreshments. Gratefully, most of the house party guests had joined the hunt, so there weren't many witnesses to Eleanor's embarrassment. But Mary was there. And she did not like what she saw.

Lord Pondridge pinched her bottom while Lord Sheffield gripped the poor girl's wrist, tugging her closer to him.

"Come and play with us, pretty gel. We won't hurt you."

The grimace on Eleanor's face and the way she clawed at his punishing grip with her other hand told Mary that he was indeed hurting her.

Lord Sheffield pulled harder, forcing Eleanor to fall onto his lap. "There, dearie, now we can have some fun."

A flash went through Mary's mind of that day long ago...

"Wha' should we do with 'er? Eh?"

"I think weee should t-up 'er, wot, wot?"

A shiver went down Mary's spine and she was on her feet before she could give credence to the thought. She moved purely on instinct.

"Pardon me, your lordships, but I have need of Eleanor's services."

"Aw, come now, Miss White, surely you can spare her for a few minutes."

Mary moved her hands in a gesture of helplessness. "I am afraid not. You see, if I am to perform this evening I must have my costume readied. Eleanor is taking the place of my lady's maid while we are in residence and I simply must have her assistance."

Eleanor scrambled from Lord Sheffield's lap the instant he released her, a look of such relief on her features that Mary felt an ache in her chest for what this girl must routinely suffer.

With a curtsey, Mary led Eleanor from the room. They traversed the halls in silence, passing other maids and footmen scurrying about to clean their masters' chambers. The upstairs maid cleaning Mary and Gabe's bedchamber nearly bumped into them as she rushed from the room.

"Beg pardon, miss." She was gone before Mary had the chance to reply.

Mary preceded Eleanor into the room and pulled a small trunk from beneath the bed and placed it atop the newly straightened counterpane.

"This is—"

"Beg pardon for interrupting, miss," Eleanor placed a tentative hand on Mary's arm, then quickly pulled it back. "Thank you. I cannot tell you how much that meant to me, your rescuing me like that."

Mary would ordinarily have brushed off the effusive thanks, but not only did she wish to earn the maid's trust, but something about her compelled Mary to help. So she was honest. "Someone once saved me from such a fate. I simply wished to repay the favour." She tapped the trunk with both hands. "Now. *This* is my trunk of costumes."

She opened the lid, an array of colourful, sheer fabrics, chained coin-shaped metal circles, and ankle and wrist cuffs overflowing the box.

Eleanor's eyes widened. "Cor!" she said breathily.

"I have not yet decided which one I will wear, so do you think you can manage to choose for me, and prepare it for this evening?"

"O' course, Miss White. I would be happy to."

CHAPTER 18

*G*abe watched Mary's swaying bottom with a lustful gaze as she left the room with the maid. He told himself it was purely because it was what his character would do, but somewhere in the back of his mind Gabe knew that was a lie.

It felt shameful, the way his body reacted when Mary was near...when Mary was touching him, licking him, kissing him. It was a natural response to such petting and teasing, but damn it, this was Mary!

His body wanted her; there was no question of that. It was his mind...his mind that told him it was wrong. His mind that rebelled whenever she pressed her sweet bottom over the hardness in his lap. His mind that told him she was untouchable.

It was a shame that his mind was right.

His gaze turned upwards as the butler appeared in the parlour's doorway.

"The Marquess of Hale and his lady," he announced.

Mr. Jenkins stepped aside with a bow so low that Gabe thought uneasily that the old man might not be able to right himself again.

From behind the butler came a sturdy-looking man of middling age, though rather robust in health, with greying brown hair and black eyes. He was dressed as any respectable lord would; his shirt was crisply white, his waistcoat of the finest silk, his coat and trousers a popularly chosen midnight blue, and his cravat pin as black as obsidian. Beside him stood the woman that was obviously his mistress. She was a young, frightened woman with cropped, short black curls and a demure brown travelling frock. Her eyes cast downward as her lover greeted the room with an affable smile.

Lord Hale wore a mask of wellness and congeniality, but Gabe sensed something dark lurking deep within. One look at him and Gabe understood why he was on Hydra's list of traitorous suspects.

"Greetings!"

The lords Sheffield and Pondridge rose and greeted the newest arrival. Abiding by propriety, Gabe rose from his seat and bowed as well.

"Who is this?" Hale pointed at Gabe.

"My name is Mr. Anthony Spencer, my lord."

Hale grunted.

Lord Pondridge took a gulp of his brandy and smiled unsteadily. "Spencer here is with the legendary actress, Miss White."

"The devil you say?" Hale's eyebrows rose. "That's another bet at White's that I've lost. Tell me, is she as good as they say?"

Gabe swallowed down some bile as he affected a grin. "Better."

"Lucky man, lucky man, wot? Where the devil *is* everyone? I was told this was a house party, not a boring week of watching men lay about."

Lord Sheffield laughed, his belly jiggling. "A few of the

ladies have gone for a turn about the garden and the others are out for a hunt."

"Ah." Hale turned to his mistress. "Sit."

As his mistress did as he demanded, perching carefully on the edge of a chair, Hale went to the sideboard and poured himself a healthy dram of whisky before sitting on the chaise. Hale then snapped his fingers and pointed to his lap, his mistress obediently moving to sit upon his thighs.

Where is Mary?

Gabe bowed to the room. "Please excuse me, my lords."

Without waiting for a response, he turned on his heel and exited into the corridor in search of Mary. He traversed the halls that led to their bedchamber, each moment seemingly taking longer than the last. He finally reached their room and went inside. Neither Mary nor the maid was anywhere to be seen.

He cursed under his breath and returned to the hall. He took several long strides down the corridor when he heard the telltale murmuring of voices coming from one of the adjacent rooms.

His senses alert, Gabe sidled up to the door and pressed his ear to the cool wood.

"Oh!" Mary's lowered voice said. "I'm so glad you've come. I've missed you."

Gabe felt his stomach flutter with...anger, he was certain, at the muffled male voice that replied. He and Mary were part-ners on this assignment. They were meant to be lovers, and he had no intention of being cuckolded, even if it was an artificial romantic alliance.

Without waiting another moment, Gabe burst into the room, the door crashing against the wall as it swung violently open.

Mary betrayed nary a flinch, but a footman dressed in unsightly green livery leapt to protect her, stepping in front of her, ready to defend Mary from the noisy intruder. But the moment Gabriel saw the golden-eyed man with whom she stood, he felt the complete fool.

He quickly closed the door behind him and entered the room to stand before Mary and the footman. "Sir Bramwell Stevens. My apologies. I did not know you would be here."

He shook his fellow spy's hand.

Stevens grinned. "What the devil did you think was happening in here, Gabe, to make you crash in like that? And please, it's just Stevens. I don't like this *Sir* nonsense."

"Nothing, I assure you," Gabe lied.

"Stevens' pseudonym is 'Smithe,'" Mary said. "Hydra informed us that he was a footman for the Marquess of Hale, if you will recall."

Gabe affected a mock half bow. "Anthony Spencer at your service. You already know Mary White."

Stevens' lips curved up in a half smile. "Indeed, I do." He lifted Mary's hand to his lips and gave it a lingering kiss.

Mary giggled, her other hand coming up to cover her perfect, smiling mouth.

Damn Stevens, anyway. He was as bad as Hugh and Colin, the incorrigible flirts.

Gabe grabbed Mary's free hand, pulling her to his side and away from Stevens. "That is enough of that. From this point on, we do not know each other."

Stevens bowed. "Of course, sir."

Gabe turned to Mary. "We have some searching to do."

With another wink, Stevens slunk from the room, leaving Gabe and Mary alone in the guest bedchamber. It was an exact copy of their room, except this one was ornamented not in puce, but sunshine yellow. It was too cheery for Gabe's current mood.

He was suddenly very aware that he was still holding

Mary's hand...and that he rather enjoyed the sensation. He quickly released her.

"Shall we begin with the downstairs study?" He forced a smile.

"Of course." She linked her hand around his elbow. "Do you know the way?"

"Not at all, but I imagine it should not be difficult to find. Is it not the room with a desk, a chair, and correspondence and such?"

MARY SENT GABE a sideways glance for his sarcasm. They continued down the hall, searching, for Lord Kerr's study as insouciantly as possible. This assignment would be simpler if they had come as servants, as they could come and go from rooms and bedchambers without inquiry. Mary knew better than to question Hydra's methods, however, and her role as Miss White the actress has already been established.

As much as Mary had been enjoying the sweet torture of Gabriel and the excitement of the hunt for Bonaparte's spies, she was concerned. Anthony Walstone, the Viscount Boxton was at the house party, and that boded ill. Despite having given him a warm greeting, Mary hated to admit that she was frightened of the green-eyed devil.

"This one," Gabe murmured in her ear.

She jumped slightly at the interruption to her thoughts. Goodness, had they reached the study already? She did not even recall descending the stairs.

"Are you well, Mary?" Gabe gazed down at her, a concerned frown marring his perfect brow.

Mary forced herself to smile. "Of course, Tony."

She entered first into the empty study. It was perfectly ordered, not a single item out of place. A large mahogany desk stood in the centre of the square room, and a tall leather wing-back chair behind it. One grand rouge brocade rug lay on the floor, nearly covering the entire surface of the room.

Despite the tidy appearance, the room held the odour of books, cigars, and cheap brandy.

Gabe let out a low whistle and Mary *shushed* him.

"What?" Gabe feigned innocence. "I've never seen a study so immaculate before."

"We had best be careful of what we touch. Someone as fastidious as this likely takes particular notice of the precise placement of their things."

He conceded the point with a nod. "Let us set to work."

Mary watched as Gabriel walked toward the bookshelves that lined the right most wall and ran his fingers along the spines, testing the books for a potential latch. His hands were strong and nimble as he moved. She imagined they'd be just as capable on her.

Stop it, she admonished herself. Shaking herself and focusing on her task, Mary slid her hands around the edges of the chaise lounge and rectangular table that stood before the left wall. Besides nails and the edges of the upholstery, Mary found nothing.

She quickly moved on, examining the wide sideboard that sat against the wall behind the desk between two large paintings that stretched from ceiling to the dark wood planked floor. She opened the cabinet door.

ABANDONING THE BOOKCASE, Gabe turned his attention to the desk and opened the bottommost left side drawer. He tapped it from the underside, noting the solid *thunk*. He moved to the next drawer, and then the next, each knock leading to the same *thunk*. He finally reached the topmost drawer, but it would not open.

"Mary," he whispered.

She looked up from where she searched in the vases on the fireplace mantle.

Gabe extended a hand. "One of your hair pins."

Mary hurried over, pulling a pin from her coiffure. Gabe accepted it with a nod then placed it in the lock.

"Shouldn't you use two?" Mary whispered in his ear, the warm, womanly rose scent of her very nearly making him dizzy.

"For locks in doors and safes, yes, but this...particular lock..." he bit his lip as he concentrated on his task, "aha!" He looked at her with a grin. "Just requires one."

He slid the drawer open to find it empty. Undeterred, Gabe reached beneath the drawer and knocked. *Clunk.* He looked up at Mary with a triumphant smile before searching the underside of the drawer for a finger hole. He found it and slid his finger inside then pressed the latch within. *Click.* The top of the hidden compartment popped open and Gabe lifted it to examine the contents.

Mary sighed in disappointment. "Nothing but lists of items purchased." She reached in and fingered through the slips of parchment. "The modiste, the tailor, cobbler, book-shop, milliner..." she sighed once more, "this is not at all what we are searching for."

Gabe frowned, frustration riding him, as he looked at the entirely innocent documents. Blast it! He had been so certain...

Carefully replacing the bills and closed the drawer, he used Mary's hairpin to lock it. He quickly turned his attention to the bookshelves. Mary had already searched for an opening mechanism, but men had been known to hollow out large tomes and hide documents within. Finding the thickest book on the shelf, Gabe withdrew it and flipped it open. Nothing. He found another and opened it. Nothing.

"Gabriel—er, Tony," Mary said in hushed tones. "What do you make of this pedestal?"

Gabe turned to see Mary gesture to a tall, cylindrical, dark oak pedestal that reached about waist height. It stood in the far-left corner of the room, and an enclosed display case on top that held what appeared to be a rare book. His lordship's prized possession no doubt.

"Lord Kerr must value that book a great deal," Mary murmured thoughtfully.

"Or what's beneath it," he mused. Gabe snapped the tome shut and replaced it on the shelf, then moved toward the pedestal.

Gabe watched as Mary slid her fingers along the edges of the wood. "There is a small indentation in the rear corner." She glanced up at Gabe. "You don't suppose it's trapped, do you?"

He shook his head. "Anyone with confidence enough to steal such documents has enough confidence that their hiding place will not be discovered. Hardly someone cowering in fear."

She extended her finger, pressing firmly into the indentation. There was a loud grinding and an echoing *click*. The front of the pedestal swung open on undetectable hinges and Mary knelt to view the contents.

"A strong box." Gabe knelt behind her.

Behind the hidden door sat a thick metal box with a lock holding it shut.

"This must be it," Mary whispered.

Just as she reached toward it, Gabe halted her. "*Shh*. Do you hear that?"

He tilted his head toward the study door. The murmur of

male voices sounded down the hall and his heart slammed in his chest.

CHAPTER 19

ary turned wide-eyes on Gabriel. "Someone's coming!"

She hastily closed the secret compartment, cringing at the loud *click*, then pulled at the material of her bodice, exposing a generous swell of her bosom and part of one nipple.

Gabe tossed his coat aside and growled as he fought with the knot in his cravat.

Mary's stomach twisted uncomfortably. She reached up to tug several pins from her hair, until the chignon was partially undone and half hanging to her shoulders.

The voices were upon them now. Without wasting another moment, Mary flung herself bodily at Gabe, her skirts hiking up to her thighs as she lifted one leg to encircle his hip. She wrapped her arms snugly around his shoulders and gripped Gabriel's hair in her fists. His arms came around her waist, pulling her tighter against him.

With a deep breath for courage, Mary pressed her lips to his.

Everything disappeared.

It was just Mary and Gabriel, alone. His mouth against

hers, his heated, muscular form surged against her soft curves. The tension suddenly left her shoulders and her jaw dropped, allowing him full access to her mouth.

A low, rumbling groan escaped him, pulling a sigh from her in response. His tongue traced her lips, ran along each of her teeth, then entered to tease and toy with her own. She tasted him in turn, her tongue dipping and swirling with his, their mouths dancing in a dangerous, seductive waltz. The taste of fruit, tea, and cloves was an alluring combination on his lips.

An electric thrum pulsed its way through her body, each hair standing on its end, each nerve alert and buzzing with anticipation and heated arousal. She tightened her grip on his hair, her nails scraping gently against his scalp, as she instinctively ground her *mons* against the hard ridge of his arousal.

Gabe grunted his approval.

Oh good heavens, what a sensation! Need shot through her like a whizzing bullet, both explosive and perfectly targeted to her womanly core.

She needed to do that again.

The door swung open, pulling a cry of genuine alarm from Mary as she pried her lips from Gabe's. For a moment she stood in shock, not only for the realization of what she felt within the circle of Gabriel's arms, but because kissing him had so distracted her from their purpose.

"My, my, what have we here?" Lord Hale's black eyes took in their dishevelled appearance, his expression alive with dark mirth.

Mary's leg fell, her foot returning to the ground as she quickly righted her bodice.

"What the devil are you doing in my study?" Lord Kerr was decidedly less amused. In fact, his expression betrayed nary a hint of his true feelings.

"I think what they're doing is quite evident, Kerr, think

you not?" Lord Hale sniffed, rubbing a finger along the side of his nose. "What say you share, eh Spencer?"

That snapped Gabe from whatever had him frozen in place. He stepped back from Mary, but kept an arm securely around her waist. "My apologies, my lords." He looked down at Mary with warm fondness in his eyes. "We happened to be walking by when I was overcome with a fit of passion for Miss White." He returned his attention to the two lords. "I found the nearest vacant room, not taking notice of which it was, and secreted her inside." He picked up his coat, draped it over one arm, then brought his arm around her once more.

"'Tis a shame we did not arrive later, eh? Wouldn't *that* have been a sight to see?" Lord Hale laughed jovially, and Gabe joined in, but Mary could feel the tension coiling within him. "Go on with you now, *rest* before luncheon."

With Hale's laughter ringing in their ears, and Lord Kerr's disapproving gaze following them, Mary and Gabe quit the room. They hastily made their way from his lordship's study and back to their bedchamber abovestairs.

Mary's heart thundered in her chest, shock rippling through her as the events of the past two minutes caught up to her. She hardly knew how to comport herself or what to think.

Gabe swung their guest bedchamber door closed behind them, the *snick* of the lock echoing through the grand room. Mary's heart thudded faster.

What just happened? She had kissed and touched him before, so why was this so different? So...so...electrifying? She was uncertain as to what made this so alluring, but of one thing she was certain. She wanted to do it again.

She turned to speak with Gabe about the possibility of giving it a try, but one look at his expression halted her. He was unmoved. Unaffected. He went about his ablutions as though nothing had happened, his movements brisk and precise. But surely he had felt something?

Ah yes, of course. He did not like her. He thought her a whore. How could she have forgotten?

Her heart sank in her chest. She was foolish to think that whatever act they perform at this house party could seep into real life. Gabriel would never be with her, and she did not want him to be. She straightened her shoulders and swallowed past the sudden emotion in her throat. This was purely a physical attraction that would pass. Mary could find another bloke after this assignment was complete and give it a go with him.

It was time to move on. Stop dwelling on her past friendship with Gabriel, her heartbreak...and their kisses. Yes, their kiss had been pleasurable for her, but it was not to be repeated after their assignment. She had best remember that.

Mary strode to their shared wardrobe and spotted the costume that had been hung carefully on an outer hook. A smile touched her lips. It would seem that Eleanor had chosen Mary's costume for this evening's performance. My, but she was efficient. Mary fingered the sheer material. She had done these *performances* for myriad traitorous men and gleaned countless secrets from each, but never had she danced for so large a group, with not only men but women, as well. And Gabe.

Tamping down on the nerves that fluttered in her stomach, Mary removed the costume from the outer hook of the wardrobe and placed it inside among her gowns.

Should she change for luncheon or wait until the evening meal? She was uncertain. She turned her gaze down to what she wore; it was not terribly rumpled. As a woman of modest means, Mary often wore the same dress throughout the day, excepting her costumes. She was knowledgeable on many of the traditions of the gentry, but entirely uncertain on how frequently ladies changed.

She sighed, closing the wardrobe doors. The same gown should be acceptable for luncheon. She was playing an actress, after all, hardly one that would be held to high society's standards.

Moving to sit at her dressing table, the mirror showing her the true, sad state of her hair. *Oh dear.* Poor Eleanor had gone to such trouble to put it up, only for Mary to take it down. She began removing the pins, one by one.

GABE SCRUBBED the soap against the wet rag until it formed a foamy lather. Damn Mary and her alluring scent. He scrubbed the soapy cloth over his neck and face. He *must* get the smell of her off of him and out of his nose or he would be walking around with a cockstand in his breeches for the remainder of the day. *That smell...*

Damn. He scrubbed harder, the rough cloth abrading his skin with each stroke.

Mary was trouble. She did something to him that no other woman had. She made him feel... Well, she made him *feel*. She clearly did not reciprocate his amorous feelings, for theirs was a *business association*, as she had reminded him.

He dropped the washcloth beside the washbasin and scooped some water into his hands. The cool water was refreshing on his face and neck as he sloshed it onto his skin. Without straightening, Gabe reached for a nearby towel to wipe at the droplets.

But that kiss... He sighed into the towel, his breath warming the coarse, damp material. Even the memory of it was enough to excite him all over again. Mary was skilled, that was for certain. For those moments before Lords Kerr and Hale entered, Gabe had entirely forgotten his purpose. Forgotten where they were. Forgotten himself.

Yes, Mary was indeed dangerous. He could see, now, how Mary was able to gain such vital information from traitors to the Crown. She had the ability to take a man out of himself, to want to get more from her at any cost, to do whatever it took to have her. With any leading question, Mary would certainly be able to learn whatever she wished. Hell, it likely took no question at all, for if what Gabe felt while she was in his arms was any indication, men would simply volunteer information purely for having her a moment longer.

He shook his head, agitatedly tossing the towel beside the washbasin. *Those feelings weren't real, Gabe old boy, simply a product of this assignment and Mary's considerable talents.* Best he focus on their plans.

"We need to open that strongbox," Gabe said, turning toward Mary where she sat fixing her hair.

She placed a small hairpin between her lips as she pushed another into the knot she had created at the base of her neck. "When do you propose we do that?" she asked around the hairpin. "If Lord Kerr discovers us in his study once more, he will most assuredly be suspicious."

"We will return this evening after everyone has retired to their beds."

Mary nodded and put the remaining pin in her hair, gazing at his reflection in the mirror. "It will have to be very late. I expect the gentlemen will wish to play cards or drink after my performance."

Gabe's jaw clenched. He had forgotten about the performance. Briefly. "Very well, then."

A wide smile graced her lips as she spun on her seat to face him. "Excellent. I shall bring the hairpins and you bring your lock-picking skill. Now. What shall we do once we've opened the strongbox? Surely we cannot simply remove the documents—if they are indeed within—without anyone noticing. We are the odd couple out, they will likely guess correctly that we removed them."

"Damn."

"We have several options." Mary tapped her chin. "But the only plausible course of action would be to switch the documents with forgeries and make our escape before anyone notices the exchange."

Gabe felt like rolling his eyes, but resisted the urge. "You're right, Mary, that is an excellent course of action, but as sound as that plan is, where in God's name do you suppose we could find a forger while at a house party in Eastbourne?" Mary opened her mouth, but Gabe shook his head, halting her speech. "No, we must think of something else." He began to pace.

"If I might point out—I have some experience with forging."

Gabe stopped his pacing to gaze at Mary, startled. "I beg your pardon?"

"I know how to create forgeries. Granted, I am not as skilled as someone more experienced than I, but while at the school, Samuels taught me about forging and cryptology, among other things." She shrugged her shoulders. "I chose to focus my attentions on infiltration and the acquisition of information over the other skills, but I still have knowledge on the base skill. All I need is to know what the documents look like."

Gabe was dumbfounded. Mary knew how to forge documents? Why had *he* not been given the opportunity to learn from Samuels?

"Once I manage to replicate the documents with planted false information, however, we will have to take our leave immediately upon making the switch."

He nodded. "Yes. Yes, this could work." A smile began to grow upon his lips as optimism blossomed in his chest. He could have Mary out of this den of wolves by the morrow! "It would appear that we have ourselves a course of action. Now, we simply wait until this evening to set it into motion."

THE HOT, soapy water lapped at Mary's neck as she sank deeper into her bath later that evening. Her hair was piled high in an unruly knot atop her head to ensure that it did not reach the water, though several rebellious auburn strands still managed. The room was dim, the flickering light of the fire wavering against the ceiling, and the steam from the rose-scented water filled the air. Having already completed her wash, Mary was now simply enjoying the warmth of the water. She closed her eyes.

Her performance would begin in just under two hours, which gave her plenty of time to bathe and prepare. Her costume, while voluminous in layers, was rather simple to put on.

Nerves assailed her stomach as she recalled the size of her audience this evening. She inhaled deeply and released it in a slow, measured breath, the fluttering in her stomach abating slightly. She was an actress, for heaven's sake, she had acted for hundreds at a time. Performing one of her "private" routines for a handful of high society ladies and gentlemen, with mistresses and paramours abound, should not shake her confidence.

But it did.

While doing a performance fell in perfectly with their plans, Mary's dances were designed for an audience of one.

With a shake of her head, she forced her mind from the subject and focused on her bath. Just after they had concluded supper, a group of footmen had placed the copper bathing tub behind the privacy screen in the corner of their guest bedchamber, then group after group of footmen in their sunshine yellow livery had brought in pails of steaming water to fill it. Mary fancied they held a likeness to a flock of pretty golden birds.

Gabriel remained belowstairs with the others while they lounged about playing cards or submerged themselves in sin while waiting for the performance.

Once—*if*—Gabe and Mary completed one aspect of their assignment this evening by finding and removing the documents from the traitors, then they would have to take their leave and return to London. And as much as Mary wished to leave this house of traitors, it would also mean that Gabriel and Mary must go their separate ways once more. Of course, the assignment would not yet be complete, as they would still not know the identity of each traitor, but Mary doubted that Hydra would keep both Gabe and Mary involved with the case. It was too dangerous to their own identities.

Which would mean that this was the end of Miss Mary White and Mr. Anthony Spencer.

Sadness touched her heart and she reached her hands up through the water to place them upon her chest. *Such a foolish girl. Stop this nonsense.*

The *click* of her bedchamber door opening caused her to jump, the water splashing on the floor around her.

"Hello? Who is there?" Mary concealed her breasts with one arm, crossed her legs, and covered the juncture of her thighs with her other hand in one awkward motion.

"It is I, Lady Kerr." The swishing of satin skirts and soft footfalls could be heard from beyond the privacy screen.

How rude of her to enter without first seeking permission to do so. "What may I do for you, my lady?"

"I just came for a little visit, dearie," Lady Kerr drawled.

"I am engaged at present, but if you would return in a quarter of an hour, I would be most happy to receive you."

"No."

The lady herself appeared from behind the screen and, to her shame, Mary squeaked.

"My lady!"

Lady Kerr turned her shrewd gaze on Mary. "Do not become prudish now, Miss White, we all know you are not pure."

Granted, Mary was playing the part of the *experienced* Miss White, but that did not give Lady Kerr the authority to enter unannounced. Yes, Miss White was supposed to be used to others seeing her nude, but Miss *Wright* was not. Never had anyone seen her fully nude, but for her Mama when she was an infant.

Lady Kerr was crossing the lines of propriety and she knew it.

"I have come to speak with you."

No, you have come to catch me unguarded and at a disadvantage. If the woman meant to attack and believed Mary to be unprepared, she would discover herself to be sadly mistaken. Mary was highly trained in self-defence, as Hydra ensured all female operatives were thoroughly taught in the art of hand-to-hand resistance and incapacitation.

"I await with bated breath, Lady Kerr."

The woman's black eyes narrowed briefly before she masked her displeasure. "You appear to be very *admired* by the gentlemen in residence."

Mary did not respond, for it would serve no purpose. Lady Kerr had a reason behind intruding on her bath, rendering Mary unable to stand, and Mary was determined to learn what that was.

"In fact," Lady Kerr continued, "you seem to be admired by gentlemen everywhere. Quite *de rigueur*."

Mary forced her spine to ease. "La! Me, *de rigueur*? Men admire women of all forms, my lady. I am but one of many."

"Why did you come to this house party, Miss White?"

Ah, a pointed question, then. Mary feigned being taken aback. "I was invited, your ladyship."

Her bath water had begun to cool, the lower temperature sending goose flesh over her skin.

"And your guest? Mr. Spencer?"

Miss White would be contrite. "My apologies, my lady, was I not supposed to bring him? He would not have been pleased if I had come on my own."

"Why did he choose you?"

Mary laughed, easily slipping from one reaction to the next, her character firmly in place. "La! Whatever attracts a man to a woman? Desire, I suppose." She winked.

Lady Kerr stepped closer to the brass tub, her gaze darkening ominously. "Are you a spy?"

Mary thought quickly. She widened her eyes and dropped her jaw in apparent shock. The tingling warning of danger travelled up her spine, and apprehension filled her heart. "A spy! I promise you, my lady, I would never divulge your delightful décor ideas to another's household. Or perhaps you dread my telling others of your cook's delicious desserts?" She contrived a convincing expression of honest concern. "Truly, I do not have many acquaintances among the women of the gentry. I would never reveal your household secrets. I swear it!"

A dangerous smile began to form on the lady's lips. "I see I was mistaken. My apologies for interrupting your bath, Miss White."

She turned on her slippered toes and left the room, the door clicking shut behind her. Mary's eyes narrowed. The lady had tried startling a confession out of Mary, but Mary was not easily rattled. Astonished, yes, at the woman's daringly direct question, but certainly not rattled. In fact, she now felt more determined than ever to uncover the traitors among these guests, and to investigate Lady Kerr in particular. The woman was a traitorous villain, and Mary would find proof, not only for the sake of King and Country, but to prove to Gabriel that she was as capable an agent as any man.

She rose from the bath and hastily dried herself, then pulled the costume from where it hung in the wardrobe and draped it across the foot of the bed. Mary slipped the scanty purple drawers up her legs; though they should hardly be considered *drawers*, and *scanty* was a word not strong enough to describe the small patch of fabric with thin, corded rope holding the material together. Mrs. McPhee must have designed them as a way to cover her most private area without requiring a large bolt of material wrapped around her hips, but the revealing nature of them was shocking, even to Mary.

She gazed at her reflection in the looking glass. Indeed, it perfectly hid the pertinent parts. Although the edges of her *derrière* poked out from beneath the material over her bottom, the fit was superb.

Her bodice—if one could call it that; "Modesty patches" was a better description—was simply two round patches of the same purple cotton, just enough to cover the circular dials of her nipples, held together with material that had been woven into a thin rope to wrap twice around her ribcage and knot in the front. It was scarcely enough fabric to keep her from being entirely nude, but for her purposes and the sake of their assignment, Mary would wear the revealing costume.

Mrs. McPhee had outdone herself with the detail. Mary scarcely knew how she had accomplished such a feat with only a fortnight to work.

Reaching for the first and second of five silver chains, Mary fastened them around her hips, hundreds of small coins *jingling* and *clinking* as she did and gasped at the coldness of the metal as it touched her warm skin.

The third chain was fastened just under her breasts, as it was meant to dangle just below the layers of bodice that she was to wear. Next, she donned layer after layer of sheer royal purple skirts. The thin, transparent skirts were meant to come off one layer at a time as she danced, slowly revealing her body beneath, until only one thin skirt remained.

She smiled at her reflection. Once she had completed dressing, had done her hair, and had darkened her eyes with charcoal, her costume would have the precise impact for which she had aimed. Bravura.

CHAPTER 20

*G*abe pulled his watch from his pocket and flicked it open. Ten of eleven. He covered a yawn with the back of his lace-bedecked wrist. It was early by society's standards, but Gabriel had never liked society's version of time.

The furniture in the pink floral drawing room had been moved about, giving space before the hearth for Mary's performance. Everyone had found a seat in lightly-stuffed pink floral armchairs, settees, or on a lover's lap.

Gabe had dropped out of the conversation shortly after Lady Kerr had returned to the room. The men spoke of women, drink, and cards. Frivolous conversation for frivolous minds.

Gabe just waited. Mary was abovestairs in their bedchamber readying herself for a humiliating display of hedonism.

He shifted his seat in the uncomfortable armchair. He rested one elbow upon the armrest and crossed one leg over the other in an attempt to find a more pleasing position.

"I am absolutely certain, Kerr," Boxton's voice cut

through Gabe's thoughts, "that you will hand one hundred quid to me by the end of the night."

Lord Kerr shook his head. "I do not expect to lose that wager, Boxton."

Lord Reddington chuckled, bouncing his mistress, Mrs. McArthur, on his knee. "I imagine you will enjoy yourself enough, Lord Kerr, that you will ultimately forget that you had entered into the wager from the first. Mary has the ability to take one out of one's self."

Gabe bit the inside of his cheek to keep from cursing the lot of them in rather coarse language.

Suddenly, the room fell silent, the only noise was the faint chafing of fabric on fabric and the light, rhythmic breathing of the parlour's occupants.

Gabe's gaze caught on Mary as she entered and wouldn't let go. A lightweight, drab, grey woollen cloak covered her from shoulders to the tips of her toes, and a faint jingling reached his ears as she moved.

She halted in the centre of her performing space and lowered the hood to reveal her chignon. Her hair shone a deep red, backlit by the blazing fire in the hearth. Her expression was one of seductive determination, and it was entirely unsettling.

Ever so slowly, Mary began to slide the cloak from her shoulders, revealing the dark purple, sheer layers of fabric that Mary deigned herself able to don before a room full of men.

A collective gasp cut through the silence of the room as the cloak fell entirely to the floor.

Gabe was stunned. Mary's middle was wholly exposed, from the underside of her breasts to well below her navel. All that graced that area in between were silver chains with dangling coins that jangled when she moved. The purple skirts reached the floor, but with the firelight glowing behind her, they could all see the outline of her legs. Her arms were visible beneath the long, flowing sleeves, capped by silver embroidered cuffs at the end. And her bodice... *Oh Lord, her bodice...* Not only was it indecently low, but it was evident that there were very few layers of sheer material concealing her, as Gabe could see dark round disks of some fabric or another covering her nipples.

His heart slammed in his chest. *Good God!*

With a flirtatious smile upon her lips, Mary began to move. Although *move* was hardly the word to describe the painfully alluring movement of her body. *Tease, seduce, dumbfound,* and *stun* were much more accurate.

She kept one knee continuously bent, but alternated from one to the other, the movement forcing each hip to alternately flick upward. Her upper body remained still, and her stomach moved in a bewitching rhythm, causing the coins to jingle to the beat of an alluring tune.

Despite himself, Gabe's body began to betray him. His blood thrummed with desire, and heat built under the collar of his shirt, spreading throughout his body. Just the movement of her body was enough to send his lust into frenzy.

What she did next only added to his frustrated desire.

With slow, deliberate movements, and with her hips still flicking and coins still jingling, Mary unknotted one layer of her skirts and let it gradually slide through her fingers.

Gabe's heart hammered unmercifully in his chest as he watched, enthralled as she turned on the spot, giving him a perfect view of her *derrière* and continued her *flicking*. *My God, the flicking*! With each movement of her hips, her bottom bounced...and with each bounce, his mind thought *very* licentious thoughts. Mary bent over the side of their bed... Mary bent over a chair, a desk, a table... Hell, Mary bent over anything; the world was rife with possibilities.

She turned back around, the gauzy purple material still in

her hands and the epitome of seduction written across her features.

Then his desire waned.

Mary strode swayingly toward Lord Boxton and draped the fabric across his shoulders as she leaned in to whisper in his ear. The cad's hands rose to grip her waist and Gabriel saw red.

Damn! He had been spellbound by her performance just as the other men had been. How could he have allowed himself to become so enraptured by her that he forgot where and with whom he was?

The bitter taste of resentment began to filter its way through him. He didn't like the other men sharing in the performance.

Mary drifted away from Boxton to remove yet another layer. One of the men in the room whispered "my God" beneath his breath, but Gabe heard him. One man even groaned aloud. And Gabe hated it.

He let his gaze roam around the room and what he saw made him ever more furious. Each man watched Mary with hunger, devouring her with their eyes; several even licked their lips, damn their hides. The women, while not watching in lust, were still very much captivated by each movement.

Gabe's indignant gaze returned to Mary. Her hips swayed, her stomach rippled, and her hands had begun to roam her own form in between the removal of each skirt layer. Now, as the volume of her skirts diminished, he noted that she wore naught but silver embroidered purple cuffs at her ankles and bared feet.

Abruptly, the anger that had wound its way through his heart since the moment that Mary had walked through the doors of Grimsbury Manor washed away. He wanted to glare furiously at her, to berate her, to blame Mary for joining the Secret Service, becoming an actress, and for attracting other men, because that was familiar. But what he felt was sad. She'd been corrupted. This was not the same Mary that blushed so easily and played in the open fields with him as children.

His heart sank further.

How many men had been so delighted by this display of hedonism that they retired with her to their beds? Gabe wagered there were far too many.

Perhaps Colin was right; perhaps Gabe should just take her into his own bed and be done with it. For too long, Gabe had held on to a deep, hidden belief—nay, *hope*—that Mary was still the same girl from his youth, but this overtly seductive woman was not someone that he knew. This woman was not *his* Mary, which led him to a distressing conclusion.

He needed to say goodbye.

Making love to Mary would satisfy this desire for her that had been growing within him, and it would officially put to rest any notion of his "rescuing" her from men lusting after her. For then he would *be* one; he would join the ranks of men that'd had the pleasure of taking "Miss Mary White" to his bed.

He watched as she slid her hands over her womanly curves and up until she reached her hair. With one strategic, gentle tug, her hair dropped in rivulets down her back and over her shoulders.

Yes. He would most definitely enjoy bedding her. And he was certain that she would agree to a night with him, if her kisses were any indication.

Mary started a new combination of her flicking and circular hip motions, each doing delectable things to the soft flesh of her stomach.

All that remained of her skirts was one layer, so thin as to be insignificant. Each man in the room, excepting Gabriel, wore one or more of her skirt layers over their shoulders. He tamped down on the irritation that swamped him after that realization.

Never mind them, he told himself, *you will have her in your bed and those traitorous scoundrels will not*. Of course, he would have to bide his time with taking her; finding and acquiring those documents took precedence over his lust for Mary. But, he was certain, bedding her would be all the more worth it for the wait.

Several more minutes passed in which the only sounds in the pink, floral drawing room were heavy breathing and the *tinkling* of Mary's chained silver coins. Gabriel watched, enraptured, as Mary captivated the room.

Soon, her performance was at its conclusion. She entered her final stance, the backs of her hands touching high above her head, her chest extended outward, her hip cocked, and one knee bent. Her audience remained silent for several moments, so stunned by her remarkable talents that they did not react.

Mary's expression became unsure, and Gabe was released from his stunned silence. He clapped his hands loudly, the others quickly following suit. There were several shocking whistles and shouts of "Brava!" and "Encore!" as the audience rose to their feet.

Gabe watched as Lord Kerr indiscreetly handed several bank notes to Lord Boxton, apparently having lost their wager.

MARY WRAPPED her cloak tighter around her shoulders as Lord Reddington attempted to slide his hand within.

"Come, Mary," he whispered hotly into her ear. "I promise to give you as much pleasure as you can handle...and then some more. Come to me tonight."

Mary smiled as warmly as she could. "You know I cannot."

"I am sure—"

"Shall we retire, sweetling?" Reddington appeared

distinctly disgruntled as Gabe appeared beside her. "I find myself in dire need of rest."

She looked up at Gabe with her heart in her eyes as his arm slid around her waist. "But of course, my dear Tony."

Reddington scoffed, dismayed, as *Tony* ushered her from the room.

Mary could feel the tension from Gabe as they walked to their bedchamber. He had been displeased with her position before this evening; she could not fathom the vehemence of his disapproval *after* witnessing her performance. She supposed she had no choice but to endure a stern set-down once they reached their bedchamber.

The door came up far too quickly and Mary stood aside while Gabe pressed the latch.

She entered, busying herself with finding a night rail and performing her ablutions in preparation for sleep. Several minutes passed in silence while she readied herself. She donned her night rail and wrapper, then removed herself behind the privacy screen with her toiletries.

And yet...Gabriel said nothing.

She paused in the midst of aggressively brushing tooth powder over her teeth to peek around the privacy screen. There sat Gabriel at the small round table, quietly practicing his patience. He casually flipped over a card and furrowed his brow in concentration.

Mary's eyes narrowed. *What is he playing at*? Why was he not berating her for her poor life decisions? Why was he not telling her that she could not and *should* not continue on in this manner? Something was not right.

She concluded her ablutions and rounded the screen.

"I believe I will take a nap before we set out," she said, watching him carefully for any sign of his ill feelings.

His gaze remained fixed on his cards. "As you will, Mary."

Her eyebrows rose, but she remained silent. There was

something distinctly odd about Gabe's behaviour, but Mary could not determine precisely what that was.

She should not complain, however. At the very least she should be pleased that she was not currently receiving a set-down.

Hastily removing her wrapper and draping it over the foot of the bed, Mary slid between the bedclothes and closed her eyes.

CHAPTER 21

*G*abe flipped over another card and groaned. He scarcely noticed what cards were what anymore. He was certain that Mary had fallen asleep already, yet still thoughts of her persisted. After witnessing her seductive performance, he could not get her out of his mind. He had told himself that he would wait until after their assignment had been completed before he took Mary to his bed, but something inside was urging him to join her in the bed now.

He glanced again toward the bed. She lay sprawled across the mattress, her hair splayed out in every direction. Affection warmed his heart as memories of her running free across fields of bluebells, her hair flying in the wind behind her, crossed his mind's eye.

He shook himself. *Enough of this*. Mary had made it quite clear that their past friendship was now dissolved, and any affection that she once held for him had long since withered away. She was *not* a friend. She was not a lover...though he would soon change that.

Gabe rose and strode to the washbasin. He splashed in

some chilled water from the puce porcelain pitcher, then began to disrobe.

He soaped the washcloth and scrubbed it vigorously over his bared skin. If one was to make love to a handsome woman, one must be clean. As he had no access to a bath for the moment, he would make do.

They would find the documents tonight in the strong box, have Mary create forgeries and carefully replace them, pack their meagre belongings, make their excuses, and spirit themselves away to the nearest inn so he may spend the entirety of the night—should the lady be amenable—making love to Mary in every way that his depraved mind had imagined over the past countless hours.

Quickly scrubbing his face, neck, and chest, he then moved to his arms and torso, working down his legs to his feet, dipping the cloth into the water and soaping it every few scrubs.

His stomach buzzed with anticipation, both for the near completion of their assignment, and for what he hoped to do with Mary.

Once his body had been thoroughly washed, he bent forward, dunking his head into the soapy washbasin. He blindly grabbed the soap and scrubbed it into his hair, ensuring that every strand had been washed, then rinsed.

He cast a sidelong glance at Mary's slumbering form, and despite the chilled air spreading gooseflesh across his skin, Gabe's body responded to the thought of being with her. His lips stretched in a mirthless smile as he continued his ablutions.

It took mere moments to dry himself before he removed the washbasin from its resting spot and tossed its contents out the opened window.

Just as he found his long blue velvet robe and slipped his

arms into the sleeves, a knock sounded at the door. Alarm rippled through him.

His gaze flew to the clock on the fireplace mantle as he tied the knot at his waist. It was well past one of the clock; evidently this was not a social visit.

Alertness heightening his senses, Gabe cast one more glance at Mary's sleeping form before he strode to the door. He stood with his shoulder to the wall, blocking the view of Mary from the door, before he opened it just enough to see who stood on the other side.

Anger and irritation burned quickly in a fiery twister in his gut when he saw who had come calling. "Reddington, Boxton," he hissed, his jaw clenched. "What can I do for you?"

"Spencer, ol' chap!" Boxton leaned on the door's frame. "Come to see if dear Mary has had her fill of you."

Gabe's jaw clenched ever tighter, the grinding of his teeth echoing in his ears.

Reddington licked his lips eagerly. "Thought p'raps we could have a *private performance*."

Gabe desperately wanted to knock their heads together, breaking both of their curst, handsome faces.

Instead, Gabe winked and grinned, running his fingers through his wet hair to slick it back, and allowing his robe to gape open slightly, deliberately revealing a patch of curling chest hair. "I'm afraid I've worn her out, gentlemen."

As much as he hated to do it, Gabe opened the door wider, giving the two scoundrels a view of Mary on the bed. As awareness of Gabe's implication dawned, neither man looked happy. In fact, both wore menacing expressions of hostile predators. Dark, hungry, and desperate.

Self-preservation and protectiveness bloomed in Gabriel's chest. "Perhaps tomorrow evening she will not be so fatigued," Gabe said. He knew that he and Mary would not be in residence tomorrow evening and he would rather these men be pacified now with hopes for the morrow than both furious and ravenous enough to intrude upon their solitude and Mary's rest this evening.

Wolfish smiles lit the cads' faces as they gazed past him at Mary. Gabe hated the invasion of her privacy, and quickly narrowed the opening of the door so the men were forced to look at Gabe.

"Do you give your word that we can have a go at her on the morrow?" Reddington licked his lower lip.

Gabe expanded his lungs in a deep breath, then slowly released it. "Yes."

"Say it," Boxton spat.

Gabe turned his sardonic gaze on the reprobate, abusive rake and lied through his teeth. "I give my word."

A GREAT SHIVER ran through Mary as something brushed her cheek. She felt herself frown, her bottom lip curling out in the likeness of a child's pout. She did not wish to wake.

A light puff of air on a silent laugh brushed her cheek next. "Mary." It was Gabe, whispering in her ear, the warmth of his body as he leaned over her, the smell of his sandalwood soap, and cloves on his breath...

He filled her senses.

Mary liked it.

She turned on her back and slowly opened her eyes, allowing them to adjust to the dim firelight that lit the room.

Startling blue eyes gazed back at her. "It is time."

Time? Oh! "Yes, of course."

Suddenly Gabe was gone. And so was her warmth. She sat up, one hand to her hair as it had gone wild in her sleep. She really should plait it as most ladies did, but she had never been one to habitually bind her hair.

Gabe had retreated to his solitary game of cards at the table once more, and Mary set about preparing herself. She pulled one of her travelling boxes out from beneath the bed and flipped open the lid. Pushing aside a selection of white, lacy underthings, she reached for what she sought: the false bottom to her box. Within that lay an array of weaponry: a pistol, gun powder, shot, knives, even darts. She retrieved a leather strap and sheath, a dagger, and from beneath it all, a simple, front-buttoning black bombazine frock that she used especially for sneak-work. She placed the items atop the coverlet at the foot of the bed then closed and replaced her travelling box.

The hairs at the base of her neck prickled and Mary glanced up, catching Gabe's gaze.

Her breath caught in her throat. In his eyes was something wild and unpredictable that sent both excitement and tingling nervousness through her. *Goodness.* His gaze held hers, deep blue and unmoving. Mary's heart began to thud in her chest and her breath came fast.

He wore all black and his hair still held the dampness of wash, the ends curling into tight ringlets.

Gabe's gaze turned heated, and her palms grew damp. Mary had caused many a man's arousal and was familiar with the expression on a man's face in that state. But on Gabriel it felt different. Suddenly, she lost her nerve. Breaking eye contact, Mary turned her attention to her task.

She rose from her kneeling position on the floor and gathered her things, retreating behind the privacy screen.

Coward.

With a silent sigh, Mary set to dressing herself. She slid the knife inside the sheath, then attached it to the long leather strap. With an unnecessarily surreptitious glance around her hidden corner, she lifted the skirts of her night rail and wrapped the strap tightly around her upper thigh.

She had not been prepared for how Gabe's stare would make her feel. Could he truly have been aroused or was he simply skilled at affecting the image of an aroused man? Was it part of his act? If so, why would he do it when it was just the two of them alone in the room? Had she simply imagined arousal in his gaze? But no, she was far too practiced to have been fooled. Could he *truly* have been aroused by the sight of her kneeling on the floor in her night rail? It did not make sense. Gabriel was proficient at disguising his true feelings, if he had not wished Mary to know it, then he would have hidden it.

But that would mean... *Impossible*. Gabe had *wanted* Mary to see the arousal in his expression?

Her breath caught in her throat at the thought. There could be only one reason for him to allow his feelings to be seen. He wanted her.

Her heart raced, pounding and skipping along happily within her foolishly hopeful chest.

She shook her head, forcing herself to focus. Gabe had seen her perform this evening; he was simply reacting as she had intended all the men to do. He was male, after all; it was not about her, personally, but the movement of her body and what it made his *man-parts* feel. She must remember that. This evening was about their assignment, not about passion or heated glances.

In the interest of a hasty return to bed once they made their escape from the house party and retired to an inn, Mary kept her night rail on in the place of a shift and donned her charcoal frock over top. Dressing in her nighttime spy attire was as welcome as returning home. It was comfortable, it was safe, and it did not suffocate her with corset, stays, or innumerable, hot petticoats. She felt free, powerful, and entirely dangerous.

She felt like a spy.

She finished buttoning herself up and straightened her long sleeves and bodice, and with renewed confidence Mary rounded the side of the screen. Without a glance in *his* direction, she strode directly toward her dressing table and sat to gaze at herself in the reflective glass, then set to work on plaiting her hair and tying it into a sensible knot at the base of her neck.

Satisfied with her modest appearance, Mary rose and turned to face Gabriel. His gaze was already on her, but the heat had dissipated.

Mary nodded with mute meaning and they broke off to snuff any lit candles about the bedchamber. Ever silently, they quit the room to stride side by side down the dark corridor, vigilantly careful not to make a sound.

The moan of a cat was carried through the air from behind a door, though Mary suspected it was not a cat. The *tick-tock* of clocks echoed through the still house giving Mary the eerie feeling that the grand, femininely appointed building had a heartbeat. *Tick-tock, bu-bum* went the heart, though only she and Gabe flowed through the wide halls.

Mary had the ludicrous urge to look over her shoulder for ghosts or ghouls, despite her certainty that they were alone. Perhaps the building judged her for spying on its masters.

A light touch brushed her arm and she turned her gaze to Gabe as he crept along beside her.

He pressed a finger to his lips, the signal for silence—did he think she would shout?—then moved his finger to tap his ear. *Listen*.

Voices. Very low, very quiet, but there were indeed voices coming from further down the hall, belowstairs.

She nodded in understanding and they sped their pace.

Painstakingly precautious as they were and the groaning steps of the grand staircase notwithstanding, they arrived at the Kerr House study without incident.

Gabe turned the knob and swung the door open on silent hinges before closing it soundlessly behind them.

Her eyes, having long adjusted to the darkness, immediately spotted something troublesome. Her heart froze in her chest as she swung her head toward Gabe, who stood stony-faced beside her. The pedestal was open and the strong box was gone.

CHAPTER 22

abe's stomach knotted in aggressive nervousness. Could the traitor have known that they were searching for the documents? Was Mary in danger? What of his and Mary's cover identities? Or could someone else have reached the documents before they could return to get them? And if so, who had them, how could Gabe get his hands on them, and what the devil was he to say to Hydra?

He started at the light tug to his sleeve, or more accurately, the fission of disconcerting awareness that burned its way up his arm. He turned his troubled gaze to Mary.

"*What*?" he mouthed.

Mary tapped the lobe of her ear then pointed to the wall of books.

Ah yes, he thought. *The voices.* He crept over to the bookshelves and pressed his ear to the leather spines.

"...arranged this meeting. Very clever with the house party, it was an easy enough way to gather us all together without suspicion. But enough nonsense," one man said. Damn, but it sounded like Hale. "We have all seen the documents, but what of the transfer?"

"Yes, yes! The transfer. Bit tricky, eh wot?"

Gabe's startled gaze sought Mary's. Mr. Piper!

"We've discussed it at length," another voice said; this one smooth, cultured, and entirely arrogant. Lord Reddington.

Gabe barely suppressed the urge to look smug.

"And we've decided on London on Thursday next," he continued. "Our contacts are already making the journey across the channel."

"Enough time to conclude with this agreeable house party, eh wot?"

There was a hushed murmur and Gabe pressed his ear harder against the bookshelves.

"Indeed. What should we make of the new additions?" Hale said.

Mary tapped Gabe's shoulder, then crooked her finger at him. Intrigued, Gabe sidled closer to where she knelt. She pointed toward the bookshelf and then Gabe saw what she had intended him to see. A crack! Just wide enough to peer through. He pressed his eye to the narrow opening, squinting the other. The light from the small room beyond affording him an excellent, albeit limited, view of the traitors.

Yes, Lord Reddington and Mr. Piper were indeed co-conspirators. But who were the rest? Was that Hale's leg he saw from beneath the table?

"Miss White's character is infallible."

"She's a whore, Reddington." Hale said.

Gabe sensed Mary stiffening beside him. *Interesting*.

"I beg your pardon?" Reddington said, outraged. "That angel is—"

"I grant you, Reddington," Hale continued, "she is as handsome as they come and talented in things far beyond my imagination, but she is a whore."

"I say, Hale! She is—"

"You may argue over the virtue—or lack thereof—of Miss

White another time. Tonight, we discuss business, eh wot? While I agree that Miss White is as simple as she is seductive, what of her paramour, Mr. Spencer?"

Gabe must admit that Mary played the part of the *simple* actress very well. But he knew Mary was anything but simple.

Again, another speaker mumbled inaudibly. Damn, but Gabe wished he could see the others at the table. Who were the other traitors? And what were they saying about him?

"I am not so certain on that score. He seems harmless enough," Hale said.

More mumbling. Gabe tamped down on his irritation; it was imperative that he remained alert and did not allow his emotions to distract him.

"I concur," Piper said. "Something about him screams 'liar,' wot, wot?"

Reddington grinned malevolently. "I would gladly remove him from our path."

A hand waved through the air, the owner of said hand, however, was out of Gabe's view. "You just want to take Miss White for yourself. Bastard."

Who was that? Lord Kerr? Lord Boxton? Mr. Jackson? Blast. He couldn't tell.

"If we will not eliminate the man, then at the very least we should continue to watch him, eh wot? Make a note of anything suspicious and let me know."

"It is late, and I have a soft, young woman waiting for me in my warm bed. Let us move along." Lord Hale picked up several pieces of parchment from the tabletop and gazed at each one in turn. "I must admit that your craftiness has well and truly surprised me. These documents are a testament to our strength. We will succeed if we remain united and focused."

Gabe glanced down at Mary where she peeked through the

crack below him. He knew she was taking mental note of what those documents looked like. Good girl.

"This meeting, where will it be?" Lord Hale continued to flip through the documents as he spoke. "Lord and Lady Sheffield are hosting a ball at their house in town on Thursday next. My damned wife demands my attendance..."

"A great many of us will be in attendance, as well. Quite the thing, eh wot?" Piper heaved a great sigh. "Very well. Thursday next after the ball, at the Crowned Pig's Grunt."

"Ugh," the unknown man scoffed. "I do detest that place. Filth and rats everywhere."

Hale slapped his hand hard on the table and Gabe could feel Mary flinch. "It is the only place!" He pointed his finger at the out of sight man, then roared, "I hear you complain once more and I'll reach down that curst bothersome mouth and rip your throat out!"

Bloodthirsty blighter. Quick to temper, as well.

Several rumbled replies rose up through the small room, confusing Gabe as to who was speaking and how many men occupied the room. One man rose, his chair scraping across the wooden floor. *Damn*! He and Mary were about to be spotted!

Gabe gripped Mary's hand and scrambled to find a place to hide. Mary pulled him to the study's door, then silently pressed the latch and swung it open, leading Gabe through it before closing the door behind them.

They had no chance of fleeing down the long hall without being noticed when the traitors left the study.

Mary released his hand and felt her fingers along the wall in the hallway. Apparently satisfied with what she found, she pressed the wall, sliding a hidden panel open to reveal a linen cupboard.

Further scraping of chairs could be heard faintly from the

hidden room and Gabe's heart began to pound against his ribs. They had mere seconds before they were discovered!

They clambered into the small cupboard, the space only affording them enough room to stand with their fronts touching intimately. Gabe slid the panel closed, leaving them in total darkness.

Everything was silent, but for the huffs of their breaths and the thundering of his heart in his ears. He twisted his neck, aiming his ear toward the study across the hall, and listened for any sign that the traitors had left their hidden meeting room.

Then he heard it. A faint *click* followed by distinct footfalls and hushed voices.

He turned his head back toward Mary to make a motion for silence, but what he saw arrested him. Through the darkness of the small space, Mary's grey eyes glittered with what Gabe could only interpret as desire. *Desire fer me.* It could just as easily have been fear or anxiousness, but Gabe was certain he saw need in her gaze.

Mary's breath hitched, her breasts pressing firmly against his chest. Her gaze locked with his, and his body gave an answering tug of need. Lord knew how long it would be before they had a clear opening to escape this closet...and there was something that Gabriel was burning to do.

Quelling the urge to release a beastly growl, Gabe pressed his lips against hers.

This kiss was no less delicious than their last. As impossible as it was, she still tasted of sweet tea and lemon curd.

Her slender fingers stretched out and gripped his lapel, crushing the material within her tightly clenched fists.

Gabe cupped her jaw, running his thumb over her chin. With a gentle nudge, Mary opened for him, and Gabe slid his tongue between her teeth to dip inside the warmth of her mouth. *Oh Lord, save me from this woman*! His gut clenched, his skin tightened, and his cock veritably screamed for release. Instead, he dipped his tongue inside her molten mouth, lapping and tasting over and over again

Unable to assuage his need with just a kiss, Gabe covered her bombazine-clad breast with his hand and kneaded it through the fabric.

Oh yes! She responded in kind, running her hands over his chest and waist, pulling agitatedly at the fabric that separated them.

He fumbled with the material of her modest décolletage, tugging until he freed one glorious breast. *Ah*! Without torturing himself a moment further, he crouched to take her nipple deep into his mouth, as he had so desperately fantasized about doing.

Her fingers clenched, her nails digging deeply into the flesh on his side and the back of his neck, but she remained blessedly silent. He smiled against her breast before sucking in earnest. He sucked, nipped, licked, and scraped her with his teeth.

But he was still desperate for more. He wanted her. He needed her. He *must* have her.

Her hips undulated against the hard ridge of his tightly restrained erection, the motion sending his eyes rolling in the back of his head. And that was all the invitation he needed.

His frantic fingers trembled as he grabbed fistfuls of her skirt and lifted it higher. He grazed her thigh with the last handful of bombazine and Mary twitched. *Good*.

Moving his mouth back to hers, he set to work making her want him as damned much as he had grown to want her. And blast it, he wanted her more than any woman had made him want before.

MARY WAS LOST, floating in a sea of passion. Gabriel made her feel things she had never thought possible for her to feel. She had always thought women silly when they spoke of such feelings of dizziness, swooning, and weakness in the knees. Now she found it not so silly. If Gabe and Mary had not been gripping each other as tightly as they were, Mary was certain that she would have been reduced to a puddle at Gabe's feet at the very beginning of this interlude.

His hand brushed her thigh and her muscles twitched of their own accord. She was accustomed to bringing men to fulfillment, but never had she allowed a man to provide such a service for her. Most particularly in such perilous and, dare she say it, *exhilarating* circumstances. And with a man she... Well, she did not love Gabriel any longer, but evidently she held him in high enough regard to allow him to... *Oh!*

He slid his palm further up her thigh, until the tips of his fingers reached her mound. He pulled his lips from hers to move them to her ear. Nearly inaudibly he whispered, "Open for me, Mary. Please."

Her body did as he bade, her legs spreading as far as they were able in such a confined space.

"Yes, Mary," he hissed.

She tensed, her heart fluttering wildly in her chest, as he glided his fingers between her slippery folds.

"Easy," he whispered.

But she couldn't ease. A man—*Gabe*!—was touching her intimately, and it was oh, so pleasurable.

His fingers began to move, sliding up and down her cleft, around in circles, and repeating. The motion rhythmic and exceedingly hypnotic.

His mouth sought hers once more and she eagerly attached herself to him. The combination of sensations built tension within her, coiling and wrapping itself so tightly she could scarcely breathe.

She was frantic for more.

One of her hands still clutched at his neck, but with her free hand, she reached down to tug at the falls of his trousers. She *must* feel him, hold his thickness in her hand and give him the same thirst for gratification that she felt.

His breath caught as she worked him free, his eager manhood leaping happily into her palm.

One of Gabe's fingers slid deep inside her, forcing her to break the kiss and her neck to arch on a silent cry of delight.

Finding an opportunity, Gabe slid his tongue up the side of her neck and along her jaw, sending a shiver down to her toes. She was damp, she was aching, oh goodness, she *needed*...

His fingers still worked, swirling and dipping. Her body trembled, but she forced herself to focus. She could not be alone in her pleasure; Gabe must join her.

Mimicking the motions of intercourse, she gripped him tighter and began a rhythm of her own; up, down, cup, up, down, cup. She felt him tense. He must be close, she could feel his strain.

His movements became fixated, his mouth fervent in his anxious desire to find release. Her own need had built to a fever pitch, his fingers playing her expertly. The coil tightened and tightened until, finally, it snapped.

An explosion of stars so bright as to be blinding burst behind her eyelids, her head fell back, and her mouth dropped open on a silent shout of ecstasy. She was far away, flying among the clouds high in the sky. *Oh my word!* How could something so sinful feel so, so good?

Gabe's damp fingers grabbed at the back of her neck, pulling her mouth back to his, his hips pumping against her tightly fisted hand. Finally back to earth, Mary realized her blunder. As she found her pleasure, she had entirely forgotten about him.

She moved her hand faster and he quickly released her

neck to fumble in his pocket. He removed a handkerchief and wrapped it around her hand just in time. He froze, his entire body stiffening as his member pulsed in her hand, his seed pumping into the kerchief.

The sound of their heavy breathing filled the cramped space, the smell of their mingled pleasure nearly overwhelming in its arousing intensity.

Awareness began to seep back into her mind, the hazy fog of their passion dissipating.

A loud *thunk* in the room across the hall brought her fully alert. Goodness, there was still someone there! Had they heard?

Gabriel must have heard it, as well, as he quickly buttoned his falls and fixed her skirts. Mary adjusted her bodice to cover her exposed bosom.

The clink of glasses echoed through the room.

"I must bid you goodnight, dear." It was Lady Kerr's voice.

"Yes, yes, goodnight," Lord Kerr's voice responded.

Had they only just entered the room or had they been in the meeting, as well? Mary wondered.

"Well, I had best be off to bed, as well," that mysterious voice said.

Kerr grunted. "Be good to my wife, Boxton."

Mary's eyes widened as she turned her shocked gaze on Gabe. *Boxton*! She mouthed. Oh, this assignment certainly has been productive.

It was silent for several moments, but instinct told Mary to wait and listen longer.

A soft knock sounded against the open doorframe across the hall.

"Ah. Yes, yes, I know," Lord Kerr grumbled.

"Everyone else is to bed, it is time that we were, as well."

That must be Lady Marpol, Lord Kerr's mistress.

"Or perhaps..." her voice turned sultry, and the *swoosh* of skirts could be heard. "Perhaps you remained in your study because you wished for me to join you here?"

Oh dear, please no.

Rustling fabric and loud smacking sounds echoed through the study, the sound easily reaching the closet across the corridor. Mary cringed.

"Perhaps we should retire to my bedchamber," Lord Kerr suggested.

Please, yes!

"Mmm, indeed."

Mary listened anxiously as their footfalls moved across the study toward them and retreated down the hall.

She stood facing Gabriel for countless minutes, both of them waiting until the way was entirely clear before they made their withdrawal from hiding.

When the house was still and silent once more, Mary reached past Gabe to push open the closet door. With a wordless, enigmatic glance, Gabe exited their hidden spot first. Mary awkwardly followed, her long twisted skirts hindering her movement.

She hid her shaking fingers as she straightened her frock. Mary's heart still raced with the startling force of her completion. She had never experienced a... What was it that the other actresses called it? Ah yes, the *little death*. But that had felt nothing like death. It felt like life, passion, excitement, and exhilaration. Is that what men felt when they reach their fulfillment?

Is that truly what it feels like for everyone?

CHAPTER 23

*G*abe stood, frozen. Mary's question hung in the air between them, her expression one of wonder. She could not possibly be asking what he thought she was asking.

"What *what* feels like?" Gabe whispered.

Mary's eyes widened. "Good heavens, did I ask that aloud?"

She was not... She couldn't possibly be... Gabe's eyes narrowed in suspicion. "You did."

"Well." She waved a hand through the air in apparent unconcern. "I don't know what possessed me to say it. Think no more on it."

Mary flounced down the hall, but Gabe remained still, his feet entirely immobile.

She *had* come markedly easily, but then, so had he. Her attentions to him had been well practiced, as he had expected. But thinking on it, Mary's reaction to his ministrations had been untutored and noticeably inexperienced.

Could Mary be a maiden?

Just as quickly as the notion had entered his mind, he

dismissed it with a silent scoff. In all the years of Mary's service to the crown, it was impossible for her to never have made love to a man. She was a beautiful woman and was proficient in the ways of pleasuring men; some bloke must have taken her to bed long ago. Her *innocence* was undoubtedly all but a clever act to entice lovers.

He could not help the sudden, fierce frown that creased his forehead, nor the speeding, angry tempo of his pulse. *Curst bizarre and entirely unwanted emotions.*

Mary was entitled to bed whomever she chose. But Gabe would make certain that he would be the next. Brief, and perhaps flippant, as their tryst had been, Gabe most certainly wished to continue in their physical association. He had never felt such remarkable pleasures as he had with Mary. And as green as she seemed in the ways of her own gratification...

Gabe's eyes widened as sudden anticipation leapt to his breast. Good God, why had he not realized it before? Mary had unquestionably had past lovers, but what of her *own* completion? Could every cad before him never thought to reciprocate the gift of orgasm? Had they all taken what they liked of her and never taught her the delights of her own body? Could he be the first man to ever give her such satisfaction?

He hoped he was. In fact, he was almost certain that he was.

The thought sent a burst of absurdly optimistic pride through him. And God help him, but it got him half hard again just thinking of teaching her all the ways her body could delight her.

Suddenly very aware that he was still standing in the middle of the dim corridor, already half aroused again, Gabe decided it would be prudent of him to make himself scarce.

With a grin on his lips and eagerness in his heart, he made his way through the shadowed, eerie halls and returned to his guest bedchamber, the oddly spooky nature of the house not dampening his mood one jot.

THE DOOR STOOD CLOSED, but Gabe let himself in. Mary sat writing at their bedchamber's desk, her gaze shooting up in alarm when he entered.

"Oh!" she gasped. She had lit a taper and placed it beside the ink blotter on the table. Firelight flickered dimly over the room, the candle upon the desk giving a warm light to Mary's flushed cheeks.

He grinned, locking the door behind himself. "I did not mean to startle you."

She returned his grin with a shy smile then bowed her head once more over a sheet of parchment. "Not startled," she mumbled. "I'm simply glad that I have not been caught being naughty."

Gabe's brow creased. "Naughty?" He strode toward her. "Whatever are you doing?"

"Forging those documents while they are still fresh in my memory."

Gabe nodded, "Ah."

He removed his coat and draped it over the back of a chair.

"Tell me, Gabe..." she started, her head still bent over her task. "How will we replace these documents? It is far too late tonight to make an escape before others are awake, and the traitors will be watching you."

"Yes," Gabe scrunched his face as he considered their options. "Our best choice is to replace them on the morrow. If you will distract the others, I will replace them."

Mary nodded. "Very well."

Gabe cleared his throat. "I should probably inform you

that I promised your...er...charms to Boxton and Reddington for tomorrow evening."

Her head snapped up. "I beg your pardon?"

"They came to the room while you were sleeping and I—having thought that we would have made our escape this evening—believed the best way to be rid of them would be to relent and promise them a 'private performance' tomorrow evening." He cringed. "I'm sorry, Mary. I—"

She shook her head. "Please do not fret. If we are fortunate —and I believe we are—we will have quitted Kerr House before they seek me out."

She gave him a quick smile before she bent her head over her work once more.

His thoughts wandered back to their interlude in the linen closet and a slow grin grew on his lips. Mary; so experienced, yet so innocent in the knowledge of her own body.

He glanced at the clock on the mantle. They had several hours before they were expected to appear at the morning meal. He could have her here. Now. She was amenable enough to his attentions in the closet, she would likely be most receptive to the many delights he could bring her in a bed.

His grin grew and his breath came fast. He wanted her. *God* how he wanted her!

But first he would tease her...

"Mary?" He crossed his arms over his chest.

"Mmm?"

"Why did you—"

"Oh!" Her head snapped up once more. She dropped her quill on the table next to the ink. "I must tell you, before I forget once more."

A clever evasion. "What is it, Mary?"

"Lady Kerr called on me earlier this evening, as I prepared for my performance. She—"

"Are you finished?" Gabe interrupted.

A frown crossed her brow. "I beg your pardon?"

"Your forgeries. Are you finished?"

"Er—yes." She clucked her tongue. "You're not listening, Gabe. She arrived unannounced, unwelcomed, and...in the middle of my bath."

Gabe shrugged one shoulder as he leaned one hip against the table. "Surely she left directly the moment she learned of her error?"

"Actually, no. Lady Kerr questioned me on my association with you and then—"

"Ah, yes," he interrupted, a haughty tilt to his chin. "I see. The lady sought your blessing for a romantic interlude with me, and—"

Mary clucked her tongue. "No, you arrogant arse, she—"

Swift as a thief, Gabe swept down to steal her lips in a kiss. Hard, rough, and passionate.

His heart beat wildly in his chest as other parts of him prepared for what would be most unquestionably a memorably gratifying experience.

MARY'S BODY awakened with the memory of pleasures recently discovered, while her mind raced.

Gabe. Kissing her! *Again*! Oh heavenly day! Her stomach fluttered with renewed arousal, her already satisfied feminine flesh throbbing with the desire to find fulfillment once more. She squeezed her thighs together in an attempt to ease the passionate ache. She groaned. The motion only intensified her wanton desire.

She explored his mouth, running her tongue along his teeth and over his responding tongue. It was the very same mouth that had so pleasured her breasts scarce minutes ago and the memory of his intimate touches sent her lust ever higher.

Mary knew what he wanted; they were in their guest bedchamber, alone, with their tongues intertwined. It was plainly obvious.

Gabe wanted her. In his bed and surrounding his body. Tonight. *Now.*

If she never had another opportunity to make love to Gabe she would deeply regret not having him now. He would always be her first. It was fitting in a tragically poetic sort of way. He had been her first friend, her first love, her first kiss, and now her first lover, in the true sense of the word.

Gabe wrapped his hands around her upper arms and pulled her from her seat to stand flush against him. His arousal pressed firmly into the softness of her stomach and heat washed over her body, the molten lust sending liquid desire to her feminine core.

Her hands worked nimbly with the buttons of his waist-coat, the nervousness that she had felt before their previous encounter was gone, replaced by simple, human *need*. She needed to have him within her, filling her. He must be just as eager, for he pulled roughly at the buttons on her bodice.

Their mouths locked in a wickedly passionate kiss as they undressed each other. First Gabriel's waistcoat and cravat, then his shirt. Mary nearly sighed with relief as his torso was exposed, one corded muscle at a time. Goodness, but he was a finely sculpted man! Rubbing her hands over his muscled chest and rippling stomach, Mary revelled in the sheer masculinity of him. She had burned to do this when she had seen him half nude this morning, and she would certainly not squander this opportunity now.

Pulling her lips from his, Mary half bent to boldly lick the deep crevice up the centre of his torso.

Gabe hissed a breath and she moved to scrape her tongue

over his flat male nipples. "Ye tease me something fierce, leannan."

Mary would have grinned if her blood hadn't been pounding in her ears so. This man did something remarkable to her body. With hands and tongue she explored the contours of his chest.

"I cannae take it any longer," Gabe growled.

With a deep groan, he nimbly pulled at her black bombazine sneak-work costume, effectively leaving her only in her night rail.

"I have seen ye in this nightwear too many nights in a row..." Gabe said between kisses, his practiced accent slipping, "and evera night I have thought of taking it off ye."

"Have you?" Mary breathed.

"Aye, damn it. *Aye!*"

His lips caught hers in a fervent, if not entirely sensual, kiss. She opened her mouth willingly under his as he gripped the low neckline of her night rail and ripped. The loud rent echoed off the walls of their guest bedchamber, mingling with Mary's loud gasp as her mouth broke from his.

Her breath caught as she saw his hungry gaze. She shook her now-ruined nightclothes from her shoulders to join her dress on the floor. She stood, nude, before him, allowing him to eat up every inch of her with his gaze.

Gabe's breath came faster, his chest expanding greatly with each gravelly huff. "Ye're... *God*, Mary!"

His mouth crushed hers, his kiss deep and rough.

Gabe wrapped his arms tightly around Mary and he lifted, carrying her effortlessly to the bed and depositing her atop the dishevelled bedclothes, before eagerly unfastening the buttons of his black trousers. His gaze never left her body as he freed himself, shucking his trousers and kicking them away. Mary's gaze, however, was entirely consumed with his jutting manhood. *Good heavens!* Is that what she had held in her hand? It was positively stunning. As odd-looking as the male appendage was, on Gabriel it was... beautiful.

Her gaze was locked on him as he leapt atop the bed and positioned himself above her. His hand grazed her hip and her waist, sliding further to rest upon her breast. Her skin heated beneath his scorching touch, but she exulted in his reverential attentions.

"I ken ye experienced yer first orgasm this verra evening, lass..." his voice was rough as gravel.

Mary's eyes widened in shock. How could he have known that? Oh, yes, of course. Her blunder. She opened her mouth to reply, but Gabe flicked his tongue over her hardened nipple. Her jaw dropped open on a gasp, her eyes drifting dreamily closed.

"Ye will reach many more, if I have anything te say about it."

His teeth gently abraded her and she hissed a breath.

He lowered himself to her—his tough, male skin rubbing intimately against hers—and she wrapped her arms around him, the feeling of his warmth so deliciously intimate. The sensation was electric, enticing, and dangerously addicting. She slid her hands up his back toward his shoulders, then down again until she cupped his rear, eliciting a rough, quavering gasp from him.

Then she felt it. The tip of his manhood prodding at her opening. She spread her thighs to give him better access, with nary a hint of alarm at her first coupling.

He groaned long and deep as he pushed further, the thickness of him widening her opening nearly unbearably. The dampness of her folds allowed him easy passage as he pressed ever further, and she gasped at the new sensation.

"Oh," she breathed. "I didn't know sex was so—"

"*God*, Mary," Gabe spoke over her. "Ye feel so—"

He halted, tensed. His face, first expressionless, suddenly wreathed in horror.

Concern touched her heart. "Gabe?"

He stared, unblinking, at the pillow beneath her head, his face contorted with disgust. "I have made a grievous mistake," he said, his English accent perfectly in place once more.

He withdrew from her body, but Mary grabbed desperately for his shoulders.

"No! No, Gabe! You must tell me what is the matter. What have I done to displease you?" *I've said too much.*

He freed himself from her grip, his expression cool and remote. Stepping down from the bed, Gabe retrieved his trousers and jerked them back on.

"You have done nothing wrong. My apologies, Mary, but I...I cannot..." He shook his head then retreated behind the privacy screen.

Mary sat up on the bed, the frigid fingers of painful rejection clawing at her. Her body still ached with need, the painful reminder of his rejection throbbing in her *mons.*

She could hear Gabe performing his ablutions on the other side of the screen, and shame washed over her. Had she not been enough for him? Had she not lived up to his expectations? Had she done something? *Said* something?

With a glance toward his hiding spot, Mary hurried to the chest of drawers to retrieve another night rail and quickly put it on. As confident as she was in her own skin, Gabe's reaction to her made her feel not just humiliation and hurt, but distinctly...undesirable.

She ran silently on the pads of her feet back to the bed and wrapped herself beneath the coverlet.

Her stomach knotted sickeningly as his expression flashed through her mind's eye. How could she have been so foolish as to think that Gabe wanted her?

The sting of embarrassing tears burned behind her eyes

and she cursed herself for her weakness. The dim light from the coals now scarcely lit the room, and through Mary's watering gaze, the entire room wavered.

She had known he would hurt her again, yet she had fallen for his charms regardless of that knowledge.

Fool! She swiped inelegantly at her damp eyes with the back of her hand.

Curse Gabriel Ashley anyway.

CHAPTER 24

The fire had died out long ago, but Gabe was still too warm. The dim brightness of pre-dawn began to seep between the curtains, lending a low light to the dark room. He lay flat on his back on the floor before the cold hearth, his heart ever pounding and his stomach twisting painfully.

Mary is a virgin! A sullied virgin, but a *virgin* for God's sake! How was it even possible? Every night she had a different "assignment" from whom she gleaned information. How else could she get such secrets from men if not from allowing them liberties? Had he gotten it all wrong?

None of it made sense. Both Boxton and Reddington had extoled her virtues and astounding *talents*. How could she have performed such acts and still retained her maidenhead? But she'd been so tight—*too* tight—and the shock, the *wonder* on her face ought to have alerted him before her words had.

He rubbed his hands agitatedly over his face. He had not slept a wink but for thinking of her. She was so bloody alluring, so damned seductive... How could a man resist such charms? Evidently many had. Lord knew he had gotten farther than any man before him, for Gabe knew that without astounding force of will, no other man would have been able to stop where he had. As it was, Gabe'd had to handle his own needs at the chamberpot, for he would never have been able to round the screen and see Mary laying in the bed they had both so recently occupied and not return to finish where he had left off.

Instead, he had satisfied his own needs—albeit not as *she* could have satisfied him—set his pillow on the rug, and settled himself down for several hours of discomfort. Listening to Mary try not to cry had not helped. Guilt rode him heavily, weighing on his chest with each sigh and sniffle. She had always been such a brave gel. What had happened? Had he hurt her so badly, then?

Mary had given herself freely to him...but why? *Damn*. He was not a cur. He did not despoil innocents—or as innocent as Mary could be, given her experience with men. But what *was* that experience?

The discovery sent fear racing through him. Damn him if he knew why, but it did. His reaction did not make sense. Her virginity did not make sense.

The entire thing was a muddle of confusion and self-derision and he hadn't the faintest idea where to place his thoughts.

Only one thing was certain. He was on assignment. He should never have trifled with Mary during their mission, and now more than ever he needed to focus on his task, get this assignment completed, and return to London to report back to Hydra.

He needed to get out of this room, to do something other than torture himself with the mental image of Mary's glorious nude body.

An idea struck him, and he felt a moment of swift relief. He would find Stevens and exchange information.

He rose from his position on the floor and returned the pillow to the bed. Keeping his gaze averted from Mary, Gabe went about his ablutions and dressing. He placed the forged documents that Mary had completed into his breast pocket and hid two of her hairpins in his cravat.

Without a glance in Mary's direction, Gabe strode from the room, closing the door quietly behind him.

MARY FLINCHED as the sun suddenly shone brightly across her face.

"I'm ever so sorry, Miss White," Eleanor said, turning toward Mary from the window. "I called your name, I did, but mayhap you didn't hear me." She gazed worriedly at Mary. "Would you like me to bring you some tea?"

Mary shook her aching head as she tugged the coverlet up to her chin. "Please do not trouble yourself, Eleanor. What time is it?"

"Half of nine, Miss."

Mary groaned. She had slept far past the time that she should have arisen, but she had only fallen asleep at five of the clock and... Oh, pooh. She was miserable and had absolutely no desire to face the day.

Her eyes were dry and scratchy, as though someone had lifted her eyelids and deposited sand beneath. She touched the tips of her fingers to her swollen eyelids and groaned, despising the usual result of her dissolving into a fit of tears.

There had only been two previous occasions in which she had spent the entirety of the night weeping. The first had been when Gabriel had abandoned their friendship and moved to Scotland. The second was when Mama had so tragically passed away.

This was now the third. Evidently, she had not learned her

lesson with Gabriel the first time he had broken her heart, for as she had only realized last night, she had willingly—and most foolishly—allowed him access to her heart once more. How could she have done such a reckless, imprudent thing? Curst hopeful heart.

She dearly wished her Mama and Papa were here to comfort her. Her mama would say, "*Any man that turns his back on a pretty flower like you, isn't worth his salt,*" just as she had after Gabe had left. Her papa would give her a kiss on the forehead and allow her to cry upon his shoulder for as long as she desired.

Her lip quivered, and the heated warmth of tears threatened behind her eyes, and she pulled the coverlet over her head. "Wake me in six hours," she mumbled.

"Oh no you don't, miss." The small maid grabbed at the coverlet and pulled it from atop her. "Pardon me for intrudin', but I know that expression. Don't you go lettin' a man ruin your pretty face with all that cryin'."

To Mary's mortification, she could feel her bottom lip begin to stick out. Oh heavens, she was pouting like a petulant child!

"You're a grown and experienced woman, if you don't mind me sayin'," Eleanor continued. "Whatever Mr. Spencer did most likely makes 'im a cad and not worth your carryin' on so."

Mary nodded her throbbing head and slowly rose to a seated position. "You're right, Eleanor. Of course, you're right."

The young maid smiled and Mary was struck by just how handsome the girl was. Her green eyes stood out in her soft, round face. Mary wondered what Eleanor's auburn hair would look like without her frilly mobcap covering it.

"O' course I am, miss," Eleanor said. "Now, up with you. We'll get you dressed and presentable in a trice."

Allowing Eleanor this moment to take charge, Mary shuffled from the bed and moved to sit at her dressing table. She glanced down at the carpet before the hearth as she walked past. Gabriel was gone; he must have awoken early, for his pillow was resting on the bed and there was no evidence of him being there.

Her heart lurched and she frowned, turning to gaze at herself in the mirror.

Drat. She *did* look affright. Dark rings graced the underside of her red, puffy eyes and her hair was tossed about. Her freckles had all but faded long ago, but now, under the paleness of her complexion, Mary could swear that she saw a light dusting of them on the bridge of her nose.

Eleanor was right. Mary should not allow Gabriel's rejection to have a complete monopoly over her emotions. Despite still having her virginity—no thanks to Gabe—she *was* a grown and experienced woman. And Gabe *was* a cad.

She ought to close her heart from further amorous feelings, and hope that the love that she'd come to feel would dissipate, for she deserved so much better than the way he treated her. Her Mama—rest her soul—would be right. Gabe *wasn't* worth his salt.

Mary nodded at her reflection. Indeed. She would stop this misery nonsense, pull herself together, straighten her spine, and complete this assignment victoriously.

Eleanor brought a brush to Mary's hair. "Your hair is a tangled mess, miss."

"I've never taken to plaiting it while I sleep."

"You're certainly unique, if you don't mind me sayin', miss."

Mary smiled. "I take that as a compliment, Eleanor."

"I meant it as one." The maid winked at Mary's reflection, then clucked her tongue. "There is nothing for it, Miss White.

We will have to apply powder to disguise the darkness around your eyes."

"Yes, I had thought as much, Eleanor. And please, call me Mary."

The maid smiled shyly, dipping her chin. Mary's instincts told her that Eleanor was someone she could trust. The maid was afraid of her master, and unwilling to say anything too disparaging, but Mary understood what the girl was unwilling to reveal.

"You are quite vocal this morning," Mary observed.

Eleanor's expression closed as she bit her bottom lip in distress. "I am ever so sorry, Miss White, I didn't mean—"

Mary raised a placating hand. "Oh! No, no, Eleanor! I did not mean for my words to be taken in such a way. I *like* that you feel comfortable enough in my presence to speak freely."

"You're so kind, miss—er, Mary." Her smile grew, exposing her uncommonly white teeth.

"There now," Mary returned the smile. "I think we will be fast friends."

"I should like that." Eleanor finished untangling Mary's long, auburn hair, then moved to the wardrobe to find a suitable dress.

Mary gazed at her reflection in the mirror and brought her chin up a notch. She was a spy. In the name of protecting King and Country, she would devote herself to her position.

From now until they delivered their recovered information to Hydra, Mary would be strictly professional.

She turned to look over her shoulder at the table. Excellent; Gabe had taken the documents. Now she must think of a way to give him an opportunity to make the exchange.

Should she make a scene? Faint at luncheon? She scrunched her face in thought.

Ah-ha! Oh, how plainly obvious.

Mary turned her back on her own reflection to face the petite, softly rounded maid. "Eleanor?"

She gazed at Mary from her position by the wardrobe. "Yes, miss?"

"Would you be so good as to prepare another of my costumes? I have a mind to put on another performance."

The maid inclined her head. "I have one already prepared. I hung it in the wardrobe before you woke."

Mary grinned at her. "You are so efficient, Eleanor. Thank you."

"A pleasure, Mary." She removed a deep green costume from the wardrobe. "I think this one shall do nicely." She draped it over the foot of the bed. "Just the right colour to brighten your mood and make everyone green with envy."

Mary chewed on her bottom lip, an idea taking shape in her mind. "Eleanor, have you ever considered leaving your post here and finding a position somewhere else?"

Eleanor laughed. "Oh, every day! But where am I to find one? Land owners in these here parts are chock full o' staff and most are cutting back, if you understand my meaning." She waved a hand in the air as she returned to Mary's side. "Besides, Lord and Lady Kerr aren't like to give me a glowin' reference."

"Have you ever considered making the move to town?"

"Me? London?" She affected the demeanour of a gentlewoman. "La! What a notion!"

Mary gave a short laugh. "You mimic high society ladies very well."

"Well, I should think so, I been around 'em long enough." Eleanor grinned.

"If I should say that I could get you any position you desire, would you travel to London?"

Eleanor stilled. "I'll not enter into anything unsavoury."

"Nothing unsavoury, I assure you." She squinted one eye

at the maid, considering. "But I believe I can trust you, Eleanor, and I have a mind that you could do very well in London. If you are able to acquire conveyance, you can find me at my apartments—I will give you the direction.

She nodded at Mary. "I will consider it. I am much obliged."

"Not at all, Eleanor. I believe that it is I who should be thanking *you*."

"No, I saw it this morning," the Bonaparte spy said.

"Perhaps it was a maid. They are wont to do odd things, eh wot?"

The spy shook their head. "What possible reason would a maid have for making a mess of linens in the closet? No. I believe this was our new *guest* come to spy on us from a convenient hiding spot across from the study."

"*Miss White*? I hardly believe her capable of—"

"Fool! Of course I did not mean Miss White; she is as simple minded as she is talented at seduction. I am speaking of her paramour, Mr. Spencer."

"Mmm… What do you suppose we do with the man?"

"What else but bring him to the dungeon for questioning?"

"How would you like me to—?"

"Leave that to me…"

CHAPTER 25

rack! The billiard ball struck another then rolled across the table. Gabe could only muster a grim smile at his excellent shot.

"Why so morose this morning, Spencer?" Lord Pondridge said before throwing back another two fingers of brandy.

"I'll wager it was a woman." Lord Sheffield laughed, his extra chin jiggling. "Miss White held out on you last night, eh? That woman..." he sighed. "She has a way of bewitching a man."

"Indeed, she does," Pondridge replied. "Why not avail yourself of the other ladies in residence, Spencer, and let one of the fellows here have a go at Miss White. They're all eager enough." He grinned.

"I'll second that!" Lord Hale said from his position by the fireplace as he tugged on the bell pull.

Gabe's jaw tightened and his stomach churned. Even while playing billiards with other, potentially traitorous men, he could not escape Mary and his disturbing experience of last evening.

"I've already promised Miss White to Reddington and

Boxton for this evening," he said. "You gentlemen will have to wait your turn."

"Lucky bastards," Sheffield wheezed.

A nervous-looking maid appeared in the doorway.

"Ah yes, there you are," Hale boomed. "Have one of my footmen come here at once."

The maid curtsied, and with a mumbled "right away your lordship," she was gone.

"Small maids in this house," Hale grumbled. "No good for anything; can't even take a man my size atop them."

"Aye," Sheffield pulled a cigar out of his waistcoat's breast pocket. "If you can't tup them, what's the point?"

"Of course, if they've got a big mouth…" Hale wiggled his eyebrows and the three men laughed.

Gabe felt ill.

"You called for me, your lordship?"

Gabe looked up to see Sir Bramwell Stevens standing in the doorway, wearing Hale's vomitus green livery and a powdered wig.

"Yes, Smithe. Have my horse saddled, will you? I have the urge to ride."

Stevens bowed. "Right away, my lord."

Gabe bent to take his turn at billiards, hardly noticing where the balls ended up. He needed to speak with Stevens to tell him what he had overheard last night. If something were to happen to him or Mary while he was exchanging the documents or while they were on their return journey to London, someone needed to pass the information along to Hydra.

Soon enough, Mary would come up with a distraction and Gabe would make the exchange. Until then, he must wait, and what better to do while waiting than speak with his comrade.

"Please excuse me, gentlemen," Gabe bowed to the room.

"Off to see if you can repair whatever damage you did last night, eh?" Pondridge grinned.

Gabe returned his grin and added a wink before he made his escape.

MARY'S HALFBOOTS crunched over the gravel as she walked along the garden's path. The sun shone brightly in the early June morn, birds chirped gaily, and the flowers were open, lending a fragrant, floral scent to the air.

She'd spoken to Lord and Lady Kerr's gardener, but aside from the fact that the Kerrs preferred their flowers arranged a particular way and they had a short temper with their staff, Mary had not learned anything. After that brief discussion, Mary had ventured over several hills until she'd reached the castle ruins that Lady Kerr had informed Gabriel about.

Despite her curiosity, Mary did not venture inside, but turned and made her way back to Kerr house. The afternoon meal would soon be served, and shortly thereafter, Mary would put on her second performance. She just hoped that they made the exchange before she was forced to fend off Reddington and Boxton's advances.

A frown caught her by surprise as her thoughts wandered again toward Gabriel. He would surely not approve of her wandering across the estate and questioning the gardener on her own.

But Gabriel was not here. In fact, she very much doubted that she would see him for the entirety of the day, until they made good their escape from the Kerr estate.

Mary turned her face up to the sun, taking delight in the warmth she found there. Her father would adore this garden; he had always enjoyed plants.

She *tsked* herself. There she went thinking of her father again and making herself maudlin. Perhaps she should visit him soon.

The *crunch* of gravel beneath feet and voices sounded down the path. Mary mentally cringed as she rounded a tall bit of shrubbery.

"I saw her coming along this path, but perhaps—oh!" Boxton led both Sheffield and Reddington down the path toward her. His face was wreathed in smiles, but his eyes held the threat of a predator.

Mary smiled cautiously at the three men. "Good morning, gentlemen."

Lord Sheffield puffed on a cigarillo, blowing the smoke at her then leering with the others. "I've been informed by these two fine fellows that you will be giving them a *private* performance this evening."

So she had been informed. Damn Gabriel for making such promises.

"I have come to express my...eternal envy for their luck."

Mary put aside the alarm spreading through her chest at Boxton's and Reddington's unwavering lustful gazes and gave Sheffield a coquettish grin and batted her eyes.

"Why Lord Sheffield, you sly flatterer. You know just what to say to charm a woman."

Sheffield positively beamed with pride. "I have enchanted a few skirts in my day." He took another puff of his cigarillo. "At the others' insistence, I must beg another group performance. Perhaps after luncheon?"

Mary flashed them a gleaming smile. That was precisely what she had hoped they would ask. "Why Lord Sheffield, I would be honoured to perform for you again."

Boxton stepped forward, moving with the agile grace of a cat, both deadly and deceitful. "You understand, Mary, that this request for a performance stands individually from the private encounter promised to Reddington and myself."

Impertinent blackguard. "Naturally, Tony. I wouldn't dream of reneging on our interlude." She winked at him.

That seemed to mollify Lord Boxton.

"Now wait just a moment," Reddington cut in, his troublingly eager gaze roaming heatedly over her. "We all have a moment here, why not give us that private performance now?"

The other men began to agree and panic sprang to Mary's chest. "Now, now, gentlemen. Surely you would not wish me to perform without my costume. I—"

"As a matter of fact," Boxton sneered, "that is precisely how I would like to see you."

Her heart tripped over in her chest. *Please* let her get out of this without having to resort to violence! "I am afraid, Tony, that you will just have to wait until this evening. Now if you fine gentlemen would excuse me, I must prepare my costume."

She skirted around them on the path, hoping beyond hope that they would not stop her.

CHAPTER 26

"You are a dunce, Gabriel Ashley," Sir Bramwell Stevens hefted a pile of hay, tossing it to the ground inside the horse's stall.

"Hush! My name is Anthony Spencer," Gabe hissed.

"There isn't anyone left in the stables, *Mr. Spencer*. The stablemen have gone to the kitchens for an early luncheon and *that* lofty crowd would never disgrace themselves by showing their haughty faces in here." He sat down on the hay pile and crossed his feet at the ankles. "You are safe in here for the moment."

"Very well," Gabe grumbled.

He inhaled deeply, breathing in the dull yet somehow acrid scent of horse manure and crisp hay.

Stevens flung his powdered wig down beside himself. "Pull up a pile and unburden yourself, friend. I can see that you need to."

Gabe shook his head. "I did not approach you to discuss private matters. I—"

"Oh come now, Gabe. You and Mary have been at odds

since you both began your *education*, surely you can admit to there being something between you by *now*."

Gabe clenched his jaw, keeping his thoughts to himself. He and Stevens had always been on good terms, but while the man was Gabe's junior by only one year, they had not developed as fast a friendship as he had with Colin and Hugh.

"Shall I hedge a guess?" Stevens' lips split in half a smile. "Since Mary nursed you back to health from your injuries, and—"

"Mary visited, I will grant you, but she hardly nursed me back to health."

Stevens shook his head, then stared, disbelieving, at Gabe. "Who do you suppose alerted Hydra to your absence? Found you in that cellar? And who sat at your bedside while you were unconscious, and administered to your wounds and held your hand?

"Now," Stevens continued, not waiting for Gabe to reply, "with both of you being on assignment together, you thought the two of you could have a go at it. She, being half in love with you, willingly went along with the venture."

Gabe moved to disabuse the man of his assumption.

"But," Stevens continued before Gabe could speak, "there was something vital that you were too stupid to realize."

"Oi!"

Stevens' gaze hardened. "Mary is a maiden."

"B—but," Gabe stammered, his brow creased in confusion. "How the devil did you know that? Please tell me you haven't..."

Stevens barked out a humourless laugh. "Good God, no!" He raised his arms to link his fingers behind his head then leaned back against the wall of the stable. "It is painfully obvious, old boy. Have you never seen her interrogate someone?"

Gabe shuffled his feet, discomfited. "No. Have you?"

"Of course! We've been on assignment together many times."

Gabe bit back an oath as something akin to jealousy began to fester in his gut.

Stevens clucked his tongue. "Have you ever *asked* her how she acquired information from men?"

Gabe shook his head. "No."

"You *are* a dunce."

"Now see here—"

"No, Gabe, *you* see!" Stevens rose from his relaxed position to face Gabe squarely, irritation and sudden fury lining his features and stiffening his spine. "Mary is my friend and I will not stay silent on this matter any longer. As experienced as Mary is in the art of seducing and questioning men, she knows nothing of intimacy...of passion...or of affection. Despite knowing precisely what men want, how they want it, and where and how to move her hands and body, Mary is an innocent. No man has ever returned her attentions and no man has ever given her the honest affection that she damned well deserves."

Stevens stepped forward and poked Gabe in the chest, his eyes gleaming with anger.

"You were once her friend, surely you know her well enough to understand? Mary is a *woman*, Gabe. Full of passions and emotions, needs and desires. She deserves to be treated with respect and given precisely what she wants. I've seen the way you treat her, as though she is incapable of making her own decisions or of conducting her life in a manner of her choosing—"

"That's not what I do," Gabe denied.

"That is precisely what you do, at least from her perspective, and from those around you. You constantly berate her for being an actress. Not once have you congratulated her on a job well done, not once have you encouraged her or—"

"See here!" Gabe said, incensed. "Mary is far too good for this life! She deserves a life of pampering, of warmth and love and passels of children! Not working herself to the bone and satisfying traitorous men's needs on a nightly basis, damn it!"

The man's golden eyes glistened in understanding. "Have you tried telling her that? Have you ever told her *why* you treat her and speak to her as you do?"

There his guilt went again. "No."

Stevens shook his head, his eyes narrowed in derision. "*Dunce.*"

Gabe grappled with the onus weighing heavy on his shoulders, not to mention his remorse. Had he truly treated Mary so ill? Why had he never told her all his reasons behind his treatment of her? Why had he never apologized for abandoning her and their friendship?

And last night? *Christ*, last night had been a disaster. Mary had *given* herself to him. To *him*! Why had he rejected her? What kind of an idiot man rejects such a gift from a woman like her? From *Mary*, for God's sake! *His* Mary!

He shook his head. "What is wrong with me?"

Stevens slapped a hand on Gabe's shoulder and squeezed. "You're in love."

Gabe's eyes widened, and he determinately ignored the sharp pang in his chest. "No, I am not!"

The man gently shook his shoulder. "... and in denial."

"A man like me *can't* fall in love, Stevens." Gabe knocked the man's hand away and stepped back.

"You mean a Scotsman?"

Gabe cursed soundly. "No, I mean a..." he looked around the empty stables, then lowered his voice, "a spy."

A nearby horse neighed and stomped its foot.

"Hydra is a spy and *he* is married. Happily, I might add, to a wonderful woman."

"And what happened to Hydra in the past year? What happened to his family?"

Stevens conceded the point with a nod. "He did have some difficulty with a few nasty fellows knowing his identity, but—"

"Aha!" Gabe pointed his finger at him. "That is exactly my point! What if someone discovers who we are? Who *I* am? What will happen to Mary, then? A cozy little life could be snatched away like *that*!" He snapped his fingers to emphasize his point.

"A cozy life!" Stevens scoffed. "What in God's name makes you think that a life with Mary will be anything different than it is now? Mary's life is the same as yours; the life of a spy."

Gabe grit his teeth. He hadn't considered that fact before. "That might be true, but the danger increases when we are together."

Stevens shook his head once more. "Will you live the rest of your life denying yourself the pleasures of love, Gabe?"

"JUST A MOMENT, MARY," Sheffield called after her as he hurried after her down the garden path.

Drat.

She turned and faced him with a smile. "Yes, Lord Sheffield?"

The portly man wheezed as he caught up to her, heaving great rasping breaths. He withdrew a handkerchief from his waistcoat pocket and dabbed at his glistening forehead. "Mary...my dear..." he said between gasps. "I do not...know your...direction." He paused to catch his breath and Mary waited. "I and my *horrid* wife are having a ball at Sheffield Court. It is our house in town, you see."

He took another moment to breathe and dab at his forehead and chins.

Lord Boxton and Lord Reddington caught up to them, walking down the path like lions stalking their prey. Heavens, they had positively voracious airs about them. She could not possibly participate in whatever lewd acts they had planned for her this evening. Gabe must be successful in his task this afternoon; she would ensure it.

"Would you do us the great honour, Miss White, of attending the ball?"

Mary took a moment to think on it. According to the traitors' meeting last night, the exchange of information would take place just after the Sheffield ball.

Her answer was simple.

She beamed at him. "How gracious of you to invite me, Lord Sheffield. I would be delighted to attend."

He returned her smile, his chins widening. "Very good then, very good. Capital, wot? We will see you Thursday next."

"Indeed, you shall." Mary dipped in a deep curtsey. "If you will excuse me, gentlemen."

She turned on her heel and swept down the path on swift feet. The crunch of the gravel beneath her feet, and those of the men who followed, scarcely registered in her mind above her harried feelings.

As she walked toward Kerr House, Mary attempted to sort through her thoughts, but one topic kept pushing at her. Gabriel. He filled her thoughts, which worsened the persistent ache in her chest. In fact, the more she attempted to shut him out, the more it seemed he consumed her.

She mustn't do this to herself. Gabe was a cad. He had broken her heart not once, but twice, he continuously berated her for doing what she loved, and he showed no remorse for hurting her feelings. Indeed, she must continue to remind herself of that.

Her heart flip-flopped as an image of his horror-struck expression crossed her mind's eye.

Curse Gabriel Ashley!

GABE'S HEART thudded wildly in his chest as he turned his hard gaze on Stevens. "That was precisely my plan."

Stevens looked taken aback. "But why would *anyone* deny themselves love if it presented itself? 'Tis foolish, and you know it is."

Gabe waved a hand through the air. "I've grown weary of this conversation." In fact, he had grown categorically miserable from it. "I came here to speak with you on a specific matter."

Stevens kept his disbelieving gaze on Gabe's face. "I will never understand you," he said, shaking his head.

"Have you had any messages from Hydra?"

"I have." Stevens resumed his seat on the hay pile, stretching his legs out in front of him once more. "What do you wish to know?"

Relief swamped Gabe, as apparently Stevens was willing to allow the conversation to pass with no further comments to add to Gabe's already painful volume of guilt. "Has he heard anything from Hugh? Have they discovered his location, or who has captured him?"

Stevens shook his head grimly. "I'm so sorry, Gabe, but Hydra did not mention Hugh in his letter."

"But he has been missing for weeks!"

"I know. I am sure he will be found soon."

Gabe began to pace back and forth in the stall, his movements quick and agitated, and the crunch of hay beneath his feet filling the small space.

"It is perfectly normal to worry over your friend's welfare, but you must also keep your wits about you. You are surrounded by the enemy here, Gabe."

"I know you're right, Stevens, I just..." Damn. His chest felt tight and his thoughts were muddled. This entire conversation made him feel too inept to run his own life.

Stevens thankfully changed the subject, "How fares your assignment?"

Gabe shrugged one shoulder. "We've found the missing documents but have yet to exchange them for forgeries."

Stevens inclined his head. "Mary is broadly skilled."

"She is at that." Gabe gave a short laugh. "She and I overheard a clandestine rendezvous..." He outlined the events of the previous evening's meeting.

"Hm," Stevens hummed in thought. "And you did not see the others involved?"

"No."

"Damn."

Gabe grinned mirthlessly. "Indeed. Tell me, how is *your* assignment progressing?"

His fellow spy's lips straightened into a thin line and his eyes sharpened with a dangerous glint. "Lord Hale is a vile man. He mistreats his wife and daughter while he and his despicable son torture his poor, orphaned nieces. Good God, the abuse in that family, both mental and physical, is astounding." His fists clenched. "And he is most assuredly a traitor."

"Why not hand him over to Hydra and be done with him?"

He leapt to his feet and joined Gabe in pacing. "I do not have any proof!" Stevens' knuckles whitened. "I've searched every crevice and cranny, every secret compartment, strong box... Oh, hell, Gabe, I've searched everywhere. I cannot find one piece of evidence. Oh, I've *heard* plenty of evidence confirming Hale's duplicity, from first-hand accounts to gossip from his servants, but..." He shook his head in aggravation.

"Perhaps my assignment could have the added benefit of aiding you with yours."

"How..." His golden eyes widened. "Oh!"

"They plan to rendezvous Thursday next. Mary and I will be there to observe. If Hale is there, your assignment may have reason to conclude, as well."

Stevens' typically jovial smile broke out as he clapped Gabe on the shoulder. "Capital!"

The sound of a horse's hooves echoed outside the stables and with a nod at Stevens, Gabe turned to make his exit.

"Wait!" his fellow spy hissed.

Gabe spun around to face him, eager to take his leave so as not to be caught by any of Kerr's guests.

Stevens gripped his shoulder, his expression grim. "Be wary of Hale," he whispered. "He may not appear it, but he is a loathsome creature. He and his friends—particularly Lord Boxton—have done unspeakable things with women behind closed doors. Keep Mary away from them and be wary of their attentions. The same applies to any of their acquaintances. *Do not trust them.*"

Gabe jerked his head in a nod. "Duly noted. Thank you, Stevens."

CHAPTER 27

Mary tightened the ribbon of the embroidered cuff on her wrist. This costume was vastly different from that of yesterday's.

The purple and silver of last evening were put to the side for this evening's deep, forest green. The gauzy material clung to her breasts and ribs, leaving nothing to the imagination, then flared at her shoulders to drape loosely until gathered at her wrists beneath her cuffs.

The costume was designed in such a way that instead of using a bolt of material *beneath* the gauze to cover her breasts, it had an elaborately beaded and embroidered vest that went overtop. The bodice of the costume barely covered her nipples but allowed her audience to feast their eyes on the outer globes of her breasts.

She was entirely bare from beneath her ribs to just above the auburn hair covering her *mons*. There, the gauzy material began again, sitting low on her hips and decorated with bells and coins, to drape in long, flowing, layered skirts with a long slit through each layer that ran up to the middle of her right thigh. The bottom half of her costume incorporated a green version of the scanty protection for her feminine area that she had worn last evening.

Her hair and makeup was fashioned in precisely the same way as in yesterday's performance, and once more she thought to forego the use of additional jewellery.

Opening the jar of her rose scented cream, Mary scraped out the very last of it and rubbed it into her hands.

With a last glance in the mirror, Mary turned to attend to her other task this afternoon. Packing.

She pulled her trunks out from beneath the bed and began to place things hurriedly within. She had very few moments before she was expected belowstairs and she knew she would likely not have much time *after* they exchanged the documents to pack all of her belongings.

Mary dashed over to the wardrobe and began removing frocks by the armful and carting the heavy mass of material back to her trunks. She scarcely spared a thought for wrinkling or damaging them, for Mrs. McPhee—bless her—would be glad to repair any gown that was damaged.

In an act of forethought, Mary selected one dark, front-fastening day dress and hid it in the corner of the room behind the privacy screen, along with a fresh pair of woollen stockings and a chemisette.

She moved to the chest of drawers and withdrew an armful of her underthings and brought them to her trunks.

Heavy footfalls in the hallway arrested her. Her heart beat erratically in her chest as she frantically closed the trunks and slid them back to their place beneath the bed.

With a nervous smile upon her lips, Mary dusted her hands together and then pulled her cloak off a hook near the door. It was time for her performance.

GABE DISCRETELY ENTERED the rear door of Kerr House after having taken a detour through the gardens so as to not be observed coming from the stables by any other guest. He closed the door quietly behind him and made his way quickly through the halls toward the billiards room.

He'd turned down the last corridor when Mr. Jackson and his blonde mistresses exited the dining room to his right.

"Oh! Good timing, Spencer." He ran his fingers through his bright orange hair before draping his lace bedecked wrist over one of his mistresses' shoulders. "Your lover is rumoured to be putting on another performance in the drawing room!"

Excellent. She had thought of a way to distract the others and give him an opportunity to exchange the documents. He could not claim to be pleased with her methods, but they were effective.

"I will be along in a moment." He leaned in towards Jackson, as though to impart a secret. "Got to take a piss."

Jackson tapped the index finger of his free hand against the side of his nose and winked.

With an exaggerated flourish, Gabe bowed to the scandalous dandy, and resumed his pace toward Lord Kerr's study.

He found the room empty with the door ajar. He crept in and closed the door soundlessly behind him. Removing the hairpins from within the folds of his cravat, Gabe lowered himself to his knees and set to work.

MARY SWISHED HER HIPS SEDUCTIVELY, slowly rotating them in a circular motion, her arms extended delicately above her head. Her audience was enthralled; each pair of eyes was fixated on the movement of her body.

The room was filled with the haze of cigar smoke and the scent of warm bodies. It was a nauseating combination. But

Mary's thoughts were elsewhere. Her body moved as though it was simply re-enacting previous performances while her mind was focused solely on one thing…Gabriel.

There was no way of knowing how long it would take him to make the switch, or if he'd even known of his opportunity. The blasted man had avoided her all day; it'd been impossible for her to tell him of her plans.

She wished there was some way to know.

CLICK. Gabe's lips pulled to the side in an awkward, mirthless grin as the strong box opened.

He quickly dipped his hand inside and removed the precious, sensitive documents, then slid the forged copies from his pocket and placed them within the box.

Using the hairpins, Gabe set to locking the box. He waited for the *click* of the lock before he hastened to replace the strong box into its hidden spot inside the rare book's pedestal.

MARY CURSED her costume for the umpteenth time that performance. The vest had not been designed with much arm movement in mind, unfortunately. A collective gasp rose out about the room—the men, out of desire, and the women likely out of outrage—for every time she raised her arms, her breasts were entirely exposed.

She entered her concluding set of movements. With each sway, dip, and flick of her hips she got closer to being able to find out if Gabriel had made the exchange successfully.

WITH THE CRUCIAL documents safely hidden in the inner breast pocket of his waistcoat, Gabe took one last glance around the vacant study and placed himself quietly beside the door. He pressed his ear to the seam, listening for any footfalls without. Everyone must still be in the drawing room watching Mary.

He pressed the latch and pulled, very slowly and very carefully opening the door. As no one came at him guns drawn, Gabe exited, ensuring he left the door ajar just as he had found it.

"Mr. Spencer!"

Despite himself, Gabe jumped at the sound of Lady Kerr's voice. *Fool!*

He forced a laugh and bowed. "My lady, you quite startled me. How do you do?"

She grinned broadly. "I am well now that I have found *you*. I confess I had been looking for you."

"Indeed?"

She looked up at him from beneath her lashes. "Mmm. Yes, I had thought perhaps that we might...have a *go*," she licked her upper lip in a suggestive manner, leaving no question in his mind as to what she referred.

He affected an unnatural expression of desire. "I would love to, your ladyship, but I am afraid that I must decline. Perhaps later this evening?"

Something flashed in her dark eyes, but it was gone before Gabe could interpret it.

"Call me Evelyn," she purred, sidling closer to him. "But do come. I have need of your...services."

According to Mary, Lady Kerr—er...Evelyn—had inquired several times about him. Mary's assertion that Lady Kerr was possibly one of the traitors ran through his mind, and the hairs on the back of his neck stood on end. Could

Mary have been right? Perhaps he ought to have listened when she'd expressed her concerns. *Damn.*

"As your hostess, I must insist that you join me for a nip," she persisted. "You are so...virile and handsome and..." She pressed her body against his front and reached around to cup his buttocks. "Oh! You do have a fine bottom."

If Gabe refused, he would appear suspicious. And if Mary was right, and Lady Kerr was a villain, he was certain that he could fend her off. If she wasn't, however, he would have to find a way out of the situation before she attempted to disrobe him.

"Well," he forced his grin to grow and his gaze to soften. "If you insist, my lady, I would be honoured to join you."

"Mmm, excellent."

"ENCORE!" Lord Sheffield called, a cloud of smoke billowing out from around the cigarillo held between his teeth.

Mary smiled and curtseyed with the appropriate amount of modesty. She pasted on a smile of sensuality and idiocy, allowing her gaze to glaze over as her audience clapped.

Where is Gabe? Heavens, he hadn't arrived at the drawing room yet. Was he delayed? Detained? Or, heaven forefend, *discovered*?

She picked up her hairpins from the floor and hastily fashioned her hair in a tight, serviceable knot at the base of her neck.

"Mary, that was...superb." Lord Boxton rose from his seat, a noticeable bulge in the front of his breeches, as he came to stand directly before her. He leaned in to press his lips to her ear and Mary suppressed a shiver of revulsion. "I am very much looking forward to my *private* performance. Reddington and I will likely have to fight over who gets to have you first...unless the man sees sense and realizes what dreadful fate will befall him if he tries to have a go at you before I do."

"I look forward to it, as well, Tony," she lied with a wink. "If you will excuse me..."

"Just a moment, Mary." He gripped her arm, halting her movement as she attempted to step away.

She spread the edges of her lips wide in a strained smile. "Yes, Tony?"

He lifted one side of her vest with the index finger of his free hand and Mary had to clench her fists to keep from slapping his hands away. The heated desire in his piercing green eyes deepened and for the third time since her performance began, Mary resolved to burn this costume upon returning to London.

"Wear this tonight," he growled. He licked the rim of her ear with the tip of his tongue and Mary tensed. "I want to rip it off with my teeth."

"*If* James allows you to go first," she teased.

His eyes darkened and his grip on her arm tightened painfully. "He will."

Lady Marpol giggled loudly as Lord Kerr bounced her jarringly on his lap, garnering Mary's attention. The others sat about the room with their own mistresses, though Lord Pondridge's large blonde sat, dejected, while he slept.

"Come join us!" Lord Sheffield called, lifting one arm in the air, his other wrapped around Lady Kellings. "I know a story that boggles the mind!"

"Come, Mary," Boxton hissed in her ear as his grip tightened even further on her arm. The warning was not missed. "Let us sit with Sheffield for a moment."

With a mournful glance at the doorway, Mary allowed Boxton to lead her to the settee.

"THESE STEPS LEAD TO THE *DUNGEON*," Lady Kerr whispered the last word in Gabe's ear, as though the dungeon were a place in which to find great pleasure.

He hadn't the faintest idea why Lady Kerr had decided to bring him to the castle ruins on the Kerr estate, but his curiosity had most definitely gotten the better of him. His initial supposition of her proposition had been an invitation to her bedchamber. At the very least he had thought to put her to sleep while rubbing her feet and then search her chambers for any pertinent information. Clearly that was not the case. At the most, he thought that he might have to restrain the woman if she attempted an attack the moment they were out of sight from any guests at the house party. But that hadn't happened.

The ruins could be interesting, he supposed, if the woman beside him had any useful information on the previous residence, when it was built, or what ultimately happened to the structure, but she was sadly mute for the majority of the short tour.

Crumbling walls surrounded him, vines and dirt creeping upward from the ground, and the distinct sound of flapping pigeon wings high above their heads.

"Fascinating, Evelyn."

"Shall we venture down to have a look?"

He dipped his head. "Certainly."

MARY GLANCED toward the mantle clock and again her heart hiccoughed in her chest. Something must be wrong.

She looked around her at the faces of sin and delight. The other guests at the house party sat about the pink floral drawing room, drinking, smoking, and otherwise rejoicing in the gaiety of their hedonism. None were aware, however, of the turmoil within Mary. She smiled and laughed with the others, but her body veritably vibrated with alarm.

Where is Gabe? The question gnawed at her and the cold feeling of dread began to spread through her like frost consuming a forest.

The others talked and guffawed, though Boxton paid particular attention to Mary, having pulled her down onto his lap to press kisses to her neck and shoulder. Where was *his* mistress? Should not *she* be sitting here instead of Mary?

Her gaze roamed the group; Lord Kerr sat with his mistress, Lady Marpol, and as did the others, each paired—or tripled in Mr. Jackson's case—with their lovers. Where was—?

Oh no! The pieces of the proverbial puzzle locked themselves into place in her mind and she leapt to her feet.

"Whoa-ho, darling." Boxton grasped her wrist. "Where are you going? We've only just begun our afternoon of enjoyment."

"I'm afraid that you must excuse me, Tony." She smiled down at him before gently attempting to withdraw her arm.

He squeezed her wrist tighter in a punishing grip. Mary bit the inside of her lip to keep from wincing as his fingers dug deeply into her sensitive flesh.

"I would prefer you stay, Mary." His eyes darkened slightly, though his mien remained playful.

She leaned toward him and whispered, "I must use the necessary."

With a distrusting—and dare she say threatening glance—he released her. "Return directly."

She leaned forward and pressed an unchaste kiss to his lips, with just enough promise to keep him from following after her, then turned on her heel and swept from the room. The moment she was out of sight, she swiped at the repulsive taste of him with the back of her hand.

THE SCRAPING of old wood against stone echoed through the narrow stairwell. Gooseflesh skittered along Gabe's skin. He took it as a dark omen. Perhaps these ruins were haunted.

"Step inside," Lady Kerr's smooth and deliberately seductive voice said.

Gabe did as she asked and stepped into the dark dankness of the dungeon. The only light came from the doorway in which her ladyship stood. The floor was dirty stone that was likely covered in rodent refuse. The walls were of the same stone, but they were cold with dripping moisture and sported scars from the nails of former inhabitants and the chains and manacles that graced its walls.

This was a room for torture. It veritably reeked of fear and pain... A shiver skittered up Gabe's spine, as one clear fact rang out like a knoll: death had happened here. Why the devil would Lady Kerr bring him to such a place?

The lady was silent, as though waiting for him to comment on the trappings. "Fascinating," he lied as he turned his gaze up toward the low ceiling. "And this was all built in Roman times? When did your husband's family rebuild the main—?"

Gabe stilled, sudden awareness, trepidation, and self-derision flowing through him all at once, as the *click* of a pistol cocking echoed through the room.

He spun around, alarm in his chest.

Bang!

CHAPTER 28

$\mathcal{M}$ary picked up her sheer skirts and ran through the empty halls of Kerr House. It was muffled, but she had heard it. Gunfire.

Her lungs burned and her muscles ached with the force of her effort. She ran past several startled servants, but she did not care what they thought. Gabe was in trouble.

Please don't let him be dead, please don't let him be dead!

She ran through one doorway and then another, finally coming upon the door leading to the back garden. She had to slow her momentum to pull the door open. Not bothering to close it behind her, she burst through the doorway and out into the bright sunlit back gardens.

Instinct told her where to find him: the ruins. Her feet carried her between the hedgerows, between the beds of flowers, and onward. The birds chirped, the butterflies flittered, but Mary paid them no heed; she just ran.

Rounding the hedge of a maze of some sort, Mary ran directly into a large tree—*oh dear. Not a tree. A man!*

Her head buzzed briefly as she blinked at the solid form.

"I beg your pardon," she said breathlessly, staring into the man's impeccable cravat.

"Mary!"

Her startled gaze flew upward and directly into the stunning golden eyes of her friend Sir Bramwell Stevens.

"Bram! Oh heavens, did you hear it, too?"

"Yes. I was on my way to see who it was."

Fear still gnawed its way through Mary, but an odd sense of calm stole over her at the sight of her friend. "I believe it was Gabe. I do not have the time to explain, however. I must go to the castle ruins. They're just beyond the garden walls, on top of the hill.

Bramwell nodded.

"Do me a kindness, Bram, and have a curricle prepared for a quick departure?"

"Of course. But what of Gabe?"

"Leave that to me. Just get the curricle. Please."

Without waiting for his response, Mary picked up her skirts and tore through the garden.

MARY WAS RIGHT. Gabe was wrong, and damn it, Mary was right.

Gabe let out a harsh growl, barring his teeth, as the shot grazed his leg. He exaggerated his pain, staggering on the spot before dropping to his knees, roaring at the jarring impact. "What the *devil*, woman?"

A bit of a performance would not only give Lady Kerr a false sense of accomplishment, but it would have the added effect of discouraging her from feeling the need to shoot him again to increase her accuracy.

Malicious delight flashed in her eyes. "Oh, I believe you understand my reasoning perfectly, *Tony*."

She turned to motion to someone outside the dungeon's door and a large footman dressed in canary yellow livery entered to place a chair in the centre of the dark, damp room.

"Have a seat, darling," Lady Kerr said in her deceptively silken voice.

Damn. Gabe should have listened to Mary when she had expressed her suspicions about Lady Kerr. He should have been more aware of what was going on around him, more alert, more... He shook himself internally. There was no use in berating himself for not realizing the lady's guilt. Right now, he must think of a way out of this.

Lady Kerr's giant brute of a footman—*where the devil had he come from?*—lifted Gabe bodily off the ground and sat him on the thoroughly worn chair before wrenching his arms behind the backrest to trap his wrists together with chained iron manacles. The man was strong, Gabe gave him that.

The manacles were tight and effective. The brute then moved on to tie Gabe's feet to the chair's legs with a length of rope.

With a commanding flick of Lady Kerr's wrist, the footman obeyed the silent command, retrieving the spent pistol from her hand and exiting, closing the dungeon door behind him. The scraping of wood against stone echoed around them, until with a final *clunk*, the door was shut, leaving the room entirely black.

"Mmm," Lady Kerr's voice rumbled sensually. "I do enjoy the darkness, but..."

Her voice trailed off as the sound of her footfalls replaced it. There was a scrape, the sound of stone striking stone, and then *poof*, a flame lit the end of a torch. Lady Kerr strode around the room lighting other torches with hers, before she placed it in its own ring mounted on the stone wall.

With the room brightened, it looked oddly more ominous than before. Rats skittered along the side of the walls, seeking shelter from detection, and a small heap of bones lay nestled in the corner. *Lord*, Gabe hoped it was an animal's bones, deceased of natural causes.

"Now we may have a proper discussion." Lady Kerr stood before Gabriel, her hands on her slender hips. "You must know by now who I am, and what I've done. But you have me at a disadvantage. Who are *you*?"

Gabe suppressed a smile. All at once, two things became clear. One, Lady Kerr was unquestionably a traitorous spy working for Bonaparte, and two, she hadn't any proof of Gabriel's identity, merely suspicion. He must be convincing as an innocent and, with luck, she would be disabused of her assumption and Gabe's identity would remain intact.

He had endured torture before—had trained for it, as a matter of fact—and he could certainly withstand questioning from Lady Kerr. "My name is Mr. Anthony Spencer, and I—"

Crack! Her hand connected with his cheek in a surprisingly painful slap.

"Try again," she said.

"I am Anthony Spenc—"

Crunch! Her fist connected agonizingly with his nose, the awful sound echoing in his ears, before blood began to spurt from his face. *Damn, had she knocked out a tooth?* Gabe ran his tongue over his teeth the metallic zing of blood consuming his mouth. They were all still there. *Thank God!*

"Again," she grunted.

Gabe again suppressed his grin. Instead he swallowed his pride and released a frightened whimper. "I am the youngest son of Sir Peter Spencer. I have—"

"*Argh*!" With a frustrated growl, Lady Kerr stormed to the dungeon door and opened it.

She stuck her head through the opening to speak briefly with her brute.

Gabe strained against the manacles to no avail. He might

be able to stand, but with his ankles bound to the chair and his wrists tied behind him, he was at such a disadvantage that he would never win in combat against this madwoman. He was well and truly caught.

The door scraped closed once more and Lady Kerr returned with a weapon in each hand. She dropped a bullwhip to the ground several feet away before advancing on him with a six inch, fearsome-looking, blade.

"I believe this clothing is in the way."

"I rather like it," he said.

Her face darkened as she advanced. She took the knife to his coat, slitting the sleeve from his wrist to his shoulder. Bloody hell, she must be strong!

"That was a nice coat!" he said indignantly.

Ignoring him, she slit the other sleeve and pulled the mass of wool from his person. She proceeded to remove his waist-coat, holding within it the vital documents and the hairpins that could have so helped him at this moment. That thought brought another question to mind. She had discovered him outside her husband's study; would she not have wondered if he had taken anything from within?

Lady Kerr tossed what was left of his coat and waistcoat across the dungeon to slide along the filthy floor. With a malevolent smile on her lips she leaned over him to press a punishing kiss to his tightly closed lips.

There was so much that was fundamentally wrong with his current dire situation, but one thing was certain: Lady Kerr was an abysmal kisser. Mary was far superior.

His eyes widened. *Good God, Mary!*

Had she been caught as well? Did she know of his capture? How did she fare? Did she worry? Had she heard the gunshot?

Gabe felt the scrape of something sharp against the under side of his chin, dragging him forcedly from his thoughts.

She pulled away from him, his cut, bloody cravat hanging loosely from her clenched fist and her face red with his blood.

"Mmm... I love the smell of a man's blood."

"That came from my nose," he grimaced.

"Delicious..."

Gabe closed his eyes against the disturbing image of Lady Kerr licking his blood from her lips. And he thought of Mary. *His* Mary, with long, curling auburn hair and warm, kind, shining grey eyes. Mary, with laughter that echoed gaily through a room and lightly lilting on the air, over hills and on the breeze to seep deep into his heart like a soothing balm.

Rip! Lady Kerr tore his shirt noisily from his person, a gasp of delight on her lips.

"Ooh, sweaty, bloody, and half nude. Precisely how I like to conduct my little *experiments*."

Mary, Gabe kept his eyes shut and thought of her. Mary, who played with him as a child, shared his secrets, commiserated with his pitiful woes, and always waited for him when he was away at school.

He felt Lady Kerr drift away from him, but he kept his eyes shut.

Mary, who always looked so pretty in the dresses her mother would make for her but Gabe was too afraid to compliment.

Snap! Gabe's eyes squeezed tighter and he released a roar of pain as the tip of Lady Kerr's bullwhip connected with his bared chest, slicing through the thick skin there.

Mary! His mind cried. Mary, who danced like a siren calling to sailors and kissed like a goddess personified. Mary, who made him feel things that he had never before experienced and had not the faintest idea how to put into words.

"*Who are you*?" Lady Kerr shouted at him.

He opened his eyes to gaze at Lady Kerr. How could any man find her even mildly attractive? Her dark eyes were filled only with malice, her brow marred with deep scowl lines...and her heart was shrivelled and blackened from the hellfire burning inside her. How long had she been dead inside, he wondered? And how had he not noticed it before?

"My name is Anthony Spencer, my la—"

He broke off as she swung her arm up, the bullwhip arching high into the air, and the expression of pure evil etched on her features.

Gabriel shut his eyes as the *crack* rent the air and the tip of the bullwhip made yet another slice through the flesh of his chest. Gabe roared.

Mary, he repeated the litany in his mind. Mary who had put her trust in him, who had offered him her body, which he had so foolishly refused. *Bloody hell* was he ever a fool! When he found a way to escape the vile Evelyn, Lady Kerr, Gabe would make it his duty to beg Mary's forgiveness and take her... Take her, tup her, make love to her, *God*, he would make her moan and scream with delight and beg for more. And he would delight in giving her precisely what she asked for. Repeatedly. For countless nights and eternal days for the rest of their lives if necessary.

Thud. Gabe grunted as the lady's small fist connected with his cheek. *When had she abandoned the whip?* His eyes snapped open. He could feel his face swell from each hit, each slap as her merciless attack continued.

Gabe groaned and cried out with each hit, though his reactions were mostly exaggerated. While the woman was persistent and eager, she lacked the strength and imagination to do him lasting harm—unless she decided to put her weaponry to use once again. Her attack was still painful, however, and with continued hits, Gabe could be in great danger of serious injury...or losing his life.

Finally, she stepped back to gaze at the result of her fine, ruthless progress of mauling him. She smiled foully, apparently pleased. Gabe felt ill.

The door scraped open on creaky hinges, garnering his and Lady Kerr's attention, and in strode Mary, as though jumping from his thoughts and into flesh and blood. His heart leapt. Mary's hair hung loosely around her shoulders and waist and she wore—*bloody, bloody hell, what is she wearing*?

Gabe nearly swallowed his tongue. Mary wore virtually nothing on her upper body; only a thin layer of sheer material stretched from her shoulders to just under her nearly nude, pert breasts. Each dusky nipple strained against the transparent gauzy fabric. Her arms were draped with the same material to tighten at the cuffs at her wrists. Her midriff was entirely bare; the soft skin of her pale belly veritably calling out to be licked. Her layered skirts flowed to the floor, but—*good God*!—they had a slit going from bottom to high on her thigh, just begging to be spread wide so one might sample what lay beneath.

Mary's lips curled back in an aroused grin as she placed her hands on her waist, deliberately displaying her flagrantly exposed figure. She cocked one hip, allowing her belt of shining coins and bells to jingle.

Despite himself, Gabe's cock twitched.

"Oh yes," she lowered her voice to a husky thrum. "Please tell me I can join in this erotic game."

What the devil?

Mary walked toward him, her hips swaying deliciously with each step.

Apparently, Lady Kerr was stunned into silence, for she simply stood back and watched as Mary halted before Gabe. He looked up into her bright, grey eyes, wishing he could tell her just how sorry he was for what he had done and how he had treated her.

Lady Kerr, having suddenly realized the dangers of having the two of them so close, called out, "Guard!"

Crack! Gabe grunted in shock.

He blinked his swelling eyelids rapidly to clear the stars from his vision, then stared disbelievingly at Mary's impassioned features. "You struck me!"

Her eyes rolled back as she shut them in an aroused expression that entirely confused Gabe. What was she doing?

"Oh yes," Mary moaned, earning another twitch for his still-eager member.

"Hit him again," Lady Kerr called. Apparently having decided that she could handle them on her own, she flicked her wrist to send her man away.

Mary wound her hand back and slapped him again, so much harder than Lady Kerr had. Gabe groaned as more stars danced before his eyes. The woman was going to knock him senseless!

With an aroused, yet slightly malicious grin, the likes of which Gabe had never seen grace her perfect, full lips, Mary very slowly rounded the chair. Once. Twice. Then halted at his back.

Her nails scraped his scalp as she fisted her fingers tightly in his hair. Gabe grimaced as she yanked his head backwards to hit the back of the chair. She pressed her lips to his ear.

"You've been naughty, yes?"

"N—no," he stammered.

She tightened her grip on his hair and *thunked* his head against the chair's back again for emphasis. "You *have* been naughty. You began this little game with Lady Kerr and you didn't invite me..."

Gabe felt something slide into his palm while she spoke. Oh, the sly woman. The genius! Of course his Mary would think to do something like this. But blast it, did she have to hit him so hard?

"You naughty, wicked boy, playing with the other girls and not with me."

CHAPTER 29

*H*aving given Gabriel her concealed hairpins, Mary released his hair.

Slowly, sensually, with hips swaying, she made her way to his front once more. Every moment that Lady Kerr allowed her to take control of this "erotic game" was one more moment that Gabe had to try to free himself.

Please let this work!

"I do so adore how you play with your toys, Miss White," Lady Kerr stepped forward to halt at Mary's side. "I commend you on your abilities."

Swallowing the bile that rose into her throat, Mary turned to Lady Kerr. "Why thank you, your ladyship. I am a quick study. To be shamefully honest, I...rather relished it."

Lady Kerr gestured toward Gabe. "Then please, continue."

Mary turned toward Gabe, prepared to deal another blow. But the look in his eyes stopped her. He blinked once, then looked to one side of the room. Mary understood his signal; he had picked the lock of the manacles and wanted her to move out of the way.

She winked her comprehension. In the appearance of rounding behind him again in order to "play" with him, Mary stopped behind the chair.

The moment she had repositioned herself, Gabe surged upward in a motion shocking for someone who had been as sorely abused as he had, and in one swift motion, shoved Lady Kerr with both hands, one cuff of the manacles still fastened around one wrist. Lady Kerr fell over backwards, screaming on her way down and landing firmly on her bottom, the back of her head *thudding* dispassionately on the hard surface of the floor and knocking her unconscious.

Gabe wavered on his feet before crouching down to untie the ropes at his ankles.

Despite vehemently despising Lady Kerr, Mary hurried to her side and checked for her pulse. *Thump-thump, thump-thump*. She was alive, most assuredly.

The door scraped open and the large footman rushed inside, apparently having heard their lady's shout of distress.

Gabe leapt forward, prepared to combat the man. Mary was amazed that his injuries did not appear to hinder him. His face, chest, and one side of one thigh were soaked in blood, and the flesh of his face had begun to swell.

With a bounce to his step, Gabe bounded toward the man and punched him square in the jaw. The footman howled and doubled over, giving Gabe an opening to jump on the man's back, grasping the chain for his half-opened manacles with his other hand and pulling tightly against the man's neck.

Thinking quickly, Mary retrieved the length of rope that had been used to tie Gabe's ankles to the chair, rolled Lady Kerr to her side, and bound the lady's wrists together. Just as she made the final tug, two meaty hands encircled her neck and pulled her to her feet.

With a strangled gasp and panic leaping through her

breast, Mary used one hand to pull at the man's fingers, and the other to reach behind her head. She scratched his cheek and made contact with one of his eyes, and he grunted in response.

"Goddamned *beast*!" Gabriel growled. "Won't bloody well lose consciousness."

The footman thrashed, knocking Mary off-balance.

Gabe roared in frustration. "That's enough!"

There was the *clink* of a chain, a gasp, and a loud *thunk*, and Mary was released. She stumbled forward and spun around, holding her throat and pulling in deep, relieved breaths.

With a vacant expression, the guard slowly tipped sideways until he fell to the ground with a solid *thud*, Gabe standing over him with his manacles fisted in one hand.

"Are you well?" Gabe asked, stepping toward Mary. "Did he hurt you terribly?"

She rubbed at her neck, where the guard's painful grip had been only moments before. While it still stung, Mary didn't believe that a dreadful amount of damage had been done. "I am well," she said, her voice turned gruff.

Eager to be on their way, Mary bent to check for the guard's pulse.

"Have I killed him?" Gabe sounded entirely too fervent.

"No," Mary croaked, rising. "We had best make our escape quickly."

"Just a moment." Gabe stopped her as she stepped toward the door.

Mary looked back at him and patiently waited as he used her hairpins to unlock his second wrist from the manacles.

"That was very dangerous what you did, bursting in like you did," he said with his face turned down as he focused on his task.

Mary's brow drew together in a puzzled frown. "I beg

your pardon?" Gratefully, her voice was beginning to return to normal.

He jerked his head toward the man on the ground. "That guard is enormous, he could have hurt you in any number of ways."

"Worried about me?" Mary smiled. "I assure you, I can handle myself around men, Gabriel."

"You had better hope so, coming in here dressed like…" he nodded at her attire before tossing his manacles to the floor and rubbing his wrist, "well, like a harlot."

The warmth that had begun to spread through her chest fled swiftly to be replaced by an ever-familiar aching pain.

She opened her mouth to utter a harsh rebuttal, but snapped it shut, glancing toward the rough stone floor. What was the point in arguing when he was so absolute in his low opinion of her? Embarrassment of the previous night flooded her once more and she forced it aside. Now was decidedly not the time.

"Come, we must make our escape before they awaken." She shook her head at him. "And for heaven's sake we must clean and bind those wounds before you get infection."

Mary turned toward the dungeon door.

Gabe caught her arm. "Mary…"

She turned to gaze at him questioningly.

"I apologize. It was wrong of me to say that you looked like a harlot. You saved my life, and deserve appreciation and respect, not disparagement." He shifted his feet, discomfited.

Her heart lurched in her chest and Mary swallowed past the unexpected lump in her throat. "While I appreciate your sudden attack of conscience, Gabriel, now is certainly not the time to discuss it. In fact, if we dally any longer we are likely to be killed."

Mary cursed her unavoidable chin quiver as she made her

way to the dungeon's door. Damn Gabriel Ashley and his ability to make her feel so many dratted emotions all at once.

GABE WATCHED as Mary strode purposefully toward the dungeon door, her chin quivering, and the ill feeling in his chest spread at an alarming pace.

He had hurt her. He hated that he hurt her. But confound it, she was right; now was most decidedly *not* the time to discuss it.

He bent to retrieve his destroyed waistcoat, and within it the vital code deciphers, maps, and documents outlining stratagems.

They stepped out onto the cool, dingy landing of the stairwell and Mary hurried past him to close the dungeon's door behind them.

"Lock it, if you will," she said.

With a nod of comprehension, Gabe turned and, using Mary's hairpins, slid the lock into place.

Someone would eventually come looking for them, but for the moment, they needed as much time as they could get to make good their escape.

Gabe took the first step of the dungeon's stairs and grit his teeth at the jolt of pain in his thigh.

Mary cringed as she looked at his bleeding leg. "Are you well enough to run, do you suppose?"

He gave her a half grin, the metallic zing of his blood still filling his mouth. "My injuries are not half as bad as they appear. My chest and face sting, I will grant you, but I am entirely capable of running."

With a curt nod, Mary turned on her heel, picked up her skirts, and sprinted up the jagged stone staircase. She paused half way up to retrieve something that had presumably fallen, then continued on her way.

Anxious to be on his way, Gabe followed.

THE DASH to Kerr House had not been as painful as Gabe had initially feared. Lady Kerr was either inexperienced in inflicting true pain, or she had merely intended to begin with minimal torture. Regardless of the reasoning, Gabe was grateful for his mobility and lack of serious wounds.

In fact, what pained him the most was his chest...and not the injuries upon it.

Sir Bramwell Stevens' words came back to haunt him. "*I've seen the way you treat her, as though she is incapable of making her own decisions or of conducting her life in a manner of her choosing... You constantly berate her for being an actress. Not once have you congratulated her on a job well done. Not once have you encouraged her.*"

The sun shone down hotly on his back as they snuck through the gardens of Kerr House. They hid behind shrubberies and slunk around hedges when they heard a servant, a guest, or gardeners nearby, each pause in their flight giving them further reason for concern.

"Mary," he whispered as they ducked behind a rosebush.

"Shh!" She frowned at him.

His conscience gnawed at him. He must get this out now. "Mary!" he hissed.

She pressed her index finger against her lips in a gesture for silence.

"I am sorry, Mar—"

"Not now, Gabe," she whispered in return before scurrying along the trellis and into the recessed doorway leading into the back parlour.

"I must speak to you." He followed her into the doorway.

Ignoring him entirely, she pressed a hand to the glass of the French-style door and looked within.

"Mary..."

Her head shot around as she pinned him with a fierce glare. "Shh!"

He missed her playfulness. Yes, they were attempting to make their escape from an estate full of traitors who would all most assuredly kill them on the spot if they knew who they truly were, but the Mary he had once known would have found humour in their current circumstance. He, half nude and bleeding, her in a scanty costume, her breasts all but entirely nude, crouching and scurrying through the garden... In all probability, if they were spotted they would be branded insane and thrown in Bedlam.

He must have laughed, for Mary stared at him wide-eyed and angry. "*Shh!*"

She put her hand to the latch on the French doors and pressed. The doors swung open on silent hinges and they both slipped into the nauseatingly pink floral parlour.

The house was abuzz with activity, but gratefully none of it was in the parlour. Pots banged and dishes clanged in the kitchens, the sound echoing through the halls.

There was no hiding his state of dress, but Gabe straightened his shoulders and wore his blood with pride as they strode through the corridors to their guest bedchamber. Good fortune was with them, and nary a single person saw them enroute.

Gabe and Mary both released a sigh of relief as the door closed and locked behind them. The room was bright—and still so startlingly puce—and the air was warm from the low burning fire.

Mary turned to face him, tossing a dark green clump of

fabric to the ground. It must be the *clearly* missing portion of her costume. "You dolt!"

"I beg your pardon?"

She huffed an exasperated breath at him then turned to retrieve her trunks from beneath the bed. "You are silent all across the hills and fields until the precise moment that we *needed* to be silent. *Then*, of course you decide it's the perfect opportunity for you to strike up a conversation with me."

Gabe found his own trunk that he'd packed that morning, and placed it atop the bed, flipping open the lid. "I meant to apologize, Mary," he said defensively. "You did an admirable job of rescuing me, as difficult as it is to admit to requiring a rescue."

He carefully removed the documents from his balled waistcoat pocket and gently placed them in the hidden compartment at the bottom of his trunk.

She released a barked laugh of true mirth. "Ha! I slapped you, Gabe. I pulled your hair and beat you. You believe that to be admirable?"

The corner of his split and bleeding mouth curved up in a grin. "I admit that you could have been a little lighter with your abuse, but such a display in that particular circumstance was necessary. Unfortunately. You did precisely what was required of you in order to gain my freedom. You could easily have barged in with guns held high and killed the lot of them, but it would have blown your cover and ruined our chance to discover who their contact is. This way, you maintained the illusion of your innocence, which will benefit you later."

Mary demurely nodded her head as she fastened the buckles of her trunks. "Thank you for saying that, Gabe."

He was momentarily distracted by the gentle sway of her breasts as she tugged on the leather straps.

He cleared his throat. "Perhaps you ought to change..."

She looked down at herself and laughed. "Oh, yes. Of course."

Mary fled behind the privacy screen and Gabe released a breath in a silent *whoosh*. His conscience had been weighing on him and he felt lighter after having apologized.

He quickly strode to the washbasin and splashed some cool water over a washcloth and began to wipe himself down. He had just completed washing the blood off his face when a thought struck him.

"If we are somehow successful in reaching the stables without being caught, how do you suppose we commandeer a carriage without the stable boys knowing? And the servants? The guests?" He shook his head. "Damn it, Mary, we may have to leave on foot. We would never make it off the front drive before we are caught, drawn, and quartered."

Her lilting laughter came from behind the screen, as well as a grunt and the shifting of fabric. "I have taken the liberty of arranging a curricle prepared."

"But—" Gabe straightened, water dripping from his swollen chin. "How did you—?"

"Stevens."

"Ah. But where are we to put our trunks? Curricles are not equipped with—"

"There are newer models, I assure you, that have compartments in the back for smaller trunks. If Lord and Lady Kerr do not have the newest model, we will simply have to put them by our feet or sit atop them. Come, Gabriel, use your imagination."

He nodded in silent agreement and continued to clean his wounds. He would have to strip the cloth from the bed in order to bind his wounds, but such was fine with him, as he would not have to wait long before they reached an inn, where he could dress his wounds properly.

CHAPTER 30

A groan escaped Evelyn as she brought a hand up to cup the back of her aching head.

What happened?

Her eyes snapped open as it all came rushing back to her. *Mr. Spencer*, if that was his true name, had escaped! He pushed her, the *bastard*!

Ignoring the ache to her bottom and the throb in her head, she rose, blinking as her vision briefly spotted. She pressed a hand to the filthy, damp wall of the dungeon, pausing to regain her composure.

Her gaze settled disdainfully on her hired brute and her eyes narrowed. Abandoning her spot near the wall, she strode purposefully over to his prostrate form and gave him a swift kick to the ribs.

"Up! Up, damn you!"

He groaned.

"Wake up, you oversized, mindless beast. Wake up and go after that bloody bastard and his idiot woman!"

Evelyn went to the dungeon's door and pressed the latch.

Nothing.

She shoved. Nothing.

"No," she breathed, the sound swallowed up in the think air of the death chamber.

She pressed the latch and shoved simultaneously, pressing her shoulder firmly against the thick wood.

Nothing.

"*No!*" she screeched, hitting the door with her hands that still bore the stain of Spencer's blood. "You bastard, you bastard, *you bastard!*"

"ARE YOU CERTAIN YOU WISH TO—?"

"Good heaven's, Gabriel, right now it is our only option. I refuse to leave my costumes behind." Mary set her jaw, giving Gabe a look that meant she was serious. She heaved a heavy breath, taking in the scent of hay, leather, and manure.

"Best listen to what she says, my friend. Mary is like to box you in the nose if you make her abandon her costumes." Stevens grinned as a horse whinnied and stomped in a nearby stall.

"But to sit on them?" Gabe argued. "The curricle is high enough and, moreover, it is dangerous. Adding height where there wasn't before could very well send you tumbling off the back." His eyes lit with worry and Mary felt her stubbornness melt a little. A *very* little.

She sighed. "The horse Stevens set free for the other stable hands to chase is likely to have been caught by now. We haven't the luxury of another distraction without causing further suspicion. Gabe, we have tarried long enough. Lady Kerr and her men will have roused already and others will be alerted to their plight. We have mere moments. I have saved you once today, already, I simply do not have the strength to do so again."

Stevens raised an eyebrow. "When I return to London, I expect a full account of what occurred between Lady Kerr and the two of you." He turned his gaze on Gabe. "*Especially* you. Looks like she beat the bloody—"

"Oi! You tread on dangerous ground, man." Gabe lifted Mary's trunk onto the curricle's seat and shifted it to her side.

Mary sidled up to Stevens and winked. "It wasn't all her."

Stevens' jaw dropped and Mary laughed. Gabe muttered something unintelligible, which made Stevens laugh, the loud, guttural sound rumbling through her chest.

"You two are going to cause a bloody scene," Gabe grumbled.

Stevens suddenly wrapped his arms around Mary and dipped her in an exaggerated flourish, bussing her quickly on the cheek. "I shall miss you, my dear friend!"

Mary could not help the startled giggle that escaped as she raised a hand to her falling coiffure. She had missed Stevens; he never failed to put a smile upon her lips.

He righted her just as Gabe grabbed her bodily and placed her in the curricle seat. Gabe settled himself on the seat beside her, the motion sending awareness skittering along her nerves. How could she still have such feelings for the dratted man after the way he had behaved last evening?

He apologized, Mary. Perhaps he truly is sorry for the events of last night, as well?

Beside her, he gripped the horses' reins in his hands. Mary tied her loose hair back into a serviceable knot at the base of her neck.

"Safe journey!" Stevens raised a hand to salute them.

Mary smiled and waved in response.

Gabe flicked the reins and the two bays jolted the curricle forward at a trot, sending Mary backwards. She caught herself on the side of the vehicle and on Gabe's regrettably injured shoulder. He hissed a breath, but caught her with his free hand.

"I told ye it was dangerous," he gritted out, his jaw clenched.

Mary righted herself, but kept a hand firmly settled on the curricle's side. "I am fine. I merely was not expecting such a quick start."

She could see the muscles of his jaw tighten and she forced herself to look away. Let the man be angry. The grouch.

She turned her face up to the afternoon sun, allowing the warmth to wash her worries away, if only for a moment. She watched the scenery pass by, trees, crops, estates... *What—?*

"Gabe!"

"Aye?"

"This isn't the way to London. We are going in the wrong direction!"

"Aye."

She huffed an exasperated breath. "*Why* are we not returning to London? The ride to London is no less than ten hours from Kerr House, surely you would wish to—"

"Aye, lass, but I willnae take ye there just yet." She opened her mouth, but he continued in his deep brogue, "I willnae take ye there because Lady Kerr's brutes are like te follow the curricle's tracks...and the horses' fer that matter. We will journey an hour West toward Brighton and send the curricle back. From there we will acquire alternate equipage and take the long road back te London."

Mary shut her mouth and thought on it. It was a sound plan. Dash it.

With one hand still gripping the side of the curricle, Mary sat back and decided to enjoy the rest of the journey.

"I've always wanted to visit Brighton," she said.

"We willnae be visiting, Mary. Donnae make yerself

known te others tha' we come across. Keep te yerself and let me do the talking."

Mary sat bolt upright and gave him a mock salute. "*Aye laddie!*"

There his jaw went, tightening again.

"You will lose your teeth if you continue grinding them," she said. "Grind them to a dust, you will."

He sent her a scathing sideways glance, but remained silent. It was just as well. This way she could enjoy the *clip clop* of the horses' hooves and the gentle rumbling of the curricle's wheels.

"It is about bloody time someone released us," Lady Kerr grumbled hoarsely as Cecil Piper opened the creaky dungeon door. "I have been shouting for over an hour, curse you!"

"I'm so sorry, my lady. Damned hard to hear you from the drawing room, eh wot?"

Evelyn ground her teeth together at his oft-repeated expression, the irritation of it nearly driving her mad. But for the moment, she must put it from her mind. They had more important issues at hand.

"Gather the others for an emergency meeting," Evelyn ordered, storming up the narrow stairwell leading from the dungeons. "We have much to discuss."

"*No man has ever returned her attentions and no man has ever given her the affection that she damned well deserves,*" Stevens had said.

Gabe tied the last of the bandages around his chest. Since entering their bedchamber in the inn just a few miles outside of Brighton, they had been silent. Not a word was exchanged between Gabe and Mary as they performed their ablutions and as Gabe tended to his many wounds. He sat in the only chair in just a towel tied tightly around his waist, the injuries on his leg and chest cleaned and bound, and his swollen face thoroughly washed.

They had sent Lord and Lady Kerr's *borrowed* equipage back, and a carriage was being prepared for them. It left them plenty of time to clean themselves up, possibly sleep, and prepare for the journey to London.

He looked over his shoulder at Mary as she washed the dust of travel from her beautiful, faintly freckled, heart-shaped face. What had possessed him to become so cross with her on the short journey to this roadside inn?

Having washed, Mary wheeled herself about to give him the full force of her irritated gaze. "How could you treat those nice gentlemen like that?" she asked, finally breaking their silence.

Those *nice gentlemen* had gawked and salivated over Mary the moment they had entered the innyard. They had looked her up and down and saw her as fair game.

"They were rude to ye," he grumbled. Damn his miserable temperament.

"And Stevens? And our marks?" Mary stepped closer to him, her hands on her hips in the position of a schoolmarm. A dashed attractive schoolmarm. "Was it truly necessary to behave in such a way? You were supposed to be Mr. Anthony Spencer, rakehell, ne'er do well, and inveterate gambler, not unconscionable grouch and grumbling recluse. Why, you spent the majority of the house party glaring at the other men with jaw clenched and the remainder of the time harping at *me*."

Gabe's heart tripped over itself as she spoke, his stomach in ludicrous knots.

"It is no wonder they pegged you as a spy," she continued. "Good heavens, Gabriel, did you not stop to think—"

Gabe burst. "*I was jealous*!" he shouted over her litany of charges against him.

The moment the words were out of his mouth, he realized they were true. *My God, I was jealous*! Truly, fully jealous. He had thought those feelings were merely *akin* to jealousy and perhaps concern for Mary's wellbeing, not the full, incensed jealousy that he now realized raged through his body.

Mary's mouth had dropped open and Gabe cursed soundly.

He opened his mouth to assure her that the feeling would pass and he would be his normal self soon enough, but something else entirely came out. "I want ye. I never allowed myself te believe it, or even *think* it until these past few days, but it is true. I have never liked ye te continue on as an actress and a spy because, in part, I was concerned fer yer safety, but if I am truly honest...I detested the thought of ye with another man. I still do. Everrah time ye flirt with a man, touch him, whisper to him, or allow him te gaze at ye as a stallion does a mare, I feel it," he pressed a hand to the bandages covering his stomach, "here." He shook his head. "I cannae name all th' feelings tha' ye rouse in me, Mary, but I knoo fer certain that I desire ye."

His skin was taut and his heart thudded madly in his chest as he gazed at Mary, awaiting a response. He had surprised her, of that he had no doubt. Hell, he had surprised *himself*.

Nervousness churned its way through his stomach at her silence, and Gabe found his mouth running away with him once more. "I think aboot ye. I think aboot th' way yer hips move, aboot the way yer hair would fall over yer shoulders as ye rode me. I think aboot bending ye over a chair, or a table, or any number of damned pieces of furniture te take ye from behind, and swiving ye long into th' night. I think aboot making ye scream my name, and the dreamy look in yer grey eyes as ye come. And *God*, I think aboot yer breasts. Pert and smooth with dusky nipples tha' I want te pull into my mouth and feast upon." By now his raging erection would be painfully obvious to her, tenting the towel at his waist, but he could not bring himself to care. He was laying himself out before her. And by damn, if she let him have her, he would be grateful for his second chance. "I want ye. I *need* ye."

MARY STOOD near the foot of the bed in the inn's cramped bedchamber, shock and arousal swirling around and working their way through her.

She had been so certain that he hated her. That he believed her unfit to be a spy and disapproved of her life's journey. In a way he had, but not for the reasons she had let herself believe all these years.

Her heart pumped a staccato beat in her chest as she gazed at him. He wore naught but a towel about his waist and down his thighs, his arousal beneath it all but straining in its eagerness. The sight sent another flood of warmth straight down her middle to pool at the apex of her thighs.

His face was still swollen, and the purple discolouration that came with the beginnings of bruising started to show around the cracks on his cheekbones and lips. The light of the low burning fire mingled with the brightness of the sunset shining in from the room's one window, lighting him in half wavering and half still light. The effect was beautiful.

Mary's stomach quivered as she took in his appearance. He was in earnest, standing before her, spilling his feelings on the table and waiting for her response. She could sense his desperation and fear of rejection.

As much as she wanted to ease his discomfort, she could

not help but point out the painful truth. "You could have had me last night, Gabriel. *You* left *me* in that bed. I had very obviously been willing to give myself to you, but you made your excuses *while still inside me* and clambered off the bed as though the hounds of hell were at your heels."

Remorse filled his features. "It was wrong of me, Mary. Ye surprised me. *Frightened* me."

She gave him a puzzled frown. *Frightened*?

He shook his head helplessly. "I cannae think of how t' explain." He hesitated. "I didnae ken ye were...tha' ye were a maiden, Mary."

A nervous tingle shot its way through Mary's stomach. *He knows. Damn it, he knows.* How could a man tell something like that?

"I didnae wish te hurt ye. I was confused and surprised. It took me off guard and I did wha' a coward would do. I fled. I apologize, Mary. I didnae mean te make ye feel unwanted. Because damn it, ye're anything but."

As much as she wished to take his words for what they were—both flattering and comforting—there was one more issue that remained unresolved. "What of twelve years ago? What of when you abandoned me for Scotland?" Her lip quivered. "I heard you," she continued on a whisper. "That day in the streets of Carlisle, I heard you speaking to the Misses Smithe."

Gabe grimaced. "Aw, damn, Mary, ye were nae meant te hear tha'."

She crossed her arms over her chest. "Evidently."

He tentatively gripped her hands within his, pulling her arms from their defensive stance. "I was afraid even then, Mary. I was too proud te admit my true feelings. My father had just died, and despite his absence from my life fer so long, I felt tha' I suddenly needed te be the man tha' he couldnae be fer mum. I needed te protect my mum. The second we left

Carlisle I missed ye. I deeply regretted nae speaking te ye. I said as much in my letters..."

"Letters?" Mary pulled her bottom lip between her teeth and worried the tender flesh.

"Aye. Did ye read them?"

Mary regretfully shook her head. "I burned them unopened."

His lips thinned, but he nodded. "Aye, and ye had reason te." His hands tightened over hers. "I'm verra sorry, Mary."

She gazed into his warm, blue eyes as he spoke.

"Despite how I treated ye, yer friendship meant a lot te me." He cringed. "An' despite how I behaved last night, yer offering was more than tempting." His voice deepened, "Ye make me yearn fer ye, leannan. Ye make me *burn*."

His words were a soothing balm to her aching heart. And his cockstand was very clear evidence that his words held truth.

One thing was certain. Mary would *not* waste this opportunity. If Gabe wanted her, then have her he shall.

She closed the short distance separating them and lifted her arms around his shoulders to tangle her fingers in his curly chocolate locks. "Take me, Gabe," she whispered. "However you want me."

The muscles in his jaw jumped. "Are ye certain tha' is wha' ye want, leannan?"

She looked up into his glittering blue eyes. "Yes."

His reaction was instantaneous. He wrapped his arms tightly around her to hold her anchored to him and his mouth crushed down onto hers. She released a short moan of surprise at his speed, but swiftly melted into his kiss. He fisted his hands in the fabric of her dusty day dress as he pressed her firmly into his chest.

The metallic taste of Gabe's blood entered her mouth as the split in his lip reopened. Gabriel didn't seem to mind, so neither did she. He kissed her long and hard, his tongue lapping fervently at the inside of her mouth.

With his lips still locked with hers, he withdrew his arms from about her and pulled frantically at her clothes. Mary aided him, leading his hands to the fastenings at her front. He fumbled with the small buttons, but finally twisted them open.

With tongues intertwining and breath mingling heatedly between them, Gabe pushed her dress off her shoulders to slide down her body and into a pile on the floor. Her chemisette and woollen stockings soon followed, until she stood nude before him.

He reached up to tug gently on Mary's already falling coiffure until her hair hung loose about her shoulders.

His eyes half-lidded, he reverently ran his fingers through her hair. "Yer hair," he groaned. "So fine... So pretty..."

He wrapped his arms tightly around her once more and lifted her bodily in his arms, bringing her to the bed to lay her atop the counterpane. He climbed up after her, kneeling between her legs.

"Not a little waif any longer," he said, the timbre of his voice deep and rumbling.

She tilted her head to gaze quizzically at him, but he dipped to press his lips to her neck. He licked, nipped, and teased the side of her neck, her collarbone, and the upper swells of her breasts.

Her hands found his soft hair once more and she dug her fingers in. She felt hot. Hot and eager. Her hips rose off the counterpane of their own accord, seeking his touch and the satisfaction she knew would come with it.

"Be patient, leannan." He grinned against the skin between her breasts.

He slid his lips lightly up one mound until he reached her

nipple, then leisurely sucked it into his mouth, pulling a gasp of delight from her.

He groaned, the vibration tingling across her breasts, and then scraped at her bud with his teeth. She gasped, and her hands tightened in his hair, her hips lifting up once more.

He grunted. "Damn it, Mary, ye'll be the death of me."

Lifting one hand off the counterpane and relying on the other to support his weight, Gabe slid the tips of his fingers over her waist. She quivered, gooseflesh erupting over her skin at his sensuous touch.

"I cannae wait," he ground out.

Mary whimpered as he left her breast, the air in the room sending a chill over her damp, puckering skin.

He lowered himself down her body until his head was settled between her thighs. It might be the raw need fogging her mind, but Mary was utterly at sixes and sevens as to what he might be doing.

He pressed her knees apart, splaying her wide open for his delectation. Heat spread over her cheeks as his eyes lit with fiery desire. Without preamble, he spread her feminine folds and pressed his mouth to her most private area.

"*Oh*!" She breathed. "Oh, Gabe!"

His tongue swirled around the small nub there, the feeling was similar to that which she had experienced with his fingers, but oh, so much more delicious!

He lapped and licked, swirling and flicking his tongue over her sensitive nub.

It was a shocking intimacy, but she could not complain. In fact, she could scarcely think at all. Her incoherent moans of delight echoed off the walls of the room, each one seemingly encouraging Gabe to increase the pace of his amorous attentions.

Her moans turned rapidly into short, heavy gasps as she arched her back, her head pressing firmly into the pillow.

Her fingers sought out his hair and she twined them through the ruffled locks, tighter...tighter, as he wound her closer to the explosion she knew was sure to come.

Flicking his tongue faster and increasing his pressure, Gabe eagerly coiled her need to a feverish pitch. Stars appeared behind her eyelids in a fiery display of light, her hoarse cry of gratification erupting from her as her pleasure hit in wave after crashing wave of ecstasy.

CHAPTER 31

*G*abe stared down at Mary as she rode her orgasm, his own need pushing him to the brink of his own ill-timed eruption.

"*God*, Mary," he breathed. "Ye're beautiful."

Her expression was soft, her eyelids closed, her mouth fallen open on her echoing cry of delight.

Gripping the towel from about his waist, he tugged it off and flung it aside. He could not wait a moment longer to claim her as his own, but damn it, he could not hurt her. He *would* not hurt her.

Wrapping his arms around her, he rolled both of them so he lay on his back and she was sprawled across his chest.

"Ride me, Mary." He shifted her legs so she straddled his hips, his throbbing erection straining eagerly toward the soft skin of her stomach.

She gazed down at him with foggy confusion written across her features.

"Ye set the pace. I donnae wish te hurt ye." He guided her hips upward and over him, then lifted his hips to show her. "Take me inside ye and move as ye would ride a horse."

Comprehension dawned and her eyes lit with anticipation. With one hand holding his member, she guided him inside her as she slowly lowered herself atop him.

Gabe hissed a breath as he made the valiant attempt to restrain himself.

He gripped her hips, his fingers digging deeply into her skin as he watched her. She slid slowly downward, taking in a small amount of him at a time, each fraction of an inch a small amount of torture, far more potent and effective than anything he'd endured before.

Gabe's gaze bored into her warm, grey eyes, and a sweat broke out across his brow. He grimaced, "I donnae wish to hurt ye, Mary."

She leaned forward, pressing her hands to the uninjured part of his chest. "Hush. I give this of my own will. You are not forcing me, Gabriel."

Her gaze stayed locked with his as she abruptly lowered herself onto him, taking him in to fill her completely. She uttered a small cry of pain and Gabe grimaced again.

She took a deep breath, then hushed him again. "It was scarcely a pinch. I do not know what all the fuss about maidenheads is about."

He grinned, quick and wide, relief flooding him. "Then ride me, leannan."

Gabe's eyes rolled briefly backward as she began slow, learning her pace. The leisurely movements drove him nigh mad with need.

He guided her hips with his hands, gradually increasing her pace until he had her bouncing atop him with greater urgency. Her breasts swung with each movement, her hair falling over her shoulders and around his head, creating an auburn veil of privacy for them both.

He watched her features as she grew closer to finding her pleasure once more, and he held back. It pained him, but he held back, waiting for her to find fulfillment before he did the same.

She was a Goddess. She was a revelation. How could he have gone so many years without taking her?

Her breath came in quick gasps as she sped her pace ever more, and Gabe's heart hammered against his ribs. Her nails dug into his chest and her head arched back as she cried her delight into the room, her hot sheath squeezing around him with each wave of her pleasure.

His stomach quivered and his ballocks tightened as he let out a hoarse shout of his own and spilled himself inside her.

Replete, Mary dropped forward to lie on his heaving chest. He brought a hand up to stroke her hair, clearing it away from her face, and then twining it around his fingers.

"I donnae ken wha' te say, Mary. I have ne'er experienced anything akin te tha' in my life."

"Mmm," she hummed sleepily against his chest.

With women he had always been aloof, always holding himself back from fully engaging himself with them. But with Mary... With Mary he felt it all. She evoked a plethora of emotions in him. He revelled in every movement, every sigh, every moan of delight. He felt just how connected two people could be. He now understood why they called it *making love*, because when you've found the right woman, it showed one just how much one loved—

He stilled, his eyes growing wide—even with the swelling his injuries caused—and his previously slowing heart rate picking up speed once more. *It cannae be! Love?* He felt connected to Mary as a friend, certainly, but to love her? It was far too dangerous for him to love. It caused poor judgement and opened one up to attack. Bloody hell, what if she became pregnant with his babe?

His pulse tripped over itself. Yes, he and Mary were both spies and could ordinarily defend themselves but having one's emotions rule one's thoughts could be perilous. He could not live with himself if something happened to Mary.

Wha' have I done?

"WHAT DO you suppose we should do?" Lord Hale leaned forward, his elbows on the round table in their small, hidden meeting space.

Evelyn rubbed a finger agitatedly across her eyebrows, smoothing each one into a delicate black arch, while she listened to the others talk. She had explained in detail what had occurred in the dungeons and now they thought of what course of action to take.

"We go after him, eh wot?" Cecil Piper said.

"Naturally," Hale replied. "But who shall go? What direction shall we take? And what of our rendezvous?"

"We will send Lady Kerr's giant and another loyal brute so we might enjoy the last days of this house party, eh wot?"

Hale raised an eyebrow. "You trust them to carry out the task after the failure in the dungeons?"

"Indeed." Lord Reddington tapped the table with his index finger. "How do we know we can trust them?"

Piper rolled his eyes at the others. "They will be more than eager to prove themselves capable of carrying out the task."

Hale nodded. "Excellent."

"As for where they will go," Cecil continued, "we will send them to London. It is the most obvious place for a rendezvous with whomever is higher up in the chain of command."

"But what of Miss White?" Lord Boxton asked. "Is she a target, as well?"

"No," Evelyn finally cut in. "She was just as she seemed, a harmless—albeit remarkably talented in seduction—actress. I'm certain that she thought it all a grand erotic game. We must find Mr. Spencer, however. And when we do, we must kill him."

A BIRD CHIRPING an early morning song somewhere in the distance slowly brought Mary awake. She stretched her arms languidly above her head, a satisfied smile pulling at her lips. She was, she would grant, a mite sore, particularly after their third bout of lovemaking in the night. But she was most certainly happy.

She opened her eyes. The curtains had been opened sometime in the morn—had they closed them last night?—and sunlight streamed in to brighten the small, threadbare room. It must be nearly eight of the morning, mayhap even later. Perhaps she had better rouse Gabriel so they might be on their way.

"Gabe—" She turned her head to wake him, but his pillow was bare. No Gabe.

Sitting up, she looked around the room. "Gabriel?"

His trunk sat, closed, upon the only chair in the room, but all other evidence of his presence, or of the events of last night, was gone.

She flung the coverlet aside and rose, nude, from the bed. The sun warmed her bared skin through the window, but a chill ran through her bones. Why had he left? Surely if he regretted being with her, he would not have made love to her twice more.

She internally shook herself. There was no sense in having such thoughts. Gabe was probably arranging equipage or requesting a meal or tea brought to their room... *Ooh*. In which case, she had better dress.

Quickly performing her morning ablutions, Mary set about preparing for the day. She washed her hair with the new soap she had specially bought before their assignment.

Something felt different within her. Her body veritably vibrated with joy in the aftermath of her night with Gabriel. He'd described the ways that he'd imagined having her, and they'd certainly explored some last night.

Her stomach quivered and her heart leapt at the memory as she quickly dried her hair with a towel then left it loose to dry further. She packed the dress of last evening and selected a front-fastening cerulean blue travelling frock with petticoats and stockings and put them on.

Gabriel had been nigh insatiable in their lovemaking. He'd given particular attention to every part of her body, kissing nearly every bit of skin. She'd attempted to do the same with him, but as most of his torso was covered in bandages, she'd settled for what was left exposed. He was truly marvellous.

Removing her brush and hairpins from her trunk, she sat at the aging dressing table and brushed the tangles from her hair. Within moments, she had a serviceable knot at the base of her neck, secured in place with several hairpins. She pulled a silver chain with a single sapphire pendant and she put it around her neck. It was simple and understated and she adored it. In fact, it was her favourite piece of jewellery, which was why she so seldom wore it.

With one final gaze in the mirror, she glanced at the door. *Where is Gabe?* He'd been gone for far longer than she would have imagined if he was merely acquiring a meal and a means for travel. Could something have gone awry?

Worry began to buzz in her stomach and she wrung her hands. "Where are you, Gabe?" she whispered.

"Likey tol' ye," the innkeeper said, "I cn git ol' Richie t'drive 'e an missus a' Lonnon ore ye takkey coach."

Gabe carefully disguised his disgust as the innkeeper spat on the coarse wooden floor of the taproom.

Gabe said in his practiced English accent, "My wife does not care for the stage or mail coaches. I would prefer to hire Richie to drive a hackney."

The large, aging innkeeper affected a sigh, his nauseatingly odorous breath wafting around Gabe and hovering there. "I cn see if'n Richie'll go. But it'll cost-ye."

Gabe nodded once as the lumbering oaf left.

A stagecoach or the mail coach would be far easier for Gabe to control himself within, as they would have an audience. But they were also far more dangerous to their identities and their safe escape. So a hackney it would be. Alone. In a hack. For a minimum of ten hours...with a *very* tempting Mary.

Gabe cursed under his breath. It would be more challenging than ever before; now that he had experienced Mary in his bed, he knew what he was missing if he did not take her again. And damn it, she was too alluring by half. He knew he could not resist. He had already told himself last evening that he mustn't continue on with Mary, that because of his *feelings* for her he must once more abandon their relationship.

But he couldn't... He had sated his initial lust for her and then could not resist but take his time with her. Not once, but twice more he tasted, nipped, and kissed every inch of her before sinking himself deep inside her heat over and over...

Bloody hell. He was indeed in serious trouble.

"Richie'll takkey. It'll costey fi quid."

Gabe's eyebrows slid skyward. "*Five quid*? Good God, man, I am not *purchasing* a carriage from you."

The bloated man picked something out of what few teeth he had remaining in his mouth with a thick, dirty finger.

Gabe sighed and pulled his purse out. He had no time to quibble over prices. He had already delayed returning to Mary long enough.

"Direct the maid with the food tray to our room. When we have concluded our meal, I will bring our things down. Have Richie and the equipage ready in the innyard, if you will." He handed five one-pound bank notes to the greedy innkeeper, then turned toward the stairs, taking them two at a time.

He entered their room and closed the door swiftly behind himself.

"Gabe! Goodness, where have you been?" Her spine was stiff and her voice soft.

"Were ye worried, then, Mary?"

"*Yes!*" She spread her hands at her sides and sighed exasperatedly.

Despite himself, his heart warmed at her concern. He strode forward and clasped her shoulders in his hands. "No need te fret."

She sighed again, and for the briefest of moments, he could have sworn that her chin quivered. Entirely helpless to stop himself, he opened his arms to her.

"There, now, leannan," he muttered.

She curled herself into the circle of his arms. His lips pulled back in a hiss as he clenched his jaw. His wounds had not been so painful last evening, but, he supposed his exertions might have reopened the wounds at his chest; his thoughts had been so muddled, he hadn't bloody well checked.

Pushing past the pain, he squeezed his arms a little tighter around Mary.

He pressed his mouth to the top of her head and inhaled her scent. *Mmm... Wildflowers?* She had changed her scent! Why would she do such a thing?

Although...

He took another deep inhalation. He rather liked it.

Blast. He *really* liked it, if his body's reaction to her said anything.

A light knock sounded at the door and Mary sprang away from him.

Irritated at the interruption, Gabe answered the door.

CHAPTER 32

*G*abe turned from the door with a tray of food in his hands and a smile on his lips.

"Tha' was a maid. Are ye hungry?"

At the sight of the tray, Mary realized just how ravenous she was. She had not eaten since yesterday's luncheon.

The loud rumble of Mary's stomach filled the room, and Gabe grinned, the motion pulling at the scabs forming on his lips. Mary sheepishly placed her hands over her middle and Gabe laughed.

"I will take your stomach's word for it," he said, winking an amused blue eye at her.

He brought the tray to the bed.

"Shall we use our imaginations?" he asked. "It will be an alfresco meal, but inside and atop a dishevelled coverlet."

Something about his willingness to try for humour brought a pleasing warmth to her chest.

She clambered onto the bed.

"I sent the curricle away this morning with an elderly man from Brighton."

The bed dipped with his weight as he sat atop it, the tarnished silver platter placed strategically between them.

Mary settled her skirts around her ankles and gazed eagerly at the array of cheeses, meats, breads, and fruits. The scent alone was enough to have her salivating uncontrollably.

"This man knows not to give your direction?" she asked.

He motioned for her to eat and she reached enthusiastically for a piece of cheese and bread and took a bite of both. *Oh heavens!* What deliciously fresh bread.

"As a matter of fact..." Gabe selected a handful of berries and began popping them in his mouth. "I spoke at great length about my plans to ride west. I knew better than to trust him to keep information to himself, so I gave him incorrect information in the hopes that Lady Kerr, her brutes, and the other traitors will believe him."

Mary ate a succulent slice of roasted ham, then followed that with a plump grape.

Gabe cleared his throat. "I must apologize to ye, Mary." His blue gaze rose to meet hers. "I didnae believe ye when ye suggested Lady Kerr as a possible suspect. I shouldae trusted yer instincts and watched her fer suspicious activity as well. I apologize fer nae listening. I was verra, *grievously* wrong."

Mary's chest swelled with gratitude. "Thank you, Gabe."

She unfolded a napkin and laid it on the mussed counterpane.

"I hate to cut our 'alfresco' meal short, but we must go." Gabe dabbed at his mouth with his napkin. "It will take us at least ten hours te reach London from here and it is already half of nine. We must report t' Hydra and find a way te disappear until the ball, else our identities may be compromised."

Mary placed several chunks of cheese, two rolls, and slices of meat into the napkin and folded it up.

"Excellent thought." He filled his own napkin and tucked it into his pocket. "Shall we go?"

"No."

"*No?*" He imitated her accent.

"No," she said. "I wish to have a look at your wounds to ensure they are sufficiently clean and bind them once more before we leave."

"*Ach*, Mary, donnae fash yerself. They are nae as deep as they appeared."

"I will not have you get infection while in my care, Gabriel Ashley."

He sighed. "Verra well."

He quickly rose and removed his clothes down to his breeches, stockings, and boots. Mary watched in awe and, she was slightly ashamed to say, with rapidly growing desire. His body was rippled and sculpted, hard and sleek.

There is no time, Mary dear. Keep your lustful thoughts buried deep until you have more time.

She doctored him in as detached a manner as she could manage, but for the odd hiss of breath at a particularly bad amount of bruising.

"How does it feel?" she asked as she finished cleaning the last of his wounds with a wet cloth.

"Fine." The deep cadence of his voice sent a quiver through her.

Detached, Mary. Do not allow his stunningly beautiful male body distract you from your purpose. Escape the traitors and return to London.

Mary finished binding his body with torn strips of clean linen she requested of the innkeep.

"That will do nicely." She turned her gaze up to his face and was arrested by the sight.

His no-longer-swollen but scabbed and badly bruised face was dark with the heat of desire. She had seen that expression on his face in the evening yesterday and twice through the night. He wanted her.

Her body heated in response to his lust, a quivering anticipation bubbling through her, spreading its way through her body until it settled at the heart of her feminine place. Her breasts grew heavy within the confines of her dress.

Mary licked her suddenly dry lips and his gaze dropped to watch.

His muscles twitched as he moved to take her in his arms, but another knock at the door halted him.

Gabe cursed soundly as he began dressing himself.

Placing a hand over her thundering heart, Mary moved to stand behind the door. "Yes?" She called.

"It's Richie, missus. Me master said t' tell ye when we was done hookin' up the hack n' t' see if'n ye were ready t' go."

She turned to glance back at Gabe, who stood already nearly fully dressed, then turned to call through the door, "Thank you, Richie. We will be down directly."

She listened for Richie's retreating footsteps then moved to retrieve her trunks.

Gabe left his cravat untied and ran his fingers through his hair before placing a dark hat atop his head. "Are ye ready?"

THE DIM RAYS of sun shone through the hackney's window, lending a soft glow to the dingy interior. The sounds of the horses' hooves thundered along the narrow, wet road and the ill-sprung wheels jostled the hack's inhabitants. Rain pounded the roof as they drove, echoing the deafening din of Gabe's hammering heart.

An involuntary groan escaped him for the hundredth time. *Why?* What the devil had possessed him to sit *beside* Mary when a perfectly acceptable seat was across from them? Her alluring body brushed against him with every movement of the carriage. Two damned hours he had been sitting in this hack, filled with want for the alluring woman.

He was teeming with lust, rampant with a burning, aching, urgent, smoldering desire. It was driving him mad.

Damn. Her scent filled the hack. The flowery, hypnotic aroma made him wish that he could lick it from every inch of her body.

His palms and forehead were damp with sweat, his cock was straining against the falls of his breeches and his entire body was tense. Gabe closed his eyes and allowed a litany of blasphemes to flow through his mind.

He loved her, damn it. He could not risk her safety by continuing on with her, by fogging his mind with emotion, thus endangering both of them. But by God he would do anything to have her again. And again. And again…

Another groan escaped him and his eyes snapped open as he shifted in his seat.

Mary turned her gaze on him from her view out the window and released a short, arousing gasp.

"Gabe!" She touched her small cool hand to his forehead, the contact sending a shock of awareness through him. "You've a fever!" She worried her bottom lip. "Oh, Gabe, perhaps we had better stop at the next inn and have another look at—"

"*No!*"

Her eyes widened in shock at his harsh tone.

"I apologize, Mary. We donnae have time te—"

"But look at the state of you! You are in no condition to be riding for the next eight hours in this ill-sprung hack. It'll jostle you to death!"

"It's nae the hack that will be the death of me, Mary."

"I do not understand." A delicate frown furrowed her brow and Gabe's control snapped.

"I cannae—" He broke off as he crushed his bruised lips to hers in an all-encompassing kiss.

His breath came heavily through his lust-flared nostrils as his tongue tangled with hers.

Without breaking their kiss, Gabe sank to his knees on the carriage floor before her, pulling her skirts up past her thighs. With trembling fingers he fumbled with the buttons of his falls.

"But your fever," she broke their kiss to gasp.

Gabe shook his head. "'Tis nae a fever, Mary. 'Tis want, plain and simple. I want ye...so badly."

"Oh," she breathed. "Oh, yes, Gabe."

Finally free, he reached beneath her skirts to slide her arse toward the edge of the seat. The seat was just at the right height for him to slide himself deep within her silken heat and kiss her soft mouth simultaneously. They fit perfectly.

She moaned against his lips as he reached the hilt. He responded with a soul-deep growl before pumping frantically into her, taking exactly what he craved, what he *needed*. And, by damn, did he need her.

His fingers dug into her hips as he drove into her, again and again.

Breaking their kiss, Mary's head dropped backward, exposing the soft underside of her jaw and her beautifully arched neck. He bent forward, following the line of her throat with his tongue, still pumping deep into the depths of her womanhood.

"Tha gaol agam ort, Mary," Gabe whispered in Gaelic against her neck. *I love you, Mary.*

She moaned as he thrust faster.

"Bheir mi gràdh thu fad mo bheatha. You agus cha robh duine eile." *I will love you my whole life. You and no other.*

He felt the force of his completion build to fever pitch, but he held back.

Desperate, he released her arse with one hand to rub his thumb into her sweet folds.

"*Oh*," she breathed. "Oh, Gabe!"

Her breath came in erratic huffs as she clenched around him. He watched as she came apart, her body tensing as her pleasure took her.

Gabe let himself go, holding her tightly against him as he pumped his seed deep inside her.

CHAPTER 33

ary was jolted awake as the carriage rounded a corner too fast.

"Oi!" Gabe thumped a fist on the ceiling. "Apologies, leannan." He returned his arm to its place across her shoulders.

She covered a yawn with the back of her hand. "Mmm, it's just fine, Gabe." She blinked the sleep from her eyes and looked out the window from her position on Gabe's shoulder. "What time is it?"

He squinted out the window towards the sun hiding behind grey clouds. "Nearly a quarter of seven, I would say."

Mary sat forward and out of the circle of Gabe's arm. "A quarter of seven? My goodness we must have nearly reached London!"

She settled back into her seat and smiled at Gabe. It was no wonder she had fallen asleep along the ride. The man had exhausted her with his lovemaking. Why, just the thought of it sent chills over her skin.

"Hydra will expect us te report te him directly. I have already given Richie the direction," Gabe said, running a finger along her jaw.

"Yes," she said, her eyelids growing heavy at the contact.

"Ye changed yer scent."

"Hm? Oh." She smiled. "Yes. I hadn't the chance to use my new soap and cream until I washed at the inn this morning. I found it at a shop on Bond Street just after I received my new attire from Mrs. McPhee. I loved the scent, so I bought a small crate full. Silly, no?"

"Nae," his voice had deepened and was rough as gravel. He brushed a strand of hair away from her face, hooking it around her ear and her heart fluttered. "What is it?"

"Mmm?" She closed her eyes and turned her face into his palm.

"What is the scent? It is a floral smell that I cannae place... Wildflowers?"

"Lilac."

He pressed his lips to her neck, kissing a place just under her ear and sending shivers through her. "Mmm," his hum sent vibrations through her neck.

She tilted her head back to give him better access.

"Tha gaol agam ort," he mumbled. It was the second time she had heard him say that, but she had not the faintest idea what it meant.

"Pardon?" she asked.

He stilled, then pulled her earlobe in-between his teeth. "I like how ye smell."

Somehow, she doubted that was what he said, but she simply could not concentrate with him doing—*oh*!

Gabe cursed soundly as the hack slowly bounced to a halt. Mary groaned. *Too soon*!

Gratefully Richie did not open their door, so Mary had a moment to gather her wits, press her chilled hands to her heated cheeks, and pat at her fallen coiffure.

Gabe gently gripped one of her hands in his. "Donnae fash yerself, Mary. Ye look lovely."

She grinned broadly at his praise, warmth spreading through her chest. "Thank you, Gabriel."

He nodded once at her. "The rain will likely take it down anyway."

Before she could say a word in response, Gabe swooped his head down to capture her lips in a quick, passionate kiss before he pressed the door's latch and swung it wide. With a naughty wink, he jumped to the cobblestoned ground, his boots clicking and echoing off the nearby buildings. He pulled down the step, then held his hand out to her.

With a secret smile, Mary placed her hand in his and allowed him to aid her descent, not caring a whit that the rain pelted down on them in sheets.

The air, ordinarily thick with coal smoke, now held a dense humidity, as well. The day was warm for early June, the combination creating a damp stickiness between her heavily padded breasts. Yet still, her lips curved up in a private grin as she recalled the past hours in the hack with Gabriel.

They had been ensconced in their own little pocket of heaven, tattered and jostling though it was.

Gabe then pulled their sopping trunks from the back of the hackney and flipped Richie a coin, which the driver caught in the air and placed quickly in his pocket. Mary turned toward the tavern, a familiar haunt for Hydra's band of spies, and prepared to bring her trunks down the alley and into the back door, which led to the hidden room which they always had reserved.

THE HAIR on the back of Gabe's neck rose, instinct of old catching hold of him, as Mary strolled down the narrow alley. He quickly pressed a hand to his outer coat pocket and squeezed. A small yelp told him he had been correct.

In one smooth motion, Gabe turned and knelt before an urchin boy scarcely more than five years old, his hair, face, and clothing unclean, his eyes filled with fear, and his features gaunt and dripping with rainwater.

"You will find no coin in there, lad," he said, affecting his practiced English accent.

"I aint done noffin, mister!" The child cried, his face wreathed in horror.

"I will not have you punished," he said in as soothing a voice as he could manage. "Where are your parents?"

"Me mum's a whore an' I aint got no pa. Mum don't want me 'round." The boy swiped at his dripping nose with the sleeve of his coat. "But I c'n take care o' meself, aye." He blinked rapidly to clear his eyes of water.

"I am sorry to hear that, and I'm sure you can." He loosened his grip on the child's hand, lost in thought for a moment. "I have an offer for you."

The child turned his face up at Gabe in hesitation. "Wot kind o' ffer?"

"An *offer*. What is your name, lad?"

"Mary, mister," the child said in a small voice.

Gabe's eyebrows rose. A girl! "I beg your pardon, Mary, I did not mean to offend."

"It aint noffin." The girl shrugged.

"My lady friend's name is Mary, as well."

The girl looked over Gabe's shoulder, presumably at Mary. Gabe kept his eyes on the hungry child.

"Yeah?"

"Yes," Gabe affirmed. "She has been my friend since I was a child not much older than you." He smiled down at the little girl. "Now, I have a quid for you if you do me one favour."

The girl's eyes lit with greed and worry simultaneously. "Wot faver?" Water sprayed from the child's lips as she spoke.

"I will tell you a direction. If you go to a man's house and tell him I am waiting here for him, I will send along a note that says he has to pay you one quid." He held up a hand to halt her agreement. "*If* you return with the man, I will give you a hot meal, *two* quid, and an opportunity for you to go to school."

The girl gazed at him skeptically. "No man gives away all that fer noffin, sir. Not even no toff."

"Ask my lady friend," Gabe gestured toward where Mary stood smiling at the child. "She went to the same school."

"You one o' them wot teaches at a skool?"

"No." Gabe grinned. "But a very good friend of mine is."

The girl nodded, swiping at her nose once more. "Okay, sir. Where's the man wot you need me t' talk to?"

SIR CHARLES BRADLEY placed a hand at little Mary's drenched back and led her through the side door to the tavern, through the hall, and directly into the back meeting room.

"Do not be afraid, Mary," he soothed, removing his sopping hat from his head.

"I aint afraid o' noffin," she said, though Charles knew the sound of fear when he heard it.

The door opened and both Gabe and Mary stood from their seats near the fire. Charles ushered little Mary past the trunks, which sat on the floor near the entrance, and directed her into the centre of the comfortingly familiar room.

Tension hit him like a wave as he neared his two agents. *Something has happened*. Something of a sexual nature, he would wager. It was about damned time.

"Welcome back," he said jovially.

Gabe sketched a short bow and Mary curtsied prettily with mumbles of "sir" and "Hydra."

With a smile, Gabe greeted the child. "I owe you two quid,

Mary. And a place in a very special school." He raised an eyebrow at Charles.

"Yes," Charles agreed.

"I need to speak with my friend here," Gabe continued. "Why do we not see about getting you that hot meal that I promised and then we will discuss it?"

Little Mary gave him a cherub smile as Gabe led her from the room, calling for a servant to assist.

Charles sat on the under-stuffed armchair, stretching his legs out before him and crossing them at the ankles. He was eager to return home to his *very* pregnant wife and adopted son. Not only was their meeting important, however, but he was damned curious about what had happened on their assignment. He tossed his hat atop the occasional table at his elbow.

Gabe returned to the room and sat across from Charles on the settee next to Mary.

"Well?" Charles prompted. "Shall you start with whether or not you retrieved the documents and move on to what the devil happened to Gabe's face?"

"We have the documents," Gabe said, removing the sheets of parchment from an inner pocket and placing them on the table between them. "But there is much more that we need to discuss than just these documents."

Charles examined the documents and placed them in his own pocket before he gestured them on. "Proceed."

Gabe cringed as he pointed at the damage done to his face. "Lady Kerr is to blame for my present state, sir."

"I apologize for interrupting." Mary leaned forward eagerly. "Hydra, Gabriel is in danger of compromising his identity. Lady Kerr knows his face and suspects his true purpose of attending the house party. I managed to release him from capture in such a way that Lady Kerr would not implicate me, but as she and her men remain alive, Gabriel is in danger."

"What do you propose, Mary?" Charles asked. "I require him for this assignment, and for several afterward. Shall we change his face?"

Mary shook her head, an auburn lock of hair falling out of her loosened, damp coiffure. "I propose an alternate plan. Mr. Spencer has a history in the Americas with his uncle. I propose that we send him back, then Gabe and I go into hiding until the ball at Lord Sheffield's house in town on Thursday."

"Perhaps you had better explain from the beginning."

Charles listened as the two spoke of their assignment, of the known traitors involved in this scheme, the potential for others, of their overhearing a discussion and the time and place of the traitors' rendezvous, of the exchange of the documents, Gabe's capture, and their eventual escape.

At the mention of Lord Anthony Boxton, Charles felt a surge of anger rush through him. The scurrilous dog had taken part in the very near ruination of his sister, Anna's, virtue and the near snuffing of her very life. The bastard was evil toward women and very much deserved to be removed to the Americas as his friend had been.

Charles ran his fingers through his short blond locks in agitation. "Well, Mary, you must attend that ball. Gabe, you will take her as the coachman and I will ensure Stevens attends in Lord Hale's entourage."

"It isnae safe for her to go alone, Hydra!" Gabe exclaimed.

"She will be safe enough. All my men are on assignments, recovering from their injuries, or damned well missing," Charles growled. "I cannot contact anyone else, let alone send them on this assignment. If, however, someone comes to me with a report of a completed assignment, I will add them to your party."

Charles' gaze switched between Gabe and Mary's uneasy miens, a grin on his lips. "You both did an excellent job recovering the documents. I am sorry for your injuries, Gabe. I have Dr. Claridge in town examining my wife presently, if you would like me to send him to examine you."

Gabe shook his head. "Nae, sir."

"Very well." Charles leaned forward to rest his elbows on his knees, then clasped his hands together. "I gather from what you have said that Mary is the target of the other men's attentions. As much gratification as I would find in simply putting Boxton and Reddington on a ship and sailing them off to the Americas, I must discover who else is involved in this ring of traitors. Mary *will* attend the ball—armed, naturally—and cozy up to them. Watch them. When they leave the ball, alert Stevens and Gabe and discretely follow them to the rendezvous location. Take care to be close enough to hear them, but far enough to not be caught."

"Yes, sir," they both said in unison.

"Because of your potentially compromised identity, Gabe, you will remain in hiding until the time of the ball. Mary, if you wish to avoid contact with the traitors, you are welcome to remain in hiding until Thursday, as well. I have my alternate town house set up for your needs should you wish to use it. Harris and Barrows are both still in recovery there."

"Thank you, sir."

"In the mean time, I will purchase passage for Mr. Anthony Spencer on a ship to the Americas scheduled to sail *after* the ball. If the traitors feel they have time for their rendezvous, they will not send any men away to chase after you; every traitor's presence is pertinent."

"We had best be wary, sir," Mary warned. "Lady Kerr will be incensed and looking for us. She will have known to come to London."

Charles nodded. "Noted. Remain alert and watch for tails. Inform me if you notice anything suspicious."

"Yes, sir," Mary and Gabe said in unison.

Charles moved to stand, but Mary reached toward him, halting his movement.

"My pardon, Hydra, but I must speak to you about a young lady I met at Kerr House."

Charles waited for her to continue.

"She acted as my lady's maid while we were in attendance. She is smart, capable, young, eager to learn, and in desperate need of rescuing. Lord Kerr and his cronies do unspeakable things—"

Charles raised his hand. He knew what she was going to say and he did not wish to hear it. It was a pitiful state for many young maids under their masters' control. "Can you vouch for this young lady, Mary?"

"I can, Hydra. I will. Her name is Eleanor Mable."

He nodded. "Is she receptive to our position in the Secret Service?"

Mary worried her bottom lip. "She does not yet know, sir."

"Very well." Charles understood and respected her desire to get the young woman out of such a circumstance. "I'll arrange for her withdrawal and transport. She can make a decision when she comes to London."

"Of course, sir." Mary beamed at him.

"Send a messenger 'round the town house when she arrives."

Mary clasped her hands together at her chest. "Oh, I will! Thank you, Hydra!"

"Not at all, Mary. Now, I must bid you both farewell." He placed his hat upon his head and nodded toward the door leading into the next room toward the main tavern. "I have a miniature Mary to have a talk with. We'll see if the lass has a future in the Secret Service, as well. If so, I'll send her to Hermes at the school."

Gabriel grinned. "But when you do, Hydra, refer to him as Colonel Kieran Richards, if you will. No need to frighten the waif."

Charles laughed. "Indeed." With that, he turned on his heel and quietly left the room.

CHAPTER 34

"*A*re ye ready?" Gabe pressed his lips to the side of Mary's neck as she gazed at her reflection in her dressing table's reflective glass, several days later.

The fluttering reawakening of burgeoning desire worked its way through her as Gabe continued to kiss a path up to the dangling pearl earring hanging from her ear.

She batted his hand away. "Naughty man," she scolded. "I only just managed to finish putting myself back together from your last eager bout of lovemaking. I haven't the time to do so again."

He gazed at her reflection with a wicked grin. "Just once more, lass. I will make it quick. And I promise no' te touch yer pretty hair."

She clucked her tongue and winked. "Shame on you, Gabe. We have a busy evening and I cannot be late."

His smile fled as he pushed away from her chair to pace her modestly appointed bedchamber in Charles' second house in town.

"I donnae like this, Mary."

She finished applying her powder and turned to face Gabe.

"You have said as much before, Gabriel, but I am a spy, and this is my assignment. I must follow through."

He rushed to her with exaggerated dramatic flair, falling to his knees and gripping her hands tightly in his. "Ach, Mary, donnae hurt me so! Donnae be a spy any longer. Flee with me! We can go te—"

Mary laughed. "I am not certain, but I think that might be treasonous." She pulled her hands from his and rose to retrieve her long, emerald green silk scarf, then draped it over her shoulders. "I am going on this assignment, Gabe. All will be well. I am perfectly capable of handling myself, I assure you."

He sighed and stood, leaning a hip against her dressing table and crossing his arms across his chest. "Verra well. Do ye have yer pistol?"

"In my reticule."

"Yer knife?"

"You know very well that it is strapped to my thigh."

His gaze heated. "Show me."

She shook her finger at him. "For shame, Gabriel! Now dirty your face, for heaven's sake. You are far too clean for a coachman."

He moved to sit in her place at the dressing table, but something caught his eye and he hesitated.

"My God..." he said in wonder.

She followed his gaze and knew immediately what he'd seen, and she cursed herself for bringing it to the safe house, but she couldn't resist. She'd missed it during her days on assignment.

Mary's cheeks heated embarrassingly, high on her cheekbones. Goodness, displaying her body for men to see did not cause her to blush, but *this* did? How silly of her.

She turned her gaze away and busied herself with gazing in her tall mirror as he picked up an item from atop her chest of drawers.

"Ye still have this conch shell, Mary?" he asked quietly.

She could feel his gaze at her back, but she refused to return it. She knew what she would find there, but it oddly left her feeling afraid. Somehow her secrets seemed to be revealing themselves, suddenly splayed out in the open for him to see... the long-buried softness in her heart for the boy who had given her the gift and the man who had abandoned her, taking her crushed heart with him. And it terrified her.

Nervous anxiety coiled itself in her stomach, fluttering and wavering with uncertainty. She knew that he found her desirable but didn't return her regard...her love. He hadn't said so, and she daren't broach he subject. It would scare him away, and now that she had him positively in her life, she couldn't risk losing him. Again.

"How... Why? Ye've kept this all these years, Mary?"

She knew what he wished to hear from her, but she couldn't. She just couldn't say the words.

Spinning to face him and running her fingers along the long string of pearls at her neck, she forced an airy smile. "Yes, I have. I think it's pretty. Now, will you *please* finish getting yourself ready?"

He very obviously wished to say more, his judicious gaze seemingly seeing through her veil of fear, but he wisely took a seat at her dressing table and began to apply oil to his hair and soot to his face. He was already attired accordingly in a worn, brown woollen coat and matching vest and breeches. Each article of clothing was appropriately scuffed and marked. He had spent the days since their return to London growing mutton chops specifically for his role at the ball.

He thought they looked rather dashing, but Mary preferred his face clean and—*oh pooh*. Who was she kidding? She thought him handsome no matter what his choice of facial hair. Handsome, muscled, bold, talented, kind, and oh, so arousing!

The past four days had been spent lying abed with him in one bout of lovemaking after another, with sleep and long, leisurely talks in between. She wished she could remain there with him forever, simply taking him over and over again.

She felt a heated flush begin under her layers of petticoats, chemise, corset, and green silk, and bit the inside of her cheek. Now was not the time to become distracted.

She scooped up her green, beaded reticule and slid her matching slippers on her feet.

Tonight would be simple. She had attended several balls in disguise and knew what was expected of her. This evening she was Miss Mary White. Actress and inveterate flirt.

"Success?" Gabe stood before her, his gaze hopeful, yet also full of pride. He was a dirty mess of a man, which was precisely the object.

Mary smiled at him. "Perfect."

He bowed deeply to her. "Your carriage awaits. Shall I escort you, Miss White?"

"Why yes, kind coachman. Thank you." She winked at him as she placed her gloved hand atop his dirty coat sleeve.

He led her through the corridors and down the stairs to the foyer. No one stood on guard at the door, so Gabe pulled it open before leading her down the steps and to their awaiting carriage.

Gratefully, the sky was clear and the night was cool, the lamps along the cobblestone street lending a deceptively peaceful ambiance to the otherwise perilous thoroughfares.

Gabe helped her into the carriage that sat awaiting them on the street, then climbed onto the perch, clasped the reins, and set it into motion. With each *clip-clop* of the horses' hooves and the loud rumble of the carriage's wheels over stone, they drew closer to Maison Sheffield.

Mary gazed out the window and wondered what Gabe was thinking. What an odd notion, wondering what another was thinking. She knew he did not look kindly on her going on this assignment. But it must be done. Her identity as an actress must remain intact; she simply could not refuse attendance.

Another thought that had been troubling her since they had returned to London buzzed alarmingly through her mind once more. *What am I to Gabriel*? Was she his mistress? His lover? She supposed she should not trouble herself with such thoughts until they spoke of it. But what of when this evening —and their assignment—concluded? Would he expect her to abandon her position as an actress? Would he expect her to no longer interrogate men?

If she were, indeed, his mistress, she would see the validity of such an expectation. But what if this was merely a tryst? What if he bored of her and she was left to fend for herself? Did she *wish* to continue interrogating men?

She was no longer certain. While she enjoyed the thrill of being on stage, of taking on a role so unlike herself, of the undivided absorption of her audience, it would be difficult to leave. Taking suspects into her changing room backstage, however...well, she supposed the thrill of it was beginning to wane.

It was possible that she could discontinue her interrogation of men backstage and continue being an actress, but there would always be an expectation of her from her audience... Her name was known well enough among the gentlemen of the *ton* by now, that men would continue to approach her, expecting that she would give them a *private performance*. That obstacle was not too large to get over, however. It could be done.

But now was not the time to ruminate on anything. She must focus solely on her task.

She braced herself with one hand on the hanging straps as they rounded a turn. The carriage wheels rumbled over the cobblestoned streets, the bright glow of the lanterns passing by.

Soon, they slowed and rolled to a stop before Maison Sheffield. There was quite the crush, as they waited in line to reach the front doors. Nervousness roiled in Mary's stomach, though she did not know why. Perhaps it was that she would be without Gabriel this evening, after having been with him for the past fortnight.

Ridiculous girl with insecure and doubtful thoughts, she admonished herself.

They made their way to the front of the line and one of the Sheffield servants opened her door, holding a gloved hand out to aid her descent of the carriage steps.

She thanked him and, without glancing behind her at Gabe, made her way up the grand stairs to Maison Sheffield. She pasted an airy smile upon her lips and stood waiting to address the receiving line. The foyer was filled with shuffling debutants, their simpering mamas, and proud, sniffling dandies. She saw none of the known traitors within the entry, though they were like to be found in the card room or ballroom. The card room was a quiet place in which they could converse, and the ballroom was the perfect location in which to blend in. But Mary would find them.

The air was thick with cloying perfume, masculine soaps, powders, oils, and the stench of too-hot bodies. It was nearly overwhelming in its strength.

Her turn came to greet Lord and Lady Sheffield, and she curtsied accordingly.

"Miss White!" Lord Sheffield wheezed before dabbing his glistening forehead with a handkerchief, evidently one of the many adding to the general stench. "So pleased you could come."

"Thank you, Lord Sheffield." Mary grinned back at him. "I am honoured to have been invited."

"Do go on and enjoy yourself, my dear."

He winked at her and she turned to follow the other guests toward the ballroom. As she turned her back, she heard Lady Sheffield's strident voice. "How do you know Miss White?"

Mary felt like laughing at the thought of what the man must endure from his wife tonight. Sheffield certainly deserved every syllable of the reprimand, for he was a wicked man, indeed.

She finally reached the butler as he stood regally beside the ballroom doors.

"Your name, miss?"

"Miss Mary White," she said.

The butler turned to announce over the din of the crowd, "Miss Mary White!"

A great number of the guests turned to watch her as she entered. She held her head high and kept her air of witlessness and sensuality about her as she strolled further into the room.

The crowd began to murmur, but she determinedly ignored it. She would naturally cause a stir. She rarely did anything in the public eye as Miss White, and it was expected that the members of the *haute ton* would be curious, put-off, or furious at her attendance.

She gratefully accepted a glass of champagne from a footman and took a hearty sip.

"Mary!" a familiar voice boomed.

She turned to see Lord Reddington and Mr. Jackson striding toward her.

She smiled, forcing her eyes to crinkle in the corners. They stopped before her and sketched neat bows. She dipped in a curtsey. "Why James, Mr. Jackson! How lovely to see you here this evening."

"I was about to say the same thing," Mr. Jackson said, straightening the lace cuff of his shirt beneath his coat sleeve.

"Might I say how lovely you look this evening, Miss White? Quite in the stare of fashion!"

Mary slid her palms down the front of her shimmering green silk gown, the reticule tied to her right wrist weighing it down. "Thank you, Mr. Jackson. It is very kind of you to say."

Reddington gripped her left hand and placed a kiss to its back. "The beauty of the morning sun's gentle touch over a flowery meadow in spring pales in comparison to your radiating splendour, Mary."

Mary's lips split in a genuine smile, but she had to bite her cheek to keep from laughing at Reddington's ham-fisted compliment. "A handsome sentiment, James."

His chest puffed with pride. "Tell me you will grant me a waltz this evening, Mary."

She shook her head regretfully. "I am afraid I am not dancing this evening." She lifted her wrist into the air between them. "No dance card."

"Ah, a shame indeed, for as graceful a woman as yourself. It would be like—"

"Good evening, Miss White," the Marquess of Hale moved to stand among their small group, Lord Kerr close behind, his eyes glinting with menace.

Ah, the vile group was nearly all in attendance.

Mary curtsied. "Good evening, Lord Hale, Lord Kerr. I do hope you all had a pleasant journey from Eastbourne."

"Indeed," Lord Kerr took a gulp of dark liquid from his glass, his shrewd gaze locked on her features. "It was a shame you did not stay longer. As I understand it, you left in a hurry."

Mary waved a hand through the air. "Oh, la! You know how lovers are. One moment they are eager for a little *rough* play, and the next they become timid. Poor man," she pouted jestingly, "cowered nearly the entire journey to London! I had to give him his congé when we reached town, naturally. I cannot abide a man who does not know how to have a good time. It is such a shame, too, for I truly thought I might have had a good thing in being his mistress." She winked at the small group of men around her. Despite her convincing lie, Lords Hale and Kerr still gazed at her with suspicion.

Mary's stomach knotted, but she continued anyway. "I fear I must have broken his little heart, for I understand he has booked passage on a ship to the Americas."

"What is this? Having a delicious conversation without—" Lord Boxton squeezed his shoulders between Mr. Jackson and Lord Hale. His eyebrows shot skyward, his eyes growing wide and possessive. "Mary!"

"Good evening, Tony."

His gaze travelled brazenly over her body and his neck grew red from beneath his shirt collar. "I have a mind to spirit you away from here and—"

"Ah!" Lord Reddington interrupted, displeasure written plainly on his features. "Such an amusing anecdote."

The others gazed at him in confusion.

"Tell me, Lord Kerr," Mary broke the awkward silence, "is Lady Kerr in attendance this evening?"

He shook his head and took another sip of his drink. "I am afraid that Lady Kerr had much more pressing matters to attend to this evening."

"I see. Do please send along my well wishes to her."

He rolled his eyes but seemed to give her an odd head jiggle in acceptance.

A gentleman in a finely tailored green coat strode past, and Lord Hale halted him with a hand to his sleeve. "Wycliff!" he boomed.

The man turned, a woman on his arm, to face the group.

"Hale, always a pleasure." He turned his gaze on Mary. "And who is this?"

Boxton hurried to make the introductions. "Wycliff, this is Miss Mary White. Mary, this is Sir Humphrey Wycliff."

Mary curtseyed politely. "A pleasure to make your acquaintance, Sir Wycliff."

Wycliff gestured to the woman on his arm. "This is my dance partner, Miss Lucille—"

Reddington eagerly leapt forward to point somewhere across the ballroom. "There is our friend. I wish to introduce you, Mary. Just a moment, I shall fetch him." Reddington disappeared into the crowd.

"Lord knows it is not Pondridge," Kerr murmured.

"Inebriated in the card room again," Jackson scoffed.

A small gasp escaped Mary, but she disguised it in a laugh along with the others. Panic, swift and powerful raced through her. Lord Winning was the "friend" that Reddington wished her to meet.

Oh no, oh no, oh no! Her gaze darted about for an escape. If Frederick saw her, her cover would undoubtedly be blown. He knew her as one of his crofters' daughters and from her friendship with Gabriel as children. Her identity was going to be compromised! Oh heavens, she could be killed this very night!

Suddenly the cloying scent in the ballroom was too much.

She fanned her face. "This is quite a crush! I believe I need some air. Please excuse me."

Without waiting for a response, Mary spun on her heel, weaving her way through the sea of rainbow silks and cutaway coats toward the doors leading to the portico. Bursting into the fresh air, Mary gasped a great, long breath of the crisp night.

What was she to do now? She could not very well remain at the ball, for her identity as Miss White was paramount.

She must return to Gabriel and find Hydra.

Turning once more on her heel, she bounced, unladylike, off of a large, solid male chest.

"Oh, pardon me—" She stepped back to lift her gaze up to the man and was arrested at the sight.

Lord Boxton stood, his devouring, lascivious gaze boring menacingly into her. Her stomach quivered with fear, but she smiled, forcing it to reach her eyes.

"Hello, Tony. I apologize for my abruptness in leaving the ballroom. I had quite lost myself in the heat and required a reprieve. I appreciate your concern, but I feel much revived now."

She made to move past him, but he caught her arm. "Have I told you, Mary, of my formidable temper?"

With a brittle smile she turned her gaze up into his threateningly and frighteningly lustful countenance. Mary knew that Boxton took pleasure in abusing women, and likely enjoyed them contrite and fearful. She would play along until they were in a more private setting and could defend herself, or at least until she could get away.

"You promised me one night with you, Mary." His green gaze darkened as he spoke. "And I did not receive it."

She stepped back, prepared for his attack. "Mr. Spencer swept me away so quickly, I scarcely had time to think!"

"Did he, indeed?" His grip on her arm tightened. "Shall we take a stroll in the gardens?"

She affected a quivering lip and nodded, allowing him to lead her off of the portico and onto the brightly lit garden path. They kept walking, past the light of the torches and lanterns, and into the shadows.

The night was dark and the garden was still. Even the night creatures seemed to understand the gravity of her circumstance and held their breath in wait.

Boxton roughly pushed her into the darkness behind a tall hedge and pounced at her, pressing his lips hard down on hers. Mary recoiled. He wanted her to fight back, to give him a challenge. She was most happy to oblige.

With a muffled *thump*, Mary slapped him across the face with her gloved hand. "You, sir, are entirely too forward." She pressed her fingertips to her bottom lip. "Must you kiss me so hard? You cut my lip!"

His dark gaze heated as he spotted the drop of blood on her white gloves.

"You *dare* to tell me how to kiss you?" He brought his hand back and Mary cowered believably. With an evil laugh, he brought his palm hard down on her.

That is enough of that, Mary thought.

In a quick motion, she extended the palm of her hand outward, making contact with his nose and breaking it in a sickening *crunch*.

Boxton howled in pain, holding his bleeding nose with both hands.

Mary made to escape, but Boxton grabbed hold of her bodice with his blood-soaked hands. "You *bitch*!"

Tugging her back to him, he snarled, pulling at the low neck of her gown. Boxton yanked, tearing the fine green silk down the front, the loud *rip* of the delicate material absorbed by the air around them.

Irate, Mary used the pistol in her reticule as a bludgeon and aimed a hard knock to his head. But she missed, her heavy reticule bouncing harmlessly off his shoulder.

"*Argh*!" He bellowed. "Damn it, woman!"

He pulled the reticule from her wrist and tossed it behind him. "What the devil do you keep in there? Stones?"

"Yes," she snapped. "To ward off vile men such as yourself."

"*Vile*?" He growled. "You wish to see vile, do you, Mary?"

He reached for her once more, and Mary abandoned the act of the meek, helpless, and terrified female, and let her training and instincts take over. With all the force she could muster, Mary extended her arm out, her fingers stretched and stiff, and jabbed Boxton in the neck. He scarcely had time to choke when she lifted the heel of her palm into his already-broken nose.

He released a garbled cry, and as soon as he bent over in agony, Mary lifted her knee to his head, connecting with a hard *thunk*, and sending him tumbling backward.

Rolling to his back, the man groaned and cursed.

Mary stood over him and glared. "I will *never* share a bed with you, Boxton. Best you had learn to accept when a woman says 'no.'"

With a swish of her skirts, Mary turned to walk away, but her skirt snagged, halting her.

In one violent tug, Boxton pulled her to the ground. The wind in her lungs left her in a *whoosh*, catching her off guard.

Before she could rise, he leapt atop her and sank his teeth deep into the flesh between her shoulder and neck. Mary screamed, the high notes echoing through the empty garden and blown away with the gentle wind.

"You like that, do you?" he asked, licking her blood from his lips.

Mary cringed, her heart thudding painfully in her chest. "You are evil, Boxton," she whispered, her voice quavering.

She had quickly lost control of this situation and must regain her ground.

"Evil," he hissed between clenched teeth. "Yes..."

He fisted the ends of her scarf in both hands and wrapped it once around her neck, then pulled.

Mary's breath was immediately cut off. *No!*

She fought. With everything she had, she kicked, clawed, punched, scratched, pinched, jabbed...but he took it all. He hovered over her with stony, sadistic and lascivious serenity, his teeth bared in excitement and his erection jabbing into her thigh.

I must live, she thought desperately. *I must tell Gabriel that I still love him...that I have always loved him. I cannot die now.*

Inflicting pain wasn't working. She must catch *him* off guard. She was running out of time.

She bucked high, throwing him off balance as he tumbled to his side.

Taking in deep gasps of air, she struggled to sit up.

In the distance, she thought she heard her name, but she blithely ignored it. This was her chance!

She lifted her torn skirts and quickly unsheathed her dagger. Then, she lunged. Boxton shouted his pain as she sliced him across the thigh. He threw his head back, and she took the opening, holding her bloodied blade to the underside of his neck.

He lifted a fist, and Mary nudged the blade deeper against his soft skin.

"You had better re-think that move, Boxton," she warned.

Boxton swallowed, then winced at the pain from her blade, his eyes narrowed and filled with vitriol. "You don't know what you're doing," he replied.

"Oh, I believe I do." Her heart thundered in her chest as she considered her options. The man *must* know by now that she was not a simple-minded actress. She had no choice but to bring him in to Hydra for questioning. "Now, you are going to come with me."

Heavy footfalls came from behind her.

Bang! Bang!

CHAPTER 35

*G*abe adjusted his seat in the stiff driver's perch of Hydra's carriage. He hated being the one sitting outside waiting for the others to complete an assignment. He saw the reasoning in it, he supposed, but it grated nonetheless.

The other coachmen sat about, either imbibing in a hidden stash of liquor or sleeping on their perches. Gabe, however, thought. About Mary. He thought about Mary and her flowing auburn hair and soft grey eyes, about the way her lips perked when she was lost in thought, of how she moved when she walked, the slide of her hair between his fingers, her pert, delicious breasts...

The very startling thought of what their children would look like crossed his mind. Would they have her features, or would they favour him? Or, perhaps, would they be a little of both; curling auburn hair with blue eyes, or straight brown hair with...

Gabe sat bolt upright, alarm buzzing through him. His heart began to thump wildly in his chest and his eyes grew wide.

Children! He dropped his head in his hands as countless curses and admonishments flowed through his mind. He'd had his share of lovers before, but he'd always used French Letters to protect against conceiving with them. Why the bloody hell had he forgotten with Mary?

His fists clenched, pulling at his hair. *Children. With Mary!* My God, how had he not thought of this before? Hell, he could have withdrawn and spilled his seed in a cloth or on her abdomen. What was the matter with him? Mary could, at this very moment, be carrying his child. And, damn it, she was inside among dangerous traitors while he was ordered to sit out here and wait for her!

Gabe's gut knotted and his skin tingled. He couldn't sit there any longer. He must find out if she was well, to the devil with his post.

Without a second thought, Gabe leapt from his perch and darted down the side of Maison Sheffield. He glanced in windows, looking for Mary, but couldn't find her. Slinking onto the portico, Gabe avoided detection from the merry dancers within the ballroom.

A faint scream rent the air and Gabe straightened once more. *Mary?*

It was covered by ruckus laughter coming from the ball, but he knew for certain that *that* scream had come from the gardens. And he ran. Not caring about the shrubberies tugging at his stockings and breeches, or what he crushed, Gabe dashed hell-bent through the gardens.

He thought he heard someone call Mary's name, and it drove him faster.

Passing the last of the torches, he went directly into the darkness. He rounded a hedge, and his heart stopped. Mary was covered in blood, her gown torn, and she was battling against Boxton.

Giving himself nary a second to think, Gabe withdrew his pistol, aimed it at Boxton's shoulder, and pulled the trigger.

MARY GASPED, her heart leaping to her throat and her ears ringing at the deafening din of two pistols being discharged.

She spun to see two of her favourite men standing behind her.

Sir Bramwell Stevens stood with her spent pistol in his hand, his eyes cold with lethal intent as he gazed at Boxton through the smoke coming from the barrel.

"You shot me!" Boxton sat on the ground with one hand over his stomach, and the other on his shoulder. "You're a bloody servant and you shot me! And *you*!" he spat at Gabriel. "I knew there was something wrong about you, Spencer."

"Mary!" Gabe tossed his spent pistol to the ground and rushed to her side. "Mary... My God, wha' happened te ye? What did the bloody bastard do?"

"Mary," Stevens said. His customary charming and affable nature had been replaced by single-minded, deadliness. "Are you well, Mary?"

She blinked, bemused. "No," she admitted. "Once I bathe and dress my wounds I will be a sight better, I believe."

She could see Bram's jaw clench even in the darkness of night.

"Do you require assistance to walk?" Gabe asked.

She shook her head and he nodded in understanding.

"Gabriel, return her to the carriage," Stevens growled bluntly.

"What are you going to do?" she asked.

His dark, golden gaze flicked to her then returned to Boxton. "What I should have done long ago...after this *bastard* abused Anna so."

Mary had heard about Hydra's sister, Lady Devon, Annabel Mason, née Bradley, and how Lord Boxton had courted her, which had proceeded poorly, indeed.

"*Annabel*? What has she to do with this?" Boxton cried. "Who *are* you?"

Stevens raised an eyebrow at Mary. "Return to the carriage and drive home. You require a doctor." He stealthily removed a blade from his stocking. "I will take care of things here."

With a jerky nod, Mary leaned on Gabriel as he helped her to her feet. Her torn gown caught beneath her heel, forcing her briefly to the ground once more. Gabe cursed soundly and bent to lift her bodily in his arms. She thought to fight him, but it felt rather wonderful to be carried by Gabriel.

With his lips thinned in anger, Gabe marched through the gardens, the sound of Boxton's snivelling following their retreat. Mary put her head to Gabe's chest, trying to outrun the villain's cries, the cool night air chilling her teeth as she gasped for breath.

A garbled, hoarse shout came from the gardens and an involuntary whimper escaped Mary.

He looked down at her her, his blue gaze clouded with fury.

"I *knew* this assignment was too dangerous fer ye on yer own! Ye shouldnae have been here without me. I should have been there, Mary."

She winced. "Now is not the time to quibble, Gabe. Take me home."

"AYE, LASS." Gabe's gut knotted sickeningly as he carefully carried Mary to the carriage.

How could he have allowed this to happen? Mary was a

right mess, covered in blood from head to foot, her dress torn, hair in shambles... *Damn*!

"Are ye well, Mary?"

"In pain," she murmured against the front of his coat. "But well enough, I suppose."

"Ye should nae have accepted tha' assignment."

"I did my job, Gabe, and despite the potential for injury, I like my job."

The twisting in his stomach intensified. "I ken, Mary. I donnae like it, but I ken."

They reached the carriage and Gabe gently placed her in it, leaning her against the squabs. He hesitated to leave her there alone. What if they hit a rut and she was jostled?

"I will be fine, Gabe. They are minor injuries."

He shook his head. She claimed they were minor, but he could see the bruises already forming on her upper arms, cheeks, and... *Nae*! There was a severe bruise forming under the red ring around her neck. The devil had choked her! With her own curst scarf!

Aghast, Gabe climbed in the carriage to sit beside her, and pressed his fingertips to her neck.

"Aye," he mumbled. "He strangled ye."

His gaze lowered to settle angrily on the blood-soaked injury in the flesh between her shoulder and neck, and his jaw clenched. "*Nae*. Oh, nae, Mary. Donnae tell me tha' he *bit* ye!" He touched his finger near the marks to closer examine them.

With a feral growl, he withdrew an unspent pistol from his coat pocket and leapt from the carriage.

"Gabe!" Mary called hoarsely after him and he stopped.

"Donnae try te stop me, Mary. That devil must pay fer wha' he's done te ye."

"Stevens is handling it," she reminded him.

Gabe's chest rose and fell with his furious breaths. How could a man—*any man*—do such a thing to a woman?

"Take me home, Gabe. I must change before the rendezvous."

"Ye are *nae* going te the—"

"Gabe," she whispered. "We will discuss it later. In fact, there is much more that I must tell you, but *not now*! Take me home."

He sighed, only barely keeping his sudden rage under control. "Verra well, Mary. But I am nae pleased aboot it."

MARY HISSED a breath between her teeth as they rounded a sharp turn. She had not been injured severely, but her body felt battered and bruised, particularly from her fall to the ground. Of course, Boxton's bite was rather painful, as well. She was simply grateful that she was still able to speak. Granted, she was a mite hoarse...but she was still able to speak.

She wondered what Stevens had done with Boxton. Had he taken him to gaol? Beaten him? Killed him? She supposed she would find out soon enough.

Gabe sped the horses along the lantern-lit, busy streets, weaving between angry riders and cursing coachmen.

Finally, they made the last turn onto the safe house's street, and Mary released a relieved sigh. She was nigh desperate to change out of her torn, bloodstained gown, corset, and chemise. She looked down at herself. Indeed, Boxton's bloody fingerprints marred her underclothes.

How abhorrent. She would have to burn them all.

The carriage rolled to a halt in front of the safe house and rocked as Gabe stepped down from his perch. The door swung open and Gabe's arms reached inside.

"I am able to walk on my own, Gabe. You needn't—"

"I donnae care if ye say ye are able, Mary. I *will* carry ye up those steps and into yer room."

She sighed. He was very determined and, this once, she would oblige him. When she divested herself of her blood-stained frock and cleaned her wounds, he would see that she was more than capable of moving unaided. On the morrow, however, she would likely be very sore.

Gabe gathered her in his arms and Mary was again swept away by his clean, fresh scent, his warmth, and his sheer brawn. To be able to lift her bodily in his arms without any strain... She had to keep herself from sighing aloud.

Swinging the front door open, he carried her over the threshold, then kicked the door closed behind them. She could tell that he was being careful not to jostle her as they crossed the foyer and ascended the stairs.

The home was quiet, as most of the customary inhabitants were on assignment, and those that remained were either in their sickbeds, recovering from injury, or likely training.

They arrived at her guest bedchamber, and Gabe pressed his hand—while still holding her in his arms—to the latch, but he hesitated.

"Mary?" he said in hushed tones. "Did ye lock th' door when ye left?"

"No, but—"

"Were all the suspects at the ball?"

Her eyes grew wide as she returned Gabe's fearful gaze. "Lord Kerr said that Lady Kerr was detained by appointments or some such thing." She licked at the dried blood on her cracked lip. "You do not suppose..."

They both looked in suspicion at the door and Gabe slowly lowered Mary's feet to the ground. He pressed his index finger to his lips in a signal for silence.

Gabe withdrew his pistol and slowly pressed the door's latch, careful not to make a sound as it opened. Mary watched with bated breath as the door swung wide.

He motioned Mary to remain where she was, to which she

soundlessly scoffed, removing her dagger once more from its sheath at her thigh. Did he truly believe she would miss an opportunity to catch an intruder in her bedchamber? In the *safe house*, of all places?

Signalling his intent to enter, Gabe eyed her for a response. Mary nodded.

He saw the intruder first, aiming his pistol at the shadowy mass sitting in Mary's armchair. Mary lifted her dagger, ready to throw.

"*Stand up and show yourself,*" Gabe shouted in his practiced English accent.

"Come off it, Gabe," a decidedly familiar voice said.

With a sigh, Gabe lowered his weapon and returned it to the holster hidden beneath his coat. "Bloody hell, Colin. I nearly shot you!"

Mary lowered her arm and slid her dagger back into its sheath, immense relief flowing through her. They could certainly use more help.

"But you didn't," Colin Greene drawled. "And for that I thank you."

"What the devil are you doing in Mary's room? Were you looking for me?" Gabe asked, striding toward the fireplace.

Mary closed her bedchamber door and slid the latch.

"Actually, I was looking for Mary."

Through the darkness, she could see Gabe's back tense.

"Well, you've found me." Mary said, her voice hoarse.

A flare of light lit the room as Gabe ignited the coals in the hearth.

"Mary?" Colin turned his gaze fully on Mary and released a gasp of dismay as he surged to his feet. "*Sweet, merciful Lord in Heaven*! Mary! What happened to you? Are you well?"

"I am well enough, Greene."

Gabe went about lighting candles around them, lending a

glow to the room. As the sitting room got brighter, Colin's features grew increasingly horrorstruck.

"Who did this to you?" he said, aghast. "We must alert Hydra at once!"

She shrugged her uninjured shoulder. "The man's been taken care of, and Hydra knows that I was on assignment. I am afraid that cannot sit to discuss it at the moment, for I must change and ready myself for the rendezvous—"

"Ye will*nae* come with me, Mary," Gabe interjected. "It is too dangerous, and yer already injured."

She wheeled on him. "You are injured too, Gabriel! I was there, I saw what she did to you! Is it any wonder you've gone purple and green?" She huffed a frustrated breath. Why would he not listen to her? "Stevens has taken care of Boxton," she continued, "that could pose a problem for the rendezvous. I must dress and prepare myself for any eventuality. We are wasting valuable time disputing the matter! The assignment is incomplete, and both of us are at risk. I *must* follow through."

He gazed at her in silence for several moments, the muscle in his jaw jumping. "Dress yerself," he finally grunted.

She flashed him a big smile and swept to her wardrobe to withdraw her nighttime sneak-work frock. With one last grin at Gabe and Greene, she dashed behind the privacy screen.

CHAPTER 36

Gabe watched Mary's fetching, retreating bottom as she withdrew behind the screen. He didn't know what he was thinking, allowing her to come. She was bleeding, bruised, and likely in shock from what occurred.

He shook his head. He hated seeing her in pain. Rising from his crouched position by the hearth, he strode to the settee and lowered himself onto it.

Colin cleared his throat. "You look like shit, friend. What happened to you?"

"Thank you." Gabe glared at the curst Adonis. "I was held prisoner and tortured by Lady Kerr."

"Christ," Colin muttered. "Are you going to tell me what is happening?" He stepped forward, his arms folded across his chest.

"The last I saw you," Gabe began, "you said that you didn't want me to seek you out."

Colin nodded, resuming his seat in the armchair before the hearth. "I recall."

"Why are you here?"

Water sloshed behind the privacy screen, briefly drawing Gabe's attention.

"I came to see Mary. I didn't know that you would be here, as well." Colin slid a glance toward the screen, and lowered his voice, leaning toward Gabe. "Did you take my advice?"

"I—you—damn it, that's between Mary and me."

"So you *did*. Capital, old fellow. Well done." He reached across the short space between them and clapped Gabe on the shoulder. "It's about bloody time."

Gabe nodded. Indeed, it was about bloody time. And it was entirely possible that she was *enceinte* with his child. But she could still move on, marry another.

His heart beat hard in his chest as he thought on it. It was precisely what he had wanted for her. She could settle down with a farmer or butcher or some such man, have passels of children, and never be in danger again...

But now the thought of holding her back grated. His pulse raced faster as the realization hit him. Mary could be so much more than a mere farmer's wife. She was a fountain of talent. She was caring, kind, intelligent, creative... She knew more about most things than Gabriel, and she had the genius to do anything she set her mind to.

She also possessed a wealth of beauty and vibrancy, which Gabe found highly intoxicating. She was his best friend, his lover. And, Gabe was afraid to admit, he wanted what *she* wanted.

For her to be happy... For her to be a spy.

"So, tell me, Mary," Colin raised his voice for her to hear him. "What happened tonight?"

She grunted. "It was a dreadful mistake."

"And that mistake tried to choke you?" Colin's hands clenched into fists, and he punched one against his thigh.

Gabe certainly knew that feeling. He'd like to punch

Boxton, himself; shooting him hardly satisfied his need to hurt the man.

"No," Mary called through the screen, her voice still hoarse. "That was Lord Boxton."

Colin's jaw jumped. "And where is Lord Boxton, now?"

"Stevens took care of him," she replied.

"*Took care of*," Colin mused.

"It is possible tha' he has been put in gaol, but dead is most probable," Gabe put in.

"Dead." Colin tapped the arm of the chair with his index finger.

"Aye." Gabe leaned forward on the settee, his elbows resting on his knees and his hands hanging between them.

"Here I am." Mary said from behind him.

Gabe rose to face her, and nearly swallowed his tongue. She was attired as a dockworker—with a dark, oily coat and trousers with a waistcoat to match, and an un-starched cream-coloured shirt and cravat. Mary had bound her breasts to fit in her costume, then powdered her own hair and tied it in a long, plaited queue that hung down her back.

The trousers outlined the shape of her thighs. It was arousing as hell. Why, if Colin weren't here, Gabe would pick her up and carry her to the bed, and—

Perhaps he had best not think on that.

She neared them, and Gabe could see that Mary had bandaged her bite wound, but the bruise at her neck and cheek stood out beneath the edge of her collar, in stark relief from her pale skin. He grimaced. It looked far worse in this light than it had earlier in the darkness.

Colin stood and strode toward her, clasping her hands in his and bussing her on one cheek. They exchanged a few muttered words before he turned and led Mary to the bedchamber's sitting area.

Gabe squelched the jealousy he felt watching their

exchange. He should not begrudge Mary her warm relationship with a friend and comrade, but he certainly didn't like it. The memory of her desire to partner with Colin for her assignment rushed through his mind, and he grit his teeth at the jolt of pain slicing through his abdomen.

He blinked and realized that Colin and Mary had already taken their seats, and he resumed his, as well.

"So, it was Boxton that attacked you," Colin confirmed. "But how the devil did he get you alone and into such a situation?"

MARY FELT Gabe's gaze on her, and not for the first time since she withdrew from the privacy screen did her stomach flutter with nerves. They hadn't much time, surely, before they must leave, and Gabe's intense attentions made her want to pull him into her embrace and remain there for hours.

She cleared her throat and forced her desire from her mind.

"Everything was going as I'd planned. I engaged in pleasant conversation with several of our marks, but when Reddington said that he wished for me to meet someone, and I saw Lord Winning being led toward me, I fled to the portico. Boxton followed, and I wished to protect my identity, so I went along with him when he led me into the gardens. We fought and—"

"Just a moment," Gabe leaned forward. "Ye saw my cousin, Frederick, at the ball?"

"Yes."

"Why didnae ye tell me from the first?" Gabe ran a hand through his hair. "Yer identity could have been compromised, Mary! De ye knoo wha' would have happened if he had seen ye?"

"Yes! That is why I went out of doors! But Boxton

followed me, demanding the night with me that *you* had promised him, curse you!"

"Now, just a moment!" Colin held his hands up, then turned to gaze accusingly at Gabe. "You promised Mary's body to some villain?"

The muscles in Gabe's jaw jumped. "What was I supposed te do? Mary flirted with the bastards since the moment we arrived; they had their expectations up!" He pointed a finger at her. "But that doesnae change the fact that ye are in danger of not only furthering yer injuries, but of being recognized. I've changed my mind. I donnae think ye should go tonight."

Pain and outrage surged through Mary, urging her to her feet. "You have no right to tell me what to do, Gabriel!"

He stood, as well, fury reddening his face and neck as he turned to scowl at her. "Ye donnae seem to ken tha' I want te protect ye!"

Hurt lanced through her chest. And, finally, she burst.

"*And I want to protect* you!" Mary shouted hoarsely, the back of her eyes stinging with withheld tears. "Every chance you get, you berate and try to control me, using only jealousy or your intent to protect me as an excuse, but think you that the feeling isn't reciprocated? Is it not enough that I witness *you* in jeopardy nearly every day?" She tapped her chest. "How do you suppose that makes *me* feel?

"This assignment is as much a danger to you as it is to me, and I will not—I *cannot*—stand by while the man I love is in danger! *It is not to be borne!*" She stood, fists balled at her sides, eyes glistening, and chest heaving.

Everything seemed to melt away. Nothing existed but a bewildered Gabe and Mary, her heart in her throat.

"Ye love me, Mary?" Gabe moved to stand closer to her.

Mary could feel the colour leeching from her cheeks. Her lip quivered, but she drew herself up in dignity, her chin notching higher. "I said as much when we were children, did I not?"

"I need te hear ye say it, Mary. Again, as it were."

There was no sense in hiding it any longer. It was the truth, and he ought to know. Her heart lurched, and she took a deep breath and released it, steeling herself. "I love you, Gabe. Of course I love you."

Mary shook, her heart fluttering and nervous tingles shooting through her body. She'd said it. She'd gone and told Gabriel that she loved him. A broad, beaming smile spread across his lips and Mary stared in awe. He was so handsome when he smiled like that.

Before she knew what was happening, Gabe grabbed her in a painfully crushing hug and pressed his lips to hers. Then she melted. Gabe was kissing her. She reached her arms over his shoulders and held him tightly there while their tongues tangled deliciously together.

Gabe broke the kiss and pressed his lips to her ear. "Tha gaol agam ort... I love ye, Mary," he whispered. "I love ye so verra much."

Mary gazed up at him with a broad smile of her own. She did not even mind that her lip pulled uncomfortably as she did so. Her heart had never felt so full. Gabriel loved her!

A loud clatter came from the fireplace, and Mary jumped, she and Gabe turning toward the noise.

Colin cringed, retrieving the fire poker from the ground and placing it back on its hook. "Apologies," he mumbled. "You were having a moment... I tried to sneak out, but...er..."

Mary laughed, the sound coming out as an awkward croak. "It is fine, Greene." Reluctantly, she stepped away from Gabe and turned to face Colin. "What was it that you wanted to speak with me about?" Mary asked.

"Ah, yes. Well, in light of recent events, my request hardly signifies, but I'd rather hoped that you could introduce me to one of the actresses in your next play. I saw her in passing, but there was a throng of men around her. Thought, perhaps, that you could be my way in to..." he trailed off, then cleared his throat. "This is far more exciting, however. My assignment is waning, and I'd like to see some action, and it seems as though the both of you could use some help." He eyed Mary's neck and the fresh scars on Gabe's face. "Mind if I come along?"

CHAPTER 37

*M*ary hurried to draw age lines and spread soot upon her face, and despite her haste, the effect was quite effective.

Gabe had applied the additions to his disguise similarly, though he put powder in his hair to make it white, instead of dark. He had blackened out one tooth and wore a wide-brimmed hat low on his head.

Colin remained as he was, despite Gabe's insistence that he change. The safe house was veritably brimming with costumes, paints, and powders.

"Shall we leave?" Mary glanced at the mantle clock. "The ball will be drawing to a close now; the rendezvous will be at any moment."

Gabe went to the tantalus and poured a healthy dram of port,

"Come now, Gabe. There is no time for that," Colin said.

"Indeed," Gabe dipped his hand in his glass, cupping some port, and splashed it on Colin's coat.

"Oi!" Colin cursed soundly.

"Ye might not look the part, but ye must *smell* the part."

Colin grumbled. "Bugger."

With a laugh, Mary took some for her own costume, then preceded the men through the safe house and outside to the awaiting carriage. The hour was late and the sky was dark. A low-lying fog swirled around the horses' hooves, and there was a bite to the chilled air.

"I will drive," she said, stepping up awkwardly onto the perch.

My, but her bottom was sore!

"I didn't know that you knew how to drive a team, Mary." Colin grinned at her, his obsidian eyes twinkling.

She affected an accent in a deep voice. "Aye, all workin' men ken how te lead a team." She winked.

Gabe chuckled. "Ye might want te practice yer accent, love."

Mary's stomach fluttered at the endearment, but said defensively, "I will not be required to speak while we observe the rendezvous, so my accent scarcely matters."

Gabe eyed her from beside the driver's perch, and his gaze turned concerned. "Are ye certain ye're well enough te lead a team, Mary?"

"I will admit that I am sore, but I am also determined." She shrugged her uninjured shoulder. "I will heal, Gabe. At the very least I should like to see justice done for this treachery." Her eyes narrowed. "Lady Kerr most particularly."

"Bloodthirsty lass." His lips curved up in an alluring half-smile. "Verra well. And if ye have te talk, Mary, try te mimic my accent, aye?"

Mary gave him a quick nod and he followed Colin into the unmarked carriage, pulling up the steps and closing the door behind himself.

She waited until she heard the tell-tale knock on the hack's roof before she clicked at the bays and flicked the reins, gently bringing them to a walk and then a trot. The sudden wind at her charcoaled cheeks was biting, indeed. But she did not care.

Despite the dangers shrouding this assignment, Mary relished the excited anticipation bubbling through her. She adored the thrill of the assignment. More than that, however, she was elated that Gabe uttered nary a single protest at her taking the lead—and thus being in the most danger of attack or recognition. He trusted her. And he *loved* her!

Her stomach fluttered. And that evening was not the first time he had told her he loved her; she recalled now, that he had used those same Gaelic words while they were in the carriage travelling to London.

She smiled into the cool night air, lightness touching her heart. She had Gabe for a lover. And he loved her.

GABE SAT in the front facing seat of the carriage, gazing through the window at the streetlamps passing by.

His heart still beat hard in his chest. Mary loved him! Bloody hell, it was a euphoric feeling.

But what of his earlier assertions that he could not fall in love? And of what happened to Hydra's family?

He shook his head. Even after he had discovered his love for her, he could not bring himself to let her go. He sat straighter in his seat. What if he didn't have to? What if he could have Mary for the rest of his life? Would she not be safer *with* him than without him? Two trained spies were certainly better than one.

What a fool he'd been. Using Hydra's family as an example of why he should *not* be with Mary was faulty logic. Hydra was the only spy in his family, and he carried the burden of protecting them all. Mary *was* a spy; Gabe shouldn't have to worry about her, at all. Hell, even his reaction to Mary when she'd engaged in combat with *bloody* Boxton had been faulty. She was right; she'd fought the devil off and was already in control before Gabe had shown up.

His instinct to protect her had reared its head and controlled his words and actions. He'd been a confounded arse to the woman.

Indeed. If Mary was, at this very moment, carrying their child it would behove him to lay claim to her and their unborn bairn.

A gleeful smile tugged at his soot-smudged lips and his heart began to gallop. A bairn. *Their* bairn, born to them in wedlock...

Colin shifted in his seat across from him, drawing Gabe's gaze.

"I mean te wed Mary," Gabe softly blurted.

The words felt remarkably freeing to say aloud.

"My felicitations." Colin inclined his head. "Does Mary know this?"

Gabe exhaled on a silent laugh. "No. But now tha' I ken she shares my feelings, I fully intend te ask."

The air was still between them as the carriage rolled over the cobblestoned streets of London. Gabe watched his friend with a gimlet eye. Something was off about him.

"Why did ye *really* come te see Mary today, Colin?" Gabe asked quietly.

Colin gazed out the window, his jaw tightening. There was several moments of silence before the tension in Colin's shoulders released and he sighed. "It's Isobel."

Awareness dawned, and an odd flood of simultaneous emotions rushed through him. He was relieved that the visit had nothing to do with Mary, but was concerned for his friend's sister.

"Is she well?" Gabe asked.

"I don't bloody well know! The woman has completely closed herself off. I worry about her, Gabe. She has always been ill at ease with our Spanish heritage—most particularly because she resembles our father more than I. But despite my efforts, I have not been able to speak to her about this most recent bout of melancholy. I'd hoped to seek Mary's help, perhaps send the women on a shopping trip. Lace and bonnets and so forth."

"I am certain tha' Mary would be amenable te a shopping trip."

Colin rested his elbow on the window's frame and rubbed fretfully at his lips with the backs of his fingers. "I hope it will help her."

Gabe turned his gaze out the window. "Act lively, Colin. We've arrived."

The carriage carefully rolled to a halt and rocked gently as Mary climbed down from her perch.

The door swung open, a gust of cool night air wafting in.

Mary clucked her tongue, and deepened her voice, "Come along, men. Time is wasting away."

Biting back a smile of mirth, Gabe followed Colin out of the carriage. Mary had tethered the horses to the post of a nearby building, nearly three streets from the Crowned Pig's Grunt.

Silently, the three of them walked, keeping to the shadows of the nearby buildings. When they were but one street away from the rendezvous point, Mary halted, forcing them to follow suit.

She spun around and uttered under her breath, "Recall your roles, men."

Indeed. Their intent this evening was to appear to be intoxicated men stumbling from tavern to tavern searching for women, drink, and song.

Mary turned back around and lurched forward, mumbling something incoherent to herself. She was most definitely a believably drunken lad. Gabe wrapped an arm about Colin's shoulders and the two stumbled together toward their goal.

The sign for the Crowned Pig's Grunt came up beside them and Gabe loudly slurred, "Thish looks likey good 'un!"

With a drunken nod, Mary tripped through the door, landing on all fours inside. The tavern was packed to the gills and every eye turned to stare at her. She rose ineptly from her awkward position, patted clumsily at her clothes, gazing through glazed, squinting eyes at the crowd.

The combined stench of foul, sweating bodies, fetid liquor, salty ocean water, and stale piss assailed his nostrils. Gabe fought the urge to grimace and squeeze his nose shut. Instead, he turned a bleary eye on the tavern's patrons; most appeared to be sailors.

Their quarries were nowhere to be seen. When they did come, Gabe suspected they would not wish to be observed by so many patrons, intoxicated or not, and would likely leave.

Mary, apparently coming to the same conclusions as he, hiccoughed and spun around, tripping on her twisted ankles and splaying herself upon the filthy tavern floor.

Hiding his instant worry for her welfare, Gabe laughed loudly, pointing at her sprawled upon the floor, Colin joining in after feigning a wretch.

"Oi!" a tavern wench called. "Take it ouside!"

Gabe wiped his nose noisily across his sleeve. "Aint noffin good in 'ere n'eyway."

He helped Mary stumble to her feet and lifted her arm over his shoulder, ineptly helping her back through the doors. They staggered down the walk until they were out of view of the tavern's doors and, releasing Mary, then darted into the narrow alleyway. The stink there was not much improved from inside the tavern, though the most prominent scents were piss and garbage. And likely not all of it was old.

Mary groaned, rubbing her shoulder.

"God's teeth, Mary! I cannae believe I forgot! How are ye?"

She waved him off. "Well enough for now, Gabriel. Focus on our assignment, if you will."

His lips thinned in displeasure, but he remained silent. As much as he wished to disrobe her to inspect her wounds, he knew they did not have the time, and this was most certainly not the place. But there was one thing that he must say.

"Mary," he whispered. "I was wrong about yer needing protection. Y'are a strong woman, capable of taking care of yerself, and I was beastly towards ye."

She blinked. "Thank you, Gabe. But really—"

"I ken ye donnae need me te be with ye fer protection, but I'd like te be with ye as a partner."

Colin cursed under his breath.

Mary pressed a quick buss to his lips, then pushed him against the cool brick wall next to Colin. "Thank you," she hissed, leaning against the wall beside Gabe and peering around the corner.

She signalled to Gabe and he discretely stuck his head around the corner above hers. Nearly thirty paces away walked a group of five—*no...six*—men and one woman. He could not yet see all of their faces, but he supposed the woman must be Lady Kerr.

Mary gasped and Gabe glanced down at her. She signalled him with her shocked grey eyes and mouthed the word *"Frederick."*

Impossible. He turned to look back at the advancing group and his heart stopped in his chest. There strode Frederick Ashley, Baron Winning, Gabe's own cousin, among a group of known traitors.

What the devil was he doing with them? Fred was a right bastard, and had been since they were still in the schoolroom, but a traitor? No. Could he have been coerced into joining? Did he even know what this meeting was about, or did he simply believe others in high society were finally accepting him?

Damn ye, Frederick, ye fool!

If the blighter found himself killed, Gabe would be named Baron, for the man had never sired any heirs. And that was the last thing Gabe wanted, to be known. It would ruin his life in the Secret Service...and he would lose his last living family member.

Gabe could not rescue his cousin without both compromising his, Colin's, and Mary's identities—and with it, exposing their ties to the Winning Barony—and endangering all of their lives.

They watched the group disappear into the Crowned Pig's Grunt.

"Report," Colin whispered.

Mary left the building's corner to go to Colin, on Gabe's other side. Gabe watched the tavern's door while Mary gave Colin a brief synopsis in hushed tones.

If they followed them into the tavern it could pose multiple problems: one, they would not find a suitable place to sit in order to overhear them over the din, and two, if their quarry left because of the lack of privacy, it would be suspicious for them to follow right after them.

They would have to remain where they were.

The sounds of boats upon the River Thames, and the muffled roar of activity from the tavern filled the air. The moonlight dimly stretched through the thick, coal- and fog-filled London air, dancing along the surface of the water. Gabe gazed at the dock across the street and the water beyond it. A frigate hung low in the water, likely full of goods to be unloaded or supplies in preparation for a long journey. Beyond it were others, mere shadows along the Thames.

Which one of these ships would be the one to bring the forged documents to France? And which one had "Anthony Spencer" booked passage on?

The door to the Crowned Pig's Grunt opened, the light from within shining along the damaged cobblestoned street, and the group of traitors emerged. Gabe could not help but notice that Lord Boxton was not among them, but he saw Lord Reddington, the Marquess of Hale, Mr. Piper, Frederick, and two men that Gabe did not know.

The tall, lanky man leading the group pointed toward the docks and they set off across the street.

Gabe ducked back, shrouding himself in the darkness that hid Mary and Colin.

He waited until the traitors walked down the wooden planks before he turned to whisper, "The tavern was too crowded. They have gone te the docks. They're likely to board tha' frigate, as it's the closest one."

"But how are we to follow?" Mary asked. "We would have no plausible reason to be there. We cannot very well swim to the ship and listen from the water. They would shoot us on sight."

Gabe shook his head regretfully. "We have nae choice, I'm afraid, Mary. We must remain ashore te watch them. We willnae hear them, but we will be able te see them well enough if we find the right spo'." He lowered his hat on his head, hiding his eyes. "Come along, then. We donnae wish te miss the meeting."

He led them through the darkness across the street, rushing from one shadow to another. Their quarries boarded a small rowboat and took themselves to the moored frigate, then began to climb the rope ladder leading to the deck one at a time.

"Why the devil would they wish te conduct their meeting on a boat?" Colin mumbled as they crouched against the side of the nearest dockside building.

It was as close as they were able to get without being exposed, but it afforded them a well enough view of the proceedings, provided the traitors did not go below deck.

CHAPTER 38

*M*ary worried the inside of her cheek as she leaned against the cool brick of the dockside building. She turned her gaze to Gabriel, whose jaw was clenched tight.

Was he well? Was he worried for his cousin? She wished she could ask him how he felt, but now was certainly not an appropriate time for such an interrogation.

A low fog tumbled its way over the cobblestones to seep through her boots to her feet, sending a chill through her.

Gabe leaned toward her. "Lady Kerr is handing over the documents."

Indeed. Mary looked toward the frigate and the petite, womanly figure had an arm outstretched toward a tall, slender man that Mary assumed was their leader, the forged documents clutched within her hand.

The tall man, whose face Mary had yet to see, accepted the documents and began to examine them.

"Oh dear." Mary cringed as the man began to shout, waving the pieces of parchment around.

He tossed the documents over the ship's rail, their cream

colour rippling like waving leaves as they fluttered to rest upon the surface of the water.

Lady Kerr cowered from the man, and from her waving hand gestures, Mary assumed that she was giving excuses and spouting her innocence.

The apparent leader of their group withdrew a pistol and aimed it at Lady Kerr. Without hesitation, he pulled the trigger. An echoing *boom* reached their ears and rippling far beyond.

Both Colin and Gabe cursed soundly under their breath, and Mary gasped, one hand covering her mouth as Lady Kerr crumpled.

A loud shout carried its way to them, drawing Mary's attention.

"Frederick, ye demmed fool!" Gabe muttered. "Leave well enough alone and keep yer mouth shut!"

Mary was riveted on the scene unfolding on the frigate. An incensed Lord Winning charged at the tall, slender man as another of the traitors lifted Lady Kerr bodily and tossed her into the Thames. A scuffle ensued. The leader stood calm and collected as Gabe's cousin threw punches and curses at the man.

"Leave off, Frederick, *leave off, Frederick*!" Gabe chanted, apparently trying to will his cousin to halt this foolishness.

Boom!

"*Nae*!" Gabe shouted hoarsely.

Gabe rose, but Mary gripped his sleeve. Frederick's lifeless body followed Lady Kerr's into the Thames, the hollow splash loud as a death knoll. As sorry as she was for the death of Lord Winning, she feared Gabe's reaction most.

"Nae," Gabe whispered, his voice rough as gravel.

Colin shifted beside her. "My sincerest condolences on the loss of your cousin, my lord."

Gabe cut a sharp glance at Colin. "I donnae wish te be a Baron. Donnae call me *lord*."

"Hush." Mary's stomach clenched with worry. "They are returning."

Indeed, their boat crossed the channel and was approaching the dock.

Mary watched with her heart in her throat as the traitors—once seven turned five—clambered from the small rowboat.

They could hear the traitors' voices now.

"Your men have yet to find him?" one man asked.

"Not the man, no. Quite tricky to get their hands on, eh wot?" Mr. Piper replied. "But they discovered that he is to take passage on a ship bound for the Americas, set to sail tomorrow at first light."

"Have a man on it. Do not let Spencer out of your man's sight while aboard. Have him follow the devil home to his uncle and kill the both of them."

Mary glanced at Gabe's taut features. She could not let his cousin's murder go without a suspect, and she knew that the witnesses would not speak of it to anyone. There must be something Mary could do...

An idea began to form in her mind. She did not have the luxury of time to plot it out fully, but she knew she must act.

Leaving Colin and Gabe's side, she staggered forward.

"Mary!" Gabe called in an undertone.

She ignored him and fell onto the cobblestones in the path of the traitors.

GABE'S HEART STOPPED.

Turning to Colin, Gabe muttered, "Donnae move."

He rushed toward Mary. His very skin was hurting from his fear for her safety. That man was a ruthless killer as was so very plain from what they just witnessed. And now Mary would throw herself at the mercy of that villain's compassion? Inconceivable!

Please, God, donnae let anything happen te Mary.

"Could ye spare a shilling?" he heard Mary say in a masculine tone.

"Don't give him anything, my lord," one of the unknown men said. "He's drunk and will only spend it on more liquor."

"I willnae, I swear! I'm hungry, I am..." she pleaded with them on her knees.

Their leader recoiled from her.

"Beat some sense into 'im your lordship," the other man jeered.

Staggering nearer, Gabe's breath caught in his throat as the man lifted his leg to kick her. *Nae!* He would not see her beaten.

Gabe deliberately tripped over his own feet, falling in front of her and taking the hard blow to his ribs. He was absurdly grateful for the extra padding of his bandages, though his wounds from Lady Kerr's whipping stung.

"Why'd ye hurt me, sirrah?" Gabe whimpered. "I only fell, is all!"

The leader scoffed. "Get out of my sight."

Gabe gripped Mary under one arm and stumbled away, the group of traitors continuing along the street, their shoes and boots clicking along the stones.

He waited until they were out of earshot and he wheeled on Mary. "How could ye do tha', Mary? Ye scared the devil out of me! Are ye hurt? Are ye well?"

She shook her head.

"*Nae?*" Gabe said, dismayed.

"No, no." She pressed a placating hand to his sleeve. "I am just displeased that I did not see his face."

With a cautious glance behind them, Gabe ushered Mary quickly back to where Colin stood waiting for them.

"Holy hell," Colin muttered. "When I said that my assignment was waning and I needed some excitement, I certainly didn't anticipate so *much*. Are you well, Gabe?"

"Well enough," Gabe grunted, his ribs paining him.

"Did you see the—"

"No," Mary cut over Colin's question. "I did not see the leader's face. His hat kept his features in shadow. But we now know he is a lord of the realm, at least."

"Aye."

Mary's grey gaze met his. "I *did* see the other man, though, Gabe."

His eyebrows lifted and anticipation began to replace his gut-wrenching fear. "Aye?"

"It was Sir Wycliff."

"OH, but we wouldn't wish to impose." Mary worried her bonnet's burgundy ribbons as she stood gazing at Hydra in his foyer. The early morning sun shone through the opened door and glinted off the marble floor.

They had gone directly from their spot in hiding at the docks to the safe house to swiftly clean themselves up and change, then rode hell-bent for Hydra's town house.

"Nonsense!" Hydra urged them further into the foyer. "It is no imposition at all, Mary. I was to have my family over to break their fast and Cook always prepares far too much. My sister, Anna, my wife, Bridget, and her sister, Kat, would be pleased to see you. Emaline, as you know, cannot return to London or there would be uproar among the *ton*, but I know she would have been pleased to see you, as well."

Mary felt a warmth flow through her at Hydra's words.

She had been in residence with his family during much of the past year but did not know that his sisters and wife had taken much notice of her.

She smiled at her superior. "In that case, I would be honoured."

"Gabe, Greene, please do hand Tim your outerwear and join us in breaking your fast."

Mary removed her gloves and handed them with her bonnet to Hydra's butler, then followed him to his morning room.

"I presume that all of you have information for me?" Charles asked in an undertone as a downstairs maid scurried past them.

"Yes, sir."

"Excellent." He stopped, spinning around with one arm directing her into the room on the left. "After you, Mary."

She entered the empty morning room and sat at the grand oak table.

"I had my staff arrange for a larger table in this room, as I find I am always hosting the morning meal." He smiled at them as he took his own seat at the head of the table. "I also had to find a house in town that suited all of our needs, including a very large morning room." Raking his fingers through his hair, he settled in his seat. He filled a large mug with coffee, mixing in a healthy amount of sugar, and took a sip.

Mary helped herself to a cup of tea, then poured for Colin and Gabe, who had chosen the seats on either side of her.

"Tell me," Hydra said, swallowing a gulp of his steaming brew. "How did everything play out last night?" His eyes lowered to Mary's bruised neck and bandaged shoulder, which she had attempted to hide with a scarf, and his gaze softened with concern. "Mary, you have been injured..."

Gabe growled. "Damned Boxton."

Hydra sat straighter in his seat. "Anthony Walstone, Viscount Boxton?"

"Aye. One in the same."

"By damn!" Hydra pounded his fist on the table in outrage, causing the teacups to rattle in their saucers. "Where is he? Where is the bastard? I shall have him shipped to the Americas!" He pointed a finger at them, his eyes alight with fury. "After what he did to my sister and then *this* to you, the blighter deserves to be hung!"

"Here, here!" Colin lifted his cup of tea.

Gabe cleared his throat. "I have been informed tha' Stevens has taken care of the matter."

Awareness dawned in Hydra's dark blue eyes. "Ah. Stevens was there, was he? He witnessed what occurred with Mary?"

"He was, sir, and I believe he did," Mary said.

A deep, wicked laugh escaped her superior before he took another healthy gulp of his coffee. "The bastard deserved what came to him, then. Stevens cannot abide by men who abuse women... One can only imagine what he did to the blighter." His gaze rested on Mary once more. "I have summoned Simon —that is, Dr. Claridge—to see my wife. I'm certain that he would see to your injuries, should you wish him to perform an examination, Mary."

"That is kind of you, Hydra, but I believe I am fine."

"All the same," Gabe cut in, "ye should let him examine ye, Mary."

She nodded in reluctant acceptance. "Very well."

Gabe leaned forward in his seat beside Mary. "Hydra, have you by chance received any news on Hugh?"

The man shook his head regretfully. "I am afraid not, Gabe. I will let you know the moment I hear anything."

Colin cursed.

"Ta." Gabe nodded.

They fell silent for a moment, each lost in their own thoughts.

Hydra clapped his hands together, the loud *crack* reverberating off the walls of the morning room.

"Tell me what news you have." Hydra leaned back in his chair, his coffee in his hands. "Did you learn the identity of any other traitors? Did the rendezvous go as planned?"

"Not precisely..." Mary began, and Colin and Gabe joined in, the three of them recounting the events of the previous night and early that morning.

Hydra listened with an attentive ear, seemingly absorbing every bit of information they imparted upon him.

When they concluded, Hydra sat, tapping his chin, his lips pursed. "Sir Wycliff, you say? Damn. The man's been knighted for God's sake. Whatever would possess a man to turn traitor?"

"Money? Greed? Any number of things, I suppose," Mary said. "But I am absolutely certain it was him. I would recognize his voice anywhere and I saw his face clear as day. He was introduced to me at the ball, but I've seen him several times before, visiting the other actresses backstage."

Hydra nodded. "Very well. Thank you. You have done an excellent job. Truly superior. I received notice from our man, Callum, this morning that he had concluded his recent assignment. I will put him on it right away."

"I could follow him, sir," Colin offered.

Hydra shook his head. "I have an assignment in mind for you once your current one is complete."

"Of course, sir."

Hydra cleared his throat and turned a solemn gaze on Gabriel. "My sincerest condolences to you in the loss of your cousin. And to have been there but not able to intervene..." he shook his head. "I cannot fathom..."

"Ta," Gabe grunted, sorrow touching his beautiful blue

eyes. "I didnae like the man, but he was still my cousin. It... pains me tha' he is gone, most particularly because of a bloody foolish mistake."

They sat in silence for another moment while they sipped at their steaming drinks.

"'Mr. Spencer' boarded the ship to the Americas this morning," Hydra spoke into the silence.

Apparently grateful for the distraction, Gabe leaned forward eagerly. "Who did you put in my place?"

Hydra swallowed a mouthful of his coffee. "As a matter of fact, Gabe, I found a man bound for the hangman's noose that has a startling resemblance to you. I offered him freedom with a very large stipend and one stipulation—that he take your name upon boarding—and he gratefully accepted."

"Good morning, my darling." A very pregnant Lady Bridget Bradley entered the morning room and greeted her husband in a warm embrace.

Gabe, Colin, and Mary stood to greet her.

Before she could be seated, the rest of Hydra's family members and the doctor entered behind Lady Bradley and the group jovially greeting one another, as well as Mary, Gabe, and Colin, before taking their seats around the table.

Soon they were settled with plates of food, cups of tea, and pleased expressions upon their faces.

Bridget sat across from Colin and smiled at Mary. "It has been some time since I last saw you, Mary. You look well."

"You gaze upon her with happiness clouding your sight, Bridget," Dr. Simon Claridge, the Earl of Merrington, said. "Not that anyone could blame you, in your own happy state." He turned his sky-blue gaze on Mary with a note of concern. "Once you have broken your fast, if you should like me to perform an examination, I would gladly do so."

"Thank you, Doctor."

He smiled broadly, and Mary could not help but return it with one of her own.

The conversation turned to the warming weather, plays, Kat's tailoring and modiste shops, and all of their newly adopted animals.

Colin leaned close to Mary's ear and whispered, "Might I speak privately with you later about Isobel?"

"Of course," she whispered back. "Is your sister well?"

His lips thinned. "Not particularly."

Mary nodded. "I would be happy to help in any way that I can."

With a small grin, Colin said in a low voice, "I never congratulated you on your happiness with Gabe. You two make a charming couple."

Mary caught Gabe's eye and a pleasing quiver fluttered low in her stomach. "Thank you. You are right, Colin," she said quietly, turning back to Colin. "He is my Prince Sebastian."

EPILOGUE

*C*M ary covered a giggle with the back of her hand as she watched Gabe cooking in the Winning estate's kitchens. He wore only an apron to protect his *man-bits* from the hot stove, the string from the loose knot dangling down the crevice of his finely rounded bottom.

"I can scarcely believe that a month has passed since that night..." Mary mused, staring at Gabe's bottom.

Gabe grunted. "Indeed."

"Thank you for bringing me to the Winning estate with you."

"Yer welcome!" Gabe laughed. "'Constant meetings with the family's solicitors is verra riveting, I'm certain. I'm just pleased tha' ye were able te get some time away from the theatre, te spend with me."

Mary leaned her back against the edge of the table and shifted her seat on the wooden bench that sat in the corner of the kitchens. It was ordinarily where the staff would sit to eat their meals, but the moment Gabe had entered the estate, he had relieved the staff of their duties. He was determined to remove everyone within the home that had been unkind to his mother when he was a boy.

Clearing her throat, Mary returned to the moment. "My still-obvious injuries prevented me from keeping my part in the next play, but I confess I do not miss it one jot. There will always be another opportunity. And I quite like being here with you, meetings and all."

Mary stood and strode toward him, then raked her fingernails gently over his back as she pressed a kiss to his shoulder.

"Ayaah!" Gabe exclaimed, waving his hand in the air. "Ach, yer distracting me, love."

With a laugh, Mary returned to the table. She chose the opposite side, sliding her feet out beneath the table.

"Ye may giggle, my heart, but I believe ye'll be verra pleased with these eggs."

"I love to watch your bum move when you walk about..."

Gabe laughed. "Naughty lass."

The smell of Gabe's cooking filled her senses; the eggs crackled in the hot pan over the fire and the scent swirled its way alluringly to her nose. Her stomach grumbled in response.

Mary placed her elbows upon the tabletop and smiled dreamily at him. Her love grew for him with each passing hour...particularly when he strode about nude.

"I would like to be *more* naughty, if you would join me at the table..."

His head swung around, his eyelids heavy with desire as he stared at her partially hidden nude form.

"Donnae tempt me, Mary. Ye'll make me burn yer eggs."

She rose from her seat on the bench to sprawl herself across the table's top. "I would not mind burned eggs," she purred.

His throat bobbed, but he turned back to his eggs, hissing a breath through his teeth. "Ye'll make me burn off me manhood, love!"

She laughed again.

Their journey north had been a wonderful one, indeed. While they'd not spent a single night in an inn, but posted through each night, she had slept wonderfully within the circle of Gabe's arms to the gentle rocking of their carriage.

"There we are." He turned to the worktop and carefully divided the eggs onto two plates, then removed his apron.

He added a green garnish of parsley and sprinkled the plates with a red spice before bringing them toward the table.

Mary watched his *manhood* standing proudly erect as he walked, her gaze riveted on the sleekness of him, and her body heated wantonly in response. His injuries were healing wonderfully, the still-red scars on his chest and thigh fading away, and the bruises on his face were all but entirely gone.

Gabe slid the plates on the table, one before her breasts and one in front of him, closest to her hip.

Teasingly, Mary lifted a hot piece of egg with her fingers and placed it between her lips. Her mouth exploded with flavour. Some salt, some sweet, some heat, and a new divine sensation in the combination of the three.

"Oh my! Oh, Gabe these are delicious."

She lifted her body up to prop her elbow beneath her, then picked up another piece of egg, and another, each tasting just as delightful as the last.

"I am verra pleased tha' ye like them, Mary."

"Oh, I do!"

She dabbed at her lips with the napkin he held out to her. There was something she needed to say to him...something that had been in her thoughts since they had left London.

"Gabriel, I must speak to you..."

Abandoning his own plate, he turned his gaze up to meet hers. "Yes, love?"

Her stomach quivered at the endearment, but she determinately set the feeling aside and spoke her mind. "I've thought about this often in the past several weeks... I wish to remain a spy. I do not believe there is anything that will change my mind on that score." His gaze dipped back to his plate, unreadable. "But," she continued, "I no longer wish to be an actress on Drury Lane."

He sat bolt upright. "But tha' has been yer dream, Mary."

"Yes," she said, feeling somewhat nervous. "However, I feel there is another way that I might be able to feel the delights of the stage without having to suffer the attentions of so many witless, dandified men."

His eyebrows rose, apparently intrigued. "Oh?"

She nodded her head, rather proud of her plan. "The *school*!" she said excitedly. "The war with Napoleon Bonaparte has been won, but our band of crown spies are still very much in demand. I had thought to seek an audience with Hermes to request a position as a teacher within the school for spies. That perhaps I might not only teach the students the virtues of superior acting skills in infiltration assignments, but that I might arrange for a theatrical at each year's end."

Gabe's response was to pull her into a deep, passionate kiss that sent wanton tingles over her skin and through her quickly heating body.

He pulled back, breaking their kiss. "Leannan, I cannae tell ye how truly pleased ye've just made me. Ye ken tha' I will support ye, whatever ye do. The only thing tha' I need is fer ye te be happy."

Mary grinned and popped another piece of egg into her mouth, and Gabe followed suit.

She picked at another piece, but hit something metallic on the plate.

Oh dear. Not wanting to embarrass Gabe by letting him know something had gotten into his delectable food, Mary tried to discretely remove it without his knowing. But as she picked the item out from beneath the eggs, Mary's breath caught in her throat.

It was a ring. Abandoning her relaxed position, Mary sat upright on the tabletop, her heart and stomach fluttering wildly within her.

"Oh my goodness," she breathed.

The slender gold band was topped with one large glittering sapphire surrounded by a dozen or more small, purple stones. A lump caught in Mary's throat and she swallowed heavily. It matched her favourite pendant perfectly.

Suddenly Gabe was kneeling on the cold kitchen floor before her, holding her hand in his.

He cleared his throat. "Mary. I have nae always been kind te ye, but I've always considered ye my friend. Since tha' first time I saw ye runnin' headlong across a field of bluebells, I've been enchanted. Ye captured my heart and I let it go willingly. Yer a bewitching lass with endless virtues. And I love ye. I love ye more than anythin'. I dream of building a family with ye. Making a life with ye." He took the ring from her numb fingers and held it, hovering before her left hand. "Mary. My friend, my love...will ye do me the greatest honour of becoming my wife?"

The lump stuck in her throat, preventing her from speaking, but she nodded franticly, anyway, her loose hair falling forward over her shoulders. Her pulse sped happily, and her vision clouded with unshed tears as he slid the ring onto her finger.

She leaned down to press her lips firmly to his and he returned it with a passionate kiss of his own. He stood, forcing her to tilt her head back.

"Ta, Mary. *Thank ye...*"

He skimmed his hands reverently over her waist and gently lowered her back to the table. Mary lost herself in the euphoria of his attentions, her hands gripping tightly to his strong, broad shoulders.

His lips found hers again as he slid his rigid member deep within her. He thrust quickly and intensely, each plunge driving her closer and closer to ecstasy, until she broke. Her cries of "Yes!" echoed through the room, as tears of joy slid across her temple and into her mass of auburn locks.

The Charming Spy

An Excerpt

EXCERPT: PROLOGUE

The Rookery, London, October 1801

BRAMWELL STEVENS TIGHTENED his grip on his younger sister's hand as he staggered along the ragged cobblestoned street in St. Giles. Night had long since fallen, the gin hovels full to near bursting, and pockmarked harlots lounged against building walls, lifting their tattered skirts to any man with a coin.

Did that truly just happen? Will someone notice? Could it have been a dream? Good God, what will we do now? A litany of distressing thoughts wandered through his mind as they walked. *It was all a horrible nightmare, surely...* The hard cobblestone beneath his feet and the chill bite to the air told him otherwise.

The air was cold and stank of drink and vomit, the scent almost overpowered by the acrid odour of piss and rotted flesh.

Crooked buildings towered high above them, dark and intimidating. What lurked within was likely soiled in sin.

A plump woman with deeply rouged cheeks and two missing front teeth sauntered toward them. "Gimme a penny, love, an' ye can satisfy yer young urges... an' for another ha'penny, th' lassie can watch."

Bram cringed and pulled his sister closer to his side as they continued to walk past. "I ain't interested," he grunted.

The lightskirt shouted blasphemous curses at him as they hurried away. He led his sister down an adjoining street, hoping to find a safe place to bed down for the night. The only light to be seen came from the cloud-covered moon hanging mockingly in the sky and dim candlelight flickering in the windows of passing buildings.

He suppressed a shiver.

A pistol went off in the distance, followed by a hollow scream, and Bram's hair stood on end, gooseflesh puckering his skin. Little Yvette tightened her grip on his hand, a garbled whimper lodged in her throat.

"I wanna go home," she whispered in her high, childish voice.

Bram's lips tightened into a grim line, the blood draining from his face. He was far too young for this responsibility but, tonight, he had been forced swiftly into manhood. Yvette was now under his protection, and his alone.

"We ain't goin' home," he returned. The image of two bodies slumped on the floor of Mama's bedchamber rose to his mind's eye. One was bloodied and broken beyond recognition, and the other stiff with a neck twisted at an unnatural angle. The image would be branded on his soul forevermore, of that he was absolutely certain.

His stomach lurched, threatening to cast up his accounts, but he swallowed them down. He'd not have food for Lord knew how long… Whatever was in his gut could very well mean life or death.

"We ain't got no home now, Yvie. We gotta make our own way."

A sob rose in her throat. "I want Mama."

His heart flipped, and unshed tears clogged his throat. "I do too," he croaked.

He could never go back now. He could never let Yvie see what had happened.

A group of men staggered out of a building, and one fell on his arse while the others roared with drunken laughter. The man who guarded the door shouted obscenities before telling the men they weren't to return to the establishment.

The hairs on the back of Bram's neck stood on end, and his gut knotted with unease.

Ballocks. He prayed they wouldn't see Yvie. She was a young thing, but some bastards didn't care about that, only about their own scurrilous needs. She was a bonny ten-year-old lass, and he was gaunt and lanky, his sixteen-year-old body still growing into that of a man's. He could never take on a group of men to defend her honour, whether said men were foxed or not.

Before they could be sighted, Bram led his sister in a sharp turn into an alley, the blackness enveloping them instantly.

"Bram." Yvette's soft whisper echoed off the leaning walls of the close. "I don't wanna be here."

"I know. Hush now, Yvie," Bram whispered back.

His eyes had widened in the darkness, his heart drumming wildly in his chest as they stepped hesitantly forward. Awareness prickled along his skin, tightening his shoulders. There was not a sound, no movement in the surrounding obscurity. But Bram could feel it: the unmistakable presence of another person.

They halted in their tracks, Bram's arm lowering to his

sister's trembling shoulders, pulling her close against him. He had to choose among the evils: continue on and risk whatever it was that lay ahead, stand in the darkness and wait out any danger, or put Yvie at risk with the drunken men.

He could never risk Yvie. Despite the unknown dangers of the close, Bram made his decision. He gripped his sister's hands and, pulling her behind him, placed her hands on his hips, ensuring that she held the material of his short coat in her small fists.

"Stay with me," he whispered almost inaudibly.

As cautiously as he could, he inched through the close, his sister directly on his heels.

Bram kept his ears trained, listening intently for any sign of movement around them. The end was near. The blackness fell away up ahead, where the narrow alley opened onto the next street.

We will make it.

The whoosh of fabric alerted him, but it wasn't from where he'd expected. His gaze rose to the rooftops and followed a dark, caped figure that threw itself gracefully over the edge of the building to cling against the wall of the close.

Bram's breath stilled in his throat as his feet stopped. *The caped figure cannot see us*, he assured himself. *Can they?*

His eyes widened ever further in an attempt to see the figure in the dark. Only the gentle scraping of the person descending the wall told him where they were. *Dear God*. The person had to be an agile animal to lower themselves from four stories up and not fall dead on the cobblestones.

The soft *clomp* of boots touching the ground echoed around them as the mysteriously shrouded person reached the bottom.

"It is perilous for a young man and a little girl to be out in St. Giles...most particularly at night," the disembodied, silken voice of the person in black called through the cold air.

Yvette's grip on Bram's coat tightened, and he felt her press herself against his legs and arse, her head at the small of his back. He wanted to reassure her. He wanted to tell her that he'd protect her with his own life, if it came to it. But he daren't show weakness to the caped pursuer.

His stomach knotted with fearful nerves, but a flash of bravery and determination squared his shoulders. Bram pulled his hands into fists and lifted them, ready to strike should the mysterious personage come near.

"There is no telling what horrors could happen to one so young in the darkness of night..." the voice continued, masculine and cultured, as it slowly advanced. Bram was now certain the caped figure was a man and, damn, even an aristocrat with his fancy speech.

A low chuckle floated across the darkness. "It is fortunate, then, lad and lassie, that you happened across *me*."

Bram's brows drew together in confusion and wariness.

"For I shan't harm you," the man continued. "As a matter of fact, I intend to teach you."

There was silence for a moment while Bram puzzled through the man's words. *Teach?* Why the devil would anyone want to teach two orphaned children in St. Giles?

Then it came to him. Damn if he'd submit and become somebody's pickpocket, chimney sweep, or, God forbid, brothel boy. And he damned well wouldn't let it happen to Yvie.

A shudder wracked his narrow frame at the disturbing thought, his fists tightening further.

"We'll not be nobody's—"

"I believe you've misunderstood me," the voice cut over him. "There is a school in Northampton that I believe would be mutually beneficial for you and its master."

Bram licked his dry lips, wariness hardening each beat of

his heart. "Why would a toff wanna teach a nobody like me?" His eyes narrowed. "Wot's in it fer ye?"

"Why, there's quite a lot in it for me, young lad. I would be teaching you to work for me."

Bram's suspicion heightened. "We won't work in no brothel," he asserted, "and we ain't gonna be no pickpockets or chimney sweeps."

Another soft chuckle echoed around him. "I wouldn't dream of it." The man heaved a light sigh. "Indeed, what I have to teach is rather more interesting than that. More dangerous, as well."

Bram waited for the man in black to continue, his suspicion melting into grudging curiosity.

"At the school, we teach maths, sciences, history, Latin, Greek, French..." His voice trailed off, and Bram could swear the man smiled. "We also teach cryptology, infiltration, espionage, reconnaissance, sabotage, weapons usage... The list is rather long, actually. But rest assured, it would be a very thorough education."

"Blimey," Bram breathed.

He could feel Yvette shifting behind him, trying to look around him at the man who spoke. But he knew that she could see nothing.

The cloaked man cleared his throat. "Unfortunately, this offer will be for you only. Your sister may reside in the school with you and receive a basic education, but she is yet too young for our other topics."

An unearthly cackle rose up in the street behind them, and Bram tensed. Yvie pressed herself further against him.

Nerves fluttered in Bram's stomach as he thought about his next question. "Who do ye spy fer?"

"Why, for England, of course," was his smooth reply.

There was something about the man that compelled Bram

to believe him. Relief hit him full in the chest, and he relaxed his fighting stance, his arms falling to his sides.

"Why me?" He licked his cracked lips once more. "Why would ye choose t' teach *me*?"

The man was silent for several moments before he finally spoke. "I feel...compelled to help you. I have a son about your age." Bram heard him shrug. "I also believe that you would suit our group quite nicely. You show bravery, courage, and an admirable protectiveness for your sister. What more reason could a spymaster need?"

Bram grudgingly nodded. "Wot's yer name?" he grunted.

There was a brief moment of silence before the caped man spoke. "My name is Lord Theophilus Samuels, Viscount Leeds."

"Cor," Bram whispered. He had been correct in thinking the caped man was of the gentry.

He scrunched his face in thought. He and Yvette were currently without a home. If he rejected this offer, they would sleep upon the hard ground with danger lapping constantly at their heels for possibly the remainder of their lives. If they didn't become beggars or other unsavoury things, they could very well die of starvation.

He could not allow that to happen to Yvie. He could not allow her to live such an existence, short though it would be. He wanted her to live long and one day get married and have children of her own. If accepting this man's offer of an education and becoming a spy could give her a better life, then he would damned well do it.

"Aye," he said, his voice becoming stronger. "I accept yer offer."

BRAM'S FEET ached something fierce. They must have walked clean across London. He and Yvie had never before ventured this far from home. The buildings were unsoiled in these parts, though slightly dusted with coal smoke. The straight cobblestoned streets were lit with oil lamps; proper carriages rolled down the thoroughfare carrying toffs to their balls, the opera, or other such things; and it didn't stink of death.

Bram rather liked it.

Yvette had begun dragging her heels. A shiver wracked her small frame, and her mouth gaped in a yawn.

Would that we could find a safe place to bed down for the night.

"Here we are." His lordship gestured toward the double doors of a building obscenely large to Bram's eye. He'd never been to the part of London where the toffs lived.

The building was tall and wide, with intricate carvings around the door. Every window glowed brightly with candlelight.

Yvie tugged on his hand, and he went willingly into the grand townhouse. Bram gaped. The foyer was bright with a white marble floor and staircase. The walls were a matching white and trimmed with rich gilt tones. The wide staircase had a tasteful carmine runner going up the length of its centre, which complemented the red trinkets about the space.

"Good evening, Chips." Lord Leeds addressed his butler.

Chips, who was surely not past his twentieth year, bowed properly to his master. "Your lordship."

"Have hot baths brought up to the rose room and the yellow room, if you will. Our guests will journey with us to Brampton on the morrow."

"Of course, your lordship." The butler bowed once more, then spun to stride purposefully toward the rear of the foyer and down a wide corridor.

"Father?" A crackling, youthful voice echoed in the grand space.

Bram looked up to see a finely dressed youth crest the top of the stairs. He could not have been much older than Bram himself. This must be the son Lord Leeds had mentioned.

"Father, I cannot find my sparring—oh!" He halted mid-step on the stairs, his astute blue gaze travelling over Bram and Yvie.

The lad continued to the bottom step, his heels clicking on the marble floor, then lowered in a perfunctory bow. "My pardon for interrupting. Good evening."

"Christian," Lord Leeds intoned, "this is Mr. Bramwell Stevens and Miss Yvette Stevens. They will accompany us to Brampton on the morrow. Young Mr. Stevens will be attending school with you."

How had the man known their full names? Bram hadn't told him, had he?

A strange, fervent light entered Christian's cobalt eyes at the news.

The moment passed quickly as his lordship spoke. "Mr. and Miss Stevens, this is my son and heir apparent, Master Christian Samuels."

"It is a pleasure to make your acquaintance, Miss Stevens." He nodded at Yvie before extending his hand to Bram. "A pleasure."

Bram accepted his hand and shook it. Master Christian Samuels' eyes glittered over their linked hands.

"Welcome, Stevens." He lowered his voice, the impact full of meaning. "Tomorrow shall be the dawn of your grand, life-long adventure."

Eastbourne, mid-May 1815

Predawn light shone dimly through the dingy fourth-floor window of Sir Bramwell Stevens' shared servant's bedchamber. He sat upon his narrow cot, watching the dust motes dance along the air as he tossed aside the threadbare counterpane.

He had been working as a footman in the household of Algernon Chaisty, the Marquess of Hale, for nearly a fortnight, and he had yet to find any irrefutable evidence of his lordship's nefarious, traitorous activity. Bram had nary a doubt of the man's guilt; not only was it in the way the man spoke of Prinny—His Majesty, the Prince—his views on politics, the secretive late-night meetings with disguised fellows, and the hushed whispers, but his superiors had also garnered irrefutable bruit from other agents in undercover posts. Rumour—and even witness testimony—however, was different from evidence. The man was undeniably a spy for Bonaparte; Bram simply couldn't prove it.

He shook his head, a lock of nearly black hair falling across his forehead. Assignments had never before taken him so long to complete. Most traitors had some bit of evidence or another hiding in a locked drawer, strongbox, a loose floorboard, or the like. Lord Hale certainly knew how to cover his proverbial tracks.

Brushing the hair away from his eyes, Bram rose and padded on bared feet to the cracked earthenware washbasin and pitcher sitting mournfully in the corner of the cramped room. The tall chest of drawers on which they rested had been formerly used in one of the guest bedchambers but had been broken by a past guest and subsequently sent to the servants' wing.

With a glance over his shoulder to ensure that he did not wake his slumbering roommate and fellow footman, Stewart Davies, Bram poured a dram of water into the washbasin, then gathered his shaving supplies from the locked box under his cot.

He looked into the fractured looking glass, which hung just at his eye level, gazing into his own gilt-coloured eyes. He worked up a lather in the shaving cream over his broad jaw and unfashionably tanned cheeks. He spared no expense when it came to his shaving supplies. Not many footmen were able to afford such luxuries, but then again, Lord Hale was not his only employer, and Bram could not abide a rough shave.

The faint fragrance of sandalwood floated up to tease his nose, and he grinned. He slid the blade from atop the chest of drawers and flipped it expertly between his nimble fingers before placing the blade against his cheek and sliding it down with a *snick*.

Bram was accustomed to the role of footman. He'd played the proverbial game in countless households under countless names. This was the first role, however, that he loathed enough to consider requesting reassignment. And it was for that precise reason that Bram remained. He would not allow this blackguard to continue on as he was.

Finishing his shave, Bram wiped at the remaining suds on his smooth cheeks and jaw with a worn towel, completed his ablutions, retrieved his livery from the small standing wardrobe that he and Davies shared, and began to dress. Within moments, he was fastening the last of the clashing copper buttons of his odious green livery and settling the voluminous white powdered wig atop his head. Damned nuisance of a thing.

Bram left the room, ensuring that his shining, high-heeled shoes did not wake Davies as he strode across the floor. The halls were nearly deserted at this hour, but a few maids scurried about in their duties and a select few footmen like himself made preparations for being called upon by their masters.

He trotted down the narrow servants' stairs, taking two steps at a time, the *clip-clack* of his heels echoing around him. The cook was in the kitchens, fixing the first meal of the day, and the scent of freshly baked sweet rolls wafted up to Bram; his mouth watered, and his stomach growled.

Slowing to a walk, he rambled into the kitchens. Then halted.

The room was filled with a cloud of white powder. Three red-faced maids ran hither and yon with pots in each hand while one scullery maid stood sobbing in the corner and two footmen laughed uproariously from their position next to the doors leading to the breakfast room. Mrs. Patel shouted at the lot of them, her normally rosy round cheeks now a blotched red and her short curling hair sticking out at all angles from beneath her mobcap.

"Get that pest out of here!" the cook shouted. "Lord knows what 'is lordship will do if 'e finds out about this! Lucy, Helga! Over that way!"

Bram watched as a pigeon fluttered over a mound of

dough, another plume of flour rising into the air. The maids scrambled to catch it with their pots.

"Harriet! Behind you!" One of them pointed.

The small scullery maid let out a high-pitched screech and swatted at her head, her cap falling to the floor and the hair beneath it flying in all directions.

This would get them nowhere.

Bram hurried to the larder and found a mostly empty sack of potatoes. He dumped the remainder into a nearby basket then jogged back into the fray. Quick as a flash, he located the beastie, brushed past the squealing maids brandishing pots, and captured the pigeon in the sack.

"Oh!" Mrs. Patel pressed one thick hand to her large, flour-covered bosom, releasing a relieved, gusty sigh. "You've saved me, Smithe!"

He sent her a wink and a grin, even while his nerves grated at her use of his pseudonym. "I'd do anything, madam, for one of your sweet rolls."

"You rascal." She scowled reproachfully, but the quirk of her cheeks belied the action.

The bag in his hands flapped about, so he turned on his heel, taking the beastie outside to release it.

When he returned to the kitchens, the weeping scullery maid had gathered herself enough to begin sweeping the floor, while the other maids wiped other surfaces and prepared the boiling water for the master's morning tea.

Bram cleaned his hands on a cloth before palming one of the sweet buns from the tall worktable.

Mrs. Patel opened her mouth to protest, but Bram swooped in and pressed a quick buss to her red cheek and quit the kitchens before she could utter a sound.

He tossed the warm roll back and forth between his hands before taking a big bite. Sweet warmth burst over his tongue, and he filled his lungs with a grateful breath. He hadn't lied to the woman: her rolls were sodding delicious.

Mrs. Patel's echoing voice followed him down the corridor as she barked orders to the kitchen maids. Huffing a quiet laugh, he popped the last of his small morning meal into his mouth, sucked the sweetness off his fingertips, then retrieved the white footman gloves from his coat pocket and slipped them on.

Swallowing the final bite of his pilfered treat, Bram opened the panel concealed in the grand foyer wall that hid the servants' passage, slipped through, and quietly closed it behind him.

The foyer was grand indeed, if one were wont to use any word other than "repugnant" to describe it. Tall, wide columns wrapped entirely in gilt stood in each corner of the space, while an enormous round table sporting a hideous arrangement of ill-combined flowers rested in its centre. The ceiling and doorways were outlined in gilt, the checked floor was gilt-flecked with cream and green, and each surface was shined to reflect the flickering lights of the garish chandelier hanging above the table. The room veritably reeked of ostentation. And poor taste.

Straightening his wig and tugging stiffly on his coat, Bram resumed his customary morning post against the far-right wall, staring invariably at the hideous bouquet.

After having been in residence for a sennight, Bram knew his way through the majority of the corridors. The foyer held grand doors to his left and right; the front entry to his left, and the right opened onto the courtyard. The corridor to the family wing was at the back of the space and to the right, while the guest chambers and other gathering rooms were down the corridor to the left.

He blinked, stiffening his spine.

Light footfalls came from the direction of the guest wing

and the faint scent of oranges reached him. That scent could only belong to one woman: Miss Rose Wilkinson. She and her sister, Miss Violet Wilkinson, were Lord and Lady Hale's nieces, and now permanent—if reluctant—houseguests. She came through the foyer every morning before the others in the house had awoken. Even the butler, Garrott—bloody awful name for a man; he should have changed it ages ago—had yet to rise.

Despite having been in residence for so short a time, Bram found himself becoming increasingly intrigued by the young woman each time he set eyes on her. She held herself boldly, yet also shyly. She was a paradox in the form of a handsome female.

And there she came. Her shining blonde hair was tucked beneath a tightly knotted, wide-rimmed black bonnet. She wore a modest, high-necked black bombazine day dress, but the drab material did nothing to disguise the lithe curves beneath. She was tall and slender with a bosom just large enough to fit in a man's hands but not so large as to spill out of them...

He shook himself internally. He should not be thinking of her in such terms.

Miss Rose strode quietly into the large space, sliding on her black kid gloves, then glanced up, skidding to a halt at the sight of him.

Her warm brown eyes darted warily around the foyer, her lips curving inward to worry them between her teeth.

Something in his stomach tugged at the sight. Was she fearful of him? She'd seen him standing there every morning since he'd been given the position, but perhaps she took time to become comfortable with new acquaintances? Or, perhaps, *men*?

His inner thoughts turned dark as he realised what must

be the cause of her reticence. Her uncle. The man didn't hide his cruelty; could his abuse of his nieces have caused a mistrust of men in general?

Bram cleared his throat.

"Would you care for your pelisse, Miss Wilkinson?"

Ignoring him, she slowly walked toward the courtyard door, her deep, coffee-coloured eyes fixed directly ahead and her gloved fingers fidgeting with the small onyx pendant at her neck.

Bram stepped forward and opened the door for her. Her startled gaze met his on a gasp. Her expression reminded him of a frightened deer, frozen in both shock and terror, hoping that it had not been sighted.

Anger and dismay raced through his gut, but he easily hid the emotions from his expression. Would that he could erase whatever trauma had caused her to be so skittish. Instead, he grinned in an effort to ease her worries.

"Thank you," she said dully before she scurried out the door.

Bramwell cursed inwardly as he resumed his post. Miss Rose Wilkinson was a curious mouse. What did she do on her morning jaunts? Where did she go? How could he ease her fears around him? She rarely spoke in his presence and, when she did, it was always so softly uttered he had to struggle to hear her.

Hell, but he was intrigued.

He grinned before he caught himself and carefully pasted a bland expression on his face. Such were easy enough things to learn, after all. A footman, however, knew better than to trouble himself with what the master and his family or guests were doing.

It was a good thing, then, that Bramwell was not truly a footman...but a spy.

Want to read more of Bram and Rose's story? Pick up The Charming Spy, Book 2 in the Seductive Spies series.

ALSO BY CHERI CHAMPAGNE

The Mason Siblings series

Love's Misadventure

The Trouble With Love

Love and Deceit

Final Battle for Love

The Seductive Spies series

The Thespian Spy

The Charming Spy

To Woo A Troublesome Spy

A Spy Worth Saving

The Pirate Spy

The Bow Street Wallflowers trilogy

Fear and Fortitude

Secrets and Sin

Presage and Piracy

*Coming Soon:

Regency Monsters series

The Kelpie Rake

The Gentleman Hound

The Reclusive Giant

The Rogue Green Man

The Dragon Lord

ABOUT THE AUTHOR

Award winning queer and autistic author of steamy and suspenseful romances. Cheri began writing as a child and fell in love with historical romance as an early teen. Finally, she combined her two passions and started writing heart-pounding historical romances full of danger, spice, and a guaranteed happily-ever-after.

She lives in BC, Canada with her high school sweetheart husband, their four neuro-spicy children, and their dogs. She/they.

Readers can find Cheri on TikTok, Instagram, Discord (the Champagne's Bubbles server), Bluesky, Threads, Lemon8, and Rednote. Links are available on Cheri's Linktree via her website: www.cherichampagne.com